MW01196321

the cornerstone

THE WALSH FAMILY

KATE CANTERBARY

VESPER PRESS

About The Cornerstone

Shannon Walsh is the boss.

She put herself back together again after enduring traumas no one should have to face, and now she's too strong and secure to let anything slow her down.

That includes an arrogant Navy SEAL who gives her two of the wildest nights of her life. But those nights soon turn into stolen weekends and secret holidays, and then the moments begin to matter more than the hot nights.

But Shannon's priorities are her family and their historic preservation architecture firm. She can't—and won't—sacrifice any piece of that for anyone.

Will Halsted has never walked away from a challenge.

After years spent in the Special Forces, his entire life is classified. Where he's been, what he's seen, what he's done. There is no mission too dangerous.

Falling for a fierce, feisty redhead is the last thing he expected from a wedding weekend hookup but fighting it is like swimming against a riptide.

Every minute is a glorious power struggle with Shannon Walsh but her life and her family are in Boston, and nothing will ever change that.

Not even falling in love.

CW: *History of emotional and sexual abuse by a parent; parent loss; estranged family member; caring for a side character with chronic illness; reference to a main character injured during active duty military service; brief reference to a side character who experienced homelessness; brief reference to being forced out of the home as a teenager*

Copyright

This is a work of fiction. Names, characters, places, and incidents are the product of the author's imagination or are used fictitiously, and any resemblance to actual persons, living or dead, business establishments, events, or locales is entirely coincidental.

Copyright © 2015 by Kate Canterbary
All rights reserved. No part of this book may be reproduced, stored in a retrieval system, or transmitted in any forms, or by any means, electronic, mechanical, photocopying, recording or otherwise, without prior written permission of the author.

Trademarked names appear throughout this book. Rather than use a trademark symbol with every occurrence of a trademarked name, names are used in an editorial fashion, with no intention of infringement of the respective owner's trademark(s).

Editing provided by Julia Ganis of JuliaEdits. www. juliaedits.com
Proofreading provided by Nicole Bailey of Proof Before You Publish. www.proofbeforeyoupublish.com

To the bitches —
Miranda Priestly, Olivia Pope, M, Blair Waldorf, and Hermione
Granger—may you always rule the world.

prologue

SHANNON

Now

I WAS THE FUCKING *BOSS*.

I negotiated multi-million dollar real estate deals, juggled at least six major crises before lunch every day, and tamed lions for fun.

Not *actual* lions, but my brothers came damn near close enough.

I ran marathons, wore heels no shorter than four inches, and could file injunctions faster than most people responded to text messages.

But I was a whore for superstitions.

Horoscopes, full moons, palm readings, Friday the Thirteenths, even freaking black cats. All of it.

It defied logic but I had to believe there was an order to the universe and everything—everything, everything, *everything*—happened for a reason. I needed to believe it all meant something, and that maybe if I paid careful attention, I could protect myself and my family from whatever the universe was throwing at me next.

So waking up an hour late, snagging three separate pairs of tights before they made it over my knees, and drowning my new iPhone in coffee not more than sixty seconds after the barista handed it to me were giant neon signs warning that my Monday was a special kind of cursed.

I needed a shaman and some burning sage, and I needed it now.

Sprinting up the Walsh Associates office stairs with my dead phone in one hand and a fresh coffee in the other, I tried to remember what was on the agenda for this morning's status meeting. Me and my five business partners—the ones who did double duty as my brothers plus Andy Asani, our newest architect and the object of my brother Patrick's affection—we held these meetings sacred. Lateness wasn't tolerated.

I didn't stop when I reached the landing for my office, instead yelling to my assistant while I started up the next flight, "Tom! Get me something to eat and I need a new iPhone before this meeting is over."

"On it," he called.

I cleared the last landing before the steep stone staircase to the attic conference room, slowing my steps to avoid wiping out. I could handle my heels in most situations, but these medieval stairs were thirteen feet of uneven, winding granite torture.

Especially in a pencil skirt.

I was out of breath and fully disheveled by the time I reached the conference room, but I cast a warning glare around the table and dropped into my seat without comment. I wasn't regaling Sam, Andy, Riley, Matt, and Patrick with tales of my crazy morning.

Andy sent me a questioning frown and pointed to her hair, an indication that my still-damp ponytail was more than likely a wreck and my bangs were undoubtedly askew. Shaking my head, I rolled my eyes and mouthed "Not now."

"I tried calling you," Patrick muttered. He was almost a full year older than me, and together we managed our family's third-generation sustainable preservation architecture firm. He handled the architecture, I handled everything else that went into running a business, and it had been this way since forever.

"Phone disaster," I said.

He groaned. "I believe that's your third phone disaster this year, Shannon."

"Thank you for that reminder, Patrick," I said with a saccharine smile. I'd been bossing his ass around for thirty-three years, and that wasn't about to stop. "Suck my dick."

Matt did nothing to conceal his laughter, and he ignored my raised eyebrow. He was a year younger than me, and too much of a big, happy puppy dog to let some brusque frowning kill his vibe.

"If we could focus on the agenda—" Patrick paused when Tom bustled in, a plate in one hand and his tablet tucked under his arm.

"Which size iPhone do you want?" He angled the tablet toward me, pointing at the device options. "You have small hands, so—"

"You have a directive. Solve problems without my involvement," I said.

Tom nodded, chastened. "On it."

He set a plate with two cartons of yogurt, two mixed berry muffins, and a large latte beside my other cup of coffee. Patrick watched, tapping his fingers on the table, and it was clear his patience was depleted for the day.

When Tom hurried down the stairs, Patrick said, "If you don't mind, I'd like to—"

"There is no vagina food allowed at this table," Riley interrupted. He was my youngest brother by five years, and it didn't matter that he was a full foot taller than me now, or that he could pick me up and lift me over his head. He'd always be a little kid to me.

"Riley," Patrick growled. "Sit down and shut up."

"I will puke if there's open yogurt in this room," Riley said. "I'm not exaggerating. It smells like old barf, and can someone actually explain what yogurt *is*?"

He snatched up the cartons and, in the process, knocked over his stainless steel water bottle and both of my coffees. Liquid and ice cubes splashed across the round table, and hell promptly broke loose.

Everyone shot out of their chairs, yelling and swearing, and collecting laptops and phones before much damage could be done. Andy found a roll of paper towels, and she and Sam mopped up the spill while Matt produced a set of tiny tools from his messenger bag and took apart his soaked computer.

"What the fuck is wrong with you?" Patrick shouted at Riley.

"I do not like being in the presence of yogurt," Riley responded.

"Would it not be possible to handle that in a slightly less catastrophic way?" One leg of Patrick's trousers was drenched with coffee, and he pointed to Andy's waterlogged notebook, the disemboweled computer, and the stained rug. "How is it?" he asked Matt.

"Fried," he answered. "And it smells like pumpkin spice."

"Oh my fucking God," Patrick seethed.

"It's not that bad," Andy said as she wiped laptops and phones dry. "Only a few casualties."

"I'm going to have to sand and stain the whole surface again," Sam murmured, his hand coasting over the tabletop.

Riley gestured toward Patrick. "If we could just agree that there's no yogurt at meetings—"

"Get over the goddamn yogurt," Matt said.

"If we're banning yogurt, we're sure as shit banning coffee and water, too," Patrick said.

"Shut up," I bellowed. "Everyone. Shut up. We have things to accomplish and we're not spending the next hour bitching at each other about *yogurt*. Sit down, get your status reports ready, and don't speak unless I specifically invite you to do so. Understood?"

There were more muttered comments as we dealt with soggy chairs and stained clothes. We returned to our seats and started working through property updates. Patrick tracked the fine project management details while I monitored the Boston real estate market, but I quickly zoned out while staring at the Multiple Listing Service website.

I was tired, hungry, and caffeine-deprived, and generally irritable. There was no one reason for my irritability, but a mountain of little reasons that had been building for months.

"All right, well, I think we're good," Patrick said, glancing at me. "Did you get everything you needed?"

"Um…" I skimmed the list of priorities and issues on my

side of the master status table Patrick and I shared. "I think so."

I retreated to my office and spun my chair to face the gothic arched windows. I didn't have much of a view—just the alley below and the adjacent Beacon Hill red brick row houses—but I needed a place for my thoughts beyond the four walls of Walsh Associates.

I was fierce to the bone, and it served me well. That fierceness taught me to keep it together at all costs because if I fell apart, everything and everyone was falling with me.

It gave me the strength to raise my siblings when my mother died and my father lost his mind. It kept me going when I was single-handedly covering college tuition for Sam, Riley, and my sister, Erin, funding the takeover of Walsh Associates from my father, and putting myself through law school, all while selling houses on the side. It gave me the energy to learn the law, money, architecture, and Boston, and the expertise to manage all of that with more competence than most people ever expected out of a five-foot tall redhead. It gave me the will to, at once, be everything everyone ever needed.

But somewhere along the way, I stopped being everything to my siblings.

A brisk knock sounded at my door but I didn't answer. Tom and my brothers were going to barrel right on in regardless of whether I responded. The rest of my support staff knew not to bother me unless the building was burning down, and I didn't smell smoke.

"Okay, boss. I think you're going to like this." Tom chattered on about the newest iPhone for several minutes while I stared out the window. "Boss?"

I glanced over my shoulder. "Can it wait?"

Tom pointed to my desk, ignoring my question. "Phone is charging but otherwise fully operational. I picked up your prescription and another pumpkin spice latte, and Rory ran the payables this morning."

New phone, birth control pills, coffee, and a heap of checks to sign. "Thank you," I said. "What else is on my calendar for today?"

He swiped his tablet to life and pushed his angular glasses up his nose. "Ten o'clock with the bank to close on your Louisburg Square investment. One o'clock lunch at Townsman with that development firm. They're the ones who want to buy out the Medios Building, and if their assistant can be trusted, the offer they'll make is a good one. Please be nice to them. Three thirty with Patrick to review the upcoming projects. Eight o'clock dinner with Mr. Pemberton."

Ugh.

I was more or less dating Mr. Pemberton.

I knew Gerard Pemberton through some lawyer friends, and we'd bumped into each other at several Massachusetts Bar Association networking events. He was an attorney at a firm where my law school buddy Simone worked, a firm that liked to paint itself as boutique but actually churned a massive volume of high-profile and high-priced divorces.

Gerard was good at that: portraying himself as something pleasant despite being a complete tool.

As fate would have it, Gerard was going through his own divorce now. He and his wife, Meredith, called it quits about six months ago and he was busy proving a point to her. He wanted Meredith to know that he'd moved on and he was better off without her, and he was going hard at sending those messages.

Apparently, I was good 'get back at your ex-wife' material, and he wanted to be seen all over town with me. I attributed one hundred percent of my appeal to the fact that the work of Walsh Associates was featured in seven different design and architecture publications in the past four months, and we were currently restoring a home for Eddie Turlan from the eighties punk band The Vials.

Gerard also wanted to fuck his anger away. Quite unfortunately for me, he had some trouble maintaining erections, and routinely blamed Meredith for that while we were in bed. It was charming to watch him berating his cock and cursing his ex.

That was one of the many reasons we didn't get between the sheets too often.

I didn't love Gerard, and I didn't especially like him either. He talked constantly and with no regard for whether anyone was listening. He was rude in subtle, elegant ways that most people interpreted as highbrow snark.

There was always a segment on NPR or a golf tournament worth recounting, but at the very minimum, he kept me occupied. Despite his soliloquies, I always had a dinner date at the ready. He was pleasantly reliable...and barely tolerable, but the only objective for me was moving the fuck on.

"Would you like me to reschedule anything?" Tom asked.

I drummed my fingers on my armrests and shook my head, but I didn't turn away from the windows. "No. Thank you, though."

My eyes landed on the emerald agate geode on the corner of my bookshelf. It was just a rock with something remarkable hiding inside, and it appeared in my office six years ago without a card or return address. The only identifying information was a Brazilian postmark.

There were other mysterious geodes, too. Some were no bigger than a strawberry and others were the size of a softball, and they came with postmarks from all over the world. Russia. Austria. South Korea. Canada. Zambia.

Only one person who would drop rocks in the mail and send them my way without explanation. Someone who liked to remind me that I was a self-centered bitch who needed to take myself a hell of a lot less seriously.

Well, now there were two people who knew those things.

Yeah, today was going to be special.

BEFORE SUNSET, I'd bought one property, sold another, and found two more to lust over. I wanted to snap them up before anyone else noticed the gorgeous—yet completely trashed—Public Garden-side brownstones, but this day wasn't going well enough to make quick decisions.

A dish of gnocchi sat untouched in front of me, my glass of pinot grigio was growing warm, and I was drowning out Gerard's commentary about wind farms. It could have just as easily been his position on the area's best driving ranges or how he was diversifying his portfolio, but I wasn't even close to listening.

Instead, I was debating whether we'd get a bigger payoff from merging the twin brownstones on Mount Vernon Street into a super-mansion or restoring them as they stood. This was the kind of project Matt lived for, and if I could get him on board, it would be huge for him. A twelve-thousand-square-foot structural remodel and preservation job meant an eight-figure price tag, and a sale like that translated to major publicity. It was exactly what Matt needed to finally grab some awards of his own and garner the media attention that Sam and Patrick picked up without effort.

"Dessert?" Gerard asked, gesturing to the menu the waitress was offering.

It took me a moment to realize he expected a response. Most of the time, he required no more than the occasional nod.

"No," I said. I wanted my bed, pajamas, and *Game of Thrones*. Some Jon Snow would help my mood. "I have an early meeting."

It wasn't exactly false; all of my meetings were early relative to Gerard's firm, where the partners strolled in around nine thirty. I texted Tom to get me on Matt's calendar for a Mount Vernon Street visit tomorrow, and engrossed myself in looking busy with emails.

Gerard talked the entire walk back to my apartment—something about paleontologists discovering an ancient species of birds. Whipping the babble out of him wouldn't have required much work on my part, but I didn't have the desire to fix him. Everything about this was temporary, and when the emotionless boredom of my time with Gerard left my wounds scabbed over and my heart numb, this would end.

It was misery, but it was the best I could do right now.

The prehistoric bird story continued until I pointed to a chair in my living room and said, "Make yourself at home. I'm getting some wine."

I grabbed a bottle from my pantry without concern for variety or origin and stood at the sink, gazing at the night sky. A nearly full harvest moon was shining bright over the Charles River, and it seemed too close, too heavy to be real.

Gerard called to me from the hall but I ignored him. There was probably a tennis match he thought I needed to see.

Sometimes I studied the sky and wondered about the order of it all. Who would I be if I hadn't lost my mother and been forced to grow up at nine years old? What if I hadn't been forced to grow all the way up at seventeen when my father kicked me out of the house? Would I be standing by while my brothers filled their lives with love and happiness and meaning? Would I still be negotiating the lesser evils of loneliness and limp dicks?

"*Shannon,*" he repeated, his tone more abrupt than I'd ever heard before. "Could you join me out here?"

Abandoning the wine in the kitchen, I rounded the corner and found Gerard in the front hallway with the door open. From my vantage point, I couldn't see past the door.

"There's someone here to see you, Shannon," Gerard said, and my stomach dropped into my shoes.

Nothing good ever came from an unexpected visitor at ten thirty on a Monday night, and I realized *this* was what the universe had been warning me about all day. Not a dead phone, not a showdown over yogurt. This.

I closed my fingers around the edge of the door and pulled it open, and then air was gone.

Even in a dark hoodie and jeans, even with a ball cap pulled low over his eyes, even with a clean-shaven jaw, even after all these months. I knew him. I'd always know him.

"Shannon," he said, his voice deep and commanding and filled with too many memories to manage in this moment.

Before I could stop myself, a broken, breathy sob escaped

my lips. It was equal doses of hell-sent anger and the kind of affection that drained oceans, moved mountains, and slowed time.

I wanted to hold him close, so close that he melted into me and we couldn't tell one from another, and then I wanted to slap the shit out of him.

"Will," I said.

PART ONE

Then

One

EIGHTEEN MONTHS *ago*

I MISSED the ocean so much it hurt.

When the plane descended below the clouds and I caught my first glimpse of the Atlantic Ocean in almost three years, I damn near cried. The only body of water I'd seen in months was the Kabul River, and that wasn't intended for surfing.

I took my time wandering through the Boston airport. I still didn't understand how my little sister Lauren—she'd always be Lolo to us—was getting *married*.

This *weekend*.

To a *man*.

We last spoke in August, around her birthday, and she wasn't seeing anyone then. Fast forward a few months and some highly covert ops, and I'm being shoved on a transport plane to appear at my sister's wedding.

How the fuck did all that happen?

Unsurprisingly, my mother was stationed on the other side of the security checkpoint. Her fingers were flying over her smartphone, and I realized I hadn't read her blog in months. *Shit.* As far as my mother's affection for her children ranked, it was Lo, the blog, me, then Wes.

Allegedly, my younger brother Wes was a real asshole while he was a toddler. Thirty years since the terrible twos ended, and my mother was still reminding him about that.

Mom startled when I dropped my backpack beside her, but that shock transformed into a wry frown. "Oh for the love of Pete, William, would it kill you to groom yourself once and a while?"

Apparently thirty-four wasn't too old for my mother to scold me for messy hair and an overgrown beard.

My mother's fingers fluffed my hair before they fisted, and she yanked me down for a hug. "I've been a little busy with the global war on terror and all," I said. That, and a certain amount of shaggy scruff was essential in my line of work. "And one of these days, you're going to have to tell us who this Pete guy is, Judy."

She pulled my hair a little harder; she hated it when I called her Judy. If she had her way, we'd still be calling her mama and asking her to rock us to sleep.

"He's my man candy on the side," my mother replied with a shrug. I bet my father loved hearing that one. "Keeps me young."

She shifted her hands to my shoulders, squeezing down to my biceps, elbows, forearms, and then gripped my hands. She always did this when I returned home from deployment. It was her way of checking that I was still in one piece. After years as a Navy medic, my mother knew exactly what the battlefield could take.

"I really wish you didn't tell me that shit, Mom."

She ran her hands up and down my chest, and repeated the motion on my back. "Too long, Will. Too long," she whispered. A smile pulled at her lips, but the tears shining in her eyes gave it all away. "I don't want them keeping you for another twenty-seven months straight. I'll tell that to the Joint Special Operations Commander himself if I have to."

"You do that, Mom," I laughed, pulling her toward the baggage claim. But she was right; it had been deployments, extended deployments, special deployments, all one after another. Pepper that with training ops and a couple of months with an advanced demolitions crew, and I could only count a few weeks of leave in the past three years. "I bet the Lieutenant General loves hearing from SEAL moms."

She rolled her eyes before wrapping her arm around my waist. "How were your flights?" she asked.

"Strange," I said when reaching for my bag. She pointed to the sliding doors and I followed her to the curb. "It's been a while since I stayed in an aircraft through take off *and* landing."

"You and your HALO humor," she murmured. "Wesley's parked over there. He's telling stories."

My mother gestured to the far end of the loading zone where Wes had two members of the State Police hanging on his every word. He mimed an explosion, and despite the fact we were at an airport and bombs were the last thing anyone should ever discuss, his new Statey pals were captivated. The story was effective in distracting them from his illegal curbside parking, too.

"And that's how you get out of Moscow before the Spetsnaz notices you were there in the first place," he said. With a lopsided smile, he beckoned me closer and draped his arm around my shoulder. "Boys, it's my pleasure to introduce my brother, Commander Halsted."

"It's one promotion after another with you, isn't it?" Mom asked. "Maybe now you'll get off the front lines."

Unlikely.

Once the pleasantries were handled, my mother grabbed us by the collars and towed us toward the rental car. "You two need haircuts, and anything would be better than cargo pants and old t-shirts."

I sucked in the fresh, salty air as we approached Cape Cod, and I wanted to spend every minute of the next four days in the ocean. I was raised on the beaches of San Diego, a water dog to the soul, and I believed an afternoon spent surfing was the cure for anything that ailed me.

Wes leaned on the center console and glanced to me in the backseat. "Where have you been hiding out these days?"

"J-bad." I shrugged; all told, I didn't spend much time on base in Jalalabad. "Or thereabouts. And what the hell were you doing in Moscow?"

"Started as a sneak and peek with a recon squad," he said. "Ended with a surprise extraction. Good times."

Wes was a master of tradecraft. Despite his thoroughly California looks, he could blend in anywhere and spoke enough languages to make it believable. He'd been loaned out—along with a few other SEALs and Delta Force guys— to man a covert unit responsible for preventing another Cold War. It was a classic counterintelligence program potluck, and it was a mystery who'd be cleaning it all up.

"Get it all out now," Mom said, "because you won't be talking about reconnaissance and assault teams at your sister's wedding."

"Yeah, can we talk about that? What does the

Commodore say about this?" I asked. There was no doubt that my father was not excited about seeing Lo married. "When did Lo get engaged? And who the hell is she marrying?"

Wes passed a phone over his shoulder, and I knew without looking it contained a rundown on our sister's fiancé. Thank God for Wes's fuck buddy at the CIA.

There wasn't much beyond the basics: name (Matthew Antrim Walsh), date of birth (nearly three years older than my sister), federal tax filings (architect-engineer, and his bottom line was annoyingly healthy), known associates (too many siblings to comprehend; dead parents). He was Ivy League all the way—Cornell, MIT—and he didn't even have a speeding ticket to his name.

I hated everything about him.

"I'd like to meet this asshole," I said.

My mother let out a long-suffering groan. "For your information, Matthew is a wonderful young man and you will not do anything to interfere with your sister's happiness. Is that understood?"

"What qualifies him as a 'wonderful young man'?" I asked.

"To start, he reads my blog every week and shares my posts on social media." My mother glared at me in the rear view mirror. "That's more than I can say for either of you."

Two

SHANNON

EIGHTEEN MONTHS *ago*

I WAS A MESS. A wreck of epic proportions. The crown princess of Barely Keeping It Together.

I wanted to shatter everything I could get my hands on and scream until the rage I felt was purged from my blood.

I wanted to get weepy, messy drunk and clutch my mother's handkerchiefs—the ones my father ripped out of my hands not six months after her death, right along with everything else she'd ever touched—to my chest until the pieces of her that I'd lost started coming back to me.

I wanted to fall apart—crawl into bed, hide under the covers, and sob until my body ran out of tears—but falling apart wasn't in the cards this weekend. I'd enjoy that luxury, along with plenty of crying, drinking, and screaming, when the happy couple was well on their way to Switzerland next week.

"Hey." Lauren curled up next to me on the patio loveseat

and dropped her head to my shoulder. "Let's walk and talk. Okay?"

She steered me toward the string of gray-shingled cottages at the north side of the inn while I rattled off the schedule of events for her big day. It was more for my benefit than hers: she was going to do whatever she wanted tomorrow—Lauren only pretended she liked order and structure—and I needed to stay busy to prevent myself from drowning in a bottle of whiskey.

"You are in beast mode, my friend. Don't worry about anything. Tomorrow is going to be perfect," she said as she flopped onto my bed. "And you know what will make it perfect? Me marrying Matthew. I don't need anything else."

"I still think the catering manager is underestimating the amount of appetizers necessary for cocktail hour," I said, dropping beside Lauren. "And I know he's not going to have enough of your signature drinks ready."

She rolled to her side and squinted at me. "I have a signature drink?"

"You have *two* signature drinks. Watermelon bellinis," I said, "and blueberry martinis. Actually, I've been calling them blue ball martinis and pussy pink bellinis in my head."

"We *must* call them that tomorrow." Lauren shook her head and laughed. "When did you pick those?"

Lauren and Matt selected the date (late May), the location (the far end of Cape Cod), and the vows (still under wraps). I took care of most everything else, and I treasured every minute of it. This was my family's first wedding, and I wanted to guarantee they had the celebration they deserved.

"Last month when I came down here to meet with the flower people," I said, yawning.

Exhausting didn't even begin to describe this week, and it was only Friday night. We were doing construction on the office, Patrick was being a moody bitch, I had to let a book-keeping assistant go, and I was up all last night threading ribbons through wedding programs. That one was a bad idea; I was talented in neither arts nor crafts.

"Well I hope those balls and pussies taste good," she said. We looked at each other and immediately burst out laughing.

"Lauren, you should know by now...balls never taste good," I said with tears sliding down my cheeks while I hugged my sides.

"Apparently you would know," she gasped between giggles. "But I guess my bigger concern is someone choking on the balls. No one ever chokes on pussy."

"And why would they?" I asked, shifting to lean against the headboard. "Pussy is pretty. Pussy is manageable. Balls are just awkward. They're hairy and wrinkly, and frankly, I do not know what to do with them. I'm sorry, but when it comes to cock and balls, they are separate and unequal. I feel as though balls hang there, judging me for not even attempting to meet their needs."

"Well..." Lauren's brows furrowed and she gestured toward me. "You could try—"

"Nope. Nope, not even a little bit. We are not talking about how you handle Matt's balls."

She laughed and ran her hands through her shoulder-length honey blonde hair. I'd always wanted hair like that. Yeah, every stylist who ever touched my hair told me how much people paid to get my precise shade of roasted carrot but that never stopped me from occasionally craving some-thing new. I also coveted Lauren's skin. The girl could blink at the sun and have a deep, golden tan.

I, on the other hand, blinked at the sun and turned into a crispy, blistered beet.

Even though I lusted after Lauren's beachy blondeness, my fair skin and red hair were the only tangible pieces of my mother that I carried with me, even after all this time. We shared everything, right down to the way our hair got lighter as it lengthened, as if the fire started at the roots and cooled as it moved down our shoulders.

I wished I could say I recalled that about her, that I had a store of beautifully articulate memories and moments with my mother, but I didn't. I had the misshapen, inconsistent recollection from my nine-year-old self and one photograph.

But now I knew that my father—we didn't bother calling him Dad; it was either Angus or Miserable Bastard—went to his grave without revealing he'd never actually destroyed any of my mother's things, and if it was possible, I hated him more than I had when he took it all away. He'd rounded up her possessions while we cried and screamed and begged him to stop, but it wasn't enough to rid the house of her clothes, perfume, and journals. It wasn't enough to make us watch while he threw an armload of her summer dresses in the fireplace and let them burn until nothing remained. And it wasn't enough to scrub her spirit from the house, right down to the sad little rock collection she brought with her when emigrating from Ireland.

If we hadn't found the secret passage he built at our childhood home where it was all hidden...*No*. I couldn't let myself think about that.

There were times when I knew he wanted to destroy me too.

He started coming into my bedroom a few months after she died. I was shattered then, still a sharp, uneven fragment of something that was once whole. It was always after a long night of drinking—then again, every night was a drinking night for Angus—and he'd sit at the foot of my bed. Sometimes it started with him crying quietly while I pretended to be asleep or his hand wrapped around my leg over the blankets. Other times he tore the blankets up over my face and stole every innocent piece of me.

For years—decades—I believed that I deserved it. I was the one who decided we were spending the whole day down the street at the McLaughlin's pool, and I was the one who didn't think it was necessary to check on our pregnant mother when she was obviously unwell that morning, and I was the one who was too terrified to do anything but fucking watch when Patrick and Matt found her drowning in her own blood.

So I deserved the worst punishment imaginable. I deserved it all.

It took a lot of time and a lot of counseling to recognize that none of it was my fault, but it was moments like these when I recognized exactly how evil he was that I felt the weight of it all over again.

"If you ever find yourself wanting ball-handling advice, you know where to find me," Lauren said. I stared at her, too lost in my thoughts to understand her comment, and forced a smile before shaking myself out of it.

Fall apart when the wedding's over.

"I should really check on the gift baskets," I said, shuffling off the bed. "And the tent timeline. I don't want them setting up the reception tent during the ceremony."

My priorities didn't stop there. Matt was convinced Lauren's Navy SEAL brothers were going to waterboard him, Patrick was moping like a premenstrual teenager, Sam was drunk, Riley was scamming on Lauren's friends, Andy was very, very late in getting her ass here, and Erin...all things Erin.

"You want to talk about it?" Lauren asked.

I realized I'd been staring at a sweater for no fewer than ten years and sighed. "No. Not tonight. Not this weekend."

She stood and inspected her hair in the mirror. Matt wasn't the only one who fell in love the minute he met her. She was the best friend I'd always wanted, the bad bitch who liked to drink and swear and spend obscene amounts of money on shoes, the sweetheart who always knew when I needed to cry on her shoulder.

And she was one of the few who knew all my secrets.

"Would a special project help?" she asked. "A strategic initiative to keep your mind off everything else?"

"Depends on the project," I said, pulling the baggy sweater over my head. It was a size too big, but it was the last one at the Tory Burch sample sale and I could not help myself.

Lauren rolled her eyes at my sweater—she tried to talk me out of this purchase but I wouldn't hear of it—and adjusted the sleeves. "I'll handle Patrick and Andy if you deal with Will. Chat him up, debate foreign policy, insult him, send him into town for a jar of peanut butter, whatever you want. Just don't let him out of your sight."

I gave the bed petulant a glare and nodded. "I might need to borrow your black Mary Jane Manolos," I said while slipping my credit card, room key, and phone into my pocket. "You know, forever."

"I guess that's the price I'll pay to keep my husband's balls unharmed."

"Make it stop," I groaned. I stomped toward the door,

shaking my head and covering my ears. "We're not talking about Matt's balls anymore."

Three

WILL

SURVEILLANCE WASN'T MY THING.

I hated all the waiting and watching. Don't get me wrong —keeping track of a bossy redhead who didn't know how to mind her own business was one of the easiest gigs to ever fall into my lap, but it was tedious as fuck. This was why I couldn't do protection ops. I was a scalpel: perfect for quick, quiet attacks, the kinds that were measured and rehearsed for the greatest impact.

I was about ready to bind and gag Shannon Walsh, and then lock her in a closet until the wedding was over. Listening in from the far end of the bar while she quizzed the bartender on his stock of craft beers only reaffirmed it.

She couldn't go five minutes without flitting between the Walsh encampments, and that was on top of her routine cross-examination of the inn staff. She wanted to know when they were pitching the reception tent, where the blue hydrangea centerpieces were being housed for the night, whether they'd prepared extra scallops wrapped in bacon for the cocktail hour.

Apparently those were the groom's favorite, and if her tone was any indication, the catering manager could expect Shannon's fancy high heel to find a home in his small intestine if he underdelivered.

I had to hand it to her—the bitch had balls.

And maybe I was a little punchy. I'd been traveling for the past seventy hours and my body and brain were still in mission mode. There was a gravity associated with coming off deployment. All sailors experienced it, but everyone experienced it differently. For me—after nearly three *years* hunting terrorists—it was the sudden, shocking loss of purpose. Without the constant chatter of comms in my ear, the familiar weight of body armor and weapons, the adrenaline of running exceedingly dangerous ops, the dual responsibilities of guarding my country and getting my men home safely...without all that, I didn't know what to do with myself.

Instead of figuring out how to shake off the culture shock, I fixated on Shannon. She was the expensive, refined kind of beautiful. High maintenance. Diamond earrings bigger than most mortar shells. She couldn't go thirty seconds without checking her phone.

Amazingly enough, that wasn't the most annoying part.

No, it was that this woman didn't even *like* beer. I refused to believe she could. This chick was too high society for beer, even weird hipster beer.

"What about Upper Case?" she asked. There was no hint of impatience or condescension in her voice, and that was the secret weapon. She was calm and relatively pleasant, but it was obvious in the sharp angle of her eyebrow that she was ready to climb over the bar, show this guy how to do his job, and shrivel his dick off with little more than a tight grimace. "Or Congress Street? Triple Sunshine?"

The bartender studied the taps in front of him and then crouched low to inspect the bottles lined up in the refrigerator. He stood, shaking his head. "I've got Smuttynose, and... and Slumbrew."

She drummed her fingers against the bar while she contemplated those options. I was actually concerned the bartender was wilting under her glare. She was a dictator dressed as a socialite, and I doubted she wilted under anything. "What about Sea Hag?"

He snapped his fingers and pointed at the fridge, smiling with relief. Hell, *I* was relieved on his behalf. "*That* I can do for you."

"I knew you'd come through for me, Barry." She sent him a wink as he slid the uncapped bottle toward her. He high tailed it to the other end of the bar, presumably to dislodge his nuts from wherever Shannon shoved them.

I was expecting her to dart back to Lo's side or hunt down other staff members to harass or just go the fuck to bed because it was past midnight and even the wicked required rest, but that all changed when she turned her gaze on me. She collected her bottle and marched my way, offering a bright, plastic smile as she approached.

"I have a thing for IPAs," she said, her voice a conspiratorial whisper. Skinny silver bracelets encased her wrist, and they clanged against each other whenever she moved. From where I was sitting, it looked and sounded like she was accessorizing with a Slinky. "A list of the best local breweries was published last month, and my goal for the summer is to try each one." Unbidden, she tucked herself into the seat beside me. "We met earlier, but I know there are a lot of us and things have been so hectic. I'm Shannon, Matt's sister."

I accepted her outstretched hand, and as our palms met, I realized she was a tiny little thing. She was just a peanut. At first glance, she didn't seem small, not with that feisty attitude and fiery hair, but she was the definition of petite. Slim fingers, smooth skin, trim, compact body, and...freckles. So many freckles.

It was as if Strawberry Shortcake fucked Winston Churchill, and nine months later, Shannon Walsh was born.

"Right," I said. "Will."

"Are you an India Pale Ale fan, Will?" Her eyes dropped to the Corona bottle beside me and she forced that fake smile again. It was obvious she did this with frequency—handling people, subtly manipulating them, getting her way while letting everyone think it was their idea—and it annoyed the fuck out of me. "Oh, that's just silly."

"Is it?"

"Yes," she said, then called down the bar, "Barry! Get my friend a Summer Ale."

Barry didn't react quickly enough for Shannon, and his shift was probably long since over but he didn't know how to break that news to her. With a sigh about wanting things done right meant doing them herself, she stepped behind the bar, grabbed the bottle, popped the top, and placed it in front of me.

"Put it on my tab," she yelled as she settled back into her seat. Barry gave us his best deer-in-the-headlights look and went back to restocking. It was late, and he was the only one manning the patio bar. My money was on him counting the seconds until this rowdy crew cleared out. "So I started my

IPA adventure with an Olivette from Paisley Pines and then I discovered Lost Highway Breweries, and now I'm dying to try the Veridien from Banded Horn Brewery."

Bound. Gagged. Closet.

"So tell me, Will," she said, inclining her head toward me. "What's your poison?"

An image of Shannon bent over my knee flashed into my mind, and *fuuuuuck* that had to stop right now. I swallowed it down, drowning that thought in cold beer. "Whatever's on tap," I growled.

In all fairness to my dick, this was nothing more than a natural reaction to being off-base and in the presence of gorgeous women who were free to dress however they pleased. Hell, I hadn't seen a lady in heels like Shannon's, with ribbons lacing all the way up her leg, since...ever.

I sent a silent prayer to my cock, begging it to calm the fuck down.

"There you are," Shannon said as Lo draped her arm over my shoulder.

"Hey, Will, this is my friend Andy. She works with Matt," she said, gesturing to the brunette beside her.

"Will Halsted," I said. She shook my hand without saying a word. "You're not related to this crew?"

"No," Andy said, and her gaze traveled over the patio area to settle on Patrick, the oldest Walsh. He was one stoic motherfucker. I'd only picked up general details about the family Lo was marrying into, and I knew Riley was the fool, Sam was the playboy, Patrick was the hard-ass, Nick wasn't related but came with the package, and Matt was the golden retriever: obedient, loyal, and couldn't keep his tongue in his mouth.

Andy ordered a glass of wine, and thank God Barry was

able to meet her request without much discussion. I doubted Shannon cared whether she was empowered to fire him or not; she'd make it happen.

"Finally, an impartial witness. Sit down," I said, pulling up a chair.

If I could get Andy talking, I knew Shannon would go looking for attention elsewhere. That meant I could get some history on these people and distance from Shortcake. Seemed like a win.

But Andy turned away from Patrick a second before he pivoted. A quick inspection of the patio told me that everyone else saw it too. I couldn't understand how she missed his hot stare.

So that's how it is with them.

"Are we not having a conversation?" Shannon asked, and *fuck*. Just...fuck. If I had the time or interest, her mouth would be too busy with my cock to make those comments. And no, I did not want to be interested but post-deployment horny didn't discriminate against viper-women who inspired fear in wolves and inadequate men.

"Apparently she didn't take the hint," I muttered but Andy ignored me. Incidentally, my dick was ignoring me too.

Lo shot me a venomous glare, mouthed "Be nice," and linked her elbow with Andy's. She flipped me off as they walked across the patio to where Wes was seated with Erin, or—as I preferred to call her—the quiet one.

I definitely drew the short straw in this activity.

"I don't spend nearly enough time listening to harpies." I gestured for Shannon to finish her story, and hoped my remarks were enough to send her back to her room for the night. That was my exit strategy, and she was providing more than enough material to work with. "By all means, continue. I'm certain there are some frat boys brewing their own basement lager that you haven't mentioned yet, and I won't be able to sleep tonight without your assessment of their operation."

"The things I do for my brothers," Shannon said under her breath.

I expected another book report on the history of brewing but she stayed silent. She watched as Lo and Andy returned to the inn, and then her attention shifted to Erin. Shannon was putting a lot of effort into making her glances seem casual, and failing miserably.

Her thumb swept back and forth over the bottle's neck, and for a moment, I was transfixed by an image of those fingers on my cock. They were so small and slim, I bet they wouldn't fit all the way around my shaft.

And fuck me, I couldn't stop watching her stroke that bottle. I closed my eyes, and I could feel it, I could feel her skin against mine, and *fucking hell*, it had been too long.

"Give me that," I said, grabbing the beer away. It was barely cold and I couldn't say I enjoyed beer this hoppy but I drank it anyway.

"We could have ordered you one, dearie," she said.

"Unlikely," I said. "You scared the piss out of Barry, and probably everyone else at this place."

Her laugh was a soft, breathy sound, and it was the most honest thing I'd heard from her all night. "You can't say I don't get shit done."

I couldn't stay seated any longer. I needed something to do, a way to expel the misplaced desire hammering in my veins, and I was half ready to dive into the ocean and swim until I washed up on the shore. At least then I'd be too exhausted to think about wrapping all that red hair around my fist and forcing her to her knees.

Stepping behind the bar, I grabbed our empty bottles and tossed them in the bin. Sam was drunkenly corralling his brothers—plus Wes, Erin, and Nick, the doctor who'd asked me an unending series of questions about tribal healthcare conditions in Pakistan and Afghanistan earlier in the evening—and leading them down the beach toward his cottage.

That was the bullet I was taking for this team tonight: Wes was gathering intel on Lo's in-laws while eyeing Erin, and I was left keeping a leash on Shortcake.

But then I noticed her tracking *me*, and I realized this little girl and I were playing the same fucking game. How could I have missed such overt scrutiny? And no, of course she didn't have a thing for IPAs.

Yeah, the bitch had *balls*.

"So you're the tail."

"I'm what?" she snapped, and it seemed plausible that she'd have a trophy case packed with all the assholes she'd torn up.

"The tail," I repeated. "I know my objective here...but what's yours?"

She crossed her arms over her chest, jangling those stupid Slinky bracelets in the process. "Your sister seems to believe you're going to kidnap and torture my brother. She wanted to prevent that."

"It's called enhanced interrogation," I said. "And that's not my wheelhouse."

"That's right," she murmured. "I'm told you're quite the commando."

I bristled. There was a lot of mythology surrounding

special operations teams, and most of it was inaccurate or exaggerated. "We aren't fond of that term, ma'am."

"In that case, I'm quite fond of it." She eyed me up and down, visibly taking stock of my dive watch, the Gatorz sunglasses hanging from the neck of my t-shirt, and the frog skeleton tattoo peeking out from my sleeve. "What kind of commando activities have you been up to recently?"

You wouldn't be able to sleep at night if I told you. "Afraid that's classified, ma'am."

She stared at me as if she wasn't accustomed to being refused anything, ever. And look at her. Those pouty lips, the ones that ordered everyone around as if they were on her payroll and they should be fucking thrilled to have that honor. That stubborn chin, angled just enough to communicate her superiority. And those eyes, big and dark, dark mossy green, twinkling as if she was amused by my insubordination.

This woman was lethal.

Tearing my gaze away from Shannon, I surveyed the beer selection and opted for another Summer Ale. "Why is Matt in such a hurry to marry my sister?"

Before seeing Lo or meeting her fiancé, Wes and I endured one of the most stern lectures my father had delivered in years. It seemed the Commodore was drunk on the Matthew Walsh Koolaid. At the very minimum, my mother was force-feeding it to him. He officially warned us off any initiatives aimed at interrogating or otherwise scaring the shit out of our future brother-in-law. That didn't mean I wasn't free to collect intel.

Shannon smiled, and for the first time, it was authentic. "Because they have crazy, filthy love for each other." She wandered behind the bar and inspected every bottle in stock before selecting a Sam Adams. She leaned against the counter, staring at me while she sipped.

Okay, so maybe she wasn't too much of a socialite for beer.

"Really? Do you even like beer?" I shook my head as she drained the bottle and reached for another. "And whatever happened to your blessed IPAs? You should know Barry's off crying in a corner somewhere."

She held the bottle in front of her face and studied the label. "I'll leave him a generous tip. Nothing a few months of psychotherapy won't solve." I couldn't repress the surprised laughter that bubbled up from my chest. "Now explain to me why you have a problem with Matt."

"I don't trust him," I said. "It's really fucking simple."

"Do you trust Lauren?"

"Of course," I said, reaching for my beard and once again finding it missing. "Without a doubt."

"Obviously not," Shannon laughed. She tugged her sweater's sleeves down from where they'd been bunched at her elbows, and now they hung over her fingers. There was absolutely no reason why I'd find that sexy, but...post-deployment horny. That's all it was. "If you trusted her judgment, you'd also trust her choice of husband."

I leaned back against the counter, mirroring her stance. My goal was keeping my eyes on her face and away from her legs and fingers, but then I noticed the way her sweater was always sliding off one shoulder. That shoulder...I couldn't stop staring at it. "I don't trust any guy with my sister."

She tossed the empty bottle into the trash and went for another. "You're a misogynistic meathead," she said.

"If you want to hit me with meathead, I'll own that, but

I'm not taking misogynistic. I can respect, admire, and champion the fuck out of women, but that doesn't mean I can't also protect my sister. That doesn't mean I can't make it clear he'll have to deal with me if she's ever harmed in any way."

"That was a lot of words for you all at once. I'm kind of impressed." Shannon ran a hand through her hair, and I noticed we were completely alone. "Let me tell you something about Lauren: she is a badass chick. You want to talk about torture? She put Matt through all kinds of hell."

"Good," I said. "It builds character. And he probably deserved it."

"While your last point is most likely accurate," Shannon said, "you need to lighten up, commando. Not all women-folk need looking after."

"Someone should be looking after you," I murmured before draining my beer. Too often, the world wasn't very nice to females, and yeah, we needed to deal with that shit straightaway. But no one was going to tell me to stop standing up for the women in my life.

"Erroneous." Her lips curled into a smile that walked the line between playful and demonic, and she shook her head. "If anything, I'm the one who does the looking-after around here."

"In other words, your brothers are lazy sacks of shit," I said, and I knew there was a reason I didn't like those guys.

Her pale brows drew together in a vicious scowl, and I recognized I was wrong about Shannon. She wasn't a socialite, not at all. She was a fighter, and a scrappy one at that.

"In other words," she said, "I run this town and I don't need any help doing it."

She shrugged and now that shoulder was all the way

exposed. A wild splash of freckles ran across her skin, and I was too tired, too fed up with this conversation, too tightly wound to do anything but imagine tasting her right there. I pushed off from the counter and stared out at the sea, all while searching for enough discipline to make it back to my room without doing something unbelievably stupid.

But instead of leaving the bar right then, I stopped beside Shannon and studied those freckles. "Like the tail of a comet," I murmured.

I reached out and traced a line from the ball of her shoulder across her collarbone. Then my gaze shifted to her mouth and those defiant, sinful lips, and my other hand was sliding up her neck and into her hair.

I didn't know why I did it. Maybe it had been too long since I touched a woman. Maybe I couldn't handle the post-deployment horny as well as I used to. Or maybe...maybe I wanted to get into a power struggle.

My forehead rested against Shannon's as I moved into her space, crowding her and feeling all five-foot-nothing of her pressed against me.

"What are you doing?" she whispered.

"Waiting for you to stop me," I said against her lips.

She sighed, and I couldn't tell if the sound originated from pleasure or pain. Then she shook her head and it was highly probable her knee would be connecting with my groin any minute. I felt every single second tick by, each one heavier than the one before.

"Will," she finally said, my name no more than a gasp.

I stole those last syllables from Shannon when my mouth met hers. She tasted like beer and sweetness, and just that quickly, my entire world condensed down to her skin, her hair, her scent. We dropped into an easy rhythm of kisses;

sweet and simple, and perfectly right for the dark of night at the beach.

But then she bit my tongue and the gauntlet was thrown. Lips and tongues and teeth all fought for control, and oh holy fuck, I was bringing this girl to her knees tonight. I didn't care what it took, she was going to surrender to me. I pulled that plump bottom lip of hers between my teeth, nipping and scraping as my hands moved down her body. Her ass fit right in my palms and I jerked her against me, my fingers squeezing that taut skin until she yelped.

"Not nice," she murmured against my lips. Her hands traveled up my chest and over my shoulders, and the fire in her eyes was enough to get me as hard as a goddamn lamppost.

"The last thing I'm going to be to you is nice," I said.

I lifted Shannon to the countertop, knocking over glasses, bottles, and utensils in the process. With her hair wrapped around my fist, I pulled her head back and my mouth latched onto the graceful slope of her neck. Her pulse was hammering and she offered tiny hums each time my tongue skated over her skin, but it wasn't enough to kiss her. I needed to lick, suck, bite. Her fingernails scored my neck and shoulders as I ground my erection between her legs, and what I really needed was to fuck her.

My arm swept out, clearing the remaining barware from the surface. I rocked into her again and her warmth drew a choked, ragged moan from deep inside me. I buried my head in Shannon's chest, kissing and nipping every freckle I could find while my hand slipped up her shorts. I was inches away from her panties when her fingers closed around my wrist, a warning look in her eyes.

"I am *not* fucking you on a bar," she said.

Oh, there was the spitfire.

"Let's get one thing straight right now," I said. My fingers were drawing slow circles on her inner thigh and nothing compared to watching her arousal extinguish her anger by small degrees. "I do the fucking here."

Four

EIGHTEEN MONTHS *ago*

THIS BOY WAS A *SAVAGE*.

The door to my cottage wasn't even closed and Will had my face pressed flat to the wall while he stripped me to my bra and panties. And he didn't waste any time thrusting that bulge against my ass, reminding me that *he'd* do the fucking.

Will's fingers flicked over my back and my lacy B-cup bra was gone, along with the bangles on my wrist. He curled one finger around the side of my panties, and it was enough to send them drifting down to my ankles. From there, his hands spread out, shifting until he was holding me in place with one hand on the small of my back and the other tangled in my hair.

What the hell was I thinking? Kissing him. Bringing him back to my cottage. Having an admittedly hurried birth control and STD conversation at the door. Promising we'd never burden Lauren with the events of this evening. Letting him strip me naked. And it wasn't like I could avoid him tomorrow. I could try, but...oh, fuck, his mouth was on the back of my neck.

He licked every inch of my neck and shoulders but it was his rough chin that had me panting and arching my back to feel more of his erection. That sharp scruff awakened every nerve, and I couldn't stop a shiver from vibrating through me.

Right, right, now I remembered why I was doing this: I was thinking my last decent orgasm occurred in my twenties.

"Be a good little cock tease and stand still until I tell you to move," he growled in my ear.

What did he say to me?

I was outraged and insulted and ready to shove his commando ass out the door. Regardless of whether I'd fulfilled my commitment to Lauren or not, I didn't put up with shit like this. I could survive on inadequate orgasms. I preferred my men civilized, thank you very much.

"You're such an arrogant asshole," I said, and those words weren't halfway out of my mouth when his hand cracked over my ass. He didn't deserve the satisfaction of the moan his touch garnered, but I was powerless to swallow it when his hand coasted over my backside and between my legs.

"I'm gonna keep that smart mouth of yours busy," he said. He edged my feet apart and we groaned in unison— loud, needy, and unhinged—when his thick fingers circled my clit.

No one had ever—*ever*—spoken to me that way before.

The sounds of his belt unlatching and his fly unzipping crawled over my skin and burrowed, frantic and urgent, in my muscles. He guided his cock against my folds, his breath shuddering on my neck. He leaned into me, his throbbing length right up against my ass, and said, "Now I'm going to show you what it means to be fucked."

"You talk a really big game," I said as his fingers speared inside me and his thumb came down on my clit. "It's actually very cute but—" *Oh*, those fingers. I wasn't capable of sustaining cogent arguments when those fingers were moving in and out and everywhere, and why, why, *why* couldn't the men I'd met through online dating have this kind of dexterity?

Will bit his way up my shoulder, chuckling. "You were saying something?"

That conceited bastard.

"I was saying your technique is awkward at best."

He pulled away, and the absence of his imposing warmth —and fingers—left me aching. Tossing him the most hateful glare I could conjure, I pivoted, completely impervious to the fact that I was naked in five-inch wedges and trembling with want.

His hand was gliding up and down that beautiful beast of a cock, and my tongue darted out to gather the drool that was about to spill from my parted lips. I glanced up to find him watching me, and I knew he saw every one of my hungry, dirty thoughts as if they were scrawled across my body like subtitles.

"Does your pussy taste as good as it looks?" Will asked.

I tossed my hair over my shoulder and folded my arms under my (very bare) breasts. "Better," I said. "But it's not like you're ever going to find out."

He chuckled. "I think you're wrong about that."

A smile pulled at Will's lips and he inclined his head. He was goading me, and as I yanked his t-shirt over his head and palmed his cock, I didn't care that I'd taken his bait. I was vaguely aware of tattoos and scars, instead focusing on the imprint of his scent and getting rid of his jeans. I ran my nails over his chest and legs, scratching his tanned skin and soothing those marks with my tongue.

"You've tested enough of my patience, Shortcake," he said, his hands sliding to my hips. He lifted me, set me on the bed, and crawled over me, his cock dragging along my leg like a threat.

"Don't fucking call me that," I said, my legs winding around his waist.

I tried to force him closer to me, to find some friction, but he wrapped one giant paw around my wrists and pinned my thigh to the mattress with the other. This asshole was under the impression he was calling the plays.

"But it suits you," Will said. His hand shifted from my leg to stroke his cock as he gazed at me for a slow, heavy minute. "And you're too pretty for Firecrotch."

"You're a prick," I groaned. His hips snapped forward and the bed creaked beneath us as he pushed into me. He was so much bigger than I expected, and my mind was quickly numbing to anything but the pleasure surging through my body. He was tearing me apart, thrust by thrust, and I wanted to do the same to him.

"Stop talking, Shortcake," he said. "You're ruining this for me."

The headboard knocked against the wall in a harsh rhythm, as if he was trying to fuck me into the next room. Each time he drove into me, my eyes rolled back in their sockets, and I was convinced I was about to combust, but that didn't prevent me from getting in some taunts. "Not much to ruin," I said.

"All this talking makes me think you need a dick in your mouth," he murmured.

He pumped in and then fully out, and it only took a flick of his wrist to flip me on my stomach and yank my ass in the air. I heard his hand connecting with my backside before I felt it, and when I did, the only thing I could think was *hot*. I was so hot, so hungry for his rough touch, and so, so close. I moaned—and it was a straight-up whore moan; no polite virginal sighs or gasps here—into the quilt, my hands fisting in the fabric.

"Now do us both a favor and stop talking," Will said.

He pushed inside me and I knew right then I'd be leaving a puddle of drool on this quilt. I couldn't stop the desperate cries and hushed pleas for *more, more, more, yes just like that*. He wrapped a hand around my hip and another in my hair, and then pulled just enough to send spasms through my body. A quick burst of light cascaded behind my eyes as I came, and despite Will's hold on me, I dropped like a stone. A happy, satiated stone with a savage on her back.

"What was that?" he asked. He didn't stop thrusting. He went right on rocking over every tender, pulsating inch of me.

"An orgasm," I said into the blankets. "Surely you've encountered more than your own, commando."

"If that was an orgasm, it was a pathetic one," he said, his arm snaking around my waist and hiking me up.

I looked over my shoulder at Will, horrified. "Did you just *insult* my orgasm?"

"Yes," he said, nodding. "Now get your little ass over here. You can do better."

Of course this asshole wasn't finished. "And what are you getting out of this?"

He bent me over the edge of the bed, my feet not even touching the ground as he moved in me. "If you have to ask," he grunted, "you've been doing it all wrong."

I had no leverage in this position, no capacity to steer his movements or change the pace, and I did not want to like that. Being in control was my thing.

Will's hand settled between my shoulder blades, anchoring me in place. "Would you just chill out?" he asked, each word punctuated with a long, dragging thrust. "You have to relax, baby."

"I'm not your baby." The stirrings of another orgasm started building in my belly, and as much as I wanted to tell Will to fuck off, that was not the way the words were falling out of my mouth at this moment. "Ohhh," I gasped. "Fuck, fuck, fuck...Will."

"Shannon," he panted, forcing me deeper into the mattress. "Please. *Please* just let me make it good for you."

I *really* wanted to tell him to fuck off, and for no other reason than to banish that starved tone from his voice. I knew he'd been deployed for a long time, and logically I knew he probably wasn't getting much ass on the battlefield, but as far as I was concerned, this was a baggage-free hook-up. Emotions need not get involved.

"Fuck," I moaned, my teeth closing around the quilt beneath me. I couldn't decide what to feel, what to think. Multiple orgasms belonged with urban legends like delicious fat-free frozen yogurt and comfortable high heels. The only thing that made sense was screaming into the mattress as heat poured down my spine, around my legs, and unfurled in my center. "Oh, oh, *fuck*."

I expected the warm fluttering to pass quickly—after all these years, I knew what to expect from my body—but it didn't stop. It expanded until every limb was consumed with hot, sweet bliss. It was overwhelming and nearly painful, and I didn't have anywhere for all this sensation to go so I kept on moaning into that quilt.

"That's a little better," Will said. He was moving faster now, his hips slapping against my ass while the bed grunted, and the headboard barreled against the wall.

Talk about stamina. He just did not stop.

"You're going to break the bed," I mumbled.

"I can accept collateral damage." His hand shifted from my back to cup my chin, and he angled my head to the side. "Suck," he ordered, two fingers pressed to my lips.

My eyes drifted shut and I did as he said, and I didn't even have a quippy comeback for him. My mind and body were consumed by the electricity coursing through me, and it seemed plausible that I'd drown in my own release.

"Open." Will's fingers left my mouth, and in their place, he left a biting kiss. "Let's see about that orgasm now."

I tried to protest, to explain that we were well past the point of teeth-numbing orgasm, but that would have required more than guttural babble. He continued pumping into me, panting, and whispered, "I told you that you could do better. Keep going, pretty girl, you got this." I nodded, too boneless to form words, and he bit my earlobe. "Good. So good. You're so good. Think you can give me a little more?"

I nodded again, and he growled as he slammed into me. His fingers shifted to my clit and nothing would ever be the same again. There was no way I could absorb all of this, and I couldn't take this much at once. These sensations—his cock, his fingers, his mouth on my neck, his roared release— they engulfed me, and then, *then* I fell apart.

As if he knew I needed something to hold me together,

Will wrapped his arms around me and held me while I gasped and shook. We were still bent over the bed and he was still inside me, twitching and setting off tiny orgasmic land mines, and minutes passed before the stars faded from behind my eyes.

"That was good," he murmured against my neck. "It takes you a little while to warm up, but you are not bad at this, Shortcake."

"You were on-par with my vibrator," I said. Total lie. All the vibrators couldn't destroy me the way Will did, but he didn't need to know that. "Completely adequate."

Will laughed and tugged my earlobe between his teeth. "I'd like to meet that vibrator," he said. The air conditioner switched on, and I shivered when the blast of cool air hit the fine sheen of sweat on my skin. He pulled out, smacked my ass, and tossed me to the middle of the bed. The bastard actually *tossed* me.

"You can go now," I snapped, finger-combing my hair from my face.

Will paid no attention to me, and instead of getting dressed, he kicked off his jeans from where they were bunched at his ankles. He sauntered toward the bathroom, and I listened, fuming, while the faucet ran. He returned with a glass of water and he shot a cocky grin in my direction.

"I said, you can go now."

Will flopped down beside me with a laugh. "Yeah, I'm not going to do that."

He pried the blanket away from my chest and brought his lips to my nipple, and my annoyance with him started dissolving into the background.

I dug my hands through his hair, angling him where I

wanted and yanking him back to remind him he wasn't the only one in charge. His teeth closed around me, and the sound I made—God help me, it was shameful—was one part sob, one part screech, one part newborn kitten mewl, all whore.

Will released my nipple with a gentle kiss and stared at me for a long beat. It gave me a moment to study his tattoos: a frog skeleton on his bicep, and an anchor crossed with a trident over his heart. They were tastefully done but I didn't love tattoos; just not my style. Come to think of it, I couldn't remember being with an inked guy. But Will's were nice. Different. Intriguing. Maybe even sexy.

"Here's what's going to happen," Will said, breaking me out of my thoughts. "I'm going to fuck you a couple more times, Shortcake. Teach you a few things about real orgasms. If that goes well, we'll talk about rope."

"Don't call me Shortcake," I warned.

He dropped his forehead to my belly and laughed. "But you're good with the orgasms and rope?"

I shrugged. There was no way in hell I'd let anyone tie me up. "Like I said, you talk a big game. I'll believe it when I see it."

"In that case..." Will pounced on me, sucking my other nipple into his mouth while he hardened against my thigh.

Then we heard a tremendous crack and the right side of the bed buckled beneath us. Will locked his arm around my waist as the bed teetered on a steep angle, and before we could move, the other side of the bed crumbled, too.

"That means we're doing it right," he said, and I laughed against his chest.

We broke the bed that night.

And the side table.

And the desk.

And the complimentary bathrobe belts, which that fucker definitely used to tie me up.

And that was all on top of trashing a bar.

I DIDN'T BELIEVE in avoiding issues. My philosophy leaned toward grabbing those issues by the balls and twisting until I made them my bitches. Sure, it sounded severe, but avoidance only left problems out to rot until they were too obnoxious to ignore anymore.

But I was avoiding Will like it was my reason for being.

It wasn't about after-the-fact awkwardness; I didn't believe in that either. No, it was about him pushing every one of my buttons and driving me to homicidal urges. He was rude and narrow-minded, and I didn't intend to start another feminist debate on my best friend's wedding day.

And his cock turned me into a dumb, drooling orgasm factory.

Nope, none of that had a spot at Matt and Lauren's nuptials.

Of course, I wasn't able to avoid Will or his shenanigans when it came to the post-ceremony photographs. It was as if the photographer knew exactly what we did last night and she thought, *Now this would be an awesome way to mess with people and capture it on film.* She parked me and Will together in every group shot, and repeatedly instructed us to "squeeze a bit closer."

I subtly flipped the photographer off every time, and it seemed she, and everyone else, was oblivious to my discomfort.

Sam was still drunk.

Nick was asking Erin every conceivable question about Portugal.

Riley was flirting with the photographer's assistant.

Andy and Patrick were having another one of those silent conversations I'd ignored for months. I thought they were glaring at each other. Turned out it was foreplay. Who knew?

Matt and Lauren were busy being the happiest people in the world, and a tiny, tiny fraction of me wanted this to be mine. For a split second, I wanted all of this, but more than the beachside ceremony, pink wedding dress, and champagne everywhere, someone who saw only me.

Someone who adored me.

"Squeeze in!" the photographer called.

Will's hand curled around my hip, drawing me closer to his hard body, and annoyance quickly replaced my jealousy. "Paws to yourself, commando."

"Relax, buttercup."

That voice was right in my ear, and it sounded exactly the same as when he was too deep inside me for my brain to function. Like I meant something to him. Like he wanted to mean something to me. Like all of this was more than one wild night.

Manipulative fucking orgasms.

"We are *not* doing this," I said, and then I thought better of it. We were both here for another night, right? "Not right now."

"Always so serious." He rocked against me, and I felt every inch of him, half-hard against my back. "How are you in a bad mood after last night? You enjoyed it. You *enjoyed* it six or seven times. I know. I was there."

"You're an arrogant asshole," I whisper-hissed. "My heels are bigger than your dick, and accomplish far more."

"Hmm," he said. His finger trailed between my exposed shoulder blades while the photographer switched lenses. We were on the far end of the group and close enough together so no one noticed his hand shifting from my hip to cup my ass over the layers of floaty mint green chiffon. "You phrased it differently last night."

I didn't respond because he was right about that, yet his cock didn't need another vote of confidence from me.

"Just one more," the photographer said. "Squeeze in super tight."

Will's fingers brushed down my back as the photographer clicked away, and I knew I'd be the fool grinning with her eyes closed in every one of these shots. If there was any possibility of disappearing from this reception and letting those fingers finish what they were starting, I would have snapped it right up.

But that wasn't happening. Not for me, not tonight. My brother and my best friend were getting the best goddamn reception I could conjure, and if that meant sacrificing some screeching orgasms, I'd survive. All told, I sacrificed more than my share of screeching orgasms for my family.

"Perfect," the photographer said. "Now, bride and groom only."

I huffed out a sigh of relief and stepped forward, but Will's hand tightened around my dress. "Not so fast, Shortcake."

"Would you shove the Shortcake up your ass, please?" That fucking nickname. Did he think he was the first person to call me Strawberry Shortcake? Or Pippi Longstocking? Or Little Orphan Annie? I'd heard every tired, unoriginal redhead nickname known to man, and the only less-inventive names he could throw at me would be Red or Freckles.

"You really need to loosen up," he said. "Why don't you let me help you with that?"

"Why don't you suck my dick?" I asked, my elbow landing on his stomach. I heard a soft grunt behind me, and this time, he didn't protest when I marched away.

It was obvious things were not going according to plan when I arrived at the reception area, and it was a good thing I pressed pause on today's showing of *Orgasm Hour with Will.* The bar line stretched all the way across the tent, there were no appetizers on the tables, and the band was still setting up. 'Tyrant' would be a fair assessment of my behavior when I stormed into the kitchen.

The next couple of hours flew by in a blur. I missed dinner entirely and didn't catch much of the first dance, cake cutting, or bouquet toss, but the inn staff that I deputized was finally keeping things running on schedule. For a minute there, I almost got behind the bar and handled service myself. It was days like this that convinced me I'd be able to pull off a successful jewel heist if I set my mind to it.

I shuffled toward the bar, my feet aching and my body too tightly strung with tension to register my exhaustion. With a glass of champagne in hand, I counted heads. Matt and Lauren were circling the dance floor. Sam was getting drunker. Riley was grinding on Lauren's mother—she was getting a kick out of it, thankfully. Patrick was still moping. Erin was seated at a far table with Andy and Lauren's brother Wes, and I couldn't decide whether I was relieved Erin was still here or concerned that she was telling them all our ugly secrets.

Nick waved as he approached the bar, and I responded with a chin lift. Too damn tired for words.

He tapped his beer bottle against my champagne glass and slung an arm around my shoulder. "One hell of a party, Shan. When are we doing this again?"

I dropped my head to his chest and sighed. "Beats the shit outta me."

A laugh rumbled through Nick's chest, and he said, "Let's run the line up."

Everything was a sports metaphor to Nick, and if a slot opened up on the Red Sox or Patriots coaching staff, he'd leave pediatric neurosurgery behind in a heartbeat.

He pointed his beer bottle toward Riley, who was dirty dancing all by himself now that Lauren's parents were headed back to their room. "He's still on the farm team, and not moving up to the majors any time soon." He pointed toward the opposite side of the tent where Sam and Patrick were standing together. "Now those two...definitely in the majors, but their stats are inconclusive. Outliers. We need to watch the season play out."

"You don't think it's going to work out with Andy?"

Nick shrugged. "It probably *will* work out, but I don't think we're walking them down the aisle for a few years. He's cautious. If he gets her back, he's going to take his time. And she's young as fuck. She's in no rush."

"And what about that one?" I nodded toward Erin.

"Ah, speaking of young as fuck. The free agent," Nick said. "What's her story?"

It was what everyone wanted to know: why didn't I speak to my sister? But there wasn't one reason. It started as a pebble rippling across a pond, but that ripple turned into a wave and then a tsunami, and everything that used to exist between us was gone.

"What's *your* story?" I challenged.

He chuckled and engulfed me in a warm hug. "Diversion. Good tactic."

Nick's was an easy comfort, and it came with no expectations. Really, there was *nothing* there.

We got drunk together last February when I held a Valentine's Day party at my place, and after everyone left, we made an indescribably awkward (and failed) attempt at hooking up. We blamed it on the liquor and laughed it off as the worst idea ever, but we both knew the truth: we didn't have enough chemistry to fill a shot glass.

"Sam's hosting the after-party again," Nick said. "Are you headed that way?"

I shook my head as I stared at the table where Erin, Andy, and Wes sat. "No," I said. "Tired."

"Okay," he said. "I'll make sure the kids behave themselves."

"You do that," I mumbled. Nick was good at riding herd. There were times when I wondered whether he was a sheep dog in a past life.

I rounded the bar to grab another bottle of champagne when Nick stepped away. Once the cork was popped, I reached for my glass only to find Will smiling at me from the other side of the counter.

Fuck, he was pretty. It was the wrong word for a man who was undeniably jacked, lethal by training and trade, and into some serious shit in the bedroom but...it was also very right. Those hazel eyes, that sun-streaked hair, the clean-cut, All-American look, the long, lean muscles that felt incredible under my fingers. Pretty was right.

Pretty fucking hot.

He was tanned to the darkest shade of gold imaginable, and seeing it peeking out from his shirtsleeves made me think of his hands on my skin last night. It was almost drool-worthy.

"What'll it be, commando?"

He stroked his finger and thumb over the scruff on his chin.

Yes, I had beard rash all over my thighs. And some other spots. And yes, it was totally worth it.

Will lifted his brows and swiped his tongue over his upper lip, and it was like a silent directive to drop my panties and fall to my knees.

I was doing neither, but...fuck. A part of me really, *really* wanted to.

"How's this going to go, Shortcake?" he asked.

Five

WILL

EIGHTEEN MONTHS *ago*

I DIDN'T SPEND much time in suits and ties. I lived in combat gear and camo, and I'd been trapped in this get-up for too long. I wasn't one for the long arm of the government, but there needed to be a law prohibiting suit coats and ties after the I Dos. I ditched the jacket, rolled up my sleeves, and loosened my tie during the cocktail hour, but I was still irritable.

My only distraction was Shannon Walsh and the faint mark on the backside of her shoulder that was most definitely a product of my teeth.

And now, after hours spent playing nice with every random person my mother insisted I meet at this wedding, I wanted to play dirty with Shortcake. Yeah, I knew she hated that nickname, but there was nothing better than seeing her fired up. I was sticking with it until I found something that pissed her off even more.

Her eyes darted back and forth over the reception area, and then she hit me with a condescending glare that could melt steel. "How's what going to go?"

This woman did strange things to me. I wanted to argue with her, taunt her, hit every one of her triggers, and then I wanted to fuck her so hard I forgot a time when I wasn't inside her.

It wasn't affection or anything like that. Fuck no. Just another round of this goddamn post-deployment horny, and I needed to get it out of my system. Sweat it out like a fucking fever.

"Don't weddings make chicks crazy horny?"

She rolled her eyes at the champagne bottle as she filled her glass. "Yeah, there's nothing cliché about that," she said. She turned a sympathetic smile toward me, her eyes crinkling. "Look at me, rambling on about wedding clichés. I'm sorry, honey. All this love and forever bullshit must make you realize you're old and hopelessly alone. Have you thought about a companion cactus? Your gun collection can't be keeping you very warm at night."

Oh yeah. This bitch had balls.

"I don't recall discussing firearms with you last night," I said.

"You're telling me you don't have a gun collection, Mr. Semper Fi?"

"That's the Marines, ma'am." I gave her a tight nod, waiting for her to make the next move. I wanted to get her alone, but I didn't want to look like a clingy bitch in the process.

"It bears noting that the point has been neither discredited nor refuted," she murmured, gesturing to her imaginary judge and jury. Lo had mentioned she was an attorney—yes,

I asked my sister about Shannon before the ceremony and I'm a big, squishy pussy who can't have a one night stand without making it complicated—and it looked good on her. Even when the lawyering came at my expense. "Permission to treat the witness as unresponsive."

"Your room or mine," I said.

"How about you go to your room, and if I have any interest in seeing you again, I'll find you." She bent and grabbed two new champagne bottles. "Bye now."

"Excuse me, beer wench?"

Shannon's head snapped up, and that pop of contempt in her eyes was everything I needed. I didn't see any reason to analyze my newfound fascination with insulting her and winding her up. "Where do you get off—"

"Your mouth would be my preference, but I'll settle for your tits. Or your ass. Whichever." I rubbed my chin, thinking. I really missed that beard. "No. Wait. Mouth. For sure."

"You're a disgusting" —she slammed one champagne bottle on the stone bartop— "misogynist" —and then the other— "meathead."

"We've been over that one, Shortcake, and you already know I pray at the altar of pussy." I smirked as her face heated, her anger rising by the second, and it was *game fucking on*. "But don't worry: I won't tell anyone how much you like being manhandled. You should know I'm good at keeping secrets."

She folded her arms on the bar and gestured for me to lean forward. "Unfortunately for you," she said, her index finger circling toward the tent, "I've already told everyone about your very small" —she glanced toward my crotch— "situation. You spend a lot of time in cold water, you know, being a commando and all. Shrinkage. It was bound to catch up with you."

Shannon pressed her index finger to her innocently evil smile, and I was not capable of waiting much longer for those lips to cover my cock.

"Darlin', you woke up everyone within a five-mile radius with your screaming and begging. Every living soul, and the whales and sharks, too. They know all about my *situation* and they know how good that situation was for you."

"You're sweet," she cooed, and if I wasn't mistaken, there was a hickey on the upper curve of her breast. Add another one to my column. "But, *darlin'*, if there's one thing I know, it's how to bullshit with the best of them. I knew your ego was fragile. I couldn't risk damaging it."

"Keep going," I said with a shrug. "Yeah, this is great. All your bitching is giving me time to think about whether I want you tied down while I slap your ass."

"Keep dreaming, commando," she said. She plucked the champagne bottles from the bar, tucked them in the crook of her arm, and started down the path toward her cottage. She paused, surveying the empty reception area, and tossed a hot smile over her shoulder that I interpreted as 'if you want me, come and claim me.'

Yeah, that wasn't a difficult decision, and following meant I got to watch her hips swaying in the moonlight. It was just the crash of waves not more than fifty yards away, the hum of crickets, and the click of her heels, and even if I never touched her again after this night, I'd always remember the foggy glow that surrounded her, as if clouds knew better than to get in Shannon Walsh's way. I was no romantic, but that was a gorgeous sight.

I let her get within a few yards of her cottage—the one

filled with busted furniture—before catching her around the waist and hauling her toward the door.

"It's open," she murmured against my neck.

Her fingers were busy with my tie and I already had a hand in her panties, but those two words were a bucket of ice water on my balls. What the fuck was she doing leaving her door unlocked?

"Don't do that," I said, scanning the perimeter before turning the handle. "I don't care how nice this place is, shit happens when you aren't careful. Especially to little things like you."

I put Shannon down—ignoring her antagonistic scowl as she uncorked one of the bottles and sucked the fizz from the rim—and motioned for her to stay put while I swept the cottage. She wasn't even one hundred pounds soaking wet, and for as scrappy as she was, she was no match for someone who wanted to harm her. Fuck, an excited beagle could take her down.

When it was secure, I grabbed her elbow and towed her inside. "This is exactly why you need someone looking after you. You shouldn't be leaving this place wide open," I said, closing the door behind her. "And I won't fuck you until you stop pouting about it."

"The only people at this resort are wedding guests." Shannon tipped back the champagne as she leaned against the wall. "I have two bottles of Dom Perignon all to myself. This place has HBO *and* Showtime. I don't need you, or your mansplainy dick."

I locked the door then grabbed the champagne from her hand and sipped, and a long, weird silence simmered between us. She was too busy wanting to be right to acknowledge that she was dead wrong. Eventually Shannon slipped out of her shoes and walked into the bedroom, and maybe I was the beagle who was going to take her down because I couldn't help but follow.

She was reaching for the zipper at her lower back, and I pushed her hands away to draw it down myself. "You're still here?" she said, a laugh in her voice. "Don't you have beach-front crimes to prevent? Maybe chase off some deer? Some rifles to polish?"

"Shut up, Shortcake," I said.

The dress fell to the ground, pooling around her bare feet, and she was left in nothing more than a tiny pair of purple panties. No bra was my favorite kind of bra. I shifted her hair over one shoulder, letting my fingers coast through the soft strands while I breathed her in. There was nothing like this in my world, nothing so pure and stunning and, for right now, mine. I pressed my mouth to her neck, licking and scraping and inhaling her while she melted into me.

I didn't do any of this last night. I fucked her plenty, but I didn't *savor* her. Somewhere in the deep recesses of my mind, I knew the desire to do just that had nothing to do with post-deployment horny.

With her hair loosely fisted in my hand, I brushed my lips over her ear and whispered, "Kneel."

Shannon met my eyes over her shoulder and smiled. "Ask nicely."

"Kneel *now*."

She pivoted, and her face was the most perfect mix of sweet and defiant that I'd ever seen. Right then, one thing was abundantly clear: I loved this game of beast and shrew, or whatever the fuck it was, and so did she.

Shannon anchored her hands on my waist and dropped to her knees, and that simple act of surrender nearly had me coming before she parted her lips. I didn't have a complex philosophy on women submitting to me; I just really fucking wanted it from *her*. I chalked it up to finally conquering some of her insufferable brattiness. Alternative explanations need not apply.

She was busy shoving my trousers and boxers past my knees and dragging her nails down my inner thighs, and my dick couldn't have been happier when her tongue curled around me. For a brief moment, she was hesitant, her tongue teasing over my shaft and hand pumping, but then a hot, hungry gasp echoed between us and she arched her neck to look up at me.

A victorious gleam lit Shannon's eyes, and I realized that gasp came from *me*.

"If you don't stop staring at me like that, I'm going to come all over your face."

She laughed. She actually *laughed* while on her knees with her little fingers wrapped around my dick, and I liked it. "And what's the problem with that?"

Shannon lifted an eyebrow while her tongue flicked over the head of my cock, and I was embarrassingly close to blowing it all right now. I took a calming breath and raked my hand through her hair, wrapping it around my fist again. It was a measure of control, for sure, and I needed every inch I could get. "Start sucking, Shortcake."

I thought this would be fast and aggressive, just like every minute of last night, but it wasn't, and maybe that was what I was supposed to figure out about Shannon. This was no beautiful or delicate blowjob, but it was so fucking *attentive* I forgot there was a world beyond my cock and her mouth.

Most people didn't understand the value of a thorough

blowjob. Kids today—yeah, I said it—they saw it as less intimate than sex, less meaningful, and they were wrong. Oral sex was a generous gift, a form of worship, and when it was good...it was deliverance, too.

The finer points of Shannon's technique were lost to me, but I knew this was so much better than my fantasies from the long, lonely nights on the other side of the globe. The best part was her hair. At times, those fiery strands were woven through my fingers, gliding against my skin like silk, and at others, I pulled hard, telling her exactly what I needed. And then there were moments when she nuzzled closer to me, her hair brushing my hip, and too many sensations were careening together at once.

I cupped her chin up, watching her take all of me because I couldn't feel this much without looking in her eyes, and that was the end. Those eyes, that hair, the light press of her teeth...I came like a motherfucking C-4 detonation. "Oh fucking...oh fuck fuck fuck fuck," I roared, my fingers tangled in her hair and rubbing her scalp. "You're such a good little cocksucker."

I kept babbling incoherent praise and obscenities but none of it was enough to communicate the soul-squeezing affection I was feeling for this woman. There was a wild spasm in my belly that I couldn't even begin to explain and everything inside me demanded that I wrap myself around her immediately. Hold her and kiss her and fall asleep with her, even if it was only for this strange, unexpected weekend. I wanted it more than I could remember wanting anything else.

Her fingernails cruised over the backs of my thighs, stroking just enough to bring me back down to earth. With my chest heaving like I'd just finished a marathon in full combat gear, I traced her swollen lips with my thumb. "Oh, baby—"

"I'm not your *baby*," she interrupted. "Let go of my hair."

What the fuck just happened here?

I opened my fist and the strands fell free, and that quickly, the moment was lost. We were back to being the people who only enjoyed arguing with each other, and those people didn't snuggle after emotionally exhausting blowjobs.

Shannon popped to her feet and darted into the bathroom. I flopped on the bed, too fried from that orgasm to do more than exist, and listened while she brushed her teeth. Swallowing was a bonus I hadn't expected—again, my preconceived notions about Shannon pointed to her squealing in horror at all bodily fluids—but I couldn't decide how I felt about her erasing the evidence of it now.

I wouldn't be able to kiss her and taste myself on her tongue, and I wanted that.

Shit. I needed to stop going on three-year deployments if I wanted to keep what was left of my sanity. Pet names? Cuddling? Post-head kissing? What the fuck was wrong with me?

"How do you not recognize the cues to leave?"

I leaned up on an elbow and found Shannon in a short blue bathrobe, one that was too thin and silky to hide the outline of her nipples. The makeup was scrubbed from her face and her eyes seemed impossibly large and bright against a riot of freckles. Her hair was up in a messy bun and her arms crossed over her chest, and my cock was more than a little interested in getting under that robe.

"Why can't you chill the fuck out?" I asked, patting the mattress beside me. How could she not understand that I needed to touch her right now? How could she do that to me and then think I'd be able to leave? "Stop bitching about everything. Get over here and let me eat your cunt."

Her eyes snapped shut and she jolted backward as if I'd slapped her. "Do *not* use that word."

"You're okay with 'good little cocksucker' but you draw the line at 'cunt'?" I scratched my head, frowning, and gestured to the bed again. I was ready to beg for her skin against mine. "What if I do really nice things to your cunt?"

Shannon unfolded one arm and pointed to the door, and when she spoke, her voice was more precise and final than some orders of execution I'd heard from terrorist kingpins over the years. "Get the fuck out."

The answer to the original question was *yes*. Yes, we were drawing the line at cunt.

"Hey, shh, it's okay," I said. I lumbered off the bed and dropped my hands on her shoulders. "Calm down. Shh. No reason to lose your shit, Irish Spring. It's all good. Now get on the bed with me."

She finally glanced up, and God, there was an entire fucking universe in her eyes. All the defiance I'd come to expect from her plus pain and fear, staring back at me. There was so much there, so much more than what she stowed just beneath the surface.

"What's the point? You've already destroyed it," she said, a laugh softening the edge of her voice.

"The point is I want to be inside you again," I said. My inclination was to push her buttons, but instinct told me to do whatever the fuck this girl wanted, and do it now. "And while I *can* fuck you against the wall, I'd like to take advantage of beds while they're available to me."

Shannon hesitated, and I seized that opportunity to

scoop her up and throw her on the mattress. She hated being manhandled in the sense that she hated *liking* it, and it had the side benefit of breaking the tension building between us.

"You are such an arrogant ass—"

"Yep. I know, Shortcake." I crawled between her legs and lifted one knee to rest on my shoulder. "No more talking unless it's to say 'Will, you're so amazing' or 'Will, your tongue deserves the Nobel Peace Prize' or 'Will, the only thing better than your tongue is your big, fat cock.' Got it?"

I tugged the bathrobe loose and leaned my head against her thigh. A sigh slipped from her lips but that didn't erase the sharp gaze she aimed at me. "I'm concerned there won't be enough space in this room for both your ego and oxygen."

My hand coasted over her mound and up her torso, resting between her breasts. "Relax. You can't enjoy this when you're all wound up."

Shannon blinked, and I didn't give her the chance to object. Instead, I rubbed my chin scruff against her inner thigh until she giggled and shrieked and tried rolling away from me. When my tongue finally connected with her clit, those sounds morphed into moans and purrs that traveled down my spine and lodged in the base of my cock like a hot vise.

She was soft and sweet, and again I was confronted with her tiny shape when my splayed hand fully covered the space between her hipbones. Right here, with my arm wrapped around her leg and my mouth on her cunt—nope, nope, I totally meant pussy—there was nothing else in the world.

Except a faint noise coming from the other room, and that was really fucking strange considering I locked the door myself.

I moved my hand from Shannon's chest to her lips, shifting to pinpoint the rustling sound that seemed to get closer with each breath. "Did you hear something?" I mouthed.

She shook her head, swatted my hand away from her mouth, and whispered, "Maybe you should focus on the task at hand" —she glanced between her legs— "and not interpret every gust of wind as a guerilla attack."

And maybe you need to be a whole helluva lot more careful, peanut.

"I like you better with my cock in your mouth." I listened for a few more beats while she rolled her eyes. I wanted to spank her, I wanted to fuck her, and most of all, I wanted to wipe that frustrated frown from her beautiful mouth and see her come apart in my hands. "I'll take care of you in a minute. I'm gonna look around first."

Shannon yanked her robe closed while I tugged on my boxers, and when I focused in, I could hear someone in the other room. I flattened myself against the wall to get a feel for the location of the breathing, and I sensed footsteps moving toward my position.

I gestured for Shannon to stay on the bed, and she responded with another eye roll.

Then a crash sounded from the hall and I rounded the corner, my fist immediately connecting with bone and soft tissue. He crumpled to the ground, howling in pain, and I secured his hands against his lower back with the not-so-gentle pressure of my knee.

Shannon flipped on the light—so much for staying on the goddamn bed—and she cried, "Riley!"

"Riley?" I rolled him over and sure enough, Shannon's little brother and his busted nose were bleeding all over the slate floor. She stomped into the bathroom and emerged with a damp towel for him.

"Son of a bitch," he groaned, clutching the towel to his face.

"What are you doing here?" she asked.

"I couldn't remember which room was mine and Patrick kicked me out, but I had your key from when I was bringing in the gift baskets last night. I was just going to sleep in your bathtub but then I heard...well, I was going to trying to leave quietly but I tripped on your shoes, Shan."

"How long have you been here?" I asked.

He eyed me up and down, not missing the fact I was in his sister's room wearing only my underwear. An uncomfortable scowl was obvious beneath the growing rush of bruises that would dominate his nose and eyes tomorrow. "Long enough."

Shannon fussed over him until the bleeding stopped, but that didn't prevent her from casting several irritated glances over her shoulder. For my part, I stood with my arms crossed over my chest, trying to figure out why a grown-ass man was creeping into his sister's room at three in the morning and letting her wipe his fucking nose. It wasn't unlike the scene I observed at the reception tonight, where she kicked everyone's asses into gear and didn't sit down once. She did everything short of busing the tables after dinner service.

I couldn't explain why, but it didn't sit well with me. I knew I didn't like it.

"Go snuggle up on the couch," she instructed, gesturing past Riley to the small living room. "I think I have some ibuprofen, and I'll get you some ice."

You have to be fucking kidding me.

"What?" I snapped.

"What do you mean, 'what'? Look at what you did to him." She glared at me, nodding toward the bloodied towel as if I'd ripped off the guy's arm and not simply knocked his nose off-kilter.

"And I'd do it again," I said. "When it's the middle of the night and something isn't right, I shoot first and ask questions later."

"Yeah, that's brilliant," she said. "You and your itchy trigger finger can go now. You've done enough."

"No, no, I'm good," Riley said, wobbling to his feet. "I'll crash with Sam."

"That's the smartest thing you've said all night," I murmured.

Shannon's little fist shot out, landing square on my bicep. "It's rude to be an asshole after breaking someone's nose."

"It's also rude to creep into someone's cottage in the middle of the night," I said. "I think we're even now."

"Not exactly how I'd define even," Riley murmured, wiping his nose again and grimacing at the trail of blood on his hand. "Anyone want to point me in the direction of Sam's room? Wouldn't want another beat down tonight."

"He's three cottages down," she said, patting Riley's shoulder.

"Great. Thanks." He moved toward the sliding glass door near the beachside patio. "And I didn't see anything. I never do," he muttered. He shot me another glance, but between the bruising and swelling, I couldn't discern much from it.

Shannon followed and I trailed close behind her, my hand resting on her hip when Riley stepped out onto the patio. He turned toward Sam's cottage but soon stopped, groaning. "Why do I always walk in on this shit?"

Shannon joined him, pulling her robe tight to her body as the damp air surrounded her. I stepped beside her, and surveyed the beach plum shrubs and sandy dunes connecting the string of cottages to the shoreline. Only a few feet away, I spied the doctor kicked back on a lounge chair.

With Shannon's sister on his lap.

And his hands under her dress.

"Could you not wait until you got inside?" Riley yelled. "This fucking night...I'm tellin' you. I just want to go to sleep but no, I get punched in the goddamn face and swallow a pint of my own fucking blood, and I don't even get to stay on the couch!" He glared back at Shannon and me, shaking his head. He shifted to face Nick and Erin, and now that he wasn't crying about his busted nose, I realized that Riley was built like a pile of bricks. If he wanted to knock me on my ass, he had a decent shot at it. "You really want Matt to blow a gasket on his wedding night? Really? Because that's what would happen if he saw this. I can't even go there with you two. Can't. Even."

"There's no reason to tell Matt," Erin said.

"Don't tell Matt?" Riley shouted. "Are fuckin' kidding me, E? You're here *one day* and you're starting shit like this? No, no. No one is telling Matt a fucking thing about *any* of this." He gestured to both his sisters, and this time, I didn't miss the fire in his eyes. "We're all pretending none of this happened. We're pretending there's no attention-whoring or hate-fucking going on right now."

"I think you might be exaggerating the situation, buddy," Nick said. "Really, we're just having some drinks and hanging out."

Somewhere between the blowjob that made me hear colors and laying Riley out, we must have fallen into an alternate, cock-blocking reality. It was like every one of these assholes knew I was half-desperate to be inside Shannon again, and they were inventing obstacles in my path.

"You might be a smart guy, Nick," Riley said, "but right now, you have no idea what you're talking about. And you —" He pointed at Erin. "If you don't want shit storms everywhere you go, don't stir them up."

I watched Riley's fingers curling into fists, unclenching, and repeating the motion. I had no idea who he wanted to pummel more—me, the doctor, or his sisters—but I wasn't letting that shit go down tonight. I stepped in front of Shannon, forcing some distance between her and whatever the hell was going on with these people.

Alternate. Fucking. Reality.

"Riley," Erin said, and his gaze snapped to her. "I got this."

"You fucking owe me," Riley called as he walked past Nick and Erin, his head shaking and his hands fisted at his sides. "*All* of you fucking owe me."

Riley disappeared into the night, and that seemed like the perfect opportunity to stop watching the doctor and the quiet sister get it on. Shannon didn't object when I led her back inside, and she didn't even roll her eyes when I checked all the locks. She just stood in the center of the room, her arms wrapped around her, gazing into the darkness.

She was thinking hard, if the frantic fingers tapping against her elbow were any indication. The doctor—the one who had his arm around Shannon only a matter of hours ago—had something to do with this, but the sister was most of it. Erin might be the quiet one, but she was the troublemaker.

I pointed to the robe. "Off."

She continued staring for a moment, her fingers never quite stilling, then shrugged out of the fabric that I was torn between loving and hating.

The robe dropped to the floor but she didn't meet my eyes. I gestured to the mattress. "Bed."

She slipped between the sheets at my command, rolling to her side and curling her arms around the pillow. Her body was tight, coiled, and I saw it all vibrating through her. At once, she was tired and tense, and those merged into a vulnerability I couldn't ignore. Shannon was so much—loud and nosy, spoiled and bossy—but she was so much more, too. If I watched her all night and through the rest of this weekend, I wouldn't be able to categorize it all.

Instead, I spanked her until she begged for my cock.

"DOESN'T Kaisall have a house in the Hamptons now?"

I glanced over at Wes from where I was marooned on the shore. The North Atlantic in May wasn't toasty warm, and after years away from salt water, I was reminded how hard it was to swim against ocean currents.

Oh, and I'd spent the past two nights fucking and fighting with Shannon.

"He does," I said. "Why?"

"Let's catch a ferry over to Montauk," he said. "There's good surfing out there, and I want to hear about the firm he's running these days."

Jordan Kaisall was a good SEAL but a better business-man. He pulled one deployment, during which he took a bullet through the kneecap when a mission went tits-up, and went on to open a private security firm. He was a good friend and he never stopped recruiting me to help run the tactical side of his operation. His protection details ranged from Washington insiders and CEOs to the occasional heiress or celebrity.

"Yeah, I'll give him a call," I said, feeling my heart rate gradually edging into normal territory.

Getting the fuck away from Cape Cod and mouthy redheads with delicious thighs was probably for the best. That, and the mouthy redhead in question was leaving for Boston this afternoon.

She'd yanked the blankets off sometime before dawn, and tossed my trousers at me. "You're leaving now," she announced.

Her hair was wild, her lips kiss-swollen, and her expression told me there was only a slim chance that she'd let my cock change her mind.

"Here I thought check out wasn't until noon," I said.

"And I thought you'd be a grower, not a shower," she said. "Guess we were both wrong."

"Hmm," I murmured, scratching my chin while I stared at her. "You need me to tie you to the headboard again, don't you? Maybe a good, hard fuck to start the day? We can bend that bratty attitude of yours into shape."

Shannon murmured to herself, a small smile lifting her lips, and she narrowed her eyes in my direction. "That's a charming offer," she said, "but I don't think your dick can reach my *attitude*, let alone bend it. I'm also leaving for Boston soon, and I'd like you to get the fuck out of my cottage."

I kept my eyes on Shannon while stepping into my wrinkled clothes. "Have you ever met anyone with bigger balls?"

She tilted her head and offered a smile intended to eat

my soul. "Hate to break it to you, but I've seen bigger blueberries than the set you're rocking."

"I meant you," I said, pulling her against my chest. "Have you ever met anyone with bigger balls than *you*?"

She requested that I fuck off, and slammed the door behind me.

I stood and stretched out my hamstrings. "Where'd you find yourself last night? You weren't with the little sister long."

Wes laughed and leaned back in the sand on his elbows. "That crew knows how to have a good time. They give each other a ton of shit, and they could drink with any Team guy," he said. "It pains me to say this, but I like them."

With that thought, I dove into the waves and swam to the sandbar and back. I didn't want to think about the Walshes, and I really didn't want to think about my burning abs and quads either. I didn't want to think about *Shannon* anymore. I lost my fucking mind with her, and the problem was, I wanted to lose it again.

When I emerged from the water and plunked my ass on the sand, Wes threw a peculiar look at me. "Did you take some shrapnel?"

"What? No," I said. He nodded at my back, and I glanced over my shoulder to find half-moon punctures and long, shallow abrasions. "It's nothing. Just a few scratches."

Shortcake. Another reason to keep her tied up next time.

Yeah. *Next time.* She might have kicked me out of her bed before sunrise, but that didn't mean this was over. It was fucked up beyond belief considering we got off on taunting each other, but it wasn't over.

He eyed me while a slow smile twisted across his lips. "That's one way to taste the local flavor," he said, laughing.

I tried telling myself this was a one-time thing—sure, technically it was more like multiple times but all in the course of one weekend—and she annoyed the shit out of me. But there was no reason to pretend I wasn't coming back for more of Shannon Walsh.

I didn't know when and I didn't know how, but I wasn't nearly finished with that peanut.

FIFTEEN MONTHS *ago*

I DIDN'T KNOW whether I should be proud or embarrassed that I didn't learn to drink tequila until I was in my thirties and met Lauren. I'd always thought it involved worms and the most heinous hangovers in life, and I stuck with my beer, wine, and whiskey.

"To the last weekend of the summer," Lauren said, lifting her margarita glass in salute.

"I'll drink to that," I said. I leaned back in the massaging seat and sipped my beverage while the technician scrubbed last month's dark plum paint from my toes.

Lauren knew how to find all the hidden gems, and this cozy spa with its happy hour pedicures was the best of them. Neither of us was particularly good about taking time for ourselves. We gave everything to our careers and our people, but we were good about forcing each other to breathe once in a while.

Our version of breathing involved liquor, cupcakes, swearing, and shopping.

"You should come to dinner tomorrow night," she said while flipping through an old copy of *Glamour*.

"What are we having?" I asked.

Lauren studied an article about sex positions to drive her man wild. She chuckled and shook her head before turning back to me. "I don't know yet. Might just order paella."

"Ohhhh, paella," I said. "I'd be down for that."

"Everyone loves paella," she said. "It's like spicy rice crispy treats for adults. With chorizo."

We clinked our glasses together again, and I went back to debating between polish shades. I was a creature of habit, and if I was painfully honest with myself, I didn't love change. I preferred consistency, knowing what to expect, knowing what was around each corner.

I stuck with dark plum.

"Are you sure you don't want to come to the Cape with us this weekend?" Lauren asked.

She and Matt were spending the long Labor Day weekend on Cape Cod, at the same inn where they were married three months ago. I kept telling them I didn't want to crash their second honeymoon, but I was nowhere near ready to return to the scene of my wedding weekend crimes.

"Do you not find it strange that you're trying to bring me along for a romantic getaway?" I glanced around and lowered my voice. "Tell me: what's wrong? Are you bored with each other? Is the spark already dying? Is married sex that bad?"

Lauren swatted me as she doubled over laughing, and my drink splashed down the front of my dress. "No!" she said. "On all counts."

"Then why would you want me hanging out with you? Do you really want me barging in, in the middle of your sexytimes, asking if you want to go biking or paddle boarding or some outdoorsy shit like that? Or snuggling up between the two of you to watch movies and hog the popcorn?"

Lauren sipped her drink and tucked her hair behind her ears, nodding to herself. "Honest?"

I gulped. Nothing preceded by an offer of honesty was ever good. "Always."

"It seems like I haven't seen you all summer," she said. "This is the first time we've talked, just you and me since... since the wedding. You only dodge people when you're trying to figure something out by yourself. But I miss you. I'm worried about you."

I waved her off. I hadn't been avoiding her. Not completely. "There's no need to worry about me—"

"Don't even start," Lauren said, laughing. "But you spend enough time taking care of everyone else that you spend no time taking care of yourself."

"I just..." My voice trailed off while I skimmed through my appointments for the rest of the week.

Tomorrow was packed but Friday was wide open after visiting some properties in the morning. *Good.* I needed that time to catch up on budgeting for Walsh Associates' next round of investment purchases, and I owed wedding gifts to a handful of business acquaintances and once-upon-a-time friends. Everyone had some of those: people you used to be tight with, but now only saw via social media and the occasional get-together.

"I'm not going to force you to talk to me," Lauren said. "But I know you have your hands full at the office. I also know that sorting through your mom's things is emotionally exhausting and super stressful—"

Yesyesyes. I can feel the weight of it on my shoulders and in my heart, and I am doing everything in my power to keep it together.

"—and you insist on doing it by yourself."

Because I can't let anyone else do it. I have to own this and I have to do it my way.

"And I know Sam has been a whiny bitch for months."

That whiny bitch is headed for an epic breakdown if he doesn't start taking care of himself.

"You know I think taking a break from online dating is really positive, because hello—weirdos—but the dry spell must be rough. So I worry about you."

It was a miracle that I didn't choke on my margarita. When it came to Lauren, I rarely censored the details of my love life but I'd been selective recently. I didn't want the "Hey, I fucked your brother" bomb slipping out between stories about the guy who kept at least eighty Glo-Worm dolls in his bedroom or the guy who insisted on wearing a wool beanie cap during sex. In the summer.

I continued scrolling through my emails, hoping this line of questioning would be replaced by anything else. I hated being the object of concern. I was the one who did the worrying and checking on people. If someone noticed that I was off, even my best friend, I wasn't doing enough to keep it together. I didn't know how to be the person others worried about, and I rarely knew what to do with their concern.

"What are we celebrating? Tomorrow night?" I asked, changing the subject while shooting a quick response to Tom's messages.

"Lots of things," Lauren said. She shook her head at me,

annoyed that I was dodging her questions. No, she never forced anyone to talk to her, but she had that severe teacher stare down hard. She could force a mime to break character with that stare. "We're celebrating eating outside on warm summer evenings, and sangria, and long weekends." She paused while the server refilled her glass. "Oh, and Will's in town."

This time, I did choke.

I blamed it on the stiff tequila and slapped away Lauren's hands when she rubbed my back like a colicky infant. "I'm fine, I'm fine," I said and knocked back the rest of my drink. "Didn't you say he was deployed?"

I was going for vague curiosity. I didn't want to know what was happening in Will's life; I was only asking because she brought it up and I was polite like that.

Even though he was an arrogant asshole.

She hummed and held up a finger for me to wait while she sent a text to Matt. "Yeah, a three-month tour. *Most* SEAL Team guys go through cycles of deployment, training ops, and leave. Will isn't most team guys. There's always another mission, another training op, another promotion. He can't get enough of it. Just like my dad."

Since I was working damn hard at my vague curiosity, I paged through Instagram for a minute. It was the only thing I could do to keep from firing off fifteen questions about Will.

"You must be excited to see him. Will, that is." I glanced over at Lauren. "How long is he in town?"

"Um, I think he's planning to head out on Friday. He said something about surfing somewhere."

"Surfing is good," I murmured. "How long is he on leave?"

She was too busy texting Matt—the two of them were ridiculous with the texts—to care that I was looking for a detailed accounting of her brother's whereabouts. And it wasn't like I was going to do anything with that information.

We had our fling, it was over, and there was nothing more to it.

And side note: I didn't even like the guy.

"Not long. The weekend, maybe a bit longer," she said, smiling at her screen. Seriously, I've seen the mobile phone bills. Those two could clear five hundred texts per day without breaking a sweat. "But he's running training missions with new SEALs for the next six months. A lot safer than the missions he was leading overseas. My mother's happy about that."

"I can imagine," I said. My knowledge of all things military was limited to the stray details Lauren shared about her wildly overprotective father and her life growing up near the naval base in Coronado. "So where do these training missions take place? Is that in California?"

Maybe my curiosity was more than vague.

"No, he went through BUD/S—it's like SEAL 101—in Coronado, but he's based out of Little Creek, Virginia. He's never there anymore. He's been overseas for the past few years, and I don't even remember the last time he was stateside, aside from the wedding."

"Huh," I said. For someone accustomed to direct questioning, this vague curiosity bullshit was strenuous. "Must be tough, you know...not getting home often. Probably hard on his friends...or girlfriend."

She frowned at the creamy orange shade on her big toe. "Do you have anything a little brighter? More a tangerine?" The technician fetched every polish between yellow and red, and Lauren studied each while my question lingered between us. After much consideration, she selected a new color and sent another text.

Chuckling, she typed out a few more messages and I was convinced she was ignoring my original comment. It was probably the best avenue for everyone involved; I didn't need to fall down the Will Halsted rabbit hole again.

As I said, I didn't even like the guy. Total douche waffle.

"He doesn't have a girlfriend," she murmured. "Hasn't since he finished the second leg of SEAL training and shipped out to Afghanistan."

I hid my smile behind the margarita glass.

The discussion turned to Lauren's school and the last-minute preparations necessary to start the year. Her teachers were busy setting up their classrooms and getting familiar with the warehouse-turned-schoolhouse, and she was eager to finally open the doors to new students.

We loitered on the sidewalk when the toenail polish was dry, debating whether we'd survive another round of drinks. Considering we both had early morning meetings and we'd already put away several margaritas, we decided it was time to call it a night.

"Come over around seven tomorrow night. We'll make sangria and sit on the terrace and soak up the last seconds of summer," Lauren said as she started walking backward toward her place. "Oh, and you might like to know Will has been asking about you, too."

I WAS AIMING for casually late. I landed closer to offensively late.

When the office started clearing out around five, I dug into some property value research in preparation for my Friday morning appointments. The title history was more complicated than I expected, and when I looked up from my work, it was almost eight thirty.

"This wasn't the plan," I yelled to my empty office. I gathered my things and headed for the garage, aggravated that I didn't have time to stop at my favorite wine shop to grab a few bottles.

Traffic was heavy and street parking was a nightmare, and it was after nine o'clock when I reached Matt and Lauren's loft. I let myself in and dropped my things in the entryway, and heard laughter coming from the terrace.

I didn't give myself a moment to hesitate and marched straight to the screen door. "Sorry I'm late," I said, settling into a seat between Matt and Lauren at the round patio table. "I was buried with research on the Commonwealth Avenue property."

"We didn't think you were coming," Matt said.

"Shannon *always* comes," Will said, his eyes trained on me as if Matt and Lauren didn't exist. "Sometimes it takes her a little longer to get there, and there's nothing wrong with that."

And there he was. The same obnoxious, sun-bleached blond prick who gave me two of the best nights of my life and vanished without so much as a 'Thank you, ma'am.'

"Well then," Lauren said under her breath. "Sangria?" She didn't wait for my response, and set a glass in front of me.

"Will," I said.

"Shannon," he replied.

I glanced around the table, ignoring Will's cool, steady gaze. "What did I miss?" I asked.

"We were just telling Will that we're thinking about getting a kitten," she said, gesturing to Matt. "Or a puppy."

"Because you two don't have enough to do?" I asked.

"Because she," Matt nodded to Lauren, "always gives me shit about growing up without pets."

"Every kid should have a pet. At least a freaking goldfish, dude," Lauren said. "And I think we can handle a kitten."

"We are *not* getting a cat," Matt said. "We need a black lab or a beagle, maybe a bulldog. Something loyal and fun. I don't want some moody cat."

"He's right," Will said. "Cats are assholes."

Cats are assholes? What kind of statement is that?

"Why don't you explain that one to me," I said.

Will shrugged and lifted his beer bottle. "Real men have dogs. Dogs do as they're fucking told, and they're happy to have your company. Haven't you ever seen a dog when you come home at the end of the day? It's the best moment of their lives. Every day, they have a new best moment of their lives. Cats are selfish. They don't give a shit whether you're coming or going."

"So you're looking for submission," I said. The corners of Will's mouth tipped up into a smirk. "The dog bows to its master. The cat *is* the master."

"There can only be one alpha, Shannon," he said, and I *felt* those words like no others. It was as if he was speaking directly to my clit, saying, 'Come on, my little pet. It's time to play.'

"Yeah…" Lauren said. "I wasn't so much worried about power dynamics. I was more concerned with the number of times we'd need to walk a dog each day and that we don't currently have a backyard."

"We can change that," Matt said. "Say the word and I'll build you that house."

Lauren held up her hands. "Don't rush me," she said.

"You don't find that argument a bit misogynistic?" I asked. I knew I was baiting Will. "Considering that cats are typically associated with women—how many sexy cats do you see on Halloween, right?—and dogs are associated with men, isn't hating cats equivalent to hating women?"

Will's tongue peeked out and painted his bottom lip, and my eyes went straight to his mouth.

"We've had this conversation before, and you're well aware that I don't hate women," he said. Lauren gasped out a quiet laugh and turned to Matt, asking him what they'd name a bulldog. "Not at all. I like my dogs loyal and my woman fiery."

The debate over canines and felines transitioned to the house Matt was planning to build for him and Lauren—when she was ready for a house, of course—and I was surprised to find Will speaking in complete sentences. He didn't growl at Matt once.

I picked at the dish of gelato Lauren placed in front of me while the men discussed football. I could hold my own in sports talk but I preferred observing Will. I'd never had the opportunity to watch him before, taking in the way he carried himself, understanding his mannerisms. He projected strength and control, yet his presence was commanding without being oppressive. He was unshakably chill, and the way his eyes cruised over the terrace gave me the impression he was aware of absolutely everything. His beard was fuller. Without thinking, my legs squeezed together at the memory of his scruff on my thighs.

I never expected to be face-to-face with him again. At least not this soon.

And I still didn't like him.

"I'll be right back," I said when the conversation shifted to World Series predictions. I only liked talking baseball with Riley. That kid was a stats savant.

I slipped inside and busied myself in the kitchen, loading the dishwasher and wrapping up the leftovers. The loft was spacious, and only a few rooms were carved out of the open space. I wandered down the hall, ducking into the bathroom under the staircase.

Will was waiting for me when I opened the door. "How've you been, peanut?"

Crossing my arms and leaning against the doorframe, I smiled at him. "Can't complain." He stared for a long moment, and I realized I'd missed the way his gaze felt on me. *This* gaze, not the detached, watchful stare I saw outside, but this hot, lazy intensity only a surfer boy could pull off. "How's the military industrial complex?"

"Business is brisk," he said.

I inclined my head down the hall, toward the terrace. "You're being unusually amenable."

Will rubbed his palm over his jaw, grinning. "He grills a decent steak," he said, "but I got eyes on him. The second he steps out of line—"

I shook my head and placed my hand on his chest. "Take it down a notch, commando."

He glanced at my hand and then up at me, smirking. That fucking smirk. It was his quiet way of making it damn clear that he was in charge here, and he wasn't about to let that change. "Where do you want me to take it, peanut?"

I wasn't sure who moved first, but within the next breath,

my hand wrapped around the back of his neck, the bath-room door was slamming shut behind us, and my mouth found Will's. His hands gripped my thighs, boosting me up and pressing my back to the wall.

"You should know I don't have sex in bathrooms," I whispered against his lips. "Apparently that's a thing people do, but I'm not one of those people."

"I have no intention of fucking you here," he said. His fingers traced the edge of my panties but never dipped inside. "Just wanted to see if you tasted as good as I remembered."

"And your game is just as weak as it was in May," I said.

Will kissed me again, and this time it was slow. Patient.

Then he slapped my ass, set me on the ground, and walked away.

That asshole.

I stared at myself in the mirror, assessing my swollen lips, disheveled hair, askew sheath dress, and ragged, desperate breaths. My entire body was pulsing with need, and I could barely see beyond that wild hunger. If I didn't get an orgasm right now, I was going to implode.

I got myself back in order, constructed a reasonable excuse for leaving early, and departed without making eye contact with Will. I drove home, frustrated and impatient, thinking up all the things I should have said to him.

What gave him the right to kiss me like that and walk away as if it was nothing?

And if he wasn't interested enough to finish what he started, he shouldn't have kissed me in the first place.

My apartment was dark and quiet, the only noise coming from the cyclical hum of the air conditioner, and I didn't turn on any lights. I stomped toward the master bedroom, heading straight for the attached bath. My clothes fell in scattered heaps, and I stopped only long enough to turn on the shower and drop my bracelets and earrings beside the sink. The water was cool, the perfect balance to my over-heated skin. I leaned against the chilly tile until my body was soaked.

Reaching for the detachable showerhead, I clicked over to my favorite setting, perched my foot on the built-in bench, and positioned the spray exactly where I needed it. My eyes closed, I dropped my forehead to the shower wall, and sighed as the first sensations rolled through me.

Shower orgasms weren't especially powerful but they were quick, and they always took the edge off. I didn't have time to pick out a vibrator, find the lube, cozy up in bed, and engage in thorough self-love. I'd do that later. Right now, I couldn't forget the way Will's hands gripped my ass, the feel of his weight against me, the pressure of his lips. I couldn't forget the way his body pinned me with such intent, a reminder that he knew how to bring me pleasure I didn't know was possible.

I slouched against the wall as I came, and the shower-head slipped from my fingers. The sounds of running water and my hammering pulse rang in my ears, blocking out everything else, and I stayed there, lingering in the small relief of an inadequate orgasm. My mind filled with to-do lists and odd thoughts of budgeting issues and reminders I needed to send Tom, and any tension that might have dissolved just now was replaced with even more.

On a defeated groan, I set the showerhead in its cradle and stood under the spray. I needed the water to wash it all away, to offer me a reprieve from the overwhelming ache inside me, to turn off my racing mind. Instead, I was left with shriveled fingers.

When I stepped out of the shower, I slathered on moisturizer, shrugged into a light robe, and twisted my hair into a bun. I required my bed, a glass of wine, another orgasm, and some *Friends* reruns, and stepped out of the bathroom with that checklist in mind.

"That was hot as fuck."

I shrieked and reared back against the bathroom door, one hand pressed against my thudding heart. Will was sprawled on my bed, the remote control in one hand, a half-eaten apple in the other. He continued flipping through muted sports stations while my stomach did terror-convulsions.

"I was tempted to join in but I couldn't interrupt something that incredible. It was like watching an act of God," he said around the apple. "Hot. As. Fuck."

"What the hell are you doing in my apartment?" I screeched.

He shrugged. "I let myself in."

"You're a presumptuous dick." I couldn't believe this guy. One minute he was slapping my ass, the next he was breaking and entering. Oh, and watching me give the downtown a thorough rinse. "Is that a commando tactic of yours?"

"Yeah, and you want to know another one?" I rolled my eyes. "You have to sit on my face for me to show you."

"Choke on my dick," I said.

"You have that one backward, peanut. You're supposed to choke on *my* dick," he said. He tossed the apple core into the wastebasket on the other side of the room. Of course he made the shot. He was unbearable like that.

"No, I'm pretty sure I had it right the first time," I said.

"You mean this drawer of dildos?" He pointed to the short chest beside my bed. I couldn't believe he went through my things. Any second now, I was going to start chucking those dildos at his head. The idea of pummeling him with the long fat one was quite appealing. "Quite the collection, but since the real thing is right here" —he motioned to his crotch— "hop on and give it a ride. Save the rubber for another day."

"No, not when the real thing" —I frowned at his pants— "only performs for two minutes at a time."

"That mouth of yours," he growled, pressing the heel of his palm between his legs. It was probably an indication that we were both a special brand of crazy, but hurling insults was the most effective form of foreplay we knew.

That was precisely what this was: the hottest fucking foreplay I'd ever had. It was like dirty talk. Slightly evil, highly effective dirty talk.

I yanked the robe tighter to my chest and collected my phone from the dresser. For once, I didn't have a landslide of new emails and texts waiting for me, and I thanked the universe for holiday weekends. "You are one creepy mother-fucker. Is this what you do now? Show up in women's apartments with your dick in your hand, expecting to get laid?"

Will tossed the remote control aside and sat up, swinging his legs over the side of the bed. "My dick was never in hand. That's your job."

I squeezed my eyes shut and slammed my phone down. "You watched me! In the shower! When I was, I mean, I was…"

"When you were hot as fuck," Will said. "It's a compliment. You should learn how to take them."

"I'd like to know," I started, edging closer to the bed, "why you came here."

He reached for the silky belt holding my robe shut, pulling me between his legs. He threaded the fabric through his fingers, tugging until the knot at my waist loosened. The robe parted, exposing a narrow strip of skin. He leaned forward, offering a quick glance up at me, then ran his lips from my collarbone down to my belly button. His whiskers tickled my skin, and as much as I wanted to call him names and yell at him for being such a beast, I wanted to feel this.

I wanted to feel *good*, and I didn't want to care about anything else.

"Shannon," he said, my name heaving out in a sigh that ignited a wave of goosebumps across my chest. "You know why I'm here."

Will's hands moved under the robe and over my shoulders, and the fabric fell to the floor with a soft rustle. He caged me between his legs, his thighs tightening against my hips, and my fingers dove through his hair as my mouth met his.

He reached between us, unfastened his belt, and popped the buttons on his jeans open. His clothes soon joined mine on the floor. He brought me to his lap, his erection tucked against my belly, and kissed up my neck and over my jaw to my mouth. My body had plans of its own, rocking against Will's cock and drawing rough gasps and grunts from him.

"You want this?" he said with clenched teeth.

His jaw was locked and his fingers were digging into my hips, nearly painful, and I pressed my lips to his throat. "You went to the trouble of breaking into my apartment. *You* must want this," I said against his skin.

Will's hands moved from my hips to my shoulders, and

he pulled me away from him. Light from the television flickered around us but neither of us stopped to turn it off. He cupped my face, angling me until we were eye to eye. "If you don't want it, I don't want it. Simple as that," he said.

I nodded, and pressed myself against his chest. His arms came around me and I bit down on my lip to keep it from trembling.

There was a second where I nearly lost my balance, where I almost dropped all the balls I was juggling. That tiny drop of decency from him threatened to bring me down right here, and I was this close to sobbing in his lap.

I was lucky; I had incredible therapists who helped me escape the mental stranglehold of my father's abuse. They taught me to conquer the degradation and crippling powerlessness, and they made me believe that I deserved a healthy sex life. It required years of reminding myself that sex wasn't dirty or wrong, and there was no shame in wanting it, either.

That didn't mean the paralyzing fear never paid me a visit. It stayed in the background, always reminding me to protect myself.

Until Will told me I was safe with him.

"Use your words, peanut. I know you have them."

I fought my way back from that dark corner of my mind to focus on the heat of his cock against my belly, the security of his arms, the desire throbbing in my veins. He was right; I had the words now, and with those words, I was always in control.

Even when I let him take charge.

Pumping his cock twice, I shifted and sank down over him. "Yes." My head lolled back on my shoulders and I released a deep, starved moan that had been burning for the satisfaction of feeling Will seated inside me again. "This." My nails raked over his scalp and fisted around his hair, jerking his head back. "You."

Will's eyes drifted shut as I started rocking into him. His hands found my waist and held me, letting me take everything I needed.

"I hope you're enjoying this," he said on a shuddering breath.

"Not going to last?" I asked.

"All right, peanut, that's it," he murmured, his palm connecting low on my ass.

The moment I was about to grind into him, he lifted me off his lap and tossed me on the bed. I landed in a contorted pile of girl, my body folded in the least sexy pose imaginable, my hair sliding from its tie, and my head buried between a stack of pillows. Before I could right myself or hit Will with a bitchy comeback, he yanked the blankets and sheets out from under me. He spanked my ass *hard*, flipped me over, and anchored my hands above my head.

"You're done talking. You're done thinking. Close your eyes and shut it all down." His other hand trailed down my inner thigh, and with one quick movement, he slapped my pussy. *Slapped.* "I'm the boss here."

Oh.

Yes. Yes he was.

Seven

FIFTEEN MONTHS *ago*

REGARDLESS OF WHICH country or time zone I was in, I woke up with the dawn. It was a habit that annoyed the shit out of me when I was on leave, but today was different.

Today I opened my eyes and found Shannon's head on my chest, her hair spilling over her shoulders and her lips pursed in the sexiest pout I'd ever seen.

Spending the night with her wasn't part of the plan. Neither was fucking her again. Hell...I didn't even think I'd see her. It was within the range of possibilities when I'd landed in Boston, but I figured she'd have her hands full disemboweling slow-talkers or castrating banker boys or hosting a regatta gala. Why would I expect Shannon to show up at my sister's place on a Thursday night when she could be out serving up verbal gut punches to her minions?

Yeah, I was going to keep telling myself that. It was pure coincidence.

But then she stepped onto the terrace last night, shot me one of those looks intended to fry testicles, and the bell sounded for round two. Nothing could stop us from going hard at each other, even with her brother and my sister as an audience.

Waiting for her outside the bathroom made all this about much more than fighting words. It made this tangible, and I knew where it would go from there...but I wasn't letting that comment about submission go down easy.

I didn't care whether she had the world by the short hairs. She didn't scare me with her balls-out attitude or her cobra venom glares. If anything, that shit turned me all the way on. I'd spent the better portion of last night with one of my sister's lime green cloth napkins over my lap because my belt was strangling my dick.

By the time I made it to Shannon's apartment, I was ready to throw the fuck down.

None of this was part of the plan. This was supposed to be an easy weekend, some time to unwind before leading a string of training ops. A quick visit to keep an eye on my sister's new husband followed by lots of beer, surfing, and sleep. That sequence of events didn't involve bullshitting with a doorman, picking a lock, or watching Shannon put a showerhead to work.

I'd spent a solid minute with my jaw on the ground, and another five convincing myself to keep my pants on. Only the structured brutality of football was enough to stop me from getting into that shower and giving her what she needed.

Instead, I wanted Shannon to come to me.

I thought about leaving after she fell asleep last night. I wasn't the guy who stayed over, but there never came a point when it felt like we were finished. Every time I got her off, I was thinking about what I wanted to do to her next.

Right now, I wanted to grab her ass and go back to sleep. I was in no rush to leave this bed.

Hours later, I stirred when Shannon murmured something incoherent and rested her hand an inch from my dick. He was a good sailor and snapped to attention, lengthening and twitching and just fucking desperate for her touch.

A part of me knew it would always be that way.

I rolled Shannon off my chest and positioned myself between her legs. She tasted different after a night of rowdy sex, and I liked that shit. It was a wicked kind of heaven. Her hips stirred as my tongue circled her clit, thrusting against me as her body found its natural rhythm. A raw moan slipped from her lips, and I glanced up to see her watching me with sleepy eyes and a rosy flush on her cheeks.

It was a good look on her.

I licked and sucked until she came against my tongue, then I pushed inside her and we rocked together, slow and gentle and the complete opposite of everything we did last night. No demands, no spanking, no swearing. Just sighs and hums and the subtle language of bodies that understood each other.

It didn't matter that we hated each other. My cock craved this little spitfire.

We stayed tangled together, kissing and stroking while morning light filled Shannon's bedroom. I was half hard again and fully convinced that I wanted *this* for the next four days. Beer, surfing…they could wait.

"Mmmm, that was nice," she purred, stretching beneath me. She glanced at the clock and groaned. "Fuck, it's late.

Time to get up. Busy day. I'm going to shower first, and then you can hop in."

She wiggled out from underneath me, tossed the sheets off, and sat up, and if there was any doubt about whether I was a greedy prick, it was put to rest when I wrapped my arm around her waist and hauled her back. "That won't be happening."

I trapped her on the mattress with my legs on either side of her torso and my cock between her breasts. With my hand fisted around my shaft, I dragged myself over her nipples, and those sweet little peaks perked up for me. A thin streak of fluid painted her skin. "You're staying right there."

"You're cute. This is really charming, the whole jerk off on my tits and brand me with your spunk routine," she said, a disapproving look aimed at my dick. "But I have to work today, and you're not on the short list of people from whom I take orders."

"You took plenty of orders from me last night," I said. I kept stroking, slower now but much, much harder.

"Will," she sighed. "Seriously. I have appointments. My brothers are going to wonder where I am."

"Your brothers have already taken off for the weekend." I pulled her hand away from twisting in her hair and placed it on my cock. She threw a sour scowl in my direction but immediately caressed me like she was trying to prove a point. "Yeah, I got the whole rundown from Matt last night," I said, groaning. "You're the only one punching in today, peanut."

I knew what I was doing when I tailed Shannon home and convinced her doorman I was one of her brothers last night, and I knew what I was doing right now.

I wanted her all to myself.

And this didn't require analysis. I mean, fuck...after three years of near-continuous deployment, wasn't I *supposed* to drown myself in pussy? It was probably listed in the Navy's official Rest and Recuperation Policy as a suggested activity.

Visiting loved ones, hunting and fishing, comfort food, consensual sex.

But I couldn't blame this on post-deployment horny anymore. The past three months hardly qualified, considering they were spent in the scorched Nevada desert, teaching a team of rookie SEALs how to survive the dry heat.

This was—oh, hell, her fingers were fucking incredible—this was too complicated to figure out right now. My only priority was hidden somewhere between prolonging this as much as possible and exploding *right this second*. "I'm leaving for Montauk this afternoon. Come with me."

She stared at me, her brow furrowed and a frown pulling at her lips. "What? Why?"

Her hand stilled, and I covered it with mine, urging her to continue.

"I have a buddy who has a house there. He's away for the weekend," I added.

I could handle her saying no, but I could also throw her over my shoulder and kidnap her. It wasn't like her kicking and screaming didn't turn me on.

"Why?" she repeated. Our hands were moving together, fast and firm.

"Don't you ever want to disappear? Leave this all behind for a few days?"

I didn't know where those questions came from, but they were the right ones. She blinked at me twice, that fierce poker face dissolving, and I saw the same flash of vulnerability I'd seen months ago. Her eyes shifted to her phone—the one that didn't stop vibrating and chiming all damn night—and her teeth sank into her bottom lip. There were instances when she dropped the bitch boss act, and even though the bitch boss was hot as hell, the real Shannon was addictive. I couldn't get a taste of her like this without wanting it again.

Something snapped inside me, and those hot, prickly sensations clawed their way down my spine. I couldn't even choke out the words to tell her I was coming.

Gripping her velvet-upholstered headboard for support, I groaned and panted until my eyes were capable of focusing again. I couldn't look down yet. I couldn't see my seed splashed over her creamy skin and not spend the rest of the day worshipping her sassy little ass.

Shannon's phone skittered across the bedside table, singing with alerts for a minute straight. Snatching it up, I keyed in her password and powered down the device. "You're not turning that thing on again until Tuesday."

"How did you unlock my phone?" she snapped, trying to tear it away from me. I held it out of her reach and tossed it under the bed.

"Commando tactic," I said, scooping her up and marching toward the shower. "We're leaving in half an hour. Don't pack any underwear."

"I WOULD LIKE MY PHONE BACK," Shannon said, her voice cold and shrill. "Now."

I admired how hard she worked at that attitude. She put everything into being pissed off, and it made me want to throw her up against any of the cars in this underground garage and fuck her while she insulted me.

"Not happening," I murmured.

"Motherfucking meathead," she huffed, stomping away.

"Could you change that to lawyer-fucking meathead? I really prefer precise insults."

It was a prime opportunity to study her ass in a tiny pair of yellow shorts. And those legs. Fuck me, those legs.

I was almost too preoccupied with the thick freckle clusters on her hamstrings to notice she'd opened a Range Rover's rear gate and was busy piling her things inside. Stopping beside her, I grabbed the bags from her and stowed them myself.

"Hand over the keys, peanut," I said while I tossed my backpack beside her brightly colored quilted bags. "Unless you'd like to see some more commando tactics."

Shannon chucked the keys at my head, growling and murmuring to herself as she pivoted, marched to the passenger side, and flung the door open. She was still fuming when I settled beside her in the driver's seat. She really wanted that phone.

"What?" I asked, gesturing to the car's tricked-out interior. Why a little girl needed a badass SUV was beyond me. "No up-armored Humvees available?"

She crossed her legs and stared out the window. "You can suck my dick, William."

Fuuuuuuck. She made furious look too hot for words. I was ready to blow off Montauk and drag her upstairs for angry sex, but we'd agreed upon a disappearance. We both needed a reprieve from who we were every day, and we weren't going to get that in the middle of her city.

"I would, Shannon," I said, "if you didn't have it shoved up my ass at the moment."

She leaned back, tapping her finger against her lips, a predatory smile breaking across her face. "Hmm. I've heard your sister enjoys ass play too. Like, *really* enjoys it."

My groan vibrated through the car and Shannon covered her mouth as evil giggles spilled out. "You didn't fucking go there."

I shook my head and drew a deep breath. I could accept my little sister being married. I could tolerate the general concept of her having sex. I could not handle specific details about her sex life, and I was morally obligated to execute her husband if they were having anything other than bland, infrequent, missionary sex.

"Tell me you didn't go there. You know why? Because if you fucking went there, I'll have to scramble a wet team to dispose of your brother's body when I'm finished with him. And that's not on our agenda for today, peanut."

"I could be bluffing," she said. I spared her an impatient look while backing out of the parking space. "Could be. But you'll have to give me my phone back."

I didn't respond until we were on the highway and well past the city limits. Everything seemed brighter out here, greener and less congested. I hated the closed-in feeling of urban areas, the wall-to-wall concrete, the noise. The beaches and wide-open spaces were for me.

"You can go a few hours without screwing around on your phone," I said.

Shannon shifted, tucking her foot under her leg, and faced me. "Do you have any idea what I do?"

"Explain it to me," I said. I met her glowering expression with a shrug.

She sighed and leaned against the center console. "My brothers—and Andy—handle the architecture. They draw the designs, they manage the builds, and they select the materials. They're phenomenal at what they do but that's *all* they do. I handle the purchase and sale of all our investment properties, manage billing, accounting, and payroll, file taxes, titles, and permits, and keep the office running so my brothers can focus on their projects. I handle the legal shit, too. Plus," she said, tucking her hair behind her ear, "I'm the point person for everything external. That includes media, branding, and dealing with the local bullshit. The preservation societies, the city council, the planning boards, the neighborhood committees…and there's never a moment when one of them isn't going apeshit over something."

"You're a beast. I know." I scratched my chin. "Can none of that rest for one weekend?"

"I buy and sell properties on the weekends, too," she said. "And family businesses are—they're about more than business. Running this operation is just as much about scheduling Sam's medical appointments and getting Riley's trousers dry cleaned as it is managing a revolving line of credit and making sure our contracts are water-tight."

Shaking my head, I frowned at Shannon. "Fucking ridiculous."

"Excuse me?"

Shannon's indignant face was enough to make my jeans feel too tight. "You're ready to claw my eyes out over dry cleaning? Do you tuck your brothers into bed, too? Maybe wipe their noses or read stories until they fall asleep?"

She held up a finger, her mouth still twisted in an angry pout. "That's not what I was saying—"

"Do me a favor," I said, "and don't tell me you can't take a weekend off because you need to fetch some goddamn dry cleaning. I've known for a long time that you're too good for that. Your brothers are adult fucking men. They might even be smart guys, though I have my doubts. They'll figure it out, and it annoys the shit out of me that they let you do all of that on top of everything else you just listed."

"But they don't have any—"

"Dry-cleaned pants. Yeah, you mentioned that," I said. "The world won't fall apart if you step away this weekend, peanut. It might teach them something about handling their own shit."

"It's charming that you think you can walk in and explain my life to me, but you know *nothing*," she said. "Maybe I do too much, but there is one thing I will never stop doing, and that's taking care of my family."

Shannon turned her attention out the window. She didn't speak again until we boarded the ferry in New London. The journey across Long Island Sound would last about an hour, and while I was interested in getting some ferry head, Shannon hopped out of the car, slamming the door behind her, before I pulled the parking brake.

I found her on a bench near the bow. It wasn't hard to spot her. The wind caught her ponytail, and my eyes snapped to those flowing red strands. Big, dark sunglasses hid her eyes. Her feet were propped on the railing and her arms were folded over her chest. A smart man would have handed over the phone and walked away. Fuck, a smart man would have bailed last night and been surfing right now.

I sat down beside her without a word.

The ocean air wrapped around me like a loving embrace. Minutes passed with nothing more than the sound of wind and water, and that was enough for me. I leaned against

Shannon, hungry for her warmth. I was kidding myself if I thought this was only about sex.

Shannon glanced in my direction and then jerked her chin toward the bridge. "Can you drive one of these? Is that one of your commando skills?"

"A ferryboat?" I scratched my chin and scanned the deck. This vessel was a hell of a lot smaller than the pirate-held oil tanker my team assaulted some years back. "If I had to, yeah."

"That would probably be strange for you," she said, the sarcasm heavy in her voice. "You probably aren't used to handling something this size."

My thumb passed over the callous on my trigger finger. "I'm pretty sure you say that so I'll pull out my dick and prove otherwise."

She shrugged and stared off into the Sound. "So there's ferryboats, stalking, and breaking into apartments. What else does a commando do?"

"Whatever it takes," I said.

A sharp laugh slipped from her lips. "Right, me too."

"Yeah," I said. "I've got the global war on terror. You've got the war on lazy pussy-men. By comparison, I have it easy."

She sighed, and her shoulders shook with silent laughter. "Do you ever wish you could take a break from your life? Like…run away, even for a minute?" She glanced at me, and if it were possible, her eyes were the greenest I'd ever seen them, even through the dark layer of her sunglasses.

"I think that's what we're doing right now."

She frowned. "Is that why we're doing this?"

"Yeah," I said. "Maybe we both need a break from life, and…and that's all this is."

"Just a break? From life?"

"Yeah," I said, and as we stared at each other, we knew it was a lie, just like all the others that'd brought us to this point.

KAISALL'S PLACE was on the north end of Ditch Plains, the legendary Montauk surfing destination known for its rocky-bottom shore. The house sat on a narrow slice of beachfront property, with a dense cluster of trees and bushes hiding it from the main road. The interior was simple and comfortable, and the screened-in porch with its wide lounge chairs and sea breezes was the closest thing to heaven New York could offer.

The only reason I knew any of this was because I'd been here before. We could have been in any city, any house. It didn't matter where we were because all I could see was Shannon. I had her half-naked, on the floor, and riding my cock before the front door clicked shut. From the sound of the waves crashing on the beach below, it was an ideal surfing day, but the ocean wasn't going anywhere. The clock was running on this weekend, and the real world was waiting for both of us on the other side.

Day passed into night while we indulged in each other, and if it weren't for my growling stomach, we would have stayed in bed straight through to morning.

The walk into the heart of town was short, and filled with Shannon's commentary on area property values. She stopped in front of a real estate office with glossy fliers advertising local homes for sale in the front window, her head cocked to the side and her lips pursed as she read. I didn't see a single listing for less than seven figures.

"Huh," she murmured, frowning.

"None of these up to par?"

She shook her head and stepped away from the window. "Not my style."

I stared after her, captivated by the flex of her lean calves as she walked. It was strange seeing her without the neck-breaking heels. They seemed like her trademark, right along with her vibrant hair and infinite freckles, and the dark purple flip flops belonged to a side of her only I knew.

She darted into a gifts and home goods shop, the door chimes clanging in her wake, and I followed. A display of silver bowls in the shape of starfish and sand dollars drew her in.

"Hang onto this," she instructed, handing over a large dish.

"Yes, ma'am," I replied, and I didn't miss Shannon's smirk.

The woman could hold her own, and it was hot as hell. Giving orders and expecting obedience was natural to her, much like it was natural to me. It made this battle of wills even sweeter because I earned her surrender every goddamn time.

"Can you get that one?" Shannon pointed to a long tray on the top shelf. It was a good arm's-length beyond her reach.

"Yes, ma'am," I repeated, passing her the tray. "You going to start calling me your errand boy now?"

"No," she said, "that's what I have Tom for."

"Tom? How many brothers do you have? Which one is Tom?"

Shannon knelt to the bottom shelf and selected three sets of miniature knives, each adorned with a silver lobster handle. "Tom's my assistant. Or...he's more like a chief of staff who also gets coffee and anything else I ever need."

Maybe I was a dickhead with an overactive sense of possession, but I didn't like this jack-of-all-trades already.

"*Anything else you need?*"

"Oh, aren't these to die for?" We glanced over when an aproned woman appeared at the display. "These are from a local silversmith. Everything is one of a kind." Her gaze dropped to the items in our hands. "Can I get these boxed up for you?"

"These are wedding gifts," Shannon said. "Can you gift wrap and ship them directly?"

"Of course," the clerk said. "You keep browsing, and I'll get started."

When the clerk was out of earshot, I leaned into Shannon and said, "So what's in a chief of staff's job description?"

She rolled her eyes and inspected a shelf filled with regional photography. "Not what you think, commando. He's my consigliere, and a little brother to me. And we've..." Her voice trailed off as she fingered a small print of Montauk Harbor. "We've been through a lot of the same things. Things other people don't understand."

The photography no longer held her interest, and she wandered off. It was her way of telling me that, yes, her comment demanded further explanation but no, she wasn't saying a damn thing more. Her hand glided down a rack of afghans and quilts, then over the surface of a fully-dressed dining room table. Finally, she stopped at a carousel of jewelry.

"What's the deal with the wedding presents?"

Shannon's index finger traced a row of silver and gold charm bracelets. "People got married. I owed them gifts. Before you kidnapped me for the weekend" —she sent a purposeful glare over her shoulder, which I summarily ignored— "I was planning to go shopping."

"You strike me as the type of guest who wouldn't dare show up empty-handed."

She tried on several bracelets. Replaced all of them. "That's usually the case. I didn't go to any of these weddings, though."

"Why not?" I shook my head as she held a hideous pair of octopus earrings to her lobe. "I thought you loved weddings."

She returned the earrings to the carousel. "Everyone says that," she murmured, almost to herself. "I don't understand why."

"Because the first time I saw you, you were telling Lo's wedding planner how to do her job. Then you were bitching about flowers and appetizers and tents. And after that, you ran the reception. I could be wrong, but you might have officiated the marriage, too."

"Yeah," she said, nodding while rubbing her thumb over a thick metal cuff. "I wanted to give my brother and my best friend an incredible wedding. It was project management with cake and flowers, not wedding fever. There's a big difference." She pivoted, her arms folded over her chest. "You want to know who has wedding fever? Andy. She wants the whole damned thing, and you know what? She deserves her Cinderella moment. Not me. I don't need any of that. I've never thought about getting married, but if I did, I wouldn't want a big, frilly event."

"No buying out beachfront inns for you?"

"No." She walked away to pay and sign the enclosure cards for her gifts, but I was insane. I wanted to know everything about Shannon, and I wasn't done with this topic.

"What would you want?" I asked.

She paused, then returned to writing the cards.

"I don't know," she admitted. "I haven't given it much thought, but...the wedding is just one day. I don't believe in that one day being the best day of your life. That's a lot of pressure for the universe. It's too easy for little things to go wrong, and make it seem like the marriage started on the wrong foot. I want the best day of my life to be a lazy Sunday morning with raspberry pancakes and open houses and *my person*. The wedding is a party with legal documents, and I don't want a party to matter more than a marriage. But that's just me."

With a shrug, Shannon slipped each card into its matching envelope and placed them beside the gift-wrapped boxes.

She couldn't make it easy on me, that was certain. She couldn't be a spoiled bridezilla brat who required a big-ass wedding. She couldn't even be a bitchy workaholic who threw tantrums when forced to take a day off. She wouldn't fit into any neat compartment, and maybe it was time to stop trying.

"I'm hungry," she announced. "Point me in the direction of food. Preferably good food, and decent adult beverages."

"Yes, ma'am."

We headed to a casual restaurant away from the town's quaint center, and sat at the outside bar. She asked me about Kaisall over dinner, and provided an oblique explanation of her refusal to eat anything off a bone. Ribs, wings, fried chicken: all out of the question.

That was no way to live.

The girl was a handful, but…it was amazing to watch her stress melting away. Some of it remained, but she was *present*. Her words softened and flowed more freely. Her body loosened, as if she wasn't bracing for battle anymore. Her gestures slowed, and her smile…that smile. The real thing was unexpectedly powerful, like a riptide.

Once the plates were cleared, she studied the dessert menu like she was being quizzed on it. I ordered another beer and let a deep sense of contentment wash over me. The salt air was sinking into my skin, there was a feisty lady at my side, my belly was full of low country barbeque, and unless there was an act of war this weekend, my time was my own until Tuesday.

"Okay, commando," she said. "I've done all the talking. Now it's your turn. What are you all about? I want the Will Halsted story."

"You should know I'm obsessed with IPAs," I said in my best lilting hipster voice. Shannon's fist landed on my shoulder, and the smiling scowl on her face told me she didn't find that kind of comment amusing. Not entirely.

"Meatheads can't handle conversation. Noted," she said, raising her arm to catch the bartender's attention. The chick with the skinny jeans and nose rings who took our order was busy at the other end, and a big, fisherman-looking dude sidled up.

"What can I getcha, sugar?"

I narrowed my eyes at the bartender. Setting aside that overactive sense of possession for a second, was it not obvious that Shannon was here with *me*? If she was anyone's sugar, she was *my* sugar.

"Irish whiskey. Whatever's top shelf. Three fingers," she said, "on the rocks."

"Sure you can handle that?" he asked while dropping ice into a tumbler with a wink. He fucking *winked* at her. What kind of asshole winked?

I cleared my throat and draped my arm over the back of her chair. That was my first warning. This guy did not want to see my version of a second warning.

"Oh I'll be fine," she said, jerking her thumb in my direction. "Muscles over here will throw me on his shoulder and get me home. He can't have a conversation, but he's really good at manhandling."

"Shannon," I growled.

"Here's my best top shelf Irish. It's a Midleton, the Barry Crockett," he said, setting the tumbler on a napkin in front of Shannon. "It's smooth. You'll like the way it feels in your mouth."

Yep, I am going to have to kill this guy now.

Shannon let out a raucous laugh. "I usually do."

"Let me know if you need anything else, sugar."

"She's good," I snapped. "Thanks."

The bartender glanced at me for the first time since arriving at this end of the bar. "Yeah, yeah," he said, backing away. "Of course, man."

"If you two want to whip your dicks out, I'll find a measuring tape," Shannon said. She lifted her glass in salute to no one in particular and took a hearty sip. "I might have an app for that. I'd need my phone, but some lawyer-fucking meathead stole it."

"Shannon," I said through clenched teeth. I continued glaring at the bartender as he moved to another group.

"That was entertaining," she said. "I always knew you were a savage, but whoa."

Her gaze skimmed up and down my body while she sipped her whiskey, and I couldn't tell if that look was contemptuous or predatory, or a little of both.

"I do like the feel of this in my mouth," she said. "It feels like it's getting me drunk tonight. You're going to tell me stories."

I groaned internally. My whole life was classified, and for good reason. Operational security was a big deal. A big fucking deal. There wasn't much I could tell her, and honestly, I didn't want to burden her with the details. "What kind of stories?"

She reclined against my arm—another benefit of relaxed Shannon: free-flowing affection—and I let my fingers travel over her shoulder. "What do you love?"

The question took me by surprise, and I paused to get my thoughts in order. "The ocean," I started. "Spending the day out on the water. My family. Being back home in San Diego."

Kidnapping mouthy redheaded lawyers.

"Has San Diego always been home?" she asked.

"Yeah, Dad was stationed there before any of us were born. I've seen a lot of this world but it's home to me. It's the only place I want to be. Even when I leave the teams, I'll stay in San Diego."

"When will that be?"

"If," I said. "I can't imagine doing anything else."

She wrapped her tongue around her straw—yeah, I was halfway hard—and squinted at me. "And what is it that you do?"

"Most of it is highly classified," I said. "But I can say I spend most of my time tracking high-value terrorist targets."

"Like...*Zero Dark Thirty*?"

I nodded. I wasn't on that raid, but that was exactly what I did.

"You kill people," she said, her words barely a whisper.

"When they put the lives of Americans in danger, yes, I do," I said.

"That's scary," she said. "Everything you just said, it's scary."

"Fear is a choice," I said. "Danger is real, but you decide whether or not you allow fear into your mind."

"But it's dangerous," she said. "Really dangerous. You have scars from...being over there. I've seen them."

"It comes with the territory," I said.

"But you could be seriously injured or, or..." She glanced up at me, her bottom lip tucked between her teeth. "Why do you do it?"

"I have a duty to serve and protect my country. I have a set of skills few others have and that puts me in more hostile regions and risky missions, but it's a challenge I willingly accept."

Shannon stared into the tumbler, her eyes tracking the ice cube as it clanked against the glass. I couldn't read her and I didn't know what to say. Most of the women close to me knew as much about SEAL life as I did. My mother and Lo lived it, my college girlfriend's brothers were Marines, and that was it. I didn't have any other women. Sure, there was the perky comm officer at the Sigonella base but that only happened a couple of times, and she knew the drill.

Shannon knocked back the rest of her whiskey and signaled for the bartender. Thankfully, Nose Ring responded this time.

With a fresh drink in hand, Shannon said, "We gave you a

nickname." A broad smile filled her face and her cheeks were pink. The alcohol was hitting her. "Only special people get nicknames. It's a thing we do. When Riley was little, he had the worst stutter. It was so hard for him to talk, and he gave up. He just didn't speak."

Tears filled her eyes but she blinked them back before they slid down her face. She reached for her glass and looked away. There were only a few emotions Shannon willingly shared: anger, derision, frustration, contempt, impatience. She kept sadness and pain all to herself, but it was obvious they were there. A dark history lived in her, and I saw it when she didn't think I was looking.

"My father refused to let the school test him for speech disorders. He said Riley was just lazy or looking for attention, and whipped him with a belt every time he heard a stutter. There were some years when Riley didn't speak at all," she said. "But he loved comic books and action figures and all that stuff, so I started reading comics to him. His job was to say some of the words with me, and he was down as long as I called him Batman and he was allowed to use the Batman voice. That was the only thing that worked for him. So we read together every afternoon for years, and in the process, he assigned superhero names to me and my siblings."

There was no correct response to Shannon's confession. It was another layer to tuck away and examine later, and I continued stroking her shoulder without comment.

Nose Ring appeared and broke the silence. "Any thoughts about dessert? The chef has a really wonderful grilled peach with brown sugar and walnut crumble. Would you like to try that?"

Shannon turned away from me and discretely wiped her

eyes. What would it take for her to look me in the eye while she cried? Would she ever let herself give up that much? Would she ever give that much to me?

"Yeah," I said. "Two peaches."

She pulled her sleeves down over her fingers and folded her arms on the bar. "He's the master when it comes to assigning nicknames, and you should feel pretty damn special that he's bestowed one on you," she said, laughing.

"I do," I said. "I'd like to hear it, and yours."

"They call me the Black Widow." She grinned over the rim of her glass, and Riley was dead-on with that one. Natasha Romanov was a nurturing assassin, and one gorgeous, ass-kicking redhead. "You're Captain America."

"Captain America?" I repeated.

"Yep, and I know *The Avengers* inside and out—hell, I'd have to after reading them, over and over and over. Steve never gets into Natasha's bodysuit. It's a sign."

"No one does," I said. Comic book knowledge didn't live in the forefront of my mind these days. "Right?"

Nose Ring returned and set two miniature cast-iron skillets loaded with grilled peaches in front of us. "They're hot," she warned.

"Right?" I repeated.

"Wes got a nickname, too," Shannon said, ignoring me as she picked at the basil leaves atop her fruit. "Thor. That one works for me. I mean, Wes is *really* hot. You're adorable and all, with your chiseled good looks and crusty personality, but if Wes broke into my apartment...well, let's just say I'd be all over that hammer."

"You are not Wes's type, peanut," I murmured.

Her little fist popped my shoulder. "What the hell does that mean?"

"My brother is gay," I said, shocked that Lo hadn't mentioned that. "Despite the fact that you demand I suck your dick, I'm well acquainted with that region of your body and know you don't have the anatomy Wes prefers."

"But…he was totally flirting with my sister at the wedding," she said, incredulous. "I saw and thought, 'Wow. He's way too old for her.' He's lucky I didn't have a few words with him about that, because let me tell you something: I've had plenty of *words* with Nick since then. That bastard's on my list. But back to Wes. If he's gay, why was he putting the moves on her?"

I definitely needed to see Shannon taking Wes to task at least once before I died. My life would not be complete without it.

"He came out to me when he was in high school but he's in the closet around our parents," I said. "My father enforced Don't Ask, Don't Tell when he was a commanding officer, and he's made enough comments over the years to let us all know where he stands. But every time I think about it, I know he wouldn't shut Wes out. He'd need some time with it, but wouldn't disown Wes." I shrugged and dug into the vanilla ice cream accompanying the peaches. "If there is anything I know to be true, it's that my mother would stage a coup before that shit went down."

"You don't think I could turn him?" Shannon forked a piece of fruit and held it up, examining it before taking a bite.

I dropped my hand to her thigh and leaned into her. "Your pussy is busy enough with me. It doesn't need another challenge."

Peach juice glistened on her lips like an invitation. My hand moved to the back of her neck and I pressed my mouth to hers, sucking the sweetness from her skin. Her fork clattered to the ground as she sighed against me.

"I like you like this," I said, my fingers twisting in her hair.

"Drunk?" she asked. "I've heard that before. All of my law school friends said I was too much to deal with until I'd had a few beers."

"Relaxed," I clarified. "You're never too much for me. But right now, you just look..." I leaned back and cupped her face, my thumb sweeping across her flushed cheek as I studied her. "Like you aren't holding up the world. Like you're as sweet and simple as summer peaches. But sweet and simple are the last words I'd use to describe you. You're smart and beautiful and really fucking complicated."

"Too complicated?"

"Probably not," I said, my lips brushing over her neck. "Why don't you sit on my face while I think about it?"

"I like you like this, too," she said.

I kissed along her jaw and cheeks until I landed on her mouth, and there was no way I could pretend this wasn't the way I wanted the weekend to unfold. I couldn't pretend I didn't want *every* weekend to unfold this way. "That's good because you're going to disappear with me in November."

"I am?" she asked. I gave her a quick nod while my fingertips grazed her collarbones. "That's a nice idea but I'll have to think it over."

"Mmhmm," I murmured against her jaw. "You can think all you want while you're sitting on my face, but know this: I'll be seeing you again, peanut."

Eight

FIFTEEN MONTHS *ago*

IT WASN'T easy leaving Montauk.

We stayed in bed until Monday morning turned into afternoon and then evening, and though we'd planned to catch an early ferry, we agreed a later one was equally good.

I never revisited Will's mention of November, and now, standing on the ferry with his chest against my back and his arms locked around my waist, I found myself in the awkward position of wanting to *talk.*

But also, I didn't.

"Stop it," Will growled against my hair. "You're stressing. It happens when you think. Just chill the fuck out."

"How does the government trust you with top secret information when your answer to is everything is 'chill the fuck out'? Is there anything you take seriously?"

"Mmhmm. And I can take a mission seriously but find a

way to be relaxed when I'm on the water with a pretty girl who happens to be rubbing her ass against my cock. Worrying doesn't solve anything. Look at the ocean. Be calm." He bent and pressed his lips below my ear. "And I didn't tell you to stop rubbing all over me."

I wanted it to be that easy—be calm—but it was *never* that easy for me.

We were quiet when the ferry docked in New London, but our embraces were tighter, our touches were firmer, as if we were trying to leave marks on each other. Proof this happened.

Traffic was heavy following the holiday weekend, and it only clogged my thoughts with reminders of all the work I hadn't accomplish these past few days.

"I see you're busy freaking the fuck out despite my direct orders to the contrary," Will said when the city came into view. "Still worried about getting those trousers dry cleaned?"

I yanked his hand away from its resting place on my knee. "Why are you such an asshole?"

"Mostly because it annoys you," he said. His hand moved back to my knee, and it stayed firm there.

"Can't believe I wasted an entire weekend with you," I said to myself, crossing my arms.

"You did, but I'm sure you forgot some of it," he said. "You blacked out a couple of times. My cock is talented like that."

"Right, if you call coming within fourteen seconds a talent."

"I do, Shannon. I really do," he said. "Those fourteen seconds are why you're walking with a limp today, right? And why you groan every time you sit down?"

"Don't you have some guns to polish or a tomahawk to sharpen?"

"Yes to both, but first," he said, pulling into my garage. "The second weekend in November. I'll figure out where."

I started to argue but Will pressed his fingers to my mouth and cupped his hand on the back of my neck. "Yeah, I know, I'm gonna choke on your dick, and I'll enjoy it, too. And you...you will be seeing me in November." He met my eyes, pausing, and slipped his thumb between my lips. "Now let's go upstairs and get you on your knees where you belong."

———

"IT IS bizarre to be doing this on a Tuesday," I said, settling into my seat at the attic conference room table.

Neutral. I was aiming for neutral this morning. No one was going to notice me wincing as I sat—Will's parting gift was fucking me hard enough to leave my ladybits throbbing his name—and no one was going to notice that I was slowly coming down from the wild rollercoaster of this weekend if I kept it locked on neutral.

"It would be less bizarre if you were on time," Patrick muttered.

"I'm five minutes late. Does that warrant a debate?" I asked. "Or are we going to start the meeting?"

"All right, people. Shannon's here, so we can start."

"Thank you, Patrick," I said, rolling my eyes. Bickering was expected; for this crew, it was the definition of neutral. I glanced at Matt, Sam, Andy, and Riley, ready to turn the attention away from me and onto them. "How was everyone's long weekends?"

"We went to a seafood festival in New Hampshire," Andy said, nodding toward Patrick.

I loved them together. It shocked the shit out of me when I realized they didn't hate each other, and now, whenever they talked about all their foodie endeavors or weekends spent geeking out over *Harry Potter*, I wanted to coo all over their dorky cuteness. I wanted them to have a cute, dorky wedding, and loads of cute, dorky babies, too.

"You went to a *seafood* festival?" Riley asked.

"He ate the fish," Andy said, jerking her thumb at Patrick. "I drank the beer."

They exchanged a quick high-five before he said, "I was bartending down in Rhody. Newport kicks ass on long weekends."

"Are we not paying you enough?" Patrick asked.

"I was filling in for a buddy, and I just like it," Riley shrugged. "But if you're looking to unload some cash, I won't stop you."

An instant messenger window opened on my screen.

Patrick: Are we paying him enough
Shannon: Yes
Patrick: You're sure? His shirt has a hole in the armpit and he's not wearing socks.
Shannon: I'm sure.
Shannon: That's his look. It's RISD chic.
Patrick: In other news – Sam has a black eye.
Shannon: Either a chick decked him (probably deserved) or he got it stumbling around drunk.
Shannon: Or, a chick decked him because he was waving his dick around while drunk

Patrick: That's more like it
Patrick: This kid is going to send me to an early grave
Shannon: Have you seen my white hairs?

We'd started messaging in meetings over the summer. It started with me pinging him a link to a property auction, and snowballed from there. Finding time to discuss all the business matters that Patrick and I handled without the involvement of the group was challenging, and it was nearly impossible to get time to plan agendas and collaborate on our approach to strategic issues. This was the best alternative, even if it meant we were essentially carrying on a side conversation through the entire meeting.

"And what about you, Sammy?" I asked.

I glanced at him over the lid of my laptop, and sipped my coffee. I sent Tom an instant message to get me another because I knew one hit of espresso wasn't going to get me through. All told, I probably caught less than three hours of sleep last night. I woke up alone—I expected that part; Will was supposed to be in Virginia by noon—and totally fucking overwhelmed.

I didn't want to have *feelings* for this guy. Desire and attraction were fine, but that was where it ended. I wasn't interested in the pang of sadness that came with an empty bed, or the urge to snap a snarky comment in his direction because he never hesitated to fire back. I wasn't interested in any of that.

We'd had sex, it was good, and it was over.

Maybe we'd have more sex, but…we weren't a *thing*, were an arrangement of sorts, and feelings weren't coming along for the ride.

But they were.

"My weekend was sensational, Shannon," Sam said. He was glaring at me, and any hope of him forgetting about the appointment I missed with him on Friday was lost. "I went to six different music festivals in four states, got drunk at the Feast of St. Anthony, passed out in Cambridge, and almost died in a goddamn elevator crash. Where the fuck were you on Friday and why the fuck weren't you answering your phone?"

The table fell silent, and eventually Riley said, "Did you get to the Thomas Point Beach Bluegrass show? I heard that was good this year."

Patrick: WTF?

Patrick: Is this real?

Patrick: Regardless of whether it's real...I've said it before,
     n saying it again: he needs regular appointments with
        t psychiatrist, the one who helped him with the OCD

          on: Yes, because that will go over so well.
          n: Why don't YOU have that convo with him?

              a metaphor for something? Or are you talking
              ual elevator?" Patrick asked.
                  at do you mean, you almost died?" Matt said.
                   went out in the Back Bay, and I was trapped
                   t the Comm Ave. property for eight hours,"

        We
        ming
                   anded like a fist to the gut. The one
                   d myself I could sneak away was the
                   rld had to implode.

Patrick: There must be more to this story because this sounds ridiculous

Patrick: Sam doesn't go to music festivals. He must have gotten into RISD's special brownies again.

Patrick: I'm almost fully convinced this entire story is a hallucination.

Patrick: And you were supposed to meet him there? What happened?

"The same elevator that slammed into the basement of that building?" Matt asked. "The one I read about, with the massive system failure compounded by the outage?"

"Same fucking one," Sam said, his eyes locked on me. "So I'd love to know, Shannon. How was your weekend?"

I could almost hear Will's voice telling me that my brothers were codependent children, and Sam's insistence that I offer up an explanation worthy of abandoning him only confirmed it.

"Did you go somewhere?" Patrick shifted in his seat, staring at me. "You didn't mention anything...I thought you were staying in town."

"That's because I don't need you to approve my weekend plans, Patrick," I said. "I don't have to tell you where I'm going, or what I'm doing, or who I'm with."

Okay, my attempts at neutral were not working out such that I was now sliding into screechy bitch territory.

Patrick: Was that really necessary?

Shannon: Quiet down over there.

Patrick: What? I thought we agreed we weren't throwing down in meetings anymore

Patrick: United front? No fighting in front of the kids?

Shannon: Oh right, right, I forgot about that when you made my weekend plans a topic of this status meeting
Patrick: If you're going dark for a weekend, prep me for that. I'll support you but don't send me in blind
Shannon: Noted.
Patrick: So…? Where'd you go?
Shannon: Away
Patrick: …and?
Shannon: I was getting back to neutral

"But it would be good if you tell me, so I don't wait around at a property and get stuck in a fucking elevator," Sam said.

"Jesus Christ, Sam, I'm sorry! I lost track of things, okay? I'm sorry." I set my coffee cup down and took a deep breath. "I went away with some friends, and I forgot about the appointment at Comm Ave., and—"

"The only person you spend time with who isn't presently accounted for in this room is my wife," Matt said, and I was ready to fling my computer at his head. It was lovely hearing about my hollow, anti-social existence at such an early hour. "And she was with me, on the Cape."

Sam turned to Matt. "Do you ever get tired of saying it with that sanctimonious tone? *My wife?*"

He shot Sam a smug grin. "Never."

Shannon: Either you rein Juggernaut in or I will
Patrick: Ignore Matt. He's just being a shit stirrer
Patrick: But the runt is off his fucking rocker this morning. He might actually want a pound of flesh for ditching him
Shannon: If he wants a pound of flesh, he'll need to bite off my dick to get it

Patrick: There are times when you really scare me. This would be one of them.

"But you're okay, yeah?" Riley asked. He pointed to the bruise on Sam's face. "Is this from the elevator or blacking out in Cambridge?"

"Elevator," Sam said.

"Why didn't you call one of us?" Andy asked him, angling her pen at Riley, Patrick, and Matt.

Sam shrugged, and shifted his focus to his coffee cup. It was odd, considering the past ten minutes were loaded with a dramatic retelling of his weekend. I expected the tirade to continue, for the rest of the group to come under attack as well, but he smiled to himself, like there was a secret he was keeping safe.

Patrick: There is so much more to this story than we're getting
Shannon: Yep
Shannon: But he's mad that no one noticed he went missing for a weekend and I blew him off, and he's withholding the details
Patrick: Yep
Shannon: We don't have time to pander to this. Move on.

"All right," Patrick murmured. "Let's get back on track here. Sam's alive. Shannon can't manage her appointments. Moving on."

It was Patrick's favorite long-running quip: I could manage everything except my own schedule, and that was amusing because a thread of truth ran through it. I'd dedicated years to coordinating everyone else and forcing them to use a consistent, office-wide calendar system, and it was perfect for the nature of their work. Mine, not so much. Few were the days when I wasn't overscheduled to the point of neurosis, but I made it work. I was everywhere, all the time, but something was always falling off.

While the boys talked properties, I paged through my calendar until I came to November. Thinking about another weekend with Will was reckless. I was tempting fate as far as ridiculous incidents involving Sam were concerned, and Lauren would hear about this soon enough, which was a bundle of awkward if I'd ever seen one.

And I had an event that weekend. Or, more precisely, *Sam* had an event that weekend. He was arguably one of the most talented, sought-after young architects in the region, and he was in constant demand for speaking engagements and conference appearances, not to mention the awards that came his way. But he hated it. He did everything to wiggle out of attending, and when he did, it was because I was dragging him.

Maybe this was a good time to change that routine.

"Sam…" I searched my notebook for the Architecture Society of New England's invitation. I couldn't remember whether it was black tie, and if I was bailing on him, I was at least going to remind him to get his tux pressed. "I can't go with you to the ASNE event in November."

Patrick: When you said 'move on' I thought that meant we were moving on
Patrick: Didn't realize we'd be kicking hornets' nests…
Shannon: Shut up

"And where will you be?" Sam asked.

I murmured, "It's personal. If you need me to find someone to go and hold your hand, I will, but don't pout over it."

Patrick: I needed him to work on a flow issue with the Castavechia restoration
Patrick: Now he's going to spend the day being petulant
Patrick: Well done.

Sam snapped his laptop shut and stood, and his chair crashed into the brick wall at his back. "You're being a dick, Shannon," he called.

We listened as he stormed down the stairs, and the table was silent until Riley burst out laughing. "He's such a fucked-up diva," Riley said.

Matt leaned back in his chair, one arm crossed over his chest. "What are we doing about this? I think it's obvious that he's not doing well, and I don't think we can sit here and watch it get worse."

"We can't drop him off at a psychiatric hospital. As much as I'd like to," Patrick added under his breath. "Until he's willing to admit he needs some help, all we can do is keep the boat from rocking." He glanced over at me. "And not blow off appointments with him."

"He shouldn't have flipped out like that," Riley said. "Sam blows off everyone else and gets away with it because he's a tortured soul and creative genius. That elevator was coming down regardless of whether Shannon was in it with him. I want to hear more about the rest of his weekend. It sounded like a great time, and it's fucking weird because he doesn't do shit like that."

"Exactly," Patrick said.

"Go right ahead," I said. "Report back."

"I think it's my turn to check on him," Matt grumbled. "I'm giving him five minutes to get over his shit."

"No, no," I sighed. "I'll deal with him. He wants to be pissed at me, so let him be pissed at me. And," I continued, tapping Patrick's arm, "I'm going to talk to him about that project. The restoration and remodel for the musician's house. If that doesn't blow his skirt up, I don't know what will."

"All right," Patrick said, nodding, "everyone get back to work."

There was a time when Sam was my best friend. We were inseparable, and when we weren't together, we called and texted constantly. There wasn't a thought that drifted through his mind that he didn't share with me. He appointed himself my chief stylist and online dating coordinator, and was my primary brunch-and-open-house companion. He even invited himself to pedicures with Lauren and me on occasion.

But then Angus died last winter, and though it should have alleviated the pressure on Sam, it made everything worse. He pulled back, curling in on himself, and pushed everyone away by small degrees. He cut me off slowly, and at first, I didn't think much of his absence at pedicure night or the shortage of text messages bitching about temperamental clients who deigned to challenge his ideas. Drinking and meaningless sex were his solutions to everything, and he plastered on a smirk that dared anyone to question his happiness. There were days like today when I was certain he wanted someone to pick a fight with him just so he could unleash some of the emotions building up inside him.

The thing about Sam was that he only understood

through experience. No one could tell him how to grapple with his issues; he had to live them. And I was starting to suspect he needed to feel the cold stone of rock bottom before he'd be able to take a step forward.

That scared the shit out of me. Sam always required so much *more*. He was born premature, and struggled from his first breath. The universe wasn't kind to him, hitting him with diabetes, immature lungs, digestive issues, plus the challenge of arriving too early, too small. Nearly four months passed between his birth and his first day outside the hospital. For the first years of his life, he spent nearly as much time in the hospital as he did at home, always fighting off infections or learning to control blood sugar spikes or evaluating his slow growth.

I was almost four when he was born. I was always helping my mother with something. Folding clothes. Cleaning up the playroom. Mixing bottles. Rubbing Sam's belly when he whimpered in pain. My mother relied on me, and when she died, I was the only one who could care for my siblings, Sam in particular.

His rock bottom was far worse than that of Patrick or Matt. Those two could drink until they pissed pure whiskey and live to tell about it. That was why we were all hovering around Sam: we knew the fall was coming, and we knew it wouldn't be a smooth landing.

Instead of parking myself at his side, I gave him time to cool off. I sent Tom to Sam's favorite cold-pressed juice shop in Kendall Square to grab one of those horrid blends he and Andy enjoyed so much. He'd be hungry at some point, and then I'd deal with him.

SAM WAS HUNCHED over his desk, deep in his design when I stopped at his door later in the afternoon. The world quieted when he was working, and it wasn't until I knocked on the door that he looked up and glanced at me over the frame of his glasses. "I come bearing gifts," I said, raw pistachios and an old-fashioned glass bottle of swamp water in hand. "You have to be hungry."

Sam stole a glimpse at the clock and nodded, beckoning me inside.

"I wanted to apologize about Friday. There's nothing else I can say other than I'm sorry." I set the bottle down, and dropped into a chair angled in front of his desk. "Carrots, honey, lemon, and celery. Andy said you were loving all things carrot."

"Thank you," he said. "I was going to stop for lunch soon."

At four in the fucking afternoon?

"You can't be skipping meals. I'm going to have Tom start placing a lunch order for you every day. You're going to get yourself sick," I said, biting back a surge of frustration. If I didn't know better, I'd think he enjoyed the extreme bouts of hypoglycemia that followed his irregular eating.

"Save the nutrition lecture for another day, Shannon."

Pick your battles. Don't show up to every fight that sends an invitation. Lunch isn't the hill to die on today.

"Fine." I flattened my hands on my skirt and took a breath. "I'm sorry about the ASNE event. It's the only event I'll miss this season."

"Actually, skip them all," he said around a mouthful of pistachios. "I'm sure you have better things to do."

I plucked a strand of hair from my hem and swallowed a grimace. If only Will was here to observe this exchange, he'd understand what I meant about family businesses involving much more than business. "Is this about Angus?"

"What? No. No, this has nothing to do with him, and if it's the same to you, I'd rather we not continue bringing him up."

"That sounds like it's definitely about Angus," I said.

"Shan, stop trying to psychoanalyze everything I say. I have a shit ton of designs to finish today, and I need to get my ass on the treadmill tonight, and then I'm going out. Thank you for lunch, but unless there's something else, we're finished with this conversation."

I wasn't leaving until he ate every one of those nuts, and the swamp water, too. "There's one more thing. Something I hope will make you happy."

My eye caught the framed snapshot from his desk, the one from the Boston Marathon finish line two years ago. I was in the middle, with Patrick and Matt on one side, and Riley and Sam on the other. Arms linked over shoulders, we leaned together, smiling. It was hard to process all the things that had changed since then.

Riley finished school and moved back from Rhode Island.

Matt met Lauren, and now they were married.

Angus died.

We hired Andy, and Patrick fell in love with her.

"Am I supposed to guess, or are you planning to say something?" he asked.

And I was here, as always, holding it together.

"It's a good thing you're cute, Sam. Otherwise I'd slap you upside the head for this shitty attitude." I shook my head and flipped open my tablet. "I renewed your driver's license for you. It will show up in a week or two. Oh, and I adjusted the automatic order for your replacement parts. When I went through the supplies at your place last week, it seemed like you were running low on infusion sets and insulin cartridges, but had enough skin preps and test strips for an eternity. Just let me know if you want more or less, or something different."

Sam brushed the pistachio shells from his desk and glared at me, as if me keeping his life in order was a huge inconvenience to him. "Where were you this weekend?"

"I went away with friends."

Just going to study my split ends while the runt attempts to interrogate me. No big deal.

"Where?" he asked.

It's sweet how he's allowed to ask questions and I'm not. So sweet. "Nantucket. I took the ferry."

Sam arched an eyebrow. "Who did you go with? What did you do?"

He wants a story; I'll give him a story. "Simone and Danielle, and it was a regular girls' weekend. Beach, brunch, booze. What else would we do?"

And he knew it was a story. I kept no secrets about disinterest in girls' weekends, or my shortage of affection for my law school friends. The honest communication train ran both directions, and if he was locking me out right now, I was doing the same.

We'll see how you like it.

"Why aren't you sunburned?"

"Sunscreen," I said with a shrug.

"Why don't you cut the shit," he said. "What is the purpose of this exercise, Shan? Does it not seem ridiculous that you're keeping something from me? From all of us? And you do notice that you're making a bigger deal out of it by lying about going to Nantucket, right?"

Kind of like how it's ridiculous that you don't talk to me anymore? Or you only take care of yourself when someone forces you?

"Since you have a busy afternoon, I'd rather get down to the reason I came in here," I said. "We were approached last month by a real estate agent who was representing a very private client. Since the agent was absurdly vague about her client's interests, Patrick and I decided not to engage."

He blinked, annoyed with my deflection. "Okay."

"The agent came back, saying the client really, really wanted to work with us. It seems the client saw the *Boston Globe* spread on the future of green restoration." I motioned to where the freshly framed newspaper feature showcasing one of his projects leaned against the wall. Another reminder to get Tom on that project right away. "And the client insisted on working with you."

"I don't have much free time, Shannon," he said. "And no offense, but I don't have a lot of patience for dealing with agents."

I bit back a quip about being the agent who put him through college. I needed him to take this project. It was the type of all-encompassing restoration that he adored. It would give him the meaning and focus he required to gain his footing again, and if it worked out the way I was hoping, I could put another pair of eyes on him at all times.

"Well, it gets better." I toggled through a few screens on my tablet, then turned it toward Sam. "Turns out the client is Eddie Turlan, from The Vials." I pointed to a picture of the punk band popular in the eighties.

I toggled to the street view map, and showed Sam the red

brick house. Once he saw the gorgeous façade, I knew he'd fall in love. "They want you to design it, and they offered to go well beyond your standard fees." I swiped to another screen, and handed the tablet to Sam. "Here's the most recent communication from the agent."

He read the email, his eyes widening when he saw the budget, and handed the tablet back to me. "I still don't have time."

"You could make time if Riley moved off Matt's projects and started working with you." Sam's expression turned pained, and I held up my hand. Riley was the resident fuck-up, and he'd spent the past year and a half bouncing between Patrick and Matt's projects as he refined his skills. Neither of them had any success in training him to consistently zip his pants. "I think you've argued with me enough today. Just listen. He's come a long, long way in the past eight months, and you have to admit that."

Sam grumbled out a sigh and I was taking that as agreement.

"I was also thinking this could be a phenomenal opportunity to partner with the roof garden girl," I said, angling for the last slice of Sam's resistance. I didn't know Magnolia Santillian, but Sam hadn't stopped raving about her work since the spring. For reasons I had yet to comprehend, Patrick hated roof gardens and shut down every one of Sam's attempts at weaving them into his designs. "If there's ever been a property that needs a roof garden, it's this one."

He reached for the tablet again. He wouldn't believe it until checking out the roof himself. After all, I was just the lawyer. I didn't know anything about architecture or preservation or design. "What's the timeline with all this?" he asked.

"They'd like to know as soon as possible. They close on the property in forty-five days or so, and want to start construction immediately. I promised them we'd follow up by Friday."

"I'll call Magnolia and find out whether she has any flexibility in her schedule," he said. "I need Riley freed up in the next couple of weeks, and I want the blueprints pulled from City Hall by noon tomorrow. Get your errand boy, Tom, on that one."

Miracles worked, mountains moved.

"Yes! I knew you'd be all over this. There's just one more thing." He groaned and flopped back in his chair as I held out my hands. "Actually, two things. One: why can't we just call her Roof Garden Girl? I really prefer that to Magnolia. I mean, please. Who names a child Magnolia? It requires her to be a landscape architect, or own a flower shop. And two: there's a strict non-disclosure agreement attached to this client. You can't go tweeting about working on Eddie Turlan's house."

"I don't tweet, and you'll need to talk to Magnolia about that. I don't think we know her well enough to give her a nickname yet."

"But you'd like to know her a little better, right?" I asked, lifting my shoulders. "You'd like to get on a nickname basis."

"You're reading into this rather far, Shannon."

I didn't know much about Magnolia beyond the stray details Sam shared, but I couldn't help wondering whether he needed someone as creative and strange as him. Anyone who designed roof gardens for a living had to fit the bill.

I paused at the door, and glanced back at him. "I really do want you to be happy, Sam. We all know the past year has been difficult for you, but we can't help if you don't let us."

"I know," he said. "I'm trying."

With a nod, I returned to my office. I had nineteen urgent items on my list, and it didn't matter how tired or sore I was, I wasn't leaving until I had this place under control.

That was the price of disappearing, and I'd pay it again.

FIFTEEN MONTHS *ago*

Will: Chicago. Second Friday in November.

Shannon: That's where you'll be masturbating to Katy Perry videos and crying into your Muscle Milk?

Will: Putting up with your shit requires conditioning. I should be hitting the weights harder just to prepare myself for you

Shannon: Mmm. Best wishes.

Shannon: Oh and when did you put your number in my phone?

Will: While you were in the shower with your little helper

Shannon: Can we stop talking about the shower yet?

Will: That was a religious experience for me. It was better than surfing at sunrise.

Shannon: I don't know what to do with that information

Will: While you contemplate it, go lock your doors

Shannon: I live in a very secure building, and before you remind me that you got in, I'll remind you that you're not the average criminal

Will: Lock your fucking doors or I'm sending one of my guys to do it for you

---

Will: Hey. What's instagram

Shannon: Is that a serious question?

Will: No, I'm just testing you to see if you can summarize things on demand. It's on my checklist, right after "Uses shower heads but gets very dirty"

Will: Of course it's a serious question! Answer me.

Shannon: You are a douche waffle.

Will: I thought we agreed on lawyer-fucking meathead…

Shannon: Bad things happen when you bring up the showerhead…

Will: I'm authentically curious about this instagram thing. My mother keeps sending me emails about her travel blog having a "super huge IG following" – direct Judy quote, btw – and telling me to get on it

Shannon: It's a photo sharing app. Selfies, pets, kids, food, landscapes.

Shannon: What's the story with the blog? Matt's always sharing it on Facebook

Will: Sigh.

Will: When my parents retired, they decided to travel. National parks and all that shit. No surprise to anyone, my mother was bored off her ass within 15 minutes.

Will: She was a navy medic, served in Kuwait, nurse on base until a few years ago. You get the picture. Always busy.

Will: She figures we all need to share in these travels, and starts taking an actual fuck ton of pictures. Lo introduces her to a blogging site. Instead of emailing the fuck ton, she's posting it.

Will: Joke's on us because people like this shit. She's got paid advertisements and product placement now, and a "super huge IG following" but she guilts the fuck out of us if we don't read and tell her how great it is, and believe me, it's actually really fucking awesome and I'm happy for her

Will: But holy fuck, who can keep up with all those posts?

Shannon: Do you even have any social media accounts?

Will: No. that shit's terrible for opsec

Shannon: For what?

Will: Operational security. It's not smart to publicize where I am or what I'm doing.

Shannon: Right. ok.

———

Shannon: So I read the blog. Entire hours of my day—gone.

Shannon: Your mom is adorable. I knew she was when I met her at the wedding, but she is too fucking adorable for life.

Shannon: She has all these sassy things to say and there are all these little inside jokes. And her photos are amazing

Shannon: I love how she refers to your dad as the Commodore

Will: That's no term of endearment. That's what he wants to be called.

Will: Like that episode of Seinfeld, with The Maestro

Shannon: Even better!

Will: Did you notice Sailor 1 and Sailor 2? We don't come up much

Shannon: And why would you? It's not like you read the blog

Will: Watch it, peanut.

Shannon: It's just so adorable! She refers to Matt and Lauren as Mr. and Mrs. Honey. Too much cuteness.

Will: Yeah she's pretty great

Will: She'd like you.

Shannon: Yeah?

Will: Totally. She loves stone cold bitches with hearts of gold.

Shannon: Invade any sovereign nations today?

Will: Why are you awake right now? It's the middle of the night

Shannon: It bears noting that you are also awake.

Will: No. I can respond to texts while I sleep.

Will: Commando tactic.

Shannon: Hilarious

Will: Seriously. Why are you up?

Shannon: Had a lot of coffee today.

Will: Yeah?

Shannon: The pumpkin spice latte has returned for fall. I'm a fan.

Will: And now you could run to Ohio and back?

Shannon: Pretty much

Shannon: I've been thinking about going jogging.

Will: Please don't

Shannon: Is this where you get all patronizing and tell me that girls should stick with their pilates and zumba? Don't trouble yourself with that. I run every morning, to and from spin or barre class. I've finished the last six Boston Marathons. I don't need any advice from a penis, thanks.

Will: It's 2:21 a.m. I get that you're tough as fuck but I wouldn't even jog at 2:21 a.m.

Will: And if my penis is giving advice, it's saying "come to North Carolina and put your mouth on me"

Shannon: How is it any different from jogging to the gym at 4:30?

Will: Common sense?

Will: Sunlight?

Will: How about the fact most psychopaths decide to pack it in by then? And the feral animal quotient goes down too.

Shannon: Pfft. I can handle that shit.

Will: Yes, Shannon. I'm certain that stray dogs and fisher cats make it their job to stay the fuck away from you.

Shannon: Oh yeah. It's a redhead thing.

Will: Ok so you run marathons and drink too much coffee. Tell me something else about you.

Will: Since you're awake

Shannon: Quid pro quo, commando.

Will: You know, pulling out the Latin at this hour is kind of like using trigonometry during beer pong. Don't be that guy.

Shannon: Yeah. Being chased by a fisher cat would be soooo much more entertaining than this

Will: I've never seen Titanic. Not a fan of romanticized shipwreck.

Shannon: Do I need to define quid pro quo for you? Or are you just giving me lame shit to work with?

Will: You need to calm down.

Shannon: Has no one told you that telling a woman to calm down is like trying to baptize a cat?

Will: If cats weren't assholes, it wouldn't be that difficult

Will: And if you'll calm your tits, I'll tell you something

Shannon: Spare me the suspense.

Will: I had a double major. Art history and finance.

Shannon: Is that so? Did you always want to be Charlotte York from Sex and the City when you grew up?

Will: Do you ever take a break from ripping assholes?

Shannon: Nope. I have bullshit to call and standards to enforce.

Will: Now tell me something else

Shannon: I once dated a guy who always carried a tin of sardines with him. He kept them in his shirt pocket and ate them before meals. Like an appetizer

Will: Nope. Not weird at all

Shannon: I have a track record with the weird and weirder

Will: I'm not weird.

Shannon: You are the weirdest

Will: Mmm I think you are. In a hot way.

Shannon: Fuck you

Will: You have no idea how much I'd love to

Shannon: Yeah? Maybe you should call me. Tell me.

FOURTEEN MONTHS *ago*

THE RATIONAL PART of me knew this game of insult-foreplay Shannon and I were playing was getting out of hand when it transcended secret weekends and snark-filled texts. The irrational part of me—the one that served at the pleasure of my cock—couldn't get enough. It started with wanting to hear her hurl obscenities at me rather than reading them over text messages, and it turned into me detailing how I'd fuck her if I was there.

Short answer: thoroughly.

Another time, I caught her while she was reviewing financial statements, and in some very strange, very desperate turn of events, my pathetic ass demanded she tell me about them. She did...in the sexiest voice conceivable. Thank God I wasn't sharing a bunk with anyone that night because I came like a geyser when she started talking about cash flow and asset ratios.

Soon, it turned into talking her through an orgasm that I ached to taste plus odd details about our days, or her critique of Judd Apatow films or my reminders to lock her doors. I learned she ate brunch with my sister most Saturdays after they visited the farmers' market, and she only watched reruns because she found it too time-consuming to keep up with new programs. She was handling an exclusive remodeling project for a musician, or as she preferred to call it, *her* classified mission.

She heard about my near-religious reverence for fish tacos and college football. She knew I *technically* lived with my parents in Coronado, in the cozy blue bungalow they bought almost forty years ago when the only things on the island were the Hotel Del and the naval amphibious base.

We still gave each other a *ton* of shit *all* the time but...I missed her when we didn't connect.

Will: True story - my brother had drinks with your sister today
Will: In Italy

Shannon: Run that by me again

Shannon: My sister, Erin?

Will: And my brother, Wes

Will: Apparently, they know a lot of the same places overseas, and were in the same area. They're hanging out now

Shannon: That's Erin. Making friends everywhere she goes

Shannon: You're sure he's gay?

Will: Positive.

Will: She gave him a tour of a volcano.

Shannon: That's special.

Will: He seemed to think so. She took him to an old school mafia speakeasy where, says Wes, they treat her like family

Will: Or whatever the Italian equivalent of a speakeasy is

Will: Maybe they were at a mafia den, and if that's the case, we should talk about whether your sister is actually deep cover foreign intelligence

Shannon: She is so odd

Will: Odd is one way to put it

Will: Is there a short explanation on the odd?

Will: I'm game for the long explanation too

Shannon: there's a thing. I don't want to talk about it

Will: A thing?

Will: Did you kill a guy in Reno?

Shannon: Something along those lines.

Will: But you don't talk anymore. You and Erin.

Shannon: No

Will: Stretch that out for me

Shannon: Nooooooo

Will: You're fucking comedy, peanut.

Shannon: I'm not getting into it with you. Stuff happened, things were said. She's happiest when I'm not part of her life.

Will: So the cone of silence is her choice?

Shannon: I'm not getting into this with you.

Will: On a scale of chicken on a bone to that C word you dislike so much, where does this fall?

Will: Still there?

Will: Ok so it's up there. Understood.

Will: You know, your blowjobs have ruined me

Shannon: …are you drunk?

Will: No. Nostalgic.

Shannon: While also being drunk?

Will: No.

Will: But I am thinking about your mouth on my cock

Shannon: Seems unwise

Will: Trust me, so unwise.

Shannon: You know what's amusing about your balls?

Will: Amusing?

Will: I don't think amusing is the word I'd go with, but please, share.

Shannon: They're aging well. They're in good shape for an old man like you. They haven't given up yet. You know, all those white hairs make it a distinguished dick. Like George Clooney.

Will: Come on. You say that to all the boys.

Shannon: Erroneous

Shannon: Are you thinking about my mouth on your balls now?

Will: Nah, I'm not into that

Shannon: And how do you know I'm not?

Will: I know how freaky you are

Shannon: Oohhhh so you know me now? Like, you understand my wants, desires, and dreams?

Shannon: Be honest: are you actually a fortuneteller? Instead of reading palms, you read pussy? Is that a commando tactic?

Will: Dudes are exactly as freaky as their women let them be.

Shannon: Don't intend to alarm you or anything, but I'm not your woman.

Will: Ahhhhh peanut. You have ruined me.

Shannon: This Chicago thing isn't going to happen

Will: Cute

Shannon: Excuse me?

Will: I find that statement cute. Like unicorns and fairies and other imaginary bullshit

Will: Explain to me why this isn't going to happen

Shannon: I'm slammed with work for a new project. I'm dealing with a high-maintenance owner who happens to have his own PR squad and as luck would have it, they're even more high maintenance than he is. I spend 80% of my day on the phone with these ass-lickers

Will: Fuck that noise

Shannon: Believe me. I've tried.

Shannon: Plus - Sam is getting an award for one of his restorations this weekend

Will: Bravo to Sam

Will: I'll see you Friday

Will: And don't pack any panties, unless you want to spend the entire weekend handing them over

Ten

SHANNON

TWELVE MONTHS *ago*

I PROBABLY WOULDN'T ADMIT it to anyone, but I missed insulting Will in person.

I was looking forward to enslaving his cock for the weekend.

And now…I was going to strangle him. That bastard was going down.

I'd delegated tasks to Tom that were a couple of rungs above his level. I'd bought new lingerie, even though I hated spending that much money on underwear. I *waxed*.

And Will didn't show up.

There was some explanation that I was not interested in hearing, and I'd spent the weekend in Chicago ordering room service, drinking wine straight from the bottle, and watching a *Law and Order: SVU* marathon in my room at The Langham. All the anticipation I'd collected over the past months shattered, but I was still holding the shards. It was the worst combination of sexual frustration, abandonment, and rejection I'd ever experienced. I was totally fucking miserable.

"The Castavechias went to Scotland over the summer," Patrick said. "They visited castles."

And now I was listening to my siblings talk about their projects, and I couldn't form whole words. All I had were growls.

Riley frowned and nudged Matt's shoulder. "Why is that an issue?"

"They'd like to redesign," Andy said. "Again."

I tuned out the conversation as my mind wandered back to last night, when Will called. It was long past midnight and he sounded painfully tired, and he told me the only thing in the world he wanted right then was to pull my hair and lick my clit, and somewhere in the middle of all that, I agreed to meet him in New Mexico next week.

But some dirty talk, a hand in my pajama pants, and a slightly above average orgasm wasn't erasing any of my misery. It only took the edge off. There was an obscenity-laced monologue about my dissatisfaction with the week-end, too.

"Are they being charged the dicking-around fee? What is this? Version nineteen?" Matt asked.

"Yes," Andy said. "But the bigger problem is that we're already halfway through a Dutch Colonial restoration. The project shouldn't become a Scottish castle, and…"

"And they want us to go to Scotland with them." Patrick waved his hand dismissively, and I opened an instant messenger window. "Something about recovering stones and floorboards."

Shannon: If you go to Scotland, you are expensing every cent of that trip right back to the client. These people are crazypants…and I'm sort of expecting them to ask you to move in soon. Resident architect.
Patrick: Yeah. I know.
Patrick: Side note – you look awful
Shannon: Do not doubt that I will throw this chair at you
Patrick: I don't but I thought you were unplugging for the weekend.
Patrick: You know, getting back to neutral
Shannon: Yeah, neutral was busy assassinating warlords
Patrick: I don't follow that reference

"They want us to go this weekend," Andy said.

"Wait. Does that mean you're actually going along with this? You're stuffing a medieval castle into a Dutch Colonial?" Sam asked, dropping his uncharacteristically chipper vibe for the first time since sitting down. "Does no one care about concept anymore?"

Shannon: You need to jump in there and calm his tits before we have another concept tantrum
Patrick: We need to talk about the girl he had with him on Saturday night
Shannon: Do I even want to know?
Patrick: YES

Patrick texted me Sunday morning, mentioning something about Sam bringing a date to the ASNE event, and I assumed he was talking about Magnolia. All Sam ever talked about was Magnolia—who Riley had nicknamed Gigi —and how insightful, helpful, and wonderful she was with the Turlan project. Of course he brought her to the event. It wasn't as if he did the relationship thing.

"It's like a turducken," Riley said.

"We wouldn't do that," Patrick said while Matt laughed. "We can work with floorboards and stones, but we won't be digging any moats."

"So you're going to Scotland," Sam said. "This weekend."

Patrick shrugged. "Possibly."

Riley leaned to Sam, asking in a whisper that wasn't especially quiet, "What are the odds they come back married?"

Patrick blushed—hard—as he glanced to Andy and then immediately back to his laptop screen.

Shannon: Something you need to share?

Patrick: No

Shannon: You're not allowed to get engaged unless I'm notified well in advance

Shannon: Or married

Patrick: Are you under the impression I'd be able to manage either of those things without you?

Shannon: Just checking

Sam passed a twenty-dollar bill to Riley. "I'll take that bet, and my money is on no," Sam said, his gaze on Andy. "Princess Jasmine looks like she's about to castrate you and Optimus might hold you down while she does it."

"Yeah, Riley," I said. "Not everyone needs to get married fourteen minutes after they meet."

Growly. I was very, very growly. I ducked back to my screen, and my search for a direct flight to Albuquerque.

Matt leaned forward, his arms folded on the table, and he glanced at Riley and Sam. "Did she just insult me?"

"Sam, why don't you tell us about Tiel?" Andy said. She waved at the table, and a smile that I could only describe as devious pulled at her lips. "I know everyone would love to hear about her."

"Or maybe we should talk about Thanksgiving, Shannon. What's the plan?" Sam asked.

He wasn't going to like the plan. None of them were, and I was stuck dealing with that. Add it to misery's tab.

Shannon: Don't hate me for this
Patrick: What the fuck now?
Shannon: Just go with it

"I'm not going to be in town for Thanksgiving. I have reservations at a spa in New Mexico, and considering the shit you all put me through on a daily basis, I don't want to hear any whining about it either," I said. For years, Thanksgiving had been my show. I didn't cook, though it was one of our few family traditions, and I worked hard at keeping it going. A twinge of remorse tightened my shoulders. "I'll order everything from the farm like I usually do, and I can have Tom pick it up, but I won't be the one reheating it. You're grown men. Figure it out for yourselves."

Patrick: The next time you do that, give me more than 3 seconds to prepare
Shannon: Sorry
Patrick: It's okay but Jugger looks like he's about to run through a wall headfirst

"So I'm hearing two things," Matt said. He pointed to me. "One, it's really shitty that you're just now mentioning this a week before Thanksgiving. Lauren and I will have Thanksgiving at our place, and fuck you very much for waiting until Sam brought it up. It's not like you've hosted for the past fifteen damn years or anything."

"See? The newlyweds want to do it. Let them trot out their new crystal and china. Crisis averted." I shrugged and turned my attention back to finding a direct flight because no, I was *not* interested in stopping at JFK.

Patrick: What's in New Mexico?
Shannon: Neutral

Matt pointed to Sam. "Two, I think we'd all like to hear about Tiel."

Sam was twisting the titanium ring on his thumb and shifting in his seat. Definitely uncomfortable. "I'm seeing someone," he snapped. "Her name is Tiel."

Patrick: Listen up. You'll want in on this story
Shannon: What happened to Gigi?
Patrick: Who's Gigi?
Shannon: Roof Garden Girl. Riley calls her Gigi, and I thought that was who Sam brought to the event
Patrick: No
Shannon: Shit. I really wanted it to be Gigi
Patrick: She probably realized roof gardens are dumb and closed up shop
Shannon: You have issues. I freaking love roof gardens.

"And she's a *college professor* and a *violinist*," Andy added.

"She's *very* pretty and wasn't even wearing hooker heels. And I'll go out on a limb and say they've known each other for a while."

Riley snapped his fingers and pointed at Sam. "Is this the same chick you drunk dialed last week?"

Shannon: What the fuck?
Shannon: What is happening right now?
Patrick: Fuck if I know but I'm telling you, he was WITH this lady.
Patrick: I was ready to start buying some Cape Annes off Ciccannessi too
Shannon: What's Ciccannessi doing with Cape Annes?
Patrick: Tearing them down and building condos
Shannon: Motherfuck.
Patrick: Yeah. But Sam was out of there. I've never seen him act like that. Even Andy thought it was fucking strange

There had to be a full moon to blame for this chaos.

"Oh. *Oh*," Matt said, frowning at Sam. "So we're talking about a real girl? An appropriate, adult, professional woman?"

Sam's glare could have cut class. "She's a couple months older than me."

Patrick: He's either fit as a fiddle or lost his fucking mind, and I have no idea which one it is
Shannon: It's probably an unfortunate mix of the two, plus some passive aggression and quiet retaliation
Shannon: At least we know she's a real girl, no hallucination, and we don't have to inventory Riley's brownies again
Patrick: For what it's worth, she seemed nice

Patrick: Polite. Maybe a little quiet.
Shannon: That's an improvement

Objectively, I knew this had nothing to do with me. There was no way in hell that Sam was dating a woman—he lived for the nameless, faceless hookup; the last time he dated, he was in his first year at Cornell—with the intent of proving to me that he was perfectly fine. It wasn't about proving that he was so fucking fine, he could handle a relationship when I hadn't made it past a second date in months.

Sneaky weekends didn't count, obviously.

"She didn't look anything like his usual syphilitic crew," Patrick said to Matt and Riley.

I sat back in my chair, holding up my hand for quiet. "And how long has this been taking place?"

Sam sent me an impatient glance. "A little more than two months."

"Is that why you've been so pleasant recently? I assumed it was some new meds or a colonic or a fucking juice cleanse or something, but this is great news," Matt said. "Good for you."

Shannon: You're telling me you knew nothing about this until Saturday night?
Patrick: Not a word.
Patrick: I've been watching him as close as you have, and I've been touching base with Riley every day.
Patrick: This came out of nowhere
Patrick: Or he's getting good at being secretive.

"Oh no, no, no. We don't do secret affairs in this office.

Not after the shit these two" —I pointed to Patrick and Andy — "pulled last spring."

Sam lifted his shoulder with a quick sneer. "I wouldn't say there's been any secret."

"You're saying this is a legitimate thing," I said. "Dating and the whole normal relationship? Seriously?"

"Yeah, Shan. Pretty much."

"The universe must really fucking hate me if *you're* in a healthy relationship," I mumbled. "Just wait, RISD will be next, and I'll start hoarding cats and learning how to knit because what else is there to do with my time? Soon enough, you'll all have kids but you won't let me near them because all I'll want to do is smell their little heads and make them promise not to let you assholes put Auntie Shannon in a home."

"We already discussed this," Andy said. "No one is letting you start a cat colony. Cool it with the end of days talk, or I'm cutting off your caffeine supply."

"Bring her to Thanksgiving," Matt said.

Patrick: Everything ok over there?
Shannon: I might be a little growly
Patrick: Yeah. You are.
Patrick: Don't worry about Thanksgiving. Go to New Mexico, eat some fry bread and Hatch chiles for me, and get your neutral.
Patrick: It sounds like you need it
Shannon: Thank you
Patrick: And when you're ready, tell me what the hell neutral is

"Yeah," Andy said. "Maybe she'll like Lauren more than she liked me."

"You can't hold that against her," Sam said. "She's the friendliest person I know. We did not expect to run into you two. We were on our way out and Patrick was his usual jovial self, and she wasn't wearing any—"

"Oh shit, son," Riley yelled. He clapped Sam on the back before rolling away from the table, laughing. "I need to meet this girl. Anyone who goes commando at an Arch Society gathering is a keeper."

Shannon: I thought she was polite and quiet!
Patrick: She can be polite and quiet and still walk around without underwear. Not mutually exclusive
Shannon: Are you speaking from experience?

"She didn't—no, I mean, I ripped her—fuck," he groaned. "Never mind."

"I've never had that much fun at any event put on by the Arch Society," Matt said. "I might start attending more frequently."

"Definitely a keeper. At the very least, she should come drinking on Black Friday," Andy said. "We'll see if she still hates me then."

Shannon: She hated Andy?
Patrick: No...
Patrick: Not really
Patrick: Maybe a little
Shannon: Outstanding...but it's worth noting you have a consult in half an hour, and after ten this morning, I'm

booked straight through until Friday night with no free time to eat or pee so maybe we should move this circus along

Patrick: I saw a documentary about people who "rescue" alligators when they get into yards and pools. These guys basically lasso the alligator but it always fights and does this death roll thing. These meetings are a lot like that.

Shannon: Does that make us the alligator? Or are we the fools trying to catch the alligator?

Patrick: I haven't figured that part out yet

TWELVE MONTHS *ago*

THIS MONTH WAS the kind of clusterfuck only the military could manage.

First, I was pulled off a stateside training op to lead a last-minute overseas mission. I was fast-roping from an Apache helicopter when I was supposed to be meeting Shannon in Chicago for another weekend away.

She was already airborne when the orders came through, and spent two days alone in the city. A text with a picture of her middle finger positioned over her lace-clad breasts summed up her feelings about the change of plans. I shared those feelings.

When I was back on base and the mission was fully debriefed, I got her on the phone. She yelled at me about fucking with her meticulous schedule after everything she went through to get away that weekend. She was reasonably pissed and lonely, but I persuaded her to let me listen while she fingered herself. I hated this war, the military, and every inch of earth separating me from Shannon when she started panting and humming into my ear.

I capitalized on her post-orgasmic bliss to convince her that she wanted to spend Thanksgiving with me in New Mexico. There was a long pause punctuated only by her shuddering breath, and I imagined the rosy flush of her skin and the tiny beads of sweat drying on her chest. She put up her usual quantities of sass and swearing, and threatened to ditch me if I was even five minutes late.

Then, during a close-quarters hostage recovery simulation at an unmarked black ops facility, one of my guys blew a mannequin's head off. If there was a good time to make his accuracy issues known, it was definitely before the dummies were replaced with live team members, but it sure as shit fucked up my day.

Any time a drill involving live rounds went off book, everything stopped. We walked the whole damn thing back, replaying every step, every move, and every decision until we isolated the error. Once that protocol was finished, I tasked my men with disassembling and cleaning every firearm in the building.

Twice.

No one was enjoying a holiday weekend—myself included—until the lesson was clear: know where your shot is going to land before you shoot it.

By the time I hit the road, I was five *hours* late. Five fucking hours, and if Shannon wasn't already on a flight back to Boston, she was going to bitch up a storm until I put her mouth to work. The girl got off on tearing assholes and busting balls, but I didn't allow myself the time to consider how much I enjoyed that.

The hotel she selected near the outskirts of Taos, in Ojo Caliente, was nestled against an ancient hot spring. The interior was all cowhide and antlers, all day. I suffered through an extensive explanation of the on-site spa services and farm-to-table dining options before the front desk attendant handed over my room key. If I'd known where Shannon was, I would have saved myself this annoyance and worked some magic on the lock.

"Just tell me which room," I said. I was too fucking impatient for this. Once I had the key, I took off in the direction the attendant pointed.

And now, five hours late to our rescheduled weekend, she was nowhere to be found.

Her designer luggage was parked in our room's closet, and her phone charger was plugged in beside the bed, but she was gone. I stood in the center of the room, staring at the untouched bed while I ran through the possibilities. She didn't go into town; too sleepy and deserted at this hour. She didn't go to the gym; she was an early bird.

That left the restaurant, and it didn't take more than a quick glance to spot her hair when I burst through the doors.

She was seated at a rustic bar overlooking the hot springs with her back to me, her laptop to her left, and a margarita glass to her right.

And two guys standing beside her, laughing and gesturing as if they were old college pals.

Fuckers.

I stood in the doorway, watching from a distance. Her hair was tucked behind her ear, smooth and styled into precise waves, and I wanted to mess it all up. The dark purple v-neck sweater and long gold chain studded with small stones—my guess was diamonds—showed off her creamy skin. I wanted to touch her and haul her back to the room, but I also wanted to admire the way she handled those guys.

Shannon was intelligent and gorgeous and really fucking intimidating, and every fool with a pick-up line was drawn to her. They didn't notice her patronizing nods or bright, fake smiles. They didn't hear the poison-laced honey when she said "Oh, that sounds *fascinating*" or "That's an *amazing little story.*"

She could handle them, of that there was no doubt. She could handle everything.

But that didn't mean she had to, and when the fucker leaning against the bar placed his hand on her knee while he laughed at the other fucker's comment, nothing could have stopped me from intervening.

"And this guy damn near falls off the boat trying to reel in his marlin," The One I'd Kill First said, gesturing to The One I'd Kill Second. "And it was a small one, just a pup—"

"Excuse me, boys." I stepped between those assholes, took Shannon's face in my hands, and whispered, "I am so sorry I'm late, peanut."

There was a fiery glint in her eyes before my lips met hers, a blend of anger and amusement. Her teeth sank into my tongue when it pushed past her lips.

Okay, mostly anger.

In a move only a few steps above licking her neck or pissing on her leg, I locked my eyes on Shannon, snatched her glass and drained the sweet liquid. It was clear signal for the fuckers to peddle their marlin stories elsewhere.

"If I could have gotten a flight back to Boston tonight," she said, a whisper so soft I almost missed it. Her shoulders were stiff, and her hands still folded in her lap. "Believe me when I say I would have."

"Did Air Traffic Control not take your call?" I asked, rubbing my knuckles down her spine. "Those bastards."

She looked good, better than I remembered. Deployment had a strange way of eroding memories, turning some unrealistically perfect or morphing others into dim, faded artifacts. Somewhere in the last ten weeks—seventy-one days, if anyone was counting—I lost the sharp force of her. Maybe it was my mind's way of tricking me into believing this girl wasn't creeping her way into my everything.

"Come," I said, holding out my hand to her.

She didn't take my hand. Of course not. She took her precious time wishing the marlin idiots a happy holiday, signing the check, closing her laptop and placing it in her bag, and then wrapping her scarf around her neck before scooting off the chair. She didn't reach for me once, and it was obvious she was making me work for the right to touch her.

She wasn't high maintenance; she was complicated. It was probably a good thing. Shannon was too smart, too fearless, too much fire to let just anyone in her company. She needed to be *won*, and that was no easy feat.

I pointed up at the night sky. "A lot of stars out here," I said.

"Suck my dick," she murmured.

"Does that mean you'll stop, breathe, and notice the stars while I'm sucking your dick? Or do I have to suck your dick first, and then you'll be ready for stars?"

The walk to our room was silent and separate. She was working hard at staying angry, and as much as I enjoyed the game, I couldn't relax until she did, and I wanted to fast-forward to the point where we could just *be*. Instead of kissing me back, she bit me. Instead of accepting my hand, she demanded I blow her. Instead of letting me hold her, she was going to shy away from me and throw a tantrum until I tied her up and fucked the fury right out of her.

And she wasn't even furious. No, she just didn't know how to let herself unwind.

"Stop thinking so hard," I said as I held the door open for her.

"I realize it's difficult for you to understand, but someone has to think around here," she snapped. She tossed her scarf to the chair and kicked off her heels.

She liked to think of herself as grounded. She thought she had her hands wrapped around everything, but she was five hundred miles ahead and flying in her own stratosphere.

"And what would you like me to think about?" I asked. She paced the length of the room. "I know what *I'd* like to think about, and it involves fucking you with your pretty wrists tied behind your back."

"Do you have any clue what I had to do to get here, Will? And for what? So you can stand there and tell me how you're going to fuck me?"

"You love it when I tell you how I'm going to fuck you," I said. She really did.

"My assistant knows. He totally knows. And your sister, fucking hell, nothing gets past that girl. They all know, and you're just staring at me like you don't care."

I knew I wasn't Shannon's usual, but I couldn't comprehend why her assistant—or my sister, for that matter—got a say in who she fucked.

"That's probably because I *don't* care," I said. I cleared

my throat. This wasn't the night to unravel her bizarre family dynamics. "There is zero reason to worry about any of that right now. You know, you don't have to be so tough all the time. It's okay to not have all the answers."

"I could say the same thing to you." Shannon lifted her chin, her quiet little "*fuck you*", and stared at me. "I'm missing important family events, you know. And I've been sitting here, thinking you were blowing me off because apparently that's your thing. You know what? That's not how this will end."

"Ignoring the fact I did not blow you off, peanut, and you're being an overdramatic pain in the ass, tell me how this will end."

"I'll blow you off," she said, her shoulder jerking hard to punctuate her statement.

"I think you're waiting for me to force you to drop that act." My fingers curled around her waistband and I pulled her toward me. "Enough bullshit out of you. Get naked."

"Don't fucking tell me what to do," she said. "How about 'Thank you for flying during the busiest travel week of the year' or 'Thank you for coming all the way to freaking New Mexico' or better yet, 'Let's get some something to eat and talk like normal people because I haven't seen you in three months'?"

"Yeah, no," I said. I had her hands pinned behind her back and her cheek flush against the wall in an instant, and her trousers shoved down to her knees. "Eat later. Talk later. I haven't seen you in three months and I need to be inside you right now."

I hiked her knee up, kicked her pants off, and took my cock in hand. Putting everything else out of my mind, I surged into her hard, drowning in the hot perfection of Shannon.

"Is that the best you can do?" she taunted.

I anchored my hand low on her abdomen, pressing my palm to the narrow space below her belly button. Her muscles flexed and squeezed under my fingertips, and she was strung tight enough to bounce quarters. "You feel how tense you are?" I asked, my hand pushing down. "Relax, baby. Just relax. Loosen up for me, right here."

"Enough with the coaching," she snapped. "Shut up and fuck me."

"No," I murmured against her neck. "No. You're not giving me another one of those wimpy little orgasms. You're going to come for me until you can't stand, then I'm carrying you to the bed and doing it again, but not" —I thrust into her, slamming us hard against the door— "until" —Again— "you stop" —And again— "fighting me."

Her fingers twined around mine as she moaned, the sound bouncing off the door and around us.

"Let me do good things to you," I sighed as her body sagged against mine. "My cock wants to take care of you."

"And what do you want?" she said.

My fingers slid down her tummy until they brushed her clit. "Same."

IT WAS ALMOST a shame to wake her. Sunlight glinted off the red rocks outside, bathing her skin in a pinkish glow. But if I didn't get her out of this bed now, we wouldn't leave it for the next four days.

It seemed counterintuitive that, after these months since

Montauk, I'd want anything more than her body in my arms, but I was struggling with this arrangement. Shannon wasn't one of those women who blindly chased any guy with a frogman tattoo and some dog tags. They deserved the same level of respect, yeah, but it was also fair to classify them as a different breed than Ms. Walsh.

To say I wanted to see her only for sex was a shallow representation of reality. I didn't like her thinking that, and I didn't like operating that way. And admitting that didn't mean I had to turn in my man card, either.

I enjoyed her company but we weren't carrying on meaningful conversations while we were naked. No, that was limited to swearing, insults, and demands. There was plenty of that while we were clothed, too, but it wouldn't be any fun if there was no foreplay.

"Peanut," I said, slapping her ass. "We're going hiking."

"We're *what*?" she groaned into the pillow.

"Shower. Breakfast. Hike," I said, punctuating each word with firm slaps.

"If you fucking spank me again, I will punch you in the nuts so hard you'll have to swallow around them."

"Yeah, I've seen your scrawny arms," I said, folding her beneath me to prevent fists from flying. "That's not happening anytime soon."

"And just for that," she said, "I'm showering alone."

We hit the trailhead about an hour later. She didn't say much for the first mile, and she stayed far on her side of the path.

Her skintight running pants and matching jacket were distractingly sexy. Though it made no logical sense, I assumed she jogged in baggy sweats or old t-shirts. In my head, it was easier to deal with the idea of her sweating in non-descript clothes than looking like a *Sports Illustrated* swimsuit model all over Boston.

I kept stealing glances at her legs, and when she noticed, she shook her head at me, smiling.

"I thought you knew how to be covert," she said.

My hand brushed against hers, a subtle invitation. I could demand many things from Shannon, but I only got them when she was willing to give.

"Can you tell me where you've been since I last saw you?"

For the first time in years, most of my activities weren't highly classified. "I've been training new SEALs. We did an advanced cold water excursion, then some desert survival drills, and this week we were running simulated operations."

"You're teaching the baby SEALs?" she asked, laughing.

I frowned and shook my head. "They go through at least a year of hardcore training. They aren't exactly delicate when I meet them."

"I'm sticking with baby SEAL," she said. "So you must have gone through that hardcore training." I nodded and she continued, "What's that like?"

I tried to think back nearly fifteen years to when I was out of college and getting my first taste of the frogman's life. *Intense* and *grueling* didn't begin to describe BUD/S. My body morphed during that time, changing from fit and strong to powerful. My mind changed, too. I learned to be perceptive and calm, but ready to strike in an eye blink.

"There's a lot of water," I said, and she rolled her eyes at me. Fuck, I wanted to spank her in the middle of this trail. That fire really did it for me. "Seriously. Entire days are spent ocean training. Treading water for six hours. They park us in the sand, arms linked, and let the Pacific Ocean do its worst. Then there's drown-proofing, where your ankles and wrists are tied. They throw you in a pool and hope for the best."

"I must say, it's nice that you survived," she said.

"It is, yeah. Good to be alive," I said. "The worst part—worse than the tear gas exposure drills, worse than being awake for one hundred and thirty-two hours straight, worse than blacking out at the bottom of a frigid pool—was the Underwater Demolition Team shorts. When you're in BUD/S, the dress code is very strict, and it usually involved these awful shorts. They're ugly beige and thin. Too thin. Awkwardly thin."

"I get it, honey," Shannon said. "And you should know: there aren't many fabrics that can conceal the heat you're packing."

"I'm sorry. What was that? Did you say something complimentary about my cock?"

"I have no idea what you're talking about," she muttered. "Now, these shorts."

"Don't lie: you love my cock," I said, and Shannon snorted with laughter. "These shorts are obscenely short. They've been around since World War II. They've only ever been issued to SEALs, and I think it's just a long-running hazing ritual. You know what's insane? I'd always see people in San Diego who were training to get into BUD/S wearing them. Like they were getting a running start on the full SEAL experience by flashing the furry side of their balls."

"What do you miss most about home?" she asked. She knew I'd spent the majority of recent years overseas, and about a decade before that was consumed with similarly grueling cycles of deployment.

I lifted my baseball cap from my head and ran a hand

through my hair. "Many things," I said. "My life is regularly irregular, and I'm good with that but there are times when I miss consistency. I'd like to sleep in the exact same place for a month, just to remind myself what that's all about." I shot her a smile. "It would be even better if you were sleeping there with me."

"Save the horseshit for another time, commando. I'm here and I'm not leaving, so stop trying to be cute."

"You think I'm cute?" I asked.

"Let the record reflect that I never suggested you were, in fact, cute. I claimed you were attempting to *be* cute," she said. "And annoying the shit out of me while doing it."

I laughed and slapped her ass. "I mostly miss home cooking, or having a kitchen. And that isn't to say Navy food is bad. It's not. It's just not home. My brother loves pickles. He's a pickle freak, and yeah, I've told him that his fondness for dick probably started there. He used to make his own pickles when we were in high school, and no matter where I go, I can't find anything like Wes's. It's that sort of thing I miss."

"In other words, you miss people cooking *for* you," she clarified.

"No, actually," I said. "I can cook pretty well. I make a mean pancake."

"I prefer my pancakes sweet," she said. "Keep your mean pancakes to yourself."

"Duly noted."

"I don't cook," she said. "I've tried, but…yeah. It's just not my thing. I never have the right ingredients either. Grocery stores annoy me. I don't have the patience to babysit a simmering pot or turn a piece of meat at the right time. I just want it" —she waved her hands in front of her— "I just want it *done*. I've tried, but instead of making food, I summon demons."

"I can see that," I said.

Shannon stayed quiet until we rounded a steep bend. "There's one thing I can make, though," she said, almost to herself. I glanced at her, wanting to hear more. "Even when I was younger, I was a wreck in the kitchen. I was good with measuring things for recipes. My mother made butternut squash pie. She did it all from scratch, roasting the squash and rolling the dough and everything. She grew the squash, too. She had a garden in the yard. I never understood why she grew such random things like green beans and pickling cucumbers and zucchini. I never thought to ask her why she chose those, and not bell peppers or strawberries."

We were headed toward the trail's high point, but the incline didn't seem to bother Shannon. She was pushing forward and barely breaking a sweat. Nothing should have surprised me about this city girl.

"Lo said she died when you were really young."

She veered off the trail and climbed some boulders to look out at the valley below. "She did," Shannon said, nodding. "She had undiagnosed preeclampsia. It's a pregnancy complication. She bled to death."

With her hands braced on her hips, she stared ahead, silent. Her words were too crisp and efficient. They weren't real. This was the hard-ass version of Shannon, the one who liked to pretend she was too tough to let anyone else know she cared or felt.

She hopped off the boulder and marched back toward the trail, and I was right behind her.

"How old were you?" I asked.

Her shoulders tensed when those words hit her. Another

mile passed without a response from her, and I was ready to shift gears into less sensitive subject matter. Sometimes I got lucky and she shared freely, but other times she closed right up.

"Nine," she said, pulling her cap lower. "I was nine when she died. Erin was only two, and God, she was so confused. She wandered around the house for months, looking in my mother's bedroom, her sewing room, the kitchen. Everywhere. She didn't understand, and how do you explain death to a baby? What do you say?"

I stopped to tie my shoelace. Shannon *never* talked about Erin. I asked her about that situation once, and she clammed right up.

"She's the only one who isn't involved in the business," I said.

"She never wanted that," Shannon said. "She's independent and selfish, and she took a lot of joy from flipping off my father." She loosened her ponytail and then retied it, all with her back to me. "Not that he didn't deserve it. So anyway...she was a baby, and she didn't understand anything that was happening. She was convinced my mother was in the house, and all you'd hear was her crying and screaming." She tugged at the hat again, until the brim fully shielded her eyes. "My father lost it one night. He couldn't handle hearing 'mama, mama, mama' all over the house so he locked Erin in a basement closet. It was dark and freezing, and he nailed the fucking door shut. It took Matt and me almost three hours to get it open, but I guess it worked because I've never heard her say 'mama' since that night. It was like the word vanished from her vocabulary."

She sucked in a watery breath and turned her face toward the sun. She still wouldn't cry in front of me. I knew this wasn't information she readily shared, and I knew there was something about getting away from her world that made her open up. I loved and hated it in equal measures. She was with *me*, and telling *me*, and that gave me a surge of victory I hadn't known I wanted. But these stories were horrible, and I wanted to hug her, kiss her, and ask a million questions about why no one ever put an end to this shit. She shouldn't have dealt with this then, and she shouldn't be mothering all over her siblings to make up for it now. Someone had to end this.

"Was it always Erin and Riley?"

She wrapped her hand around her ponytail, smoothing the strands and then repeating the motion. "No, but my father was worst to the youngest ones. Well...maybe that's not accurate." She took a sip from her water and offered it to me. "He hated us all in different ways. Riley and Erin have scars you can see, but...it's what you can't see that does the most damage."

This was the second time Shannon mentioned her father's abusive behavior, and she didn't have to say anything else for me to know he harmed her, too. It wasn't simply the trauma of seeing a brother beaten or a sister trapped, and I found it hard to breathe around the weight of that knowledge. I wanted to find his remains so I could have the pleasure of killing him again.

I lived with an intimate knowledge of the unimaginably gruesome awfulness that existed in the world, and though it was easier to believe that awfulness was extraordinary, that it was exception, I knew it wasn't exclusive to the war-torn regions I frequented. The unimaginable happened to ordinary people every day, and often, the people you least expected.

I didn't want it to be *my* person.

"But he didn't take on Matt or Patrick, and they were better at not triggering my father. Sometimes I thought Erin wanted to piss him off. When she was older, she went out of her way to do it, as if she wanted to know how far she could push him. She was willing to go all the way to the edge, and there were times when I thought she wanted to go over just to see what the fall was all about. She's fearless like that. I mean, she'd have to be. She walks on fucking lava."

I handed the bottle back. "What exactly does she do? Other than infiltrating the bedrock of the Italian mafia?"

"She's a geologist now. She studies volcanoes, and travels all over the world doing research. She's been published in journals, and even a few science magazines. She's smart, really smart," Shannon said, and I had to pause and study her for a second. The pride in her voice was measurable, and all of this was coming from the woman who routinely refused to speak about the sister in question. "When she told me she wanted to go to the University of Hawaii, I figured that was just her way of telling everyone to fuck off. Then she got there, and she took some geology classes, and she was a convert. It's probably the right field for her. There aren't many options for people like Erin. It's either village witch or head of the Holy Roman Empire, and I think that ship has sailed. Somehow volcanologist is right in the middle."

We continued along the trail, following the Bosque River, and even though the silence was heavy with history, it wasn't uncomfortable. A desert cottontail rabbit charged across the dusty path and into a cluster of low juniper bushes, then scrambled over the footbridge ahead. I tracked its movements while organizing the shards of childhood Shannon just placed in my hands.

Everything inside me demanded that I wrap my arms around Shannon and hold her until those memories faded into the background, but she wouldn't allow that. Going to her now would result in a brush-off, a brash comment, and even more ground to cover until I earned my way back.

"So I can make a pie," she said, her voice high and shaky. "I have to get three or four squash because something always goes wrong, and Patrick and Sam give me a ton of shit about it. I only burnt one this year." She laughed and started down a narrow path off the trail. "I hope Lauren remembers them."

"I can guarantee you that Lo will not forget about a pie," I said. "Pie is a major component of her world."

"Fair point," she murmured.

This path led toward a large, flat rock the size of a gazebo. She climbed up and stood in the center, then turned back and beckoned me to join. That was the invitation, and I was taking it. I jogged to the rock and grabbed her around the waist, turning her upside down while she laughed and shrieked.

"You're going to drop me," she screamed.

"I'm giving you a new perspective on the valley," I said, my arms banded around her torso as she wiggled and kicked. I pressed my teeth against her backside and bit. "You're supposed to be appreciating nature, peanut."

"Are you *biting* my ass?" she yelled.

"It's a nice ass," I said, kissing the same spot before setting her on her feet.

We settled on the rock and shared the lunch we'd picked up before leaving the hotel. She tossed eighty percent of the turkey from her sandwich aside, explaining that she preferred sandwiches composed mostly of vegetables and cheese.

"If it were up to me, I'd skip the bread and stick with cheese and fruit," she said, gesturing to me with her water bottle. "And nuts. Cheese, fruit, nuts. That's all I need. There's a market in Chestnut Hill that makes these perfect little cheese plates, but it's a pain in the ass to get there from my place. Sometimes I send Tom to get me one for lunch, but I can't really justify him spending that much time on cheese."

I gazed at her, smiling. "When am I going to see you again?"

She capped her water and reclined back against her balled-up jacket. "When would you like to see me again?"

"Soon," I said. I shifted to lie beside her, and wove our fingers together. There was an extended deployment on my horizon, and I wanted to steal every single moment of time between now and then with Shannon. "Really soon."

"Why?"

I wasn't sure what prompted the question, but it wasn't like we spent much time defining this relationship or our feelings for each other. I only assumed she had feelings for me, and that was why she agreed to continue seeing me. "You're so much," I said, dragging my finger across that comet of freckles on her collarbone. "And I want all of it."

———

SHANNON WAS quiet on the drive to the airport. She sat beside me, her fingers laced around mine, staring at the scenery as it passed.

I hated it.

"I noticed that it's the end of November," I said. "And December comes next."

"A shrewd observation," she mumbled. "Are commandos expected to memorize the sequence of months, or is that one of your special tricks?"

I hiked up my sleeve and made an exaggerated glance at my watch. "I had you biting a pillow two hours ago. You need me to pull over and fix that attitude?"

SEALs liked to say *anything worth doing was worth over-doing* and this thing with Shannon—this power struggle—was definitely worth overdoing.

Shannon shook her fingers free with a snicker. "You don't want me to hop on?"

She gestured to my crotch, and as if the mere suggestion of her silky skin against mine was enough to turn me on, an ache rolled down my dick. Four days of unrestricted access to this woman wasn't enough, and as I caught sidelong glimpses of her now, her hair wavy and wild, a splattering of new freckles fanning out across her nose and cheekbones, her lips arched in a scowling pout, I knew there wouldn't be a time when I wanted anyone other than Shannon.

"I want you to spend Christmas with me."

I wanted to piss her off and fuck her hard. I wanted to laugh with her and hear all her awful stories. I wanted her vicious insults and the purring sighs she made before she came. I wanted it *all*.

"No," she drawled. She huffed out a laugh and glanced at me, her brows furrowed. I knew she was searching for a caustic comeback, and when she found none, she crossed her arms over her chest. "No."

"And by no you obviously mean yes," I said. "We're going to Mexico, a little place on the Baja coast."

Shannon propped her sunglasses up and pressed her fingertips to her eyelids. She exhaled, as if this topic was inflicting pain. "You've omitted some critical details."

"Like what?" I asked. My hand moved to the nape of her neck.

"You're being obtuse," she murmured. "Your entire family goes to Mexico for the holidays. I know this because Lauren's told me all about it, and Matt went with her last year." She met my blank stare, and raised me an eye roll. "And they're going this year, too. I'm not interested in any part of that. No."

"There will be plenty of pillow biting. Did I mention that?" Another eye roll. "Do you even have a reason? Or are you too busy glaring at me with all your hell fire?"

"I have several reasons," she cried, knocking my hand from her neck. "First, *my* family is in Boston and *my* family has its own traditions. I took enough shit for ditching them this week—"

"And that's exactly why you should spend a week with me in Mexico," I interrupted, "where I'll keep you drunk and naked."

I fucking hated her brothers. Those lazy bastards dumped everything on Shannon. I wanted to sit each of them down and have a few words about how I expected them to treat their sister, and by *words,* I meant kicking the shit out of them until we reached an understanding.

"Yeah, being surrounded by your parents, Wes, Lauren, and Matt sounds like the perfect time to be drunk and naked," she snorted. "We're not talking about this anymore."

"There will be moments when clothes are tolerated," I said. "Few and far between, but they'll exist, and you can hang with Judy, and tell her how much you love the blog.

She will promote you to favorite in a fucking second. And you can give Wes shit about everything, because you can and I want to watch that."

"What you're talking about isn't what we have going on," she said, her hand circling the space between us.

"Let's renegotiate the terms," I said.

"You don't want to negotiate with me," she said.

"Maybe I do," I said.

"Listen. I wouldn't challenge you to a commando contest. You shouldn't challenge me to a litigation duel."

She continued sighing and murmuring about me losing my damn mind, and I returned my hand to her neck. She was tense, all tight, wiry muscles bunched between her shoulders, owed entirely to me messing up her universe again.

Her land mines were everywhere. Some I could spot, others were hidden, and all of them required caution. Patience.

And fuck me if patience wasn't my middle name.

"Then let's talk about some road head."

Twelve

ELEVEN MONTHS *ago*

I USED to think whiskey taught me everything I needed to know about hangovers.

Whiskey was nothing when compared to a long weekend with Will Halsted.

Those glorious days in New Mexico came crashing down when I woke up Monday morning. A crunchy layer of snow covered the roads, the sky was gray, and my bed was void of delicious men in need of insults.

A dull ache throbbed at the base of my skull, and I frowned at my empty text message inbox. There were a fuck ton of messages when I landed last night—mostly Lauren and Andy sharing the holiday highlights, Patrick blasting me with questions about the status meeting agenda for this morning, and Will requesting confirmation that I was safe and snug at home. He sent a picture, too, one he snapped of us on the tail end of our hike. It was at a steep, rocky part of the path, far from the marked trail, with the snowcapped mountains framed in the distance. Will's lips were pressed to my temple, and he was smiling. I looked sweaty and blotchy, and the angle gave me an extra chin, but I kind of loved that image.

When he delivered me to the airport, he swept me off the curb and kissed me harder than was polite for such a public setting. Then he explained he'd be leading training missions all week. He'd be off the grid, and the absence of his texts and calls made the hangover much worse.

I avoided the office, distracting myself with buying and selling properties, and walking through our current job sites under the guise of listing preparation. It was a good diversion. It gave me time to think, and though the distance from Will was hard, it was healthy.

I couldn't keep doing the rollercoaster routine: the eager-anxious build-up before seeing him, the incredible lightness associated with great sex and good company, the sharp plummet when it ended, and then getting in line to do it all over again. It was too much—drama, travel, emotion, all of it —and over the course of this week, I refined a persuasive argument to end things altogether.

But I wasn't going to.

If I was brutally honest with myself, I *couldn't* do it.

I wanted these weekends, and even if there were costs and challenges associated with them, they weren't substantial enough to get me off the rollercoaster.

MY INSTANT MESSENGER pinged while I was rewriting an injunction on Thursday morning.

Patrick: Got a second
Shannon: Yep
Shannon: You're welcome to walk down the stairs and have this conversation in person. People still do that.
Patrick: Can't. I'm on a conference call with the Castavechias and their interior decorator, who might be one of the horsemen of the apocalypse.
Shannon: Please tell me Andy's doing the talking
Patrick: Yes.
Patrick: What have you heard about Thanksgiving?

I glanced at the clean crockery on the corner of my desk. Matt dropped the dishes off earlier, and thanked me for the butternut squash pies. Apparently, Lauren ate half of one for breakfast on Thanksgiving morning, and the others were demolished before the holiday bowl games ended.

Shannon: That my pies were best in show
Patrick: Not going to argue that
Patrick: But there's more to the story. Sam brought Tiel
Shannon: That's still happening?
Patrick: Oh yeah.
Shannon: I got some texts from Lauren and Andy. They said it got a little tense.
Patrick: That's a good assessment. I wouldn't say it went badly, but I wouldn't call it good either. There were some uncomfortable moments. She might just be socially awkward, in which case, they're a good pair.
Shannon: Uncomfortable how?
Patrick: My gut says she's a nice girl but she was really prickly.
Patrick: She said some unusual things to Lauren and Andy.

Shannon: How drunk were you?

Patrick: Only a little. I can't remember exactly what she said, and all in, she was pretty quiet, but when they left, we all looked at each other and we were like, wow. That was really fucking strange

Shannon: Maybe you could tell me what made it so strange…details never hurt anyone.

Patrick: She kind of bit Nick's head off. And she yelled at Lauren.

Shannon: About what?!?

Patrick: Lauren invited her to lunch.

Shannon: And she yelled at Lauren about that?

Patrick: You should talk to Sam. Find out where his head's at. See about getting him an appointment with that counselor.

Shannon: I thought we weren't kicking hornets' nests anymore…

Patrick: Talk to him. He's not going to talk to me and I'm getting nothing out of Riley.

Patrick: Let him bitch about something. That always opens the floodgates.

Shannon: Awesome. I'm popping some headache medicine before I go in

Patrick: Wait. You never told me about New Mexico.

Shannon: It was good. Really good.

Patrick: Did you try any fry bread?

Shannon: No…

Patrick: Back to neutral?

Shannon: All the way.

"KNOCK, KNOCK." I leaned against Sam's door while he pored over the blueprints on his desk. "Have a minute to spare?"

He nodded, and rolled up the plans. "Sure."

I waved a take-out menu. "I was going to place a lunch order. Did you want anything?"

"I'm good," he said, pointing to a covered glass bowl that appeared to contain kale and apples. He hadn't said much, but his tone was decidedly cool. He wasn't interested in this chat. "What's up?"

"Just a few things." I studied my palm while thinking through the list of things I wanted to cover before getting to the 'Hey, your girlfriend is kind of a bitch. What's that all about?' discussion. "Your dry cleaning was dropped off this morning, and it's in the back seat of your car. I checked in with your endocrinologist's office, and your appointment is next Monday afternoon. They'll have you do some blood work too, so I blocked that time on your calendar. I sorted out your expenses from last month, and assigned costs to clients as best as I could determine. I'll need you to look it over, but that will be quick. And I had Tom arrange your travel to that conference in January, the one in Arizona." I traced the circumference of my bracelets before glancing up. "I was really bummed that I didn't get to meet Tiel. Everyone said she was…intriguing."

His expression shifted from disinterested to sharply defensive in an instant, and I swallowed hard. I hated fighting with Sam. He interpreted everything as a personal attack, and while I was often hit with the 'holds a grudge forever' stick, he was the one who really struggled to let things go.

"Tiel *is* intriguing," he said, his eyebrow arched. "I've

never met anyone with so many accomplishments, and I have to practically beat them out of her. It's refreshing to meet people who don't view themselves as gifts to this planet."

"And some people are attorneys, Sam." I held up my hands, resigned to the fact I was playing the part of the enemy today. Might as well embrace it.

"So it wasn't rose petals and rainbows," he continued. "I seem to remember you going all corporate commando the first time Matt brought Lauren here."

"That was because Riley was being a juvenile delinquent." I shifted in my seat, girding myself against the blowback that was bound to come next. "Look. I've heard several times that dinner was tense, and your guest was a hard pill to swallow. I'd just like to hear about it from you. Are you trying to prove a point, or going through some kind of angry girl phase?"

I picked at the hem of my skirt while anger—fast-breathing, wide-eyed, jaw-twitching anger—rippled through Sam.

"Has it occurred to you that *we* are a bit intense, and not everyone handles this tribe the same way?" he asked.

"No, not really." The last thing he wanted was me invading more of his space, so I did exactly that and scooted closer, folding my arms on his desk. "It has occurred to me that you might be having some difficulties coping with stress. We've been talking about Angus's estate and the work at Wellesley a lot, and I know those are triggers for you. I don't think adding a toxic relationship with this girl is going to help you, and maybe it's time to get an appointment with Dr. Robertsen."

"Shannon, I'm going to say this once."

His breath whooshed out as he stood, his palms flat on

his desk, and I couldn't decide whether his fury stemmed from talk of Tiel or his generally irritable disposition these days. I was no stranger to macho chest-thumping, but this seemed more complicated than standing up for his lady.

Sam closed his eyes, his chest heaving, and pointed to the door. "Get the fuck out of my office."

Riley stood in the doorway, his fingers raking through his thick hair. "What did you do?" he mouthed.

"Nothing good," I whispered.

"And thank you kindly for that," Riley said under his breath, his gaze on Sam. "Now I get to spend the afternoon with the Hulk."

Sam blew out a long breath and looked up at us. He did that a lot—counting, deep breathing, tuning into his heart rate—but it didn't appear to be working today.

"Hey," Riley said, slow and friendly, as if he was trying to coax a skittish puppy to his side. "We're walking properties this afternoon, right?" He made a show of looking at his notebook, and back up at Sam. "Yeah, you wanted to check out the Turlan basement now that the power washing is finished. We also have five others to see."

I waited while Sam tossed his things into his messenger bag and stormed out of his office, and then I glanced back to Riley. "That was productive," I murmured.

"Don't do this to me, Black Widow," he sighed. "He's going to be a hellcat all night and I don't have time to babysit his ass. My fantasy football team is last in my league right now."

"Do you think he's all right?"

Riley tucked his notebook away, shrugging. "The only thing I know is that I know nothing."

I nodded. "Same."

Shannon: Any chance you're around?

Will: At your service, ma'am

Shannon: When did you get back?

Will: Couple of hours ago

Shannon: Did everything go well? What's the preferred outcome for these things?

Will: Decent training op. Everyone came back, and with all limbs.

Will: Fucking tired though.

Shannon: You should sleep. I'll talk to you later

Will: You'll talk to me now.

Will: What's up?

Shannon: You know what I hate

Will: Chicken on a bone

Shannon: Well, yes, but other things too

Will: The use of the word cunt

Will: Which, I have to tell you, I don't understand. I figured you'd be all over that one. Think of the inventive ways you could mix up your insults.

Will: I'd be excited about you calling me a rusty old cunt or something.

Shannon: You finished?

Will: Yes ma'am.

Will: Tell me all the things you hate

Shannon: I hate when people expect me to be the bitch. Like, they just assume my cold, dark heart beats for the sole purpose of being awful.

Shannon: And yes, sometimes, I have to strap on the balls and be the bitch because that's what I do here but I hate when people can't see that there's a difference between me and my role.

Shannon: It's really fucking messy because my family and my work are indistinguishable. Right now, Sam thinks I'm the most evil bitch in the world because I suggested he talk things through with his psychiatrist

Shannon: And because he's too busy being a man to acknowledge that a lot of things are changing in his life right now and he needs some help processing it all

Shannon: Not because I think he's mentally ill, deranged, or unfit for society. Because it helps to talk things out

Shannon: But no. to him, therapy is for pussies and he freaks when he thinks people are criticizing him, and I'm the worst

Shannon: He's gone out of his way to avoid speaking to me for the past four days because of this.

Will: You want me to kill him?

Shannon: No but I appreciate the offer

Will: Anytime

Will: You're not a bitch, peanut.

Shannon: I'm pretty sure you've been telling me otherwise for months

Will: I'm allowed to insult you. I make up for it in orgasms. Those other fuckers are not, and God help them if they upset you again.

Shannon: Why do you say that?

Will: What? That I'll kick their pathetic asses?

Shannon: Yes

Will: Because I will

Shannon: But why?

Will: There are a lot of reasons.

Shannon: Give me some of them

Will: I care about you. I don't like it when you're upset and stressed. I'd like to teach your brothers something about not being dickheads

Will: Come to Mexico. Please.

Shannon: I just told you how fucked up my life is right now and you want to make it more fucked up by telling our families about this arrangement of ours?

Will: We don't have to tell anyone anything.

Shannon: No, we probably do

Will: Then let me handle it while you drink tequila and chill the fuck out

Will: Think about it

Will: Still thinking?

Will: Shannon?

Will: I think you're forgetting that I can see when you've read my messages...

Will: Just tell me when you intend to ignore me.

Shannon: I'm ignoring you.

Will: Fucking finally! thank you! Now think about Mexico while you ignore me.

Thirteen

WILL

ELEVEN MONTHS *ago*

Will: Where are you right now?

Shannon: What? Your spy satellite isn't working?

Will: The word you're looking for is drone, and no, it is not tracking you

Will: Not yet

Will: Where are you?

Shannon: A town council meeting outside of Boston that is testing my patience for humanity because they've been debating the local ordinance relative to shrub trimming for 90 minutes and they won't get to my proposal to update the structure of a property until midnight because they have to approve every time someone changes a light bulb around here.

Shannon: Why do you need to know?

Will: Because I'd like to have a chat with your pussy and I don't want anyone else to hear you come

Shannon: Am I supposed to be down for that?

Will: Here's what I want.

Will: I want your panties in my hand. Without me even asking for them.

Will: And I want your skirt around your waist

Will: And I want to inhale that sweet scent

Will: And I want to lick you until you can't speak

Will: I love the way you taste.

Shannon: What part of "at a town council meeting" did you misunderstand?

Shannon: I'm surrounded by people and I have to stay here until they get to my proposal, and you're waxing poetic about the ladybits

Shannon: I don't call you while you're blowing up oil pipelines, do I?

Will: All right fine. Call me when you get home.

Will: But for the record, I'm usually preventing the oil pipelines from being blown up.

Will: I want to talk about the holidays

Shannon: Awesome.

Will: Why won't you consider it?

Shannon: You're extrapolating quite a bit from a one-word response

Will: Yeah, I am. I can hear text sarcasm from 3000 miles away

Will: What's wrong, peanut?

Shannon: Nothing

Will: Save us both the time and energy of wading through the bullshit and tell me.

Shannon: I've fucked things up with Sam

Will: What happened?

Shannon: I've handled the whole thing wrong. Everything. I've taken a lot of shit for coddling him over the years, and I should have kept doing it. Never should have backed away or gotten into this fight about his issues and his strange girlfriend or any of it. I should have snuggled him up and doubled down on the coddling.

Will: Ok, so move on. If you want to do things differently, go ahead.

Shannon: Yeah, unfortunately, Sam's busy being furious at me and he interprets everything I do as manipulative or malicious or whatever, and he's not having it

Will: I know what you should do

Will: COME TO MEXICO

Shannon: omfg would you stop it?

Shannon: Allow me to be abundantly clear: I am not going to Mexico with you. I have articulated my reasons and I'm finished with this topic.

Will: Your reasons are shit

Shannon: They're still my reasons and I'm serious about being finished. I'm not talking about this anymore.

Will: And here's why your reasons are shit

Will: You're in a war of hearts and minds with Sam. You need to let the insurgency run itself into the ground. Let it blow up, burn down, and when there's nothing left to lose, you can get in there and fix things

Shannon: I can't let Sam blow up or burn down

Will: At the minimum, you need some distance from that shit.

Will: Matt and Lo will be in Mexico, so you'll have family. Also: Judy will love you.

Shannon: Don't you think Judy will require some kind of explanation as to why I'm joining the Halsted Family Festivities?

Will: Let me deal with Judy

Shannon: And you're going to deal with Lauren, too?

Will: Stop obsessing about that. Come to Mexico. Stay with me. There's nothing more to be said.

———

Will: Care to explain why you aren't answering your phone?

———

Will: Here's the situation. I've called you 6 times and left 5 voicemails. That means it's time for you to call me back.

———

Will: Just talked to Tom. He confirmed you're alive.

Will: He's a treasure, btw. Gave me your entire schedule for the week.

———

Will: Peanut. talk to me.

Fourteen

SHANNON

ELEVEN MONTHS *ago*

"WHAT'LL IT BE?" Riley asked.

His shirtsleeves were rolled to his elbows and his collar was open at the throat, and he seemed truly content tending the makeshift bar in Patrick and Andy's apartment on Christmas Eve. The glassware was arranged in neat rows, his lemons and limes were beautifully segmented, and all the bottles were lined up like an army of liquor.

"I'd like to shed some brain cells tonight," I said.

His fingers tapped the bottle tops for a moment. "Who's getting you home?"

I scowled. "I can get myself home, thank you."

"Hmm," he murmured, grabbing the rum. "Sounds like someone isn't feeling the spirit of the season."

I crossed my arms over my chest and sank further into my scowl. "Nope," I said, "not really."

He continued pouring liquids into the stainless steel container, and asked, "Didn't want to spend the holiday on the beach?" I looked up from his rhythmic shaking with a frown. "I figured you'd be seeing Captain America since you've been spending most holidays with him recently."

What happened to not seeing anything?

"Be a good boy and stop talking about things above your pay grade," I said, wincing.

Spending Christmas in Mexico with Will and his parents, Wes, Lauren, and Matt was crazy and out of the question. I wanted Will time. I didn't want to deal with Lauren's knowing grins or Matt weirding out, or focusing my energy on not swearing my ass off in front of his parents. And it seemed so sudden and public and official, all the things I wasn't convinced I wanted right now.

This was scheduled sex. Easy, uncomplicated, not an issue-for-me-to-manage, along-for-the-rollercoaster-ride scheduled sex.

I liked the vague, gelatinous nature of things with Will, mostly. I didn't love sneaking around and I was nearly at my breaking point when it came to the secrets I was keeping from my brothers—or not keeping, in Riley's case—and Tom and Lauren, but there was something wonderful about leaving this off the books. It was as if we had something no one else could interfere with. As long as it stayed between us, it was our little insults-and-hate-sex bubble, and that was kind of perfect.

Of course, those feelings changed every time I was alone in my bed, missing him and beyond desperate for a steady stream of affection.

And dick. Let's not pretend I didn't appreciate the easy access to dick.

Riley pointed to his nose. "Next time you see him, you should tell him it still feels a little out of whack."

Glancing around the open floor plan, I noticed Sam helping Andy in the kitchen, Patrick and Nick talking with some of their marathon training group friends near the television. No one was close enough to hear us.

"How are you always creeping on people like this? Do you get a sixth sense for it?"

Riley laughed as he handed me a glass. "I know I'm not the smartest guy in the bunch, but I'm pretty sure I know what I walked in on last summer," he said. "And you're a little obvious in your refusal to discuss your recent travels. The lady doth protest and all."

"Great," I mumbled around the straw. "What is this?"

"Comfortably Numb," he said. "And like I said, I never see anything."

"I'm not sure whether that's a good thing or not," I said. "I'm getting a distinctly extortionist vibe from you right now."

Riley wiped his hands on a bar towel, and draped it over his shoulder. "I don't have the attention span for those shenanigans." He waved me off, saying, "Go sit in a corner, and be Grinchful. It's not Christmas without somebody trotting out the melancholy."

I sagged into a chair near the fireplace, scowl still intact, and sipped my drink. I wasn't melancholy; I was a masochist.

Will went a little spastic when I told him I wasn't interested in the yuletide festivities. He seemed to believe we wouldn't have to explain anything about our relationship to anyone, and I called bullshit on that proposition. There was no way in hell that I could show up in Baja without getting a beat down from Lauren. She'd want the Complete History of Shannon and Will, or at least she'd give me sweet, smiling gazes and say she was happy for us, and that was basically the same thing. It would be a topic of discussion at our regular Saturday lunch outings, a *thing* open for collective analysis. And later, when Will and I stopped scheduling secret weekends, she'd look at me with sympathetic eyes and promise not to mention him, and I couldn't deal with being the object of pity and concern.

But more than anything, I wasn't willing to share him. There was never enough time, and I knew his family got even less, but I still wanted him all for me.

Will wasn't interested in acknowledging any of my reasoning for this, though. All he heard was that I wasn't going to Mexico. Over the course of nine days, we argued about the whole holiday mess via text. I knew he'd turn on that firm, demanding voice and make me tell him how my pussy felt if we talked, but sending his calls to voicemail only annoyed him. Neither of us got what we wanted, but a bouquet of plum calla lilies appeared in my office later that week and I texted him a picture of my (mostly covered) boobs and it was over.

We weren't back to normal—or whatever qualified as normal for us—yet either. Will had been tied up most of the week, and I hadn't heard anything more than a quick text since he arrived in Cabo San Lucas last night.

I spent the evening tucked beside the fireplace, drinking away my brain cells and picking at the food Andy repeatedly forced in front of me.

"There are too many depressed people here," she muttered. "Tonight's supposed to be fun! Joyful!"

"How did I not know that you were a secret holiday fanatic?" I nodded at her crimson trousers. "I don't think I like this. I prefer Andy the ice queen." My phone started vibrating in my pocket, and she arched her eyebrows when I yanked it out to see my surfer on the shore. "I'll just take this…somewhere else."

I handed the plate back to her, and ducked into the bedroom. "Hello?"

"Shannon," Will said. He stretched my name out into a long, rumbling sigh, all kinds of "Stella!" and *A Streetcar Named Desire*. "You aren't in Mexico."

There was a party on the other side of the door, with music and laughter and people happy to spend time together, but I didn't want to be there. I moved deeper into the bedroom, and headed for the bathroom. The door clicked shut behind me. "Are you drunk?"

"Yes," he drawled. "My sister ordered shots. Lots of shots. Like, all the shots. I can't believe I taught her to drink tequila. And you know me. I can't let a little girl drink me under the table."

"Of course not," I laughed. "If this is the state you're in, how's she holding up?"

Will laughed. "She grabbed Matt's dick and said a few things I never thought I'd hear out of my sister. I kept drinking with the shady hope I'd forget the whole experience."

"Oh yeah, she's a dirty bird," I said, settling on the edge of the tub.

"Please don't tell me those things," he said. He grunted, and if I listened closely, I could hear waves crashing.

"Are you on the beach?"

"I'm looking at the Pacific Ocean and my ass is in the sand," he said.

"It's a rough life," I said, threading my necklace between my fingers.

"I hate you right now. You know why?"

I laughed. "I believe the tequila will tell me."

"Because I've spent eleven days with you in the past eight months and that's all it took for me to fall for you. Because I've sent you over five thousand texts and called you two hundred and eighteen times and you know what I have to show for all that? I fucking *love* you, and you're there and I'm here and that's why I hate you."

The necklace was wrapped tight around my fingers, the delicate gold chain digging grooves into my skin that bit enough to keep those words from hitting my heart all at once. "The tequila isn't going to remember this conversation tomorrow, honey."

"That's where you're wrong. Tequila never forgets," he sighed. "You were wrong. You should have come."

"That's where we still disagree," I said. I wanted it to sound pleasant and light, but it came off harsh. Cold.

"You should have come," he repeated. "My parents would probably fight over which one of them liked you more. They'd just chop you to pieces and eat you because you're so perfect. And this place...I could've taken you out sailing or diving. Or shots. You're a fun drunk. And there's a huge bed in my room, too. I can't look at it without thinking about you."

I stayed quiet. He was drunk and rambling, and he didn't mean any of this. It didn't matter whether those words—the ones I didn't want and certainly didn't need—were wrapping me in a painfully sweet embrace right now, or that a thick, confused blob of emotion was pulsing in my chest.

"I'm tired of secrets, Shannon. You'll either fuck me in public or you won't fuck me at all."

"What?"

"That didn't come out right," he mumbled. "Shannon," he continued, almost too low to hear. "The only thing I wanted was to wake up next to you and stop this fucking game where you don't want anyone to know that you're fucking me, and it's not about the sex. I just want to be *with* you."

I dropped my head to my hand and gulped back a groan. "Will. I couldn't go."

That wasn't completely accurate, and we both knew that, but I couldn't cobble together any further argument tonight.

"There's a bell," he said, "on base, in Coronado. In the middle of the courtyard. Regular old brass bell. Almost two-thirds of the guys who go through SEAL training ring that bell. They bow out. Drop your helmet, walk away, no questions asked."

He sighed, and fell silent for several minutes. I heard his heavy breaths and the ocean, and I had to work hard to avoid imagining myself on the beach with him, his arms around me while his lips tattooed those words—still didn't need them, still didn't want them—on my skin.

"Why don't you go back to your room?" I asked. "It doesn't seem like a good idea to pass out on the beach."

A laugh burst across the line. "Peanut, I've been surf conditioned. Drown-proofed, too. I can stay underwater for more than four minutes before coming up for air. I have Poseidon's trident over my goddamn heart. The sea reports to me."

"I'm sure it does," I said, smiling.

"Shannon," he started, "I've seen that bell, and it's never once crossed my mind to ring it."

"And that's what makes you good at what you do," I said.

"No, I'm not talking about the teams," he said. "I'm talking about you. I'm warning you now: I know how to fight and I'm not giving up."

I stayed locked in the bathroom, perched on the edge of the tub, long after we disconnected.

There weren't many decisions I regretted, but in that moment, I regretted everything about Mexico. We didn't get enough time together, and even if I had to tell Lauren—and everyone else—that none of it was up for conversation, I should have gone.

When I emerged, the crowd had thinned to only Patrick, Andy, Sam, Riley, and Nick. They were sprawled on the sofa while a muted soccer match played, and I settled into the space beside Nick while Riley prepared his next round of cocktails.

"Haven't seen much of you recently," Nick said.

"That's largely due to me avoiding you," I said as I accepted an Irish coffee from Riley.

"You are nothing if not consistent," he murmured.

"Ri, this is strong enough to tranquilize a rhino," Sam said.

Nick sipped his drink and glanced at me. "Do we want him sedated tonight?"

"Probably not," I said, rubbing my brows.

I fucking love you.

He didn't mean it. Couldn't mean it. Even big, tough, drown-proofed SEALs got drunk and spouted off nonsensical things.

"It really isn't," Nick said, turning back to Sam.

"Dude, if you get hammered and piss on my wall, I'll kill you," Patrick said.

"Your tolerance is off," Riley murmured. "You haven't been hard drunk in months."

I'd digested just enough of the conversation to add, "That's positive. Is that something you're working on now?"

"Are you looking to start something with him? Jesus, woman, I didn't sign up to jump on your grenades tonight," Nick said under his breath. "Can you do us all a favor and not talk to him like he's five? So his lady has some fire-breathing dragon moments. So do you. Oddly enough, no one's tried to run you off."

The scowl returned as I shifted to face Nick. "I don't recall asking your opinion, so why don't *you* do *me* a favor and tuck it away with your little dick. Okay? Thanks."

"We don't need any more Walsh factions on our hands," Nick hissed. "And I don't appreciate this ongoing slander of my dick. I'll drop trou right now and remind you."

"Ugh, don't be horrible," I whispered. "Keep your pants up and your dick down."

"Does anyone remember the year we changed all the labels on the presents?" Patrick asked. "For the life of me, I can't figure out when that was, but we managed to peel all the tags off and rearranged them."

I stared into my coffee, blinking as that memory blew over me. It brought a dozen more with it, and if I thought about it hard enough, I could remember the way the kitchen smelled while my mother baked during the holidays.

"At first Mom was really confused but then she was *pissed*," he continued. "She figured it out within a few minutes and she was steaming mad." He pointed at me as I sucked in a breath to will back the tears prickling my eyes.

"She gave us that exact look, that awful face-melting look you just gave Nick, and stared us down until we cracked."

Sam sat up and gestured to himself. "It was Matt's idea, but he blamed it on me."

"Yes," Patrick laughed, pointing at Sam. "And he did it because he knew Mom was going to beat his ass with a wooden spoon but she'd never get mad at you."

"Do you remember when we hollowed out the cake?" I asked. "It was this big, beautiful layer cake that she made for one of those holiday parties we always had, and we cut a little piece and then scooped out the inside. We filled it with something—what was that?"

"Leftover stuffing," Sam said, and the room bubbled with laughter. "Even at seven, Matt was very concerned about preserving the structural integrity."

"Such a fucking nerd," Patrick muttered. "But God, when Mom cut into that cake and realized what we'd done...shit, we'd never run so fast in our lives."

"Why do I remember none of this?" Riley asked from the bar.

"You were two or three," I said. "You were a baby. You wouldn't have remembered."

Those memories simmered around us, and as I studied my siblings, I felt that tug of home, the one that kept me in Boston despite the admirable persistence of a certain sailor. I wanted to be here, but I also wanted to be with Will, and there was no clear middle ground.

"Come on," Nick said, tapping my elbow. "Let's get out of here."

I followed him without question, and though we hadn't been on the best of terms since the wedding and we'd snapped at each other tonight, we were still friends. We found ourselves at Sullivan's Tap, sitting side-by-side and sipping whiskey with the other lost souls long past last call.

"Where's Erin these days?" I asked.

Nick lifted a shoulder as he regarded his glass. "Not here," he said. "That's all I know."

"Consider it a gift," I said. "She's too young for you anyway."

"That's a fucking miserable thing to say," he murmured. "And the thing about age is that it stops mattering around the time you hit twenty-three or twenty-four. Definitely when you hit twenty-five." He gestured for a refill, and I slid my glass over for the same. "It's also my position that Erin knows no age. The eight years between us are—" He held out his hands as if reaching for something. "They're nothing. She's lived more lives than I have, and she knows more of the earth than I do, and—"

I wrapped my hand around his wrist to slow his motions. "If this is where you tell me how she's captured your heart, I'll need to say goodnight and walk out the door because I cannot handle that right now."

"That's not quite how it went down," he said, laughing. "No, but I'd like to point out that you've been operating under the assumption you know what happened with me and Erin that night, and believe me when I tell you that you're wrong."

I gave him my best *you can't bullshit the bullshitter* glare, and said, "Right, so you had your hand under her dress because…what? Checking for ticks? Trying to find the 'mute' button?"

He folded his arms on the bar and leaned forward, glancing at me. "It's not what you think."

Shaking my head, I said, "I don't think I want to hear any more of this. Not tonight."

"Good. I don't want to talk about it anymore."

We didn't say anything else. It was a lonely way to spend the earliest hours of Christmas morning, but it was better than being alone.

Fifteen

SHANNON

NINE MONTHS *ago*

Will: You know…it's a waste of water

Shannon: What the fuck now?

Will: What you do with your showerhead

Shannon: William. I told you bad things happen when you bring that up.

Shannon: I don't recall making any comments about you *cleaning your rifle*

Will: It's irresponsible. Most people don't have that kind of water to waste

Will: You should really delegate management of those priorities to me

Shannon: Mmhmm. I'll be over here, ignoring you.

Will: Talk to me about those toys.

Shannon: ?

Will: The deep dicking drawer.

Will: If I didn't have a handle on my masculinity, that drawer would have given me something to think about

Shannon: You're not making a lot of sense

Will: Yeah I've been awake for the past 4 days but I keep wondering which one of those toys you use when you're thinking about me

Shannon: What gives you the impression I'm thinking about you

Will: You were thinking about me in the shower

Will: And I think about you

Shannon: ....using the deep dicking toys?

Will: No. In my head you just use your fingers

Will: But I have thought about teasing you with them. Seeing how crazy I can get you

Shannon: Aren't you supposed to be thinking about commando shit? I'm uncomfortable with the idea of you jumping out of airplanes or crawling through mud on your belly while thinking about vibrators.

Will: Whoa. Hold on. Let me write this down. I want to remember the day and time you backhandedly admitted caring about me.

Shannon: I was more concerned with national security and all. I don't want you invading the wrong country or taking out the wrong dictator or whatever

Will: That's sweet but the jumping out of aircraft is a small portion of my day. There's a lot of down time where I can contemplate vibrators relative to your pussy.

Shannon: I do care about you. Don't say I don't. That's rude.

Will: Yeah whatever. You care about my cock

Shannon: I won't disagree with that statement but I would add that I enjoy other parts of you as well

Shannon: I might need you to help me hide a body

Will: I'm your guy

Shannon: You're my guy

Will: I appreciate that you've finally confirmed it.

Shannon: Maybe a few bodies

Will: What kind of damage are we talking? Frat party gone wrong or mass grave? I can handle either one but I'd want an extra pair of hands for the sake of efficiency if we're in mass grave territory

Will: And I don't usually ask this but humor me here...who are we burying?

Shannon: Sam clearly has a death wish today

Shannon: And another one of Patrick's assistants quit

Shannon: She decided she wanted to Occupy Wall Street or join Greenpeace. She said working for us was robbing her soul of its generosity and she needed purpose in her life.

Shannon: We save old homes, for fuck's sake! We're actively preventing history from being demolished!

Shannon: And for once, it wasn't Patrick's fault but fuck... there are times when I'm 93% sure I'm employing children. Actual children.

Will: Don't get me started.

Shannon: You can make them run and jump and climb things. I can't ask an intern to put paper in the copier without a story about her life's path and my contribution to deforestation

Will: Run and jump and climb? Are you confusing the special ops with playgrounds?

Shannon: Yes, William. Yes, I am.

Shannon: Do you wear a thigh holster?

Will: Mmm?

Shannon: You know. On your missions.

Will: Yeah.

Will: Why?

Shannon: I have my reasons

Will: Wait. That's the weirdest thing you've ever asked and we've had some strange convos

Shannon: Unlikely

Shannon: I was just wondering

Will: Why don't I believe that?

Shannon: They're kind of hot, all right?

Will: Wait a minute.

Will: Wait

Will: Were you watching SEAL porn?

Shannon: This conversation is over

Will: omg you were!

Will: I've turned you into a tag chaser. I want to hear all about it.

Shannon: Can you go squeal somewhere else?

Will: Hold on. You were watching porn and you didn't call me? How many movies have we watched over the phone together? At least 10

Will: You can call me when that Eurotrip movie is on but you can't call me for PORN?

Will: I expect a call when porn is involved

Shannon: Sigh.

Shannon: I never said I was watching porn

Will: And you haven't denied it either.

Will: You want me to bring my gear the next time I see you? Give you the real thigh holster experience?

Will: What does it for you, peanut? Some enhanced interrogation? Camo? Underwater knot tying?

Will: You want to watch while I do push-ups?

Shannon: Oh my jesus

Shannon: Can we please not talk about this anymore. Or ever again.

Will: Sure. Agree to one thing.

Shannon: Ugh what

Will: You're not allowed to watch porn without me. Got it?

Shannon: Yes sir.

Will: Ohhhh that was nice.

Shannon: Hey. Are you awake?

Will: Yes

Shannon: I can't sleep. Tell me something interesting.

Will: One of my guys thinks he's coined a new sex term for visiting each port

Shannon: Right there. That one. That was pretty special.

Will: He calls it "getting in 3 holes of golf"

Shannon: Gross

Shannon: Amusing, and something Riley would totally say, but gross

Shannon: He'd probably aspire to that as well

Will: I like how you automatically understood that one.

Shannon: I have 4 brothers. My office is like a locker room

Shannon: Tell me something else

Will: I want to roll over at 2 in the morning and find you, not a text message

Will: I love talking to you but I hate this

Will: Too real?

Shannon: No.

Shannon: I know exactly what you mean.

Will: I'm going down range for a bit
Shannon: Should I understand that comment?
Will: It means I'll be off the grid.
Shannon: With the baby seals?
Will: No. I have to jump on a mission.
Shannon: A real one? Not training?
Will: Real
Shannon: Oh. Ok.
Shannon: Don't take out the wrong dictator
Will: I'll try.
Will: Be good while I'm gone, peanut.
Shannon: I'll try.
Shannon: Just be careful, ok?
Will: I will.

Will: You up
Will: Fuck this has been a long week
Will: I want to talk to you
Will: I miss you
Shannon: How can you miss me? You haven't spent enough time with me to miss me
Will: Yeah it shocks me too
Shannon: That must have been some mission
Will: Affirmative.
Shannon: Nice to know you made it back in one piece.

Will: Terrorists are a lot like king salmon. Life is great until the seals show up

Will: And don't think I didn't notice you worrying about my ass

Will: You going soft on me now?

Shannon: About as soft as your cock

Will: Awwww that's sweet

Will: Completely false, but sweet

Will: Whose soul are you eating today?

Will: Do you wear one of those blinged out wrestling belts? Something with 'Soul Crusher' engraved on it? It just sounds like it would be appropriate.

Shannon: You know what they say. Send me to the wolves and I'll come back leading the pack.

Will: That you do, peanut.

Will: So who are enslaving?

Shannon: Not that it's any of your goddamn business…but Sam

Will: Well, he deserves it.

Shannon: Don't you have governments to overthrow or submarines to blow up?

Will: Yes. I'm saving that for after lunch, though.

Will: What did Sam do to earn your wrath?

Shannon: Nothing. He's just being a bitch.

Will: Is it because he discovered he's a grown man who needs someone to launder his pants?

Shannon: Would you shut the fuck up?

Will: Yeah, next time I have your pussy to suck on

Will: And thank fuck that's going to be soon

"I CAN'T HEAR YOU," I said, raising my voice though I knew it wouldn't help. I glanced at the screen. "Tom? You're breaking up. I have a good signal but I think there's something wrong with my phone. It got wet this morning, and it sounds like something is sizzling inside. Hold on, let me get into the terminal."

I blew my hair out of my face and tucked the phone against my other ear but I was still in shambles. I was morbidly premenstrual and feeling one hundred percent too bloated for these jeans and this bra. I was ready to eat six cheeseburgers and all the chocolate cakes, and I was well past *hangry*. My quick flight from Boston to Washington, D.C. hung out on the tarmac for three hours before takeoff, and it was packed with dueling high school cheerleading squads and screaming babies. When I stepped off the plane and onto the jetway at Reagan National, my ears were ringing and I couldn't get "we go tick, tick, boom" out of my head.

And it was a full moon.

This was one of those insane weeks where every item crossed off my to-do list was replaced with another five, and everyone was miserable about something. It was cold and snowy, work on our properties was taking much longer than expected, and another one of Patrick's assistants quit in a flurry of tears and drama. Oh, and Will and I hadn't been in the same state in over three months.

We made plans to spend a long weekend together in January, but a blizzard shut down the airports. Will made some noise about knowing where to find a snow mobile, but he was on the opposite end of the country and wasn't getting to me, even with all his connections. Instead, we video chatted while we both watched *The Day After Tomorrow*. I thought it was a good choice considering the whole epic snowfall situation; Will thought my humor was frighteningly dark.

Neither of us ever brought up Christmas Eve…but I replayed that conversation daily.

We lost two more weekends when he was pulled from baby SEAL training to handle an overseas mission. The certain danger he faced hit me harder than ever before, and it tore me apart. The worry was paralyzing. I scoured the Internet for incidents involving special operations, and kept cable news on the background all night. Until I heard from him and he confirmed he was perfectly safe, I was a frantic mess and the most difficult part was knowing there was nothing I could do.

When his call came through, telling me that he was alive and well and hopping a flight back to the base in Virginia, no one could have stopped me from going to him. It didn't matter that this weekend was terrible for me, work-wise, or that Sam was notably depressed, or that we only had one day together since Will was due on base Sunday morning.

"Sam is being very *strange*," Tom said.

"He's always strange. It's his signature look," I said.

"Right, yes, I know that. However," Tom said, taking a breath, "he seems really…off. I've been ordering him lunch every day like you asked, but he didn't even notice me when I walked into his office. He was just staring out the window. When I came back three hours later, he hadn't eaten anything. Also, I don't believe he's sleeping. Did you talk to him before heading out?"

A slow-moving group of cheerleaders ahead of me burst

into shouts and chants as they marched up the jetway, and I edged around them. The terminal smelled like cinnamon rolls and teriyaki, and in a perverse way, that combination sounded great. "Sometimes he does that. Staring out the window. It's his creative process. I don't know what else to tell you. We had breakfast a few weeks ago and everything was fine, but other than that, he doesn't talk to me much. And you know what, Tom? I can't chase him down every time he sneezes or frowns. Neither can you. We have a goddamn business to run and he's not a toddler."

"Business to run; no toddlers. Got it." I heard papers shuffling on his end. "Talk to me about the building you picked up in the South End."

I stared at the patterned carpet beneath my feet. "I need Matt to check it out before I decide. If nothing else, it's a hot area and I'll be able to dump it for a profit."

"Two of the properties you're watching in Cambridge were sold today."

"Motherfuck," I groaned. I tugged my bag higher on my shoulder while I scanned the terminal for ground transportation signs. Will was driving up from Virginia, and we agreed to meet at The Jefferson, near DuPont Circle. "Ask Patrick to walk the other one I was looking at, and make an offer if—"

But Will wasn't at the hotel. He was striding toward me, his hands fisted at his sides and a sharp scowl across his face. He shook his head and relieved me of my bag. "You could have canoed here faster than that fucking flight." His arm curled around my waist, tugging me close to him, and he snatched the phone from my hand. "She'll call you back next week."

He ended the call and slipped the device into his back pocket.

"You could have waited a minute for me to finish," I said, head reclined against his chest.

Will tipped my chin up and crushed his lips to mine. "They've had you all week. All month. All fucking winter. It's been ninety-seven goddamn days since I've seen you and I'm not sharing. It's my turn now," he whispered into my cheek. "I have been climbing the walls waiting for you, peanut."

"I know, I know, and my flight…" I trailed off as Will's hands landed on my hips and he wrapped his arms around me. "I'm sorry."

"No, Shannon, it's not your fault," he said, his lips pressed to my jaw. "I couldn't wait in the hotel room any longer. I was losing my fucking mind."

We made our way through the airport and into a taxi. We stayed close, always touching and leaning into each other, and this was different from the wild urgency of desire, but it was still a powerful tide of emotions, all swirling together, washing over me, dragging me from the safety of the shore. I was drowning in Will, and as he banded his arms around me and squeezed tight for the tenth time this evening, I knew this wasn't scheduled sex anymore. It was tipping into affection and concern and *other feelings.*

It was scary, but then it wasn't.

I knew scary things—death and disease, violence and abuse—and this wasn't like that. This was warm and happy and special, and maybe…maybe it was finally my turn.

Will led me to our room, and he was pretty cute with my Burberry tote on his arm. "That really works for you," I said, pointing at the bag.

"Yeah?" he asked, holding the door open for me. "You're sure it goes with my shoes?"

"And the belt," I laughed. He pulled my coat over my shoulders then dropped to his knees behind me, dragging his fingers down my sides. He stayed there, his face resting on my backside, and all the noise of *'What is this and what are we doing?'* around me quieted.

His fingers moved under my shirt and to my belly, smoothing over my skin and dipping beneath my jeans, and then he freed the buttons at my waist. The denim slipped over my hips, and I bent to help him with my lace-up boots. "What kind of shoes are these? Do these things ever end?"

"You want to talk about my boots?"

"No, I want to get your boots off, and your pants and your shirt and everything else," he said, laughing. "Maybe next time you go with the ones that zip, you know, when ripping your clothes off will be part of the agenda."

Once the boots were abandoned alongside my jeans, and Will was kissing his way up from my ankles, heat was pumping through my veins, awakening all my nerves and filling me with this need to feel him against me and pour all my words and thoughts, and hopes and fears, and the *everything* building up inside me over him, over us.

I sent my shirt and bra sailing through the air, and then I started tearing his jeans off. "I want you on the bed," I whispered.

"I love your scent," he said. "I've been thinking about this for months." His teeth scraped over my upper thigh, pausing to bite along the line of my panties. "And I love it when you start handing out orders." He stood, scooped me up, and marched toward the bed. "You're hot when you're bossy."

He set me on the bed—for once, no tossing—and immediately crawled over me. His cock was heavy on my leg, and I arched up, starved for him. An impatient, whiny noise rattled in my throat and he chuckled, kissing the valley between my breasts.

Will shrugged out of his shirt, and my eyes landed on a measure of gauze banded around his bicep. There were tiny spots of blood seeping through. I bolted up and feathered my fingers over him. "What the hell happened to you?"

He glanced at his arm, his eyebrows lifting as if he was seeing the wound for the first time. "Oh, it's nothing. Just a flesh wound."

"*A flesh wound*?" I repeated. I might have screeched. Couldn't be sure. "What does that mean?"

He tore the gauze off and balled it up, exposing a line of stitches the length of my hand. "The bullet barely hit me. I didn't even notice until we were back on base."

"You were *shot*?" Definitely screeched that time.

His face softened and he leaned down to brush his lips over mine. "It's okay," he said. "It happens, and I live to fight another day. There are far worse things than a flesh wound."

"But that's just it," I said, tears—dumb, hormone-fueled tears—threatening behind my eyes. I was bare save for my panties, my hands wrapped around Will's arm. "Worse things *could* happen, and I can't do anything to stop it. I can protect everyone but you, and you need it the most."

"Baby, no, you can't worry about that," he said, pulling me into his lap. He kissed my hair, my temple, my jaw.

"But what if something *did* happen," I continued. "Would I even know?"

I watched his throat bob, and I knew I wasn't going to like the response. "I'm sure Lo would hear." He rubbed his chin over my shoulder and held me tighter. "Listen. We can talk about this tomorrow. The only thing happening to me tonight is death by blue balls."

"You're sure you're all right?" I asked. "Am I going to find any other injuries?"

I felt him smile against my neck as he pressed my hand to his cock. "I don't know. You might need to give me a thorough inspection."

"I'm not kidding," I said, stroking him. "I want to know that you're okay."

"Peanut, everything I need is in my lap."

Will's hand traveled up my belly to squeeze my breast, and it stole my breath. "Owww," I moaned. Not a good moan. "Don't, please don't."

He leaned back, his hands suspended away from my body. "What did I do?"

I shifted in his lap. "My boobs hurt."

Will peered at me with concerned eyes. "Oh. Okay. I'm sorry."

"You didn't do anything wrong," I said. "My boobs always hurt the week before my period."

"Oh. Okay," he repeated, nodding.

"Shit," I said, noticing his pinched expression. It was the same way I looked whenever the boys talked about sweaty balls or dick chafing in my presence. "Sorry about the *ick* factor. Didn't mean to over share."

He rubbed his hands together for a long moment, and fitted his chest against my back. "There's nothing icky about a functional uterus," he said. "Tell me if this is all right."

His warm hands settled on the sore undersides of my breasts, massaging with the gentlest strokes imaginable, and I couldn't recall anyone ever touching me with such tenderness. Those hyper-hormonal tears slid down my cheeks, and I didn't try to stop them.

"Good?" he asked. I murmured in agreement and snuggled into him. "Anything else hurt?"

I shook my head. "No, I just feel fat, and I'm irritable and tired, and I'm so hungry, but none of that matters because I haven't seen you in forever and you've been *shot* and I don't want to waste any of this time because my boobs are being moody and I'm crying like a bitch. And you have to leave in twenty-nine hours."

"You're counting, too?" He kissed a line from my shoulder to my earlobe. "There's something I want you to let me try."

"If you think we're having anal sex right now, you've truly misinterpreted what I'm saying."

"You have a filthy mind, peanut. Really filthy." Will laughed against my neck, and I smiled through my tears. "That's not what I want. I want you to let me take care of you. You think you can handle that?"

Six months ago, the answer would have been a definitive *no*. Maybe even three months ago, or last week. But that desperate need for control wasn't clawing at me right now. I listened for it, waiting to hear the noise of all the things I should be worrying about, and I searched for it, waiting for the snap of anxious adrenaline to tighten across my shoulders, but it didn't come to me. All I had was the heat of Will's chest against my back, his hands on my breasts, and the bubbly pressure of feeling possessed.

"I don't think I know how," I said, sniffling, "to let you."

"Let me show you," he whispered.

I wasn't sure how long he held me, and I didn't protest when he carried me into the bathroom like a freaking doll. The tub was gorgeous, and when he filled it with water, I tried to explain that I wasn't a bath girl. I never felt particularly clean afterward. Most bubble bath formulas left my skin irritated. I got bored quickly. Will wasn't interested in my opinions on the topic, and said, "Stop arguing with me. Get in the fucking tub and relax."

But this was nice. I *did* relax, and repeatedly toed the knob for more hot water. When I emerged from the heavy steam, Will was seated on the end of the bed, watching college basketball. He was wearing the same faded jeans he wore last summer, at Matt and Lauren's place, a dark green Killer Dana t-shirt. My heart was too full to be a single organ in my chest because what I felt for him right now couldn't be contained with muscle and blood alone.

"Come on," he said. "You need to eat." He cradled my head against his chest while running his hand down my back. "And after you eat, I'm going to kiss your entire body."

We nestled up against the headboard, drinking wine, eating cheeseburgers and cupcakes from room service, and watching a marathon of *Arrested Development*. Will pointed at the television and said, "I imagine this is what your office is like."

"No," I said, studying the dysfunctional family of real estate developers. I could see the similarities when I looked at the right angle. "Well, no, not *exactly*. We're not hiding anything in a banana stand, and Patrick would die if someone called him a real estate developer."

Will turned to me, his brow furrowed. "I never asked you how you got into this work."

"Family business," I said, and reached for my wine.

His brow was still furrowed. "The family business is architecture. You're not an architect."

"Oh, you don't need to remind me," I groaned. "Every time I'm in a meeting with one of the boys and I make a comment about anything that isn't the property's listing price, someone always says 'Shan, we'll handle the building if you handle the selling.' I've learned to make them believe they come up with every idea on their own now."

Will released a long, impatient sigh that morphed into a growl. "I hate your brothers," he said under his breath.

"You do not," I said. "You don't know them. You just run around, all macho and pissed off, and threaten to kick the shit out of them when they annoy me. My brothers are a handful but they aren't that bad."

"I hate hearing about you dealing with one issue or another because they dropped some balls, or these shitty things they say to you, or all the things that happened when you were a kid and—"

I pressed my fingers to his lips and shook my head. "Not tonight, commando. We only have a few hours, and we're not leasing that time to my brothers."

He grabbed my wrist and placed a kiss on my palm, nodding. "Tell me how you got into not-architecture."

I drained my glass and held it out for a refill. "The universe opened a door, and I walked through it."

Will finished his burger and the remains of mine, and gestured for me to continue. "That's a little vague, peanut."

"Yeah, well…"

That wasn't a time I liked revisiting. Angus kicked me out not long after Patrick left for college, and it forced me to bounce between friends' homes unless I wanted to sleep in the girls' locker room at school. The friend angle was tricky, considering I didn't devote much time to friendships in high school, and convincing them to let me stay for days or weeks often required many layers of lies.

Will stroked my neck, his fingers unwinding the knots.

"I always knew my brothers were going to take over the family business. There was no question about it for Patrick and Matt, and Sam got there, too. Riley's always been special so I didn't know what to expect from him, but he's secretly great when it comes to design. Less great with structures and math and physics, but that's why we keep Matt around."

He made another growly sigh, and tugged me closer.

"Like I said, they were always going to take over the business," I continued. "I had a friend in high school, and her father was in real estate development. He specialized in converting old mills into luxury condos and lofts. Things with Angus were...difficult, and I spent a lot of time away from the house. This girl, Rosalie Goff, let me stay at her house. Her dad was making a killing on condos, and he let me pick his brain about the business. He gave me some advice, and helped me get my license."

Fred also let me live in his home long after Rosalie left for Vanderbilt, and offered me a loan to cover my licensing coursework. He was kind and generous when the world kept closing doors in my face, and I'd never found the words to summarize how much that mattered to me. How he saved me.

"He knew everyone, and pointed me in the right direction to get started."

I turned my attention to the television, watching the last half of the episode without saying anything else. I was comfortable sharing many things with Will that I usually kept locked away. But this...I didn't want all of these details spilling out and taking over this night.

"I discovered that I had good instincts when it came to buying and selling, and the market was cranking at that time," I said when a commercial started. "Everyone was making a killing on everything, and that meant we didn't have to rely on Angus anymore."

"Just tell me one thing." Will slipped his hand under the robe and over my belly. "Do your siblings appreciate everything you've done for them?"

"Usually," I said. "I do sign their paychecks."

He murmured in approval and dipped his head to my neck. His lips moved down my skin, kissing and licking, while he rubbed my abdomen.

"I should check my phone," I said, groggy.

"You should not," Will yawned.

"Sam's going through something, and I want to make sure he doesn't need me."

"You know what the guys in my unit do when they're going through something?" He continued before I could respond. "They remember they're grown men and deal with their shit. They don't go crying to their sisters."

I traced the anchor on Will's chest, and the trident woven through it. He was probably right. This thing with Sam and his girlfriend was going to be fine. He wouldn't have let a situation get that far out of control without telling me. And Riley was with him, which counted for something.

"What's really going on with him?" Will asked. "Sam. All I know is that he's been a pain in the ass who refuses to see a therapist. If I had any sense, I'd let that dog sleep but I keep chasing you so *sense* isn't part of my skill set."

"Sam and I are really close. Or...we were. He's in his own world right now. Obviously, he's noticed that I've been spending time away from the city," I gestured to Will, "and he's not pleased about me keeping the details to myself."

"Why do you?" he asked. "If that's part of the issue, why not tell him?"

"I have my reasons," I said. "It's none of his damn business to start. I've given him the space he needs to deal with his problems and date a woman who seems like she's making his life more hectic, even though I probably shouldn't have. There was a time when we shared everything with each other, but he hasn't wanted that from me for more than a year. And…fuck, Will, all I really want is one thing I don't have to share with everyone. Something I can keep all to myself without anyone touching or judging or interfering. I don't…I don't want to share you."

"That's my girl," he said.

"When will I see you next?" I asked.

Will was quiet for a moment, and I leaned up on an elbow to look at him. "I'm not sure," he said. "The next six months are up in the air right now. I'll know soon."

"Six *months*?"

"I'm up for another tour," he said. "But I don't want you worrying about that now."

Will's lips met mine, firm and deliberate, and his hands brushed down my body, over my thighs and between my legs. Though our time together was rapidly vanishing, his touch was careful and unhurried, almost reverent. He settled over me, and my heart was again overflowing when he paused to ask whether I was feeling well enough for more.

"Yes," I said, reaching up to wrap my arms around his neck. "Yes."

He kissed between my breasts and up my neck, and said, "You'll tell me if it's too much. If anything hurts."

I nodded, canting my hips toward him when he reached between us and pushed into me. "I will."

Will twined his arms around my torso, holding me tight as he moved inside me, and I anchored my legs on his waist because even this close wasn't close enough right now. We rocked together as if we had all the time in the world, and perhaps knowing that we didn't made those sweet, drowsy moments that much more perfect.

He stilled, lifting his head from the crook of my shoulder that he'd claimed as his own private destination, and smiled down at me.

"What?" I asked.

His hips rolled gently while he continued gazing at me. "You're beautiful," he said. "I don't say that enough."

Will took my hand from where it rested on his bicep, and pressed a kiss to my palm. With his eyes locked on mine, he placed my hand over his heart. He leaned down, kissing my cheeks, my jaw, and finally my lips, and the orgasm that arrived was a pleasant bonus to the wordless everything that was passing between us now.

———

I WOKE up alone on Sunday morning.

I knew Will was gone before my hand swept over the mattress, but there was something about confirming his absence that made it sting even more.

It shouldn't have. None of this should have been a surprise to me. I walked in with my eyes wide open, and I knew this weekend was going to be over almost as quickly as it started.

Going home was always the worst. It was a lot like cleaning up after a big party: the house was a mess, everyone was gone, and all the anticipation was replaced with emptiness.

And my ladybits were usually sore.

My flight wasn't until later in the day, but I went to the airport and waited until a standby seat came available. My phone wouldn't turn on and nothing happened when I plugged it in, so I spent my afternoon paging through magazines and devouring some juicy romance novels with bare-chested men on the covers.

If the commando business didn't work out for Will, he could always fall back on cover modeling.

Eventually, I got a flight to Boston. It was quick and uneventful, and as the cab barreled through the streets of Beacon Hill toward my apartment, I couldn't help thinking something was wrong. I couldn't put my hands on the source of that sense, but I couldn't get rid of it either.

My apartment was cold and lonely, and I stopped only long enough to change out of the slim, sexy jeans and lacy lingerie I brought on this trip for Will's benefit. Cotton bra and panties, old bootcuts, and a fuzzy turtleneck sweater felt instantly better, and I headed out to replace my phone.

I wandered around the store while the salesman configured my new device. "You have a lot of messages coming in," he called.

For a second, I hoped they were from Will. Maybe he was thinking about me while he drove to Virginia, or found out it wouldn't be six months until he could see me again, or maybe he just wanted to tell me he missed me.

But Will was the last person on my mind when I saw scores of frantic texts from Riley, all insisting that I call him immediately.

I skipped the call in favor of a quick text telling him I was on my way, and drove straight to the restored firehouse he and Sam shared in the Fort Point neighborhood. Riley was pacing in the kitchen when I arrived, his hands braced on his

head. His eyes were bloodshot and his body radiated anxi-
ety, and I realized something awful had happened this
weekend.

He pressed his finger to his lips for silence and motioned
for me to follow him down the hall, away from Sam's room.
At the far end, he leaned against the wall and crossed his
arms over his chest. "You were with Captain America again."

I stared at the stained concrete floors.

"It's your business. I don't care what you do," he said,
and the accusation on his face was the opposite of not caring.
"But I don't think it's too much to ask for you to answer your
phone when I call you eighty-nine times in an hour. I needed
some fucking help and this was the weekend *you* picked to
start ignoring me, too."

"My phone broke," I said. "I wasn't ignoring you."

But even if my phone was safe and sound, I wouldn't
have known. Will made a point of turning it off, and I chose
to interpret that gesture as one of concern rather than
control. He wanted me to relax; he wasn't putting a wall
between my family and me.

It was hard to convince myself it was all about relaxation
right now.

"Yeah, well, that's great," Riley said. He ran his hand
through his hair and stared at the ceiling for a moment.
"Sam's not okay, Shannon. I realize that you've been too busy
with that dude to notice, but Sam's whole fucking world
imploded last week. He didn't know it and he'll deny it until
he's blue in the face, but he was trying to kill himself. He
made me sit there and watch a fucking suicide attempt."

A million should-haves hit me at once. Should have
listened to Tom when he said something was up. Should
have fought Sam harder on seeing the psychiatrist. Shouldn't

have brought up the psychiatrist at all. Should have worked at brokering the peace. Should have forced Patrick off the sidelines and into Sam's well-being. Should have stayed home this weekend. Should have stayed home every weekend.

"Tell me what happened," I said. "Start from the beginning."

"The beginning? The beginning was months ago. You've known just as well as I have that he's been hanging on by threads, and yeah, things were better when he was with Tiel. But now Tiel's gone."

Riley shook his head and looked away.

I should have been here, and I should have stopped this.

I'd talked myself out of worrying about Sam, and let myself believe that he was better off without my interference. That he needed to struggle through it on his own. But it was entirely preventable, and Will was wrong about Sam not needing me hovering over him. These boys were my *people*, the only ones I had in this world.

"He crossed the line into alcohol poisoning, went into hypoglycemic shock, and seized six times. That was all before they pumped his stomach. I got a front row seat to that show." He rubbed his eyes and let his head fall against the wall. "Oh, and when he woke up from all that? He insisted you not know anything about it. Now I don't know what shit went down between you two—"

"Nothing happened," I shouted and Riley pinned me with an angry glare before I got the words out. "Nothing happened. I thought he needed some space to work through things after Angus died. I didn't notice anything—"

"Is it possible you've been a little busy with your new pal? A little preoccupied?"

That was exactly it, and I hated myself for putting my libido above my family.

"I'm sorry I wasn't there for you and Sam," I said. "We'll figure this out. I'm not going anywhere, not anymore."

Riley nodded and wrapped his arms around me. When he released me, he returned to Sam's room and sat by the bed. He was the most unabashedly affectionate of my four brothers, and his actions always spoke louder than his words. But his words were important, too. He didn't offer many of them, and when he did, they were either ridiculous or spot-on accurate.

It wasn't my turn. And after this weekend, I wasn't even convinced I deserved a turn.

Sixteen

SHANNON

EIGHT MONTHS *ago*

MY PHONE BUZZED on the table—the hundredth time this hour since all of Sam's clients were now calling *me* with their issues and questions—and I tapped the screen to life.

Will: Hey
Will: Back on base. Fucking clusterfuck. Sorry it took so long.
Will: I need to see you
Will: What are you doing tomorrow night?
Shannon: Fuck you
Will: Very good, fucking me.
Shannon: Ha
Shannon: That is NOT happening
Will: Peanut. Please. I know I was off the grid longer than expected and I'm sorry. That seems to be the theme around

here right now. I can get away tomorrow night but I have to be back on base the next afternoon.

Will: Need to see you.

Shannon: Believe me when I say I'm finished coming when you call

Will: Last I checked, you enjoyed the coming

Shannon: Further evidence why this is ridiculous and out of control and over

A moment later, the distant image of a surfer standing at the water's edge—the single token of our weekend in Montauk, and intentionally unrecognizable to anyone but me—appeared on my screen. I wanted to ignore his call because I couldn't manage another disaster right now, but...I didn't.

"This is over," I said, bypassing all pleasantries and introductions.

"Mmhmm," Will said. "I haven't slept in three days and I don't have time for bullshit games today, Shannon. What's really going on?"

"Nothing," I said. "We had our fun, I got some frequent flyer miles out of the deal, and now it's over. Nothing more to discuss."

The line was silent save for the wind gusting through Will's end. I could imagine him scowling at me, his eyes narrowed, his jaw locked. "Right," he murmured. "We'll see about that."

"There's nothing to *see about*," I said, exasperated.

I was mentally and physically exhausted, and I needed him to accept this as our last conversation. There were no more secret weekends for me, and I didn't have the emotional muscle to be anything more than brusque and flippant at the moment. I couldn't even think about Will without my thoughts seizing back to Sam, and how I wasn't there when he needed me most.

"I'm finished with this."

I knew what was coming next, and I didn't want to hear. I couldn't.

I hung up, blocked his number, and drummed my fingers on the table while I waited. Glancing up, I spotted a beautiful, dark-haired woman, and she had to be Tiel. There weren't that many boho chicks toting violin cases around Boston, and even fewer walking into this coffee shop at the exact time I requested we meet.

"Are you Tiel?" Or, as I was calling her, The Girl Who Broke Sam.

It didn't take much to find her. Tom pulled the activity on Sam's mobile phone, and I knew he wasn't calling and texting the same client forty times each day. She was something of an Internet celebrity, with millions of views on her YouTube strings performances, and a college professor, but looked like neither. Nearly-black hair brushed her shoulders, and beneath her burgundy coat, she wore simple black pants with a gray cardigan. The cardigan was misbuttoned, and I wasn't certain, but it looked as if she was wearing a Dark Side of the Moon t-shirt underneath.

She stared at me, her eyes roaming over my hair, my Theory suit, my Louboutin heels. Her gaze was contemptuous, as if she decided long ago that she didn't like me and this moment only served to confirm it for her.

"Yes," she said slowly.

This was risky. Digging up her number, getting her to meet me, figuring out what the fuck she did to my brother: all very risky. But this girl *broke* Sam. She didn't dither over commitment like Lauren or meltdown over power dynamics like Andy—and believe me, I was ready to start handing out the ass-kickings when those girls sent my brothers into tailspins—but she *destroyed* Sam.

He nearly drank himself into a diabetic coma, and when that was all said and done, he decided that late February was prime time for an outdoor adventure. His credit card activity placed him in northern Maine, and that was the extent of information I had on the situation. I didn't know why he ran away, how long he'd be gone, or what he was doing.

"I'm Shannon Walsh." I extended my hand, but she didn't notice or she didn't care. I let it drop to my side, and then gestured to the table. "Thank you for meeting me. Can we talk?"

She wanted to say no. It was hanging on the tip of her tongue as she rolled her eyes and shifted her violin case from one hand to another. "Can you just tell me what happened with Sam? Is he all right?"

"Can we sit? Just for a few minutes?"

I didn't wait for a response. Instead, I returned to my table and caught the barista's attention. I ordered the first thing that came to mind, but I knew I couldn't eat much. I'd been a wreck since returning from Washington. Terrorizing my brothers and best friends for information about Sam, spending most nights sorting and resorting my mother's things, hoping he'd call, hating myself for letting a guy tell me I shouldn't look after my family. It'd left me tired, overcaffeinated, and too anxious for food.

"Is Sam all right?"

I focused on the sugar cookie waiting in front of me, first snapping it in half and then tearing each piece until it stopped being a cookie and became a buttery pile of crumbs. That was exactly how I felt: too broken to qualify as whole. I couldn't press them back together. The structure and integrity were gone, and nothing could unbreak it.

"No, he really isn't okay," I said.

I didn't know whether it was the exhaustion or the stress or something else altogether, but suddenly I was crying in the middle of this coffee shop. I didn't have any pretty girl tears that gracefully streaked down my cheek. These tears were the quivering, sniffling, hiccupping kind that came with bloodshot eyes and puffy redness all over my face. I hated that I was melting down in front of this woman—the one I came here to annihilate—when I believed crying should be reserved for quiet, private moments far from the view of anyone else, ever.

Tiel grabbed my wrist and yanked my fingers away from the crumbs. "Honeybunch, you need to start talking."

I told her everything I knew about his decision to leave his home, his work, and his family behind and spend an indeterminate amount of time camping. In the winter. In Maine. And then I waited, hoping she would offer some insight into this turn of events.

Tiel smiled to herself, a small, firm pull of her lips that told me I wasn't going to get anything I wanted out of this discussion. She sat back and laced her fingers together. "You presume I had something to do with it?"

"As a matter of fact, yes. I believe you were dating my brother at one point, and now that you're not, he finds it necessary to vanish into the woods."

She ran her fingers through her hair with a sigh. "Shannon, I'm not clear how that's any of your business. Sam is an adult and he does not need you or anyone else managing every one of the minute details of his life. Anything that transpired between us was just that—between *us*."

At first, I was angry. I wasn't used to defiance.

Then I remembered everything Will had said over the past few months. Were they right? Was I doing this all wrong? All this time, the only thing I ever wanted was to give my family everything they needed, wanted, and deserved.

The tears poured out again, a loud and hysterical mess, and I knew I was causing the kind of scene people live tweeted. I made my way to the bathroom and crouched in a stall, crying into my hands until I couldn't find another drop to wring from my body.

When I returned to the table, Tiel was still there—a small surprise, all things considered—and she offered a patient smile. I saw it as an opening, and charged through it. "My mother," I started. "She died when we were young." I reached for my now-cool latte. "Did you know that?"

"Yes," she said, her voice lilting in a way that told me she knew everything about my mother, our family, all of it.

"Right, of course." I nodded and dragged my hand through my hair. "I raised my brothers and sister. I've been Head Bitch in Charge since I was nine. All I have ever done is manage the minute details of their lives. When they were kids, I made sure they were bathed and wearing clean clothes. I sewed buttons and fixed hems because there was no one else to do it. I took care of them when they were sick. I signed their report cards and paid bills. I went to work selling houses when I was eighteen so they could go away to college. I got them *through* it. And now that we're adults? I'm still getting them through it. I schedule their doctors' appointments. I file their taxes. I register their cars. I can't remember a time when my life wasn't about taking care of them. I meddle in their lives because I have been a lot more than their sister for nearly twenty-four years."

Tiel didn't say anything. She sat there, expressionless, while those words coursed through me. I'd never said any of that out loud before. I never wanted anyone to think I resented the responsibilities leveled on me. I didn't need any acknowledgement, but the orbit was changing. *They* were changing, and somehow, I was exactly where I'd always been. I wanted something different for myself—something more—but I didn't see how I could get gravity on my side.

I laughed and turned my attention to the bracelets on my wrist. My thumb swept over the anchor charm, the one I picked up during a holiday shopping marathon with Lauren. Anchors were popular right now, just like circles and horseshoes in years past. I knew no one would read anything into it, and it served as my tiny connection to Will. Just like our relationship, it hid in plain sight.

"It began with online dating a few years back. That's pretty much the worst invention in the world." I rolled my eyes and shuddered. The commercials were deceitful. One of these days, I was going to start a blog or write a book about the guys you *actually* met through those sites. "But then Matt started dating Lauren, and now she's my closest friend. I didn't know how to be friends with girls before her, and Lauren taught me," I said. "She says nice things about you."

Tiel gave me a skeptical frown. "I bet she does."

"I started seeing someone last summer." I laughed to myself. "'Seeing' probably isn't the right word. It's more like scheduled sex. Really, really incredible sex." I looked around, still somewhat concerned about live tweeting. "I can't believe I just said that out loud."

"Keep going," she demanded.

"So, this all has been occurring," I said, "and I've been trying to maintain everything else, but I haven't been able to. I keep thinking that I should have been there for Sam when your relationship ended."

"Do you swoop in when all your brothers' relationships end?"

I lifted a shoulder and sipped my coffee. "My brothers don't have many relationships. Patrick kept his a secret for months. Matt holds me at a distance. Riley's still a toddler in my eyes. And Sam...well, Sam changed this year, and I didn't notice. I wasn't paying attention, I wasn't there, and I let him down."

"But the sex? It was decent?"

I tried—and failed—to suppress a grin. "I haven't been able to get on a bike for spin class since." I laughed, but quickly remembered that good sex came with the cost of abandoning my family. "If I'm not taking care of my brothers, I don't know who I am anymore."

Tiel finished her coffee and eyed the exit, and though it was a terrible idea, I went back to my original question. "May I ask what happened? With you and Sam?"

She stared at me, and the contempt was replaced with something softer. "I hope he finds what he's looking for, wherever he is. And...I'm sorry you're going through this." She gathered her things and dropped some cash on the table. I was too defeated to argue about picking up the tab. "I know you're trying to do the right thing. I hope it gets easier."

I thought this was going to be our moment, the warm realization that we both cared about Sam and only wanted the best, and we were going to work together to get him home. This was not that moment. Sighing, I said, "When he figures it all out and comes back, give him a chance. Please don't turn him away. He's so much more sensitive than he likes us to believe."

Tiel stopped in the doorway and studied me. "Shannon, I know exactly how sensitive he is. You don't need to tell me that."

I turned back to the mountains of sugar cookie crumbs in front of me.

So completely broken.

Seventeen

EIGHT MONTHS *ago*

THIS FUCKING WEEK. It wasn't enough that one of my guys forgot the basics during a HALO jump and busted his goddamn leg in the middle of the South Dakota wilderness or that I was facing at least six months running a task force aimed at eliminating terrorist strongholds in densely popu-lated cities. No, I had to talk my way into Shannon's building—pulled the brother card again, figured there were too many of them for a doorman to actually keep track—and pick the lock.

All I wanted was my girl and a day or two to chill before shipping out, but something was up. She was quiet and distant after our weekend in D.C., and then pulled some shit about ending things.

I figured she was having a difficult day and putting me on blast because I was handy, but then she blocked my calls. It was an easy hack to get around that—just one of many tools of the trade—but I couldn't even get a reaction out of her. At the very minimum, I expected some comments about my commando tactics and some vehement "*fuck yous*" but I got neither.

I thought things were good after that weekend. Really good. I needed to know what went wrong, and more than anything else, I wanted to know that Shannon was all right.

Inside, her apartment looked nothing like I remembered. Where it was once ruthlessly ordered, there were now mountains of photo albums, boxes overflowing with blankets, and dated clothing. And it was everywhere. Every surface in the living room was overflowing.

The kitchen revealed a single wine glass in the sink and six empty bottles in the recycling bin. Her bed was made but rumpled, as if she slept on top of the blankets.

It was strange. I could accept any of these things individually, but when considered together, I couldn't make sense of it.

I didn't know when to expect Shannon, so I parked myself on the sofa and tugged my baseball cap low for a nap. I wasn't sure how long I slept, but snapped to attention when I heard the door bang shut.

"Are you fucking kidding me?" Shannon yelled.

"Hey, peanut."

Her bag slipped from her shoulder and landed on the floor with a thud. She stared at me, her hands propped on her hips, and her expression venomous yet tired. "No," she said. "I'm not doing this with you. Not anymore."

I pointed to the small blue table beside the sofa. "What's the deal with all the rocks? You've got these things all over the place. They're from Erin, aren't they?"

Her gaze flicked to the geodes clustered on the table, frowning. "Don't talk about my sister."

"Is that how it goes? We only talk about her on your terms, and the rest of the time, we pretend she doesn't exist?" I asked.

"You get off on making your own rules. I understand that, but I am not doing this tonight."

"Yeah, I have no fucking clue what's going on here, Shannon. You get that, right? No. Fucking. Clue. I'm not going anywhere until you talk to me."

She stepped out of her heels and walked into the living room, and I knew I wasn't looking at the same woman who slept in my arms last month. "This is over," she said, as if that explained everything. "Stop calling me. Stop texting. Stop breaking and entering."

She busied herself with loading the assorted clutter into boxes, muttering to herself while she stepped around me. My mother would call Shannon a worker bee. She was always doing something, never content unless she was working, thinking, moving, and my mother was the same way. She couldn't watch television without also editing photos for her blog, or reaching for her latest craft project.

But right now, Shannon wasn't working. She was avoiding, and she wasn't even doing a fair job of it.

"Yeah, and that's where you've lost me."

"I'm finished sneaking around with you," she said. "I hate keeping secrets from my family, and I'm not going to do it anymore."

"Secrets? You are the one who wanted secrets, darlin'," I said. She couldn't be serious right now. "What about Mexico? I wanted to end the fucking secrets, Shannon, if that wasn't a big enough clue for you."

"Why, Will? What are we even doing? You tell me where and when to show up, like I'm your goddamn call girl, and that's it. I'm sorry, but I'm not in love with announcing that I'm your stateside whore."

"You're my *what*?" I clasped my hands behind my head as if I could wring some sense from this conversation. "Have I made you feel that way?"

"This isn't a relationship, Will. It's sex. Secret, scheduled sex, and I'm telling you I'm finished," she said.

"I think your definition of relationship needs adjustment," I said.

"And I think you don't understand anything about me," she said.

"I'm a simple guy, peanut. You're gonna need to explain this load of shit you're spewing because I'm fairly certain I know you damn well."

She continued packing, and I rolled through every conversation we'd shared in the past months. I still didn't know where it went off the rails.

When Shannon reached for a pile of blankets, I caught her wrist and pulled her down to the sofa. I locked her hands behind her back. She still fought like an angry bull in the chutes, but I had her pinned. We were getting to the bottom of this shit whether she liked it or not.

"You have two choices, my dear. You can either tell me what's pissed you off today, or I can take you into the bedroom and torture you with my tongue."

"I'm done with scheduled sex," she said, her words quivering. "I want you to leave."

Springing to my feet, I hauled her over my shoulder and marched down the hall. "Bedroom it is," I said, slapping her ass.

"I'm serious, Will," she said, and something in her voice stuck with me. She sounded detached and cold. I dropped her to the bed and kept my hands on her hips. "We're finished."

"You have to do better than that," I said. "If you're finished, I'd like an explanation. Was it the orgasms? You just hated all the orgasms I gave you?"

Shannon covered her face with her hands and released a long, heavy sigh. Her body sagged into the mattress and her chin wobbled, and I just wanted to hold her and make this stop. "Sam almost died when we were in D.C.," she said. "He and his girlfriend had a huge fight, then he got crazy drunk and ended up in the hospital."

I lifted her arms to see her eyes. "Is he okay now?"

"That isn't the point, and I don't know how he is because he's left the city and won't share his location with anyone," she said. "Riley probably knows, but he's not saying a word about it."

"So what does that have to do with us?"

She covered her face again.

"Because you don't understand me at all," she murmured. "All I ever hear from you is how I need to worry about my brothers less. They're grown men, right? They should be able to live their lives without me, right? You don't get that my family is all I have. Taking care of them is what I do. I let you get between us once, and I'm not doing it again."

"No, I understand your relationship with your brothers perfectly," I said. "And yes, I'm sorry about what happened with Sam, but you cannot spend your entire life just waiting to catch them when they fall. You have to be able to turn your phone off sometimes or go away for a weekend, and you're not going to convince me otherwise."

"You said you wanted to take care of me, that you knew what I needed," she said. "To you, that's having me all to yourself."

"Yes, Shannon, that's exactly what it is," I said. It was possible that this was the closest range argument I'd ever had with a woman. It was intimate, and void of the yelling, stomping, and slamming I knew Shannon favored, but in a way, I would have preferred her usual. I didn't want this resigned version of her. "I want so much more of you. I want you all the time. Always. I hate it that I can't wake up with you every morning and I can't kiss you good night. I hate that, even when I do have you, I have to fucking share you with them."

"Because they are my *family*," she whispered. "I have nothing without them."

"That's not my view on the situation," I said. "You hold their entire fucking worlds together, Shannon. You do everything, all the time, and it will never be enough. Not for you, definitely not for them. If you just let me—"

"No!" she said, pushing me away. "Don't tell me how much better my life would be if I let you call the shots. Don't act like you want what's best for me. You want what's best for you, and even after all this time and everything I've told you…you still don't get me. You still don't see that I am what I am because of my family, and I don't want that to change. Maybe you need to realize that you can either earn your spot in our tribe or get the fuck out of my life. We stick together, no matter what, and—"

"Yeah? Kind of like how you stick with Erin? If that's the logic you're operating under, Shannon, please explain to me how not speaking to your sister is sticking together. I actually want to hear you make this argument."

The anger in her expression drained, and in its place was cool emptiness. It was a haunting, dead-eyed look that I never wanted to see again. "I meant it when I said this was over."

"Fight me," I demanded, wrapping my hands around her biceps. "Put on your war paint, little girl, and fucking fight me. You want to get rid of me? I want to see you work for it."

I shook her, desperate to see any flare of emotion, but nothing broke through her stoic grimace.

"I know you're upset about Sam, and I know you hold yourself responsible for" —I held my hands apart, trying to encapsulate the world Shannon managed— "for fucking everything, but where the hell do you draw the line?"

"Will," she said. "No more."

We stared at each other, minutes passing as the distance grew between us. "You should know I'm going down range for a few months. There's a comm blackout in effect with this task force. No mobile phones, no email." Shannon dropped her eyes to her hands and rubbed the pad of her thumb over her fingernails. "I should be stateside around September, and when I am: I'm coming for you."

Eighteen

SHANNON

I DIDN'T ALLOW myself the luxury of falling apart.

The weeks and months after Sam's implosion were hard on everyone, and we all hoarded reasons to blame ourselves, but a fair amount of quietly spoken censure tracked toward me. Regardless of whether Sam was an adult with advanced degrees and a successful career, I was still responsible for tending to his health and overall well-being. It was built into the mechanics of this family, and I'd never stopped to announce we were overhauling the system. Instead, I'd abandoned that post when he needed it most.

I did the only thing I could: I locked it all down. I saw every sunrise and sunset from the solitude of my office, and I worked until all the words and numbers blurred together. My mind was weight-weary, and my body was drawn too taut to recognize anything more than the deepest ends of hunger, exhaustion, pain. There was a beauty in the excess of it all: our restoration projects were selling well above asking price, my investment properties were turning wild profits, and our services were in greater demand than ever before.

But if I wasn't working, I didn't know what to do with myself. I wore through three pairs of running shoes and doubled up on my morning spin classes, and when I couldn't push my body any further, I ended up at the Public Garden or the Prudential Center, watching people as they went about their lives.

I couldn't bear to be alone. Not any more than I already was.

Sometimes I wondered whether I was going to wake up on my fiftieth birthday and realize the good men were taken, my childbearing days had passed, and the years I devoted to raising my siblings were a shiny memory of a time when I was more than the meddling aunt. I was going to wake up hollow and alone because I'd given everything, and while I was busy giving, there was no one in my life to replenish *me*.

But when September and then October came and went with no sign of Will, I knew I was already there.

IT TOOK Sam almost four months to come back to us.

He went to Tiel first, of course. He went to her and before I could blink, they were moving in together.

Another blink and they were engaged.

"Tiel and I are getting married," he announced at the tail end of the Monday morning status meeting.

He smiled to himself while he ran his hand over his tie and fished his phone from his breast pocket. He tapped the screen, and an image of him and Tiel appeared. Their faces were close together, happy and smiling like people who hadn't put each other through multiple layers of agony. Her hand was positioned between them, and on her finger sat a large peachy-pink diamond ring.

Everyone crowded around Sam, offering handshakes and hugs, congratulations and quips about Tiel making an honest man out of him. A few beats passed before I realized I was still seated, watching while Andy and my brothers lavished him in well wishes.

Sam looked up and met my eyes across the table, his frown communicating exactly how much it hurt him that I wasn't in line to share his joy. "Shannon?"

For as far as we might have drifted, he still wanted my approval. "Congratulations!" I said, rounding the table to envelop him in a squeeze. "Have you set a date yet?"

Sam patted my shoulder with a chuckle. "No, we didn't get that far yesterday," he said.

"Well, there's a ton to plan," I said, breaking away from the group. Sam's smile fell and he gazed at me, confused.

It wasn't the right response, that much I knew, but it was the best I could do. Everything was a situation to manage, a problem to solve, and I kicked the shit out of every issue that crossed our path. I didn't know any other way to show my love.

"We should get dinner soon, the three of us, and start thinking about dates, venues, themes," I said, edging out of the attic conference room and toward the stairs. "So much to do. Colors. Flowers. Everything. Let me know what works for you two, and we'll get together."

I felt like a brittle piece of antique glass that was bound to crack under the lightest pressure as I returned to my office and settled behind my desk. Dragging a breath into my lungs, I dropped my head into my hands just as my door banged shut.

"Is there something you wish to share with me?" Sam asked.

"No," I said, running my hands over my face. "A lot on my mind today. A lot of meetings. You know how it is. Mondays are always crazy."

Sam crossed his legs and folded his hands in his lap, and he nodded.

"And I'm checking out two more properties this afternoon. A pair of brownstones that were in the process of being remodeled but the developer ran out of cash so they've been vacant for a few years. Could be interesting."

He nodded again, eyeing me with cool exasperation. "If I wanted your schedule, I could have asked Tom. Why don't you cut the shit and tell me what's going on."

I stared at my dark lilac skirt and brushed some dust off the hem. "Nothing is going on. I'm thrilled for you, truly, and will do anything to help with planning the wedding."

"Bullshit," he said, and my head snapped up at his tone. "That's bullshit. You should have seen your face up there, Shan. You were devastated, and I want to know why."

An image of that ring appeared in my mind, and I knew without asking that it was one of a kind, just like Tiel Desai. It was different in an unexpectedly lovely way, and he didn't need my help picking out rings or deciding how and when to propose. He didn't need me for anything. Not anymore.

"Not devastated," I said. "Just surprised. It seems like you just moved in together, and…and I can't wait to help with the planning. You're thinking summer, right? Summer weddings are wonderful, though the best spots book up quickly. What about The Cliff House in Ogunquit? Or were you thinking somewhere in town? Oooh, what about The Lenox? There's always The Mandarin, I know you like The

Mandarin. Or maybe Crane Estate if you wanted something rural. Or Misselwood or Nantasket if you wanted the beach. Harrington Farm is gorgeous in the fall, so that's an option, too."

"Shannon." He leaned forward and flattened his hands on my desk. "Stop it. Do not handle me. Do not spin this conversation. If you have a problem with me or Tiel, or me marrying Tiel, you need to get it out or get over it right now."

"That's not it. Not at all. I know it's selfish, and I'm sorry, but…I wish you'd called me," I said. "I wish you'd told me as soon as it happened. I wish you'd asked me to go ring shopping with you."

Sam offered an impatient smile and eased back. "I didn't exactly plan it out. I didn't intentionally exclude you. And yesterday, well." Sam laughed. "We got a little carried away."

He was stingy with the details these days, and intensely protective of his relationship with Tiel. It was either respect the boundary lines or find myself locked out entirely. "I'm happy for you and Tiel. Really. Now when can we get together to celebrate? I'll bring the champagne."

"Soon, but…" he started, sighing, "I love you. You know that. But that doesn't mean you can adopt our wedding as your new pet project. You hijacked Matt and Lauren's wedding, but they were too busy to care. We want to do this our own way. Tiel will reach out to you, I can guarantee that, but she'll do it on her time. She adores you, and I really appreciate how you've given her as much time as she needed to warm up to you, and everyone else. But that doesn't mean you can smother her now."

"I wasn't trying to hijack anything. It's your day, and I just wanted to help with—"

"Give Tiel some space. If she wants your opinion on these things, she'll ask. Until then, I need you to take an enormous step back."

Clasping my hands together to prevent my nails from sinking into my palms, I nodded. "Of course, Sam. Whatever you need. If there's anything at all that I can do for either of you, just let me know."

PART TWO

now

THERE WERE rules to every engagement, and each theater served up its own set of variables. Finding myself face-to-face with Shannon's new man—if you could call this shitsnack that—was no different.

I was staring down the Lord of the House of Douche, and if I didn't know Shannon would give me a lifetime worth of shit for it, I would have killed him by now. He introduced himself as Gerard after she stared at me in open-mouthed shock for two minutes, and the longer I watched him, the more convinced I was that she'd gone in search of the biggest prick in town.

He'd fucked her, that was plain as day, and he was sitting there, his legs crossed and his hands folded over his pinstriped fucking trousers, as if he owned the joint.

As if he owned *her*.

If there was one thing I knew with certainty it was that no one owned Shannon. She owned herself and anyone who suggested otherwise was usually invited to go fuck himself. If there was anyone who could lay claim to Shannon it was me, and even that stood on shaky ground at this point. I knew showing up at her apartment was a dicey move after all this time and everything that had happened, but this tactic never failed me, and…I needed her.

The Lord of the Douches shifted in his seat, then scratched his ear, looked around, and scratched his ear again. It was a glowing invitation to interrogate this bitch while Shannon took her sweet ass time hiding in the kitchen.

"Gerard," I said, "you a Red Sox fan?"

He offered an indifferent shrug that told me he intended to blow off every question I asked. He didn't give a shit who I was or what I was doing here, and he probably sensed I wanted to get rid of him. "Yankees. New Yorker."

"Everyone has a cross to bear," I said. "Riley hasn't black-listed you? Impressive. He must be going soft in his old age."

Lord of the Douches squinted, confused. "Riley?"

He tugged at his ear again, and this guy needed to get his tells under control. Who the fuck was he? Any man who earned a spot in Shannon's life was forced to share it with Patrick, Sam, Riley, and Matt. Not to mention Nick and Tom. You got the slice she served up, and you were fucking thankful for the offering. It wasn't a lesson I came by easily, but it was one I knew as clear as my name and rank.

"The youngest one," I said, and he continued squinting. "Shannon's brother? Goes to every home game. The kid wants to get married on home plate, name his first born Big Papi, and have his ashes spread over the outfield when he dies."

I didn't know any of this to be true, but I wasn't burdening Gerard with those details. The only thing he needed to know was that his time with Shannon was over.

"I hadn't heard that," he said, leaning forward and

clasping his hands between his knees. "I'm sorry, I don't believe I caught your name."

"Captain Will Halsted, United States Naval Special Warfare Command," I said.

I didn't pull the SEAL Team card often, but it was a small pleasure to watch Gerard's reaction wash over him. How was it possible that this uptight sack of shit was in Shannon's apartment? Unless he was here appraising the place, there was no way I could believe she'd willingly spend time with him. Sure, on the surface he was her type but there was far more than met the eye when it came to her.

He pressed a hand to his hip and retrieved a shiny iPhone from his pocket. "Apologies," he said. "Call from the office." He pointed to the den. "I'll just…"

Lord of the Douches quick-stepped down the hallway, and I knew his "call from the office" would keep him busy.

Aside from the flaming asshole in pinstripes, Shannon's apartment was exactly the way I remembered it. Furniture that only looked too fancy to be comfortable. Hardwood floors topped with intricately woven silk rugs. Built-in bookshelves on either side of the brick fireplace, filled with books, old photographs, and an assortment of geodes, none of which she wanted to discuss.

It was precisely Shannon. *Intentional*. Everything had a purpose, everything meant something.

The click of her heels against the floor announced her approach before she rounded the corner from the kitchen, but it didn't prepare me for the impact of gazing at her again. The months, the distance, the resentment over the state of things between us…none of that changed the way my heart and head reacted to her. She was sexy as hell—that was nothing new—but that wasn't my first thought this time. No, this time I wanted to drag her into my lap, wrap my arms around her, and let myself be *close* to her for a long, long time.

"Did you say you wanted wine?" Shannon asked. She stared at the empty chair, blinking. "Where's Gerard?"

"I threw him out the window," I said. "I had to kill him but I didn't want to get blood on your rugs."

"Jesus Christ, Will," she hissed. She crossed her arms over her chest and I sucked in a breath. I couldn't remember seeing anything that beautiful in months, and that wasn't just because those months were filled with some of the toughest, most deadly missions I'd ever led. "That's really fucking hilarious."

"Anything to get you smiling," I said.

She sent me a withering smirk, and I was pleased to see it fall into a frown when Gerard entered the room.

You can't fool me, peanut.

"Shannon, thank you for an enjoyable evening. If you'll excuse me, I need to see to a client." He glanced in my direction. "Captain, it was a pleasure, and...thank you for your service."

I offered a tight salute as Gerard shrugged into his coat. I couldn't hear their conversation, but observed with an emotion I can only describe as glee when Shannon showed him to the door without so much as a handshake.

She kicked off her heels as the door closed, and came to a stop right in front of me. "Captain, is it now?"

We did not have time to discuss my ascension in the ranks. "Who the fuck was *that*?"

"What the fuck are *you* doing here?" she yelled. "I mean, it *is* nice of you to knock this time. Have you grown out of your breaking and entering stage yet, commando?"

I was on my feet and grabbed her around the waist before the last syllable passed her lips. "Tell me, peanut: when his name is on your lips, does it taste the same as mine?" I asked, my arms banded around her torso with her back pressed tight against my chest.

"That's none of your goddamn business," she bit out as she wriggled in my arms. My shoulder was aching and pins and needles were setting my last three fingers on fire, but I didn't care. I was going to hold her until she drew the line and told me to stop.

"Would he mind if I did this?" I dragged my lips up her neck and over her jaw, melting even further into this woman as the taste of her skin spread around me. "What if…" I brought my fingers to her chin and angled her toward me. "What if I did this?"

She knew what I was thinking while I stared at her mouth. She knew I was going to kiss her, and that, in the long, disjointed history of us, kisses were never simple, never innocent. My lips found hers, and we were both uncoordinated and impatient, biting, sucking, licking, feasting on each other. When she released a sweet, *relieved* sigh, I knew she still belonged to me.

"Kiss me like that again and your clothes are coming off," I warned, my hand tight on her hip.

When our lips met, I knew she was as desperate for this as I was. My hand ran down her thigh and then back up, and over the globes of her ass, squeezing and grinding myself into her. My lips landed on her neck and this—*this right here*—was worth crossing deserts and mountains, surviving helicopter crashes, taking a fucking ton of shrapnel.

This woman was worth it all.

"What the fuck are you doing here?" she asked. "It has been eight fucking months, Will."

"I needed to see you," I admitted, my lips on her neck. "I told you I was coming for you when my tour was up."

I couldn't talk about the failures of my last mission, the scars it left behind, or the decisions ahead of me. Not tonight. The one thing I was capable of doing tonight was crawling into bed with Shannon and holding her—

"And I told you this was over," she said. "You cannot show up at my door like this and think…I don't even know what the hell you think, but you can't do this. I've moved on. I'm *with* someone else."

She fought against me, and for a second I debated whether she actually wanted me to release her. We were rough with each other as a matter of fact, but this seemed different. I loosened my hold, and she slipped out of my arms.

"You can't do this," she repeated. "You can't be here."

When I hopped a flight back to the States with the intention of sorting out my life and visiting Shannon, I knew there were several possible outcomes.

She could straight-up refuse to see me, and that was a very real contender. Shannon was a heavyweight when it came to shutting people out and pretending they didn't exist.

She could order me to whip my dick out and fuck her until we both collapsed. Of course, she'd insult me the entire time and I'd get off on that shit.

Finally, and perhaps most realistically, she'd treat me to the coldest shoulder known to man, and once I earned the right, she'd let me touch her and taste her. I deserved plenty of that ice, and I'd take everything she threw at me. I also knew that, regardless of anything, she took care of her people. Too much. So much that she didn't take care of herself.

"I'm staying with you," I said. "Just a few days. Please. This is the only place I can go right now."

"Let's ignore the fact that your sister lives ten minutes away." She rubbed her temples, and I saw when her muscles sagged in resignation. "You know where the guest room is," she said. "Don't break anything. No commando tactics. No bomb building. No gun fights."

"That's a good reminder," I said. "Bomb-building was on my list of activities for tomorrow."

"I don't want to hear about your activities," she murmured. "I don't want you here."

"And I don't want to hear about you spending time with that asshole," I called as she walked toward her bedroom.

"Let's clarify a few things, Will." She whirled around, wagging her finger at me. "One, you don't call the shots here. Two, what I do is none of your business. Three, the only asshole in this situation is you. I had an epically awful day *before* you showed up, and I'm done. I cannot deal with the universe slinging any more shit at me. I am finished with this day."

The door slammed behind Shannon.

It was her way: she worked hard at controlling every inch of her life, and here I was, messing it all up again. She kept her emotions on lock. She required time and space to warm up, to get comfortable, to relax. And there was a lot more time and space between us now than there had ever been before. I couldn't throw her on the bed, own her pussy, and force her to chill the fuck out. Not yet. Not tonight.

So instead of tearing her door off its hinges like I wanted

to, I inspected the locks and pulled the open kitchen windows shut. The pantry door stood ajar, and I ducked inside for a closer look. Wine, bottled water, crackers, nuts, dried pasta. The refrigerator offered little more, and though I was tempted to confirm she'd eaten, I made my way into the closet-narrow guest room without stopping by her door.

With my arms outstretched, my fingers nearly touched either wall.

Shannon could undoubtedly explain all of the architectural features and provide a short dissertation on why a room of this size and shape existed, and part of me wanted to know. But if there was anything to be interpreted from the tone of that door slam, it was that she wouldn't welcome my appearance in her bedroom this evening.

I flopped onto the pillow-laden daybed and pressed my fist to the pain radiating through my shoulder and down to my elbow. Nine hours crammed in the back of a military cargo plane out of Germany had only made the situation worse, but I'd be damned if I resorted to wearing the sling. The worst part was the numbness through my forearm and part of my hand, and mostly because those fire-and-ice tingles weren't numb at all. But the real problem—the one the Navy was hoping would disappear after some leave time —was my trigger finger.

Dropping anchor in Boston wasn't the smartest idea. The best spot for me was the naval amphibious base at Little Creek, Virginia. I'd get the unit physician's undivided attention, world-class physical therapists, and unlimited time at the shooting range. No redheaded distractions there.

But the redhead was the one thing that made sense right now. I needed her, and maybe she'd let herself need me too.

Twenty

SHANNON

"THIS IS…A DISASTER," Matt said. He turned in a slow circle, eyeing the interior wreckage of one of the two Mount Vernon Street brownstones I was hoping he'd love. The last owners—a house-flipping crew that ran out of money about five seconds after stripping the property to nothing more than studs and beams—were not kind to this structure. They blew everything out, leaving behind only the bones and a massive pile of soggy construction debris in the courtyard. "I mean…epic disaster. What is even left?"

"There's nothing left, but there's a ton of opportunity," I said.

From the outside, this pair of homes looked like the picture of historic preservation. The façades were strong and solid, and save for some window box weeds and flaking paint on the shutters, spoke nothing of the abandoned shell of a home inside.

"For a masochist," he murmured.

That wasn't how I saw it. This house had a past and a future, but right now, it was lost in an odd limbo of broken emptiness. Much like our other restorations, it needed attention and patience and vision, but most of all, it needed someone to believe it was worth putting back together.

Sam liked to say that some things were worth saving, and he was right about that, but it didn't stop with preservation.

After scaling all five floors and inspecting each room, closet, and alcove, Matt and I stopped in the cave that once served as the dining room. It was dark and closed off from the rest of the living spaces, and the ceiling was warped with water damage.

"This is a shit show," he said, shaking his head.

"Your favorite kind of show," I said.

He paced up and down the room, pounding his fist against the studs and kneeling to examine the fireplace. "If we moved these walls…" Matt started, "we could run floor-to-ceiling windows along the back of the property, and open up into the courtyard."

I pointed to the brick wall at the far end of the home, the one that separated this property from its twin. "What would it take to make these two into a single, giant home? To completely reimagine the structure and floor plan?"

Matt walked to the wall and stared at it for a long moment, as if he was having a little talk with the stones to get their opinion on the matter. He ran his hands over the bricks, pressing and following the mortar lines, and this was his wizardry. Structures made sense to Matt in a manner that seemed ingrained in his DNA.

"It's a good wall," he said. "I like this wall. But…buy me a burger and you might be able to talk me into tearing it down."

We walked through Beacon Hill, discussing the current

glut of flipper-abandoned properties, on our way to The Paramount for lunch. Once we were seated, Matt waved away the menu the server offered. "I already know what I want," he said. He glanced over as I yawned into my menu. "But she might need a minute. You need some coffee, Shan?"

"That would be great," I said.

The server retreated, and Matt eyed me from across the table. "Are you okay?"

"Fine," I said, stifling another yawn. "Tired."

It wasn't as if I had a better explanation. My mind was a battlefield, and every contradictory emotion I could conjure went to war when Will showed up at my door last night. I stared at the ceiling for hours, desperate to formulate a plan for handling the unwelcome visitor down the hall. But...he wasn't entirely unwelcome, and that knowledge fired the first shot in this war.

There were so many things I felt for Will—most of which I wasn't prepared to admit—and no amount of anger could bury those feelings. But it wasn't like they were neat or organized. No, they were a jumbled mess of fondness and concern and belonging, and even as the sun rose over the city, I couldn't grab on to anything more than stomach-twisting confusion.

The Will I knew never pleaded with me to stay anywhere, he never let me go, even when I demanded it, and he never accepted sleeping arrangements that didn't involve sharing a bed.

At first, I thought his hesitant reaction was due to Gerard, but then I remembered the calm fury I saw brewing in Will, and the warning to stay away from Mr. Pemberton. On most days, I found Will's possessiveness to be nothing more than obnoxious, misplaced jealousy, but last night awakened a part of me I hadn't known was dormant.

Matt cleared his throat, and I realized I'd been staring at the menu, too lost in the memory of Will's arms locked around my body to notice his expectant gaze or the server beside our table.

"Oh, sorry," I mumbled. "Can I have a grilled chicken panini, but no chicken?"

"You just want the mozzarella and tomato?" she asked.

"Yes," I said, and held out my hands when Matt turned an arched eyebrow in my direction. "What?"

"Why do you do that? The chickenless chicken sandwich?"

"I'm particular about chicken," I said, working hard to keep the defensiveness out of my voice. "I prefer it grilled, on a real grill, and not restaurant kitchen grills. I never feel like it's cooked through all the way, and it always tastes like it was cooked right next to meat. Like, that greasy, griddly, beefy flavor. I hate that."

He tapped his phone against the tabletop, smiling. "It's funny because my greasy, griddly, beefy burger never tastes like chicken." He gestured toward me and opened his mouth, but paused, as if he couldn't select the right words.

"Let's talk about these properties," I said, more hurried than necessary. I knew where Matt was headed—straight back to my mind-wandering weirdness—and I knew I was too exhausted to build an excuse that sounded valid. "If you want this project, I'll get a cash offer out before your lunch arrives, but you have to be certain. This is a long, messy, expensive restoration, and I'm not about to continue the conversation unless you're fully behind this."

He nodded and sipped his water. "Why do *you* want it?"

"It's a gorgeous pair of brownstones," I said, "and you secretly love hot messes."

"Why *else* do you want it?" he asked.

I shrugged, turning my attention to my phone. Tom was bombarding me with several thousand quick questions in the form of texts and emails, his version of punishment for me spacing out during our regular Tuesday morning check-in meeting.

We kept that time sacred. In all the years we'd worked together, I could only remember a few occasions when we didn't meet, and it was a result of Angus dying or Tom taking a week off to climb Denali. My late arrival—I didn't want to go home and run into warm, sleep-rumpled Will after my barre class but I still hadn't mastered the art of showering and dressing for the day in the communal locker room at my gym—and complete lack of focus meant we only discussed my schedule for the week while I signed another mountain of checks.

"Those are completely adequate reasons," I said. "But for the sake of argument, let's add a few more, Matt. How about one less garish, modern townhouse where a sustainably designed restoration belongs? How about a kick-ass Beacon Hill location? How about giving you a project uniquely suited to your skill set? How about a fifteen-million dollar price tag when this is all said and done, or better yet, the cover stories and awards that will absolutely come your way?"

"Paramount burger, extra bacon," the server said as she slid Matt's plate in front of him. "Grilled chicken panini, hold the chicken. Can I get you anything else?"

"All set," Matt said. "I don't know that I want a huge project right now, and I don't mind running the engineering while Patrick and Sam handle the design on big restorations."

I took two bites from my sandwich before fishing the sliced tomatoes out. "Lean in, Matt. Don't tell me about how you and Lauren are thinking about getting a dog again, or that you want to start building that house you promised her, or any of that shit. This is *your* time."

He eyed the abandoned tomatoes and shook his head. "I'm not even going to ask what that tomato did to you."

"I like the flavor of tomatoes with mozzarella, but not the watery sliminess of tomatoes," I said. "And if you're serious about not wanting this project, I'll drop it. I mean, I *do* live in that neighborhood, and a part of my soul *will* shatter every time I walk by those brownstones. I don't know what I'll do if a development firm buys them only to tear them down or —God forbid—rip out the brick and replace it with stucco. Fucking stucco. And honestly, this isn't about money or awards or recognition for you, and that's fine. I'm sure Patrick and Sam will have plenty of projects to keep you busy. One of these days, Riley is bound to stir up some business of his own. You could help him with that."

Matt set the remaining portion of his burger on the plate and wove his fingers together, propping his chin on his clasped hands. "You play dirty."

"Thank you," I said.

I pushed the plate away and reached for my coffee. There was an inverse relationship between the number of complicated issues I could manage at any given time and my appetite: the more stressed I was, the less I ate. Those three bites, plus a nonfat latte, were the only things I'd managed to consume today. Lauren liked to make noise about that being some sort of blessing, but I hated when people noticed my erratic eating habits. I did the best I could.

"You really think it will sell for fifteen million?" Matt asked. He helped himself to the sweet potato fries on my plate.

"Fully restored and loaded with all the sexy sustainable design features?" I stirred some sugar into my coffee, nodding while I mentally ran through the recent comparable sales. "Fifteen sounds right to me. There's a five-story Greek Revival around the corner, and that sold for eleven. And a Gothic on the sunny side of Commonwealth. Same size, but it needed work. It was a closed sale with a non-disclosure but my sources tell me it sold for somewhere north of twelve-five."

"It's going to be expensive," he murmured, his fingers drawing numbers on the tabletop as he added it up in his head.

"I expected that," I said. "I wouldn't have started this discussion if I couldn't fund it."

"Okay, then," he said. "Let's buy a disaster."

"Two disasters," I corrected, "one amazing restoration."

Will: When did you leave this morning?
Shannon: Early
Will: Does that mean you'll be home earlier tonight?
Shannon: That's none of your concern
Will: That's arguable

Will: I'm fixing the hinges on your closet. Maybe slam them less?

Shannon: Get out of my bedroom

Shannon: Actually, get out of my apartment

Will: You want me to bring you lunch? No problem. What do you feel like?

Shannon: Seriously. Why are you here? What's going on?

Will: I'm on leave

Shannon: You've never wanted to spend that time in Boston before

Will: Not true.

Will: When will you be home? We'll talk.

Shannon: I don't think that's a good idea

Will: That wasn't a question. We will talk.

Will: Met your cleaning lady.

Will: And by "met" I mean she walked in while I was in the shower

Will: I paid her and sent her home

Will: Should I expect anyone else to walk into your apartment unannounced?

Shannon: Probably not.

Shannon: How traumatized was she, on a scale of your goldfish dying to finding your grandparents having sex

Will: That's an awful scale. I'm not going to think about dead pets and naked grandparents

Shannon: Grow some balls, would you?

Shannon: It couldn't have been that bad. She hasn't called me screaming, and it's not like you have much to traumatize her with.

Will: Look at you, insulting my dick like a champ

Will: Don't lie. You enjoyed that, didn't you?

Shannon: I'm ignoring you now.

Shannon: I left 2 pieces of grooved metal in the kitchen.
They're known as keys.

Shannon: These are probably new to you.

Shannon: Rather than using your black ops methods, please
use them to get in and out of the building.

Will: Understood

Shannon: And no other commando tactics either, please.

Will: Dammit. I really wanted to practice my urban rooftop
jumping

Shannon: None of that

Will: What about fast roping on power lines? Is that ok?

Shannon: No

Will: Well, shit. I'll just reorganize your vibrators

Shannon: Please don't

Will: No worries. I can diffuse a land mine. Vibrators don't
scare me

Shannon: Yeah. There's nothing weird about this convo.

I RAN out of patience for the world around two o'clock on
Friday afternoon.

My advertising and media team had the combined
common sense of an inchworm, Patrick was bitching about
his assistant again, Riley managed to flood the basement at
one of Sam's properties, Lauren was pissed that I ditched

pedicure night, Tom was complaining about every random thing that crossed his mind, and my unusually polite house-guest was fucking with my understanding of the universe.

To say Will was acting strangely would be the under-statement of the year.

I didn't know what to do with a well-behaved Will. I only knew the argumentative version who liked stripping me down and tying me up, and then going dark for weeks at a time. The man living in my guest room went to bed before ten every night, filled the refrigerator with my favorite cheeses, and made no attempt at touching me. The apart-ment was cleaner than I left it, and he took it upon himself to wash and fold my laundry.

I still didn't know why he was here or how long he was staying, and I couldn't get my head around this tentative roommate bullshit. It was a slow walk to crazy, and part of me was itching to insult him so we could get back to the place where we knew how to act around each other.

We didn't speak much earlier in the week. Not beyond chilly texts. I headed to the gym before dawn and parked myself in the office until late each night. There was always some cheese, nuts, and bread waiting for me under plastic wrap when I got home, and I would have thanked him in some backhanded way if he wasn't already in bed. The thought of crawling in beside him crossed my mind several thousand times each day, but I'd been down that path before, and I knew where it ended.

By the time this morning rolled around, Will was wise to my avoidance strategy. I nearly pissed myself from the shock of finding him seated on the kitchen counter, dressed in running shoes, track pants, and a wind shirt, hours before sun-up.

"Ready?" he asked.

It was too early to form words, let alone the sharp, snappy words I wanted right then, and I lifted a shoulder in response. He followed as I jogged downstairs and through Louisburg Square, crossing the Public Garden toward the Back Bay gym. I didn't expect him to saddle up beside me for sixty minutes of advanced cycling and borderline evil taunting, but he smiled at me as if he'd been doing this his entire life.

I took some perverse joy from the hungry gazes aimed at Will by the hedge fund wives who packed this class. Even Nina, the screaming beast who trafficked in aphorisms like 'disregard your limits' and 'use fear as your fuel' and 'move your fat ass, bitch' was drinking up the rhythmic flex of Will's thighs and the steely determination in his eyes as she increased the pace. She leaned off her bike when he yanked the wind shirt over his head, revealing a faded University of California, San Diego t-shirt, and I could almost hear her eye-fucking him.

These women were ready to kneel at his feet and beg for the pleasure of his attention, and I...I kept telling him to get the fuck out of my apartment.

"And you run home after this?" he asked when the class ended.

I murmured in agreement. It meant I saw a lot more of him in the morning, but I abandoned the gym shower routine after forgetting a fresh pair of undies on Wednesday. I stopped at La Perla and bought some on my way to the office, but then I realized I never wore new panties without washing them first. I dropped eighty dollars on a pair of basic boyshorts, and still spent the day bare-assed.

It wasn't his fault entirely, but I ranted at Tom for a good twenty minutes over the apparent lack of back-up panties in the office. I had a spare suit, heels, and stockings. Why not undies, too?

Will used the hem of his t-shirt to mop sweat from his forehead, and a collective purr sounded when his abs came into view. The four thirty spin class didn't see much testosterone, especially not Will's variety. "Fuck, Shannon, you're a machine. That was rough."

"Underestimated me again?" I asked. "It used to be funny how you did that. Now it's just obnoxious."

"I've never underestimated you, and I think you know that." He leaned forward and folded his arms on the handles. "This was like my first week at BUD/S. The only thing missing was the water cannon." He glanced at Nina. "Why would anyone choose to do this?"

"She might be a Satan soldier, but my ass is a work of art." I inclined my head toward the group of women staring and whispering in his direction. "If the commando business falls apart, you can always train the high-end stroller crew. They'd drop big money for you to yell at them."

"The Department of Defense needs to hear about this," Will said, waving his hand at the white walls and neon yellow bikes. "This would definitely change their view on women in combat."

"Yeah, I don't know about that," I said, cutting my gaze away from the t-shirt clinging to Will's chest and toward his fan club. "They can't go anywhere without reliable access to alkaline water."

He smiled, and I saw his intention before he moved but I did nothing to stop him from tucking some loose strands of hair over my ear.

"What?" I snapped, finally jerking away from his touch.

His smile dimmed and he shook his head. "I've missed talking to you," he said. "I've…I've missed *you*."

A choked, stuttering noise sounded in my throat. All the words were fighting for dominance, and I wasn't sure which would tumble out first. I opened my mouth to respond then realized we weren't alone.

"Hey," Nina said, sidling up to Will. "I don't think I've seen you here before."

"Probably not." He glanced at the stripe of pink running through her platinum blonde hair and nodded toward me. "I'm here with Shannon. I go where she goes."

"How do I sign up for that service?" she asked.

Not interested in witnessing another moment of *that* conversation, I made quick work of pulling on my running jacket and hitting the sidewalk. Will caught up to me on Tremont Street, and he was smart enough to stay a few paces back.

I took the long way home, jogging down around Cambridge Street and weaving through narrow cobblestone alleys off Charles Street to my building. This was the one moment where I could focus enough to hear my thoughts, where I knew my world didn't line up with Will's. It never would, and I wasn't letting myself settle for secret weekends or the warped argument that I needed to change my priorities.

"Hey," he panted, taking the stairs two at a time. He leaned into me as I struggled to pull my key from the hidden pocket inside my waistband. He was breathing heavy, leaving puffs of air on my neck, and I could feel heat radiating off him, wrapping around me. "We're going to talk. Tonight."

"I have plans," I said, trying and failing to get the key in the lock.

Will covered my hand with his and he pressed his chest against my back, his chin on my shoulder, and if his lips touched my neck, my resolve would be *gone*, just fucking gone.

"We're going to talk," he repeated. "You're not hiding from me anymore, peanut."

He turned the key, opened the door, and walked away without another word.

And now—hours later—the only thing I could think about was that promise. Didn't he know that he was a second away from knocking over the only supports I had left? That I was going to dissolve like a pillar of sand, and forget all about our arguments and the awful months I spent mourning the loss of him from my life? Or was that exactly what he knew?

"Holy—what the hell are you doing in here?" I looked up from the paint fan deck in my hands to find Andy staring at me. I wasn't sure how long I'd been camped out in the materials room. "Why are you sitting on the floor? In the dark?"

"I hate people," I said.

"That's my line," she said, settling beside me.

"I'm borrowing it today."

She crossed her long legs in front of her and smoothed out her dark trousers, and the marvelous thing about Andy was that she never felt compelled to fill the silence. She was comfortable sitting beside someone, completely wordless, and somewhere in the past two years, I'd learned to love that about her. She was a rock like that, quiet and steady and always, always there for me.

"Tiel came out with us last night," she said.

"Yeah, she texted me," I murmured. The shelf to my left caught my attention. "Oh dear God. Isn't Patrick's assistant responsible for organizing this room?"

Andy held up her hands. "I stay far away from that situation. She's Patrick's problem."

"That means she's my problem," I said. "How was Tiel?"

"Happy. Excited. Overwhelmed," she said. "But mostly happy. And no, she hasn't thought about wedding dates, dresses, locations, flowers, cakes, or colors. She went all snapping turtle when Lauren asked. Here's my best guess: they'll either elope or be engaged for the next three years."

I didn't know my way around Tiel yet. She only tolerated us in small bites, and sometimes, even that was too much for her. We didn't start out on the right foot, and she was skittish around us. She'd started joining us for pedicures and drinks over the summer, and it was a good first step. Lauren took the lead on the 'welcome Tiel to the family' initiative, and let's face it: she was the obvious choice when the alternatives were Andy or me.

Tiel liked Lauren but that wasn't a valid measure of anything; everyone liked Lauren.

I ended up going to Martha's Vineyard with Sam and Tiel two months ago—it was a pity invite and I'd accepted without shame—and the three of us had a great time together. Tiel and I parked ourselves in front of the fire pit one night, drank a lot of wine, and talked about everything but also *nothing*.

Somehow, we started with the annoying dudes on the subway who felt it was necessary to sit with their legs spread at a ninety-degree angle, regardless of whether that meant they were encroaching on the space of others. That snowballed into discussing the hygiene of characters in dystopian stories because they seem to wear the same clothes day after day but are never seen bathing or washing those clothes. Obviously, that segued into comparing notes on gynecologists; I was always looking for a doctor who would actually give a shit about my issues and not wave them away as normal discomfort. From there, we debated where we'd want to live if global warming flooded Boston. We didn't walk away with any solutions for that one, and we never revisited that awful conversation at the coffee shop last winter.

It was nice to spend time with her, and she was just as funny and sweet and spunky as Sam promised, but the jury was still out on how long I'd be on eggshells with her.

"Well that's fabulous," I said, reordering the stone samples. "Really, really fabulous."

"I'm going to a Yin yoga class tonight," she said. "Really low key. Super chill. Mostly meditation with some poses. Want to come?"

"Hand me that swatch panel," I said, gesturing to the board beside Andy. "Yoga doesn't agree with me."

"You don't like Bikram. Yin is nothing like that," she said. "And…it looks like you need some centering."

I turned and met her eyes. "Oh really?"

"You've been a bit jumpy this week." She shrugged and pointed at my face. "You look tired, and you know I say that with love. Come to class with me, and then we can make Patrick get us take-out and drinks. He's going to do that for me anyway. You should reap the benefits."

Sighing, I started sorting the design journals. "I'm supposed to have dinner with Gerard."

"Ugh," she groaned. "Not that dick weasel again. Is this some kind of Walsh family competition? Like when Patrick and Matt tried to see how long they could go without coffee, as if that made them superhuman or something? Or when Nick and Riley took that Pure Barre class just to see who could nail the instructor first?"

"Did anyone win that bet? The barre instructor?"

Andy rolled her eyes and blew out a breath. "No, that was more about them being morons than anything else. But Gerard—that's a contest. A really fucked-up dare. He can't be real."

"Oh it's real," I said. "I don't think he's that bad."

"He is *that* bad," Andy said, laughing.

Yeah. She was right about that. When I invited him to join us for drinks last month, he started by insulting the neighborhood pub we frequented. Then he made some quietly hostile comments about large Irish Catholic families that "didn't know when to stop" and Boston's "cultural vacancy" relative to New York City. He ended the night by butchering everyone's names and tipping Tom five dollars. The running explanation was that Tom must have given Gerard a handey under the table.

No one had said much about that evening. I knew my family didn't care for him, but they were pleased about my return to polite society after months of my anti-social work obsession. They assumed it was associated with Sam's emergence from the woods—lumberjack beard and all—and that was partially true. When Sam came home, it relieved the pressure of his absence, the suffocating fear that we'd get a call about him taking his life with nothing but the woods by his side. They didn't know Gerard was my way of closing the book on Will.

Or, closing the book, dousing it in gasoline, burning it

until only ash remained, and then punting those ashes far into the ocean.

"He's just...a dick weasel. There's no other way to describe it. He's not worth a second of your time, Shan. Is he the reason you're hiding in the materials room? I'd merrily kick his ass if you asked."

"You're not the only one," I murmured. "Maybe next week for yoga. I have to deal with Gerard tonight."

Andy stood and propped her hands on her hips. "Should we hug? Is that the proper protocol here? I never know when that's called for."

"You're so weird," I laughed, waving her away. "I fucking love you."

Twenty-One

SHANNON

GERARD WAS TALKING ABOUT SOMETHING—
SEA urchin harvesting, maybe?—and I was doing a fair job
at the appearance of listening. There were well-timed nods,
some interested murmurs, and enough eye contact to get by,
but I wanted to reach across the table and gag him with a
dinner roll.

By the time I'd finished chatting with Andy, it was too
late to cancel on him, and having a face-to-face conversation
seemed like the least bitchy path.

That was two hours ago. Now...the bitchy path sounded
terrific.

"This story you've been telling for the past forty-five
minutes is truly incredible," I said, holding up my hand to
stop his flow. "But I was hoping we could talk about a few
other things now."

"I didn't realize," he said, his eyes wide as if he was
bewildered by his own staying power. "Meredith always
said I lost track of time when I was engaged in a subject."

Dear Meredith. Sweet, precious Meredith. Gerard's ex-wife deserved a medal for the time she served under this guy.

"Yes, that's nice," I said.

My eyes dropped to the napkin in my lap, and I folded it into a crisp triangle. It was time to put this kinda-sorta relationship to an end. I'd needed someone to keep me occupied during a rough spot, and Gerard did that for me. He'd babbled me to death while I'd isolated every memory of Will and tucked them away. He'd brought me a pleasant absence of emotion, and now I could be cold and empty without urchin stories.

Eliminating the urchin stories was my only motivation; I wasn't pulling the plug on Gerard because Will was…whatever he was.

I cleared my throat and flattened my hands on the table. "It's been lovely—"

"Hi, sorry I'm late." I glanced up just as Will pulled an empty chair from a neighboring table and parked himself between Gerard and me. A devious grin tugged at his lips. There was always a shenanigan with this fucker. "I'm glad you didn't wait to order. May I?"

He grabbed my fork and sampled the untouched salmon on my plate. "What the fuck are you doing here?" I whispered.

To his credit, Gerard nodded at Will, smiling as if he was expecting him to crash our evening, and beckoned the waiter to our table. "A drink, Captain?"

"Enough with the 'Captain' business," I snapped. "He doesn't need you inflating his ego when it's already exceptionally large."

"And by *ego* you mean *cock*," Will said under his breath.

Gerard didn't hear him. Instead, he looked genuinely

shocked at my comment and leaned back in his chair, his eyes narrowed. He didn't know me to have strong reactions to anything. He knew ambivalence, and never desired much more than that.

Will sampled my wine, nodding. "I'll have what she's having," he said to the waiter. His gaze pinged between Gerard and me before digging into my salmon again. "What are you guys talking about?"

"Sea urchin," I said, pushing the plate closer to Will. I didn't need him leaning against me right now.

"Santorini," Gerard corrected. "You thought I was talking about sea urchin?"

This was the problem with handling two opponents at once: one of them was going to see your hand if you took down the other. Ultimately, it was about assessing the greatest risk. Right now, I couldn't decide whether it was Will or Gerard.

"You don't like sea urchin," Will said, pointing his fork in my direction. He turned to Gerard. "She's very particular about the fish she eats. Won't touch most of it. I'm surprised she even ordered salmon, but then again…" He looked around the restaurant. "Apparently this is a seafood place."

"You don't like fish?" Gerard asked.

"I've mentioned that," I said. *A few hundred times*.

"Do you remember that shrimp thing we had in D.C.? With the butter and garlic?" Will asked. "That was amazing." He turned to Gerard. "Best I've ever had. With this lady right here."

"How long have you two known each other?" Gerard asked.

Will jumped in before I could respond. "A few years," he

said, ignoring my eye roll. "My sister married Shannon's brother, Matt."

"And you've spent most of that time overseas," I clarified.

"Although I'm with you whenever I'm stateside," he said with a pointed look. "Always."

Gerard clasped his hands in his lap. "I should let you two catch up."

I started to protest but there was no reason. I didn't want to spend any more time with Gerard, and that mess had to end here. Whether I wanted to spend time with Will was a different story.

"I'll walk you out," I said, standing.

"I'll be right here," Will called, pointing to the table.

I flipped him off as I stepped away.

"He must have so many rich stories of culture," Gerard mused as we neared the door. "To embed one's self in a foreign land and serve the greater good, that must be a defining experience."

"Yeah, something like that," I murmured. It wasn't that I disagreed with Gerard. I just wanted to get a word in edge-wise so I could kick him out of the nest and get on with my life. "So listen. You're a smart, successful guy, and I know you've had a rough year with the divorce. You have so many interests and tons of knowledge, and a lot to offer. I want to make sure you find someone who brings similar things to the table. I'm not that person."

He ran his hands down his lapels before shoving them in his pockets. "I know," he said. "That's why I was doing you a favor."

"You were *what*?" I asked.

"I figured you wanted an arrangement that served your career," he said. His tone implied that I should have known exactly what he was talking about. "You're not going to start something traditional at your age, and you require companionship for appearances."

"That is a truly ingenious spin," I murmured.

"Of course, public appearance also supports my work, and you're attractive enough and have great contacts, so it wasn't completely one-sided."

I squeezed my eyes shut and brought my fingers to my temples. "I really know how to find the winners," I said to myself. "It was a time, Gerard. Best of luck to you."

He nodded and moved toward the door. "Give my regards to the captain."

"Yeah, of course," I murmured. I waited while he hailed a cab, returning his wave when he hopped in. "*At my age.* That motherfucker."

Shifting, I found Will staring at me from across the restaurant. He wasn't wearing the open, animated smile he used on Gerard. He was calm yet more serious than I'd ever seen him, his intense gaze taking root inside me and curling around my bones and organs. I marched back to him, plotting how I'd torture him for these antics.

"I have many questions," I said as I settled into my seat, "though the first must be this: how did you know I'd be here?"

Will ran his knuckles over my thumb, and I really wanted to ignore the electricity behind his touch. "An operator never divulges his methods."

"The universe needs to help a bitch out," I groaned. "First I get the 'Listen, lady, you're old as fuck but not so washed up that I won't be seen in public with you' line. And then it's a stubborn SEAL who's made a home for himself in my guest room. How is this my life? Which God did I anger?"

"Is that what he said to you?"

I shook off his question. I was done rehashing. "Let's review the facts, William. You've invited yourself to my gym and dinner dates. You're staying in my apartment. I believe you've been doing my laundry, which means you've touched my panties, and I don't recall inviting you to do that. I can only imagine how you've defiled them. You've offered exactly zero details about your sudden appearance, and now you're pulling the black ops card. Does that sound right to you?"

He bit into a spear of asparagus and inclined his head toward me. "Yes, ma'am."

I waved my hand in his direction, expecting more. "This would be the opportunity to expand on that."

"I believe that all depends on what constitutes *defiled* in your book," he said.

My hands curled to fists and I blew out a snarling breath. "You might be the most repulsive person I've ever met."

"Anything for your praise, peanut." He set his fork down and glanced at me. "I picked up the tab while you were talking to Lord of the Douches. Let's get out of here. You can tell me about that conversation on the ride home."

This asshole.

"You know what's great about that comment? Its complete refusal to answer my question," I said.

With my coat slung over my arm and my purse in hand, I stormed out of the restaurant. I didn't want everything about Will to drive me crazy, but it was like my judgment and self-control flew out the window when we were in the same zip code. I couldn't be near him without being a little insane, and that scared me because this man could convince me to do almost anything.

I knew he was behind me, and I was certain he was watching—all patient and amused, like I was a puppy lost under a blanket—while I attempted to navigate the North End's uneven cobblestone streets, wrestle my arms into my coat, and dig through my purse for keys, all at once. The alarm chirped when my fingers landed on the car's remote start button, and the vehicle roared to life.

Will slipped into the passenger seat without a word, and kept his eyes glued on the windshield even when I slammed my door with enough force to rock the car. I was a slammer and a stomper, and though I knew those reactions had drama queen written all over them, that was how I rolled.

He closed his hand into a fist and then splayed his fingers out, exhaling heavily as he repeated the motion, and asked, "What did you say to the Douchelord back there?"

"I'm not answering your questions until you answer mine," I said.

"You let him down easy," Will said. "How'd he take it?"

"Allow me to repeat myself: come clean or choke on my dick."

"Those are interesting choices," he murmured.

The short journey back to my apartment building seemed infinite, filled with slow pedestrians and quick-changing stoplights, and I could only assume it was the universe's way of getting back at me for letting things linger this long with Gerard.

I knew why I ignored his obnoxious tendencies, and why I overlooked our complete lack of chemistry. He was Will's opposite in so many ways, but most importantly, he never made me feel much of anything. And I wanted it that way. I couldn't function with all of this emotion rippling right at the surface. I could manage anything when it came to my family and my work, but I couldn't handle feeling fucking ravenous for one man.

After stomping from the garage to the elevator to my apartment, I glanced at Will while unlocking the door. "I'm finished with these games. No more stalking."

I headed straight for the dining room, away from the cozy sectional in the den where I wanted to curl up with some wine and *The X-Files*. The den was too centrally located and I'd been avoiding it since Will arrived; it begged for him to come in and join me. I knew the distance between us would evaporate, and I didn't trust myself to be strong when his open arms beckoned.

My coat was hanging haphazardly from a chair back while I rummaged in my bag. It served as the catchall for my necessities: laptop, small notebook, makeup bag, hairbrush, phone charger, long-forgotten Kind bars, keys to every-where, and a deck of business cards. I didn't know what I was looking for but it didn't matter. I took it all out, slammed it on the gorgeous antique Chippendale table that Patrick salvaged from a property we restored nine years ago. It was before I bought this apartment, and there was no way the twelve-seat set was fitting in my tiny walk-up rental, but I couldn't bear to see it go. Instead, it moved between our investment properties, serving as an odd—yet completely fitting—mascot for our fledgling business.

"Drop the act, Ally McBeal. Dinner with the Douchelord was about as pleasant as an anesthesia-free wisdom tooth extraction, and you were thrilled that I saved you from hate-glaring at him any longer. He annoyed the ever-loving fuck out of you, and I give you credit for sticking it out this long. You'd be an outstanding hostage." He laughed. "Now give it up: you told him you craved my cock and couldn't live without it, right?"

"You are such an obnoxious bastard." I started shoving things back in my bag, and though I was trying to organize that mess, it was much, much worse than before. "Why are you here? Why are you in *my* apartment when your sister is across town and would happily take you in? What do you want from me, Will?"

He released a humorless laugh. "Me staying with Lo is an invitation to kill your brother in his sleep. If you're good with that, say the word and I'll pack up."

I closed my eyes and drew a deep breath. "Why. Are. You. Here?"

"Pissing you off is amusing as fuck."

"Original. Really original." I threw my hands up but didn't turn to face him. "After all this time, you're at my door, and you just presume I'm going to rip my clothes off and jump into your arms. Please. I expect more from you than this."

"Get over here and sit on my face and you'll get plenty more," he said.

I dropped my back-up phone charger into my bag and stared at the table's wood grain, fuming. Then I did the first thing that came to mind. I grabbed a lime from the decorative bowl in the center of the table, pivoted, and winged it at Will's head. The element of surprise worked in my favor, and it pinged right off his skull.

"Holy mother of fucking Christ, Shannon! What the hell was that?" he cried, his fingers pressed against his forehead.

"Enough," I yelled, reaching for another lime. It shot out from my hand, and then another, and they landed square on his chest. "I've had enough of your quippy comments and your grocery shopping and your entire existence as I know it."

Will tumbled over the backside of the sofa, ducking when another lime flew in his direction. He popped up, two limes caught in his palm, and he pointed at me. "You've got a cannon for an arm, peanut," he said, laughing. "But don't think I won't throw these right back at you."

The bowl was far from empty. There were probably another twenty limes, and right now, I wasn't above chucking the Waterford crystal dish at his head either. "You don't have the balls," I said. "And I would know because the last time I went looking for them, all I could find was a big, sloppy vagina."

"You are so asking for it," he said.

The fruit flew across the room and struck my outer thigh, and fuck me sideways, those things *hurt*. I yelped, and fired another at Will, catching him on the shoulder. He dropped back behind the protective wall of the sofa and mumbled a long, imaginative string of curses. He was only down a moment, and when he reappeared, two more limes pelted my legs.

And then it was all-out war.

Fruit whizzed back and forth between the rooms while we swore and insulted each other like never before. We were sweaty and breathless, and my apartment was thoroughly ransacked. The one upside: everything smelled like fresh citrus.

"You're getting spanked tonight, peanut," he called as a lime whizzed toward me and connected with my boob. My freaking boob.

"What kind of pussy aims for my tits?" I screamed, rubbing the offended breast. I pointed to my chest. "These are off-limits to you in every possible way, you dirty hooker."

"Sorry, I was distracted by that giant dick you like shoving down my throat," he said, and sent another fruit sailing toward my hip.

"You should be thankful it's not your ass," I said, and aimed a lime at his crotch.

It missed, and he pinned me with a fierce gaze, his shoulders squared, and his arm extended in my direction. "Don't you dare," he warned. "I will take you *down*, little girl."

Of course, I fired the last three limes at the same target. He was quick, and rushed toward me as I threw, twisting and shifting his body to avoid the assault. He tackled me to the ground, his weight heavy on my hips as he anchored my hands over my head. I gulped, praying he wouldn't rock forward and press his cock to my center because a girl— even a bossy, bitchy girl who knew how to bury all her feelings under a mountain of guilt and control it all—could only take so much.

"You're a vicious little gremlin sometimes, you know that?" he murmured. "And now that you've worked that shit out of your system, we're going to talk."

A groan rumbled in his throat, a roll of thunder that rattled between us, and I held myself rigid, bracing for the bolt of lightning that was sure to come. His lips landed on my neck, and in quick succession, I flinched and tilted my head to give him better access. I couldn't be more conflicted; I wanted him but we were wrong for each other in every possible way. It didn't matter that our anatomy did nice things when it came together.

"If you have to hold me down, it doesn't exactly qualify

as a free-flowing conversation, commando. You're teetering into the land of interrogation. Coercion, even."

"Yeah? All this time, I thought you liked it," he said, his teeth scraping over my skin. There wasn't much I could refuse when I had two hundred pounds of hard, neck-kissing man on top of me. "You're probably thinking about me holding *out*." He rocked his hips against me, and that was the cock I missed having in my life. "That's it. You hate it when I hold *out*. You still love it when I hold you *down*."

There was always a tipping point when Will and I were together, a moment that crossed the line from sparring into sex. I was standing on that line now, and though the inertia of this night was pushing us forward, I leaned back. "Please. Just tell me why you came."

Will sensed the shift, pulling away from my neck. "You keep asking that as if you don't know. I might not have arrived on time, but I promised you I was coming back."

"I'm not going to change," I said. "And I'm not going to choose."

"Shannon, I've never asked you to change." He sat back on his knees, smoothing his hands down his legs. "You're the only one who thinks you have to choose."

That wasn't how I remembered it. I remembered my universe torn apart at the seams, and I remembered failing at the one thing I cared about most.

I caught a glimpse of the living room. "You better get started cleaning this up," I said. "I don't want lime juice stains on my rugs."

His eyes met mine in challenge, and that spark of something—oh, the line between love and hate had never been so fine—that I still held for him urged me to give up the fight. He saw it too.

"The Douchelord was a placeholder. A seat-filler. I don't blame you for a minute of it, but I need to know it's over. If it's not, I'm going to find him and I'm going to end it for you."

"It's precious that you're so hot for Gerard." I nodded, shifting to my feet and heading down the hallway. "Not that it's any of your business, but he's back on the market. I wouldn't put any energy into chasing him, though. I don't think you're his type. He likes them young."

Will flopped to the side and dragged a hand over his face. "Yeah, I'm gonna kill him."

My heart was *pounding pounding pounding* when I closed the door behind me, and all these emotions were crawling their way to the surface. But I didn't want to fight them anymore.

My clothes hit the floor while I changed into a cozy set of flannel pajamas. I scrubbed the makeup from my face and tied my hair back, all while telling myself that I could handle boys—even commando boys—better than anyone.

The door clanged behind me when I emerged from my bedroom, but Will didn't move. He was flat on his back with a hand pressed to his shoulder and his eyes closed. "I'm watching *Orange is the New Black*. You probably won't like it but you're welcome to join me as long as you can promise you won't wrestle me to the ground again."

"Will you be throwing anything?" he called.

"Haven't decided yet," I responded. I tossed a bag of popcorn in the microwave and poured some wine. "Aren't commandos supposed to be able to handle a few flying objects?"

Will popped to his feet when the microwave sounded,

and he followed me into the den, his gaze skeptical. "I've never had a lime thrown at me before."

I pointed at the far end of the leather sofa while I queued up the series to the last episode I watched. "You can sit there."

"And where are you sitting?" he asked.

"Over here." I wedged into the opposite end, tight against the armrest.

"I'd rather be on your side," he said. "With you. And the popcorn."

I hugged the bowl to my chest. "Get your own."

"You beat the shit out of me with citrus and called me a dirty hooker. The least you can do is share your popcorn."

I set the bowl on the cushion between us, cranked up the volume, and turned my attention to the show. It took Will a little time to stop sending me loaded glances and pay attention to the episode, but it wasn't long before he was laughing with me. He asked me to pause and catch him up on the story lines, and joined my running commentary about the characters.

"Is this what people mean when they say 'Netflix and chill'?" he asked, and I almost dropped my wine in the process. There were odd bits of pop culture that Will missed out on while he was deployed.

"No," I said. "No, that's something else. Something different."

"Either way," he murmured, "this is surprisingly good."

We watched the last half of the season, and when I announced that I needed my beauty rest, he gave me a sad smile, patted my head, and retreated to the guest room without a word.

When I plugged in my phone for the night, I was surprised to see a recent text from him.

Will: What are you doing?
Shannon: Getting into bed. Why?
Will: At least tell me what you said to Douchelord
Shannon: None of your fucking business
Will: You threw two dozen limes at me tonight
Shannon: …and your point?
Will: Have I not earned the information?
Shannon: I told you. He's back on the market. That's more than enough intel
Will: You're there. I'm in here. One of us is in the wrong place.
Shannon: You sound like you're 13 and trolling on pinterest
Shannon: Your text game has suffered

I closed the text window, and opened a new one to Andy and Lauren.

Shannon: sorry ladies. Have to skip lunch tomorrow…errr it's today now. Headed to Swampscott for an open house. Have a mimosa for me. Or six.

I often bowed out of our weekend lunches for property shopping. They wouldn't think anything of it as I'd skipped most outings in recent months, and I wouldn't have to look Lauren in the eye and conceal the fact her brother was in my apartment, recovering from a fruiting attack. It wasn't the same as concealing the fact I'd hooked up with the very same brother for months, or that I'd omitted huge portions of the truth when she inquired about my travels. She'd be pissed at me about the weekends, but she'd strangle us both if she found out he was in town and avoiding her.

Staring at my phone, I debated firing off some hostile texts to Gerard. I didn't believe in kicking corpses and I didn't have the time or patience for vengeance, but someone needed to throw a flag on the play he ran tonight.

"Such a dick weasel," I said, studying his name in my contact list. Deleting him was the smarter option. The last thing I needed was Mr. Pemberton whispering about my old, dried-up prune of a pussy all over town. "But I can send a case of herbal erectile dysfunction pills to your office."

The door burst open, and Will—wearing only boxers and a t-shirt—leaned on the handle. "What the hell are you doing in here? Who are you talking to?"

I was still amused by the idea of Gerard getting a shipment of boner stimulants in his swanky office, and couldn't shut down the giggles. "There's nothing wrong with talking to myself. It was an important conversation."

His eyes swept the room, and he shook his head before switching off the lamp. He stopped beside the bed, his fingertips tapping the duvet, and sighed. "You're the weirdest one in your family, right? Tell me it doesn't get any worse than this."

My body was committed to the giggles now, much like jumping off a diving board. All the ridiculousness of this week catalyzed into laughter, and soon I was hugging my sides while my eyes watered. "Not even close," I stammered.

Will muttered something under his breath and climbed into bed beside me. His arms wrapped around me, strong and warm and safe, and I didn't push him away. How could I? How could I find the strength to protest when my heart required *this*, when I'd spent the week stewing in my anger but wanting nothing more than *this*, when I'd spent months numbing myself to the memories of *this*.

I kept going back to that first night we were together, before the wedding, and how he could take me away from everything in my mind. I needed it then; I wanted it now.

Even if my head was busy mounting a bulletproof offensive.

"Now, listen to me," he said. "I'm here for you—"

"I don't want to talk right now," I said, hiccupping as the giggles subsided. "Just keep your shorts on, don't try to slip it in, and don't make it weird."

Will brushed my hair over my shoulder and kissed my jaw. "Sure you don't want to tell me what you said to the Douchelord?"

"Why should I start giving you what you want now?" I asked. His thumbs worked the knots in my neck, and he had my eyes crossing in bliss.

"Because somewhere in your feisty little gremlin heart, you care about me," he said. "And I'm not letting go until you remember that. I've told you before: I'm not giving up."

WILL WAS busy flipping pancakes in the kitchen when I dragged myself out of bed the next morning. He handed me a plate and turned back to the stove without discussion. We'd slept together, perfectly civil and clothed, and it'd felt like my universe was sliding into its rightful orbit again.

Not that I was sharing that sentiment with Will. Not yet.

When I took a bite, I realized these pancakes were filled with raspberries. I couldn't remember ever telling him that I preferred raspberry, or ordering pancakes with him. I stared at the wedge on my fork, confused. People didn't just toss raspberries into pancakes. Blueberries had that market on lock.

"Hey," I called. "About—"

"You mentioned it in Montauk," he yelled into the dining room. "Eat."

I promised myself it was just pancakes, nothing bigger or more symbolic, and only staged a small revolt when Will invited himself on my open house hunt.

"How does this work?" he asked as I merged onto the highway, heading north.

"What? Open houses? Or me tolerating your existence?"

Will turned his head, glaring at me. "The open house," he said. "You just walk around and decide whether you like it? Or have you already decided that you're buying? Is there a bidding war, and if so, I'm very interested in watching you eviscerate people."

"No bidding wars. Not unless it's an auction, and we aren't going to any of those today," I said, waving at the quaint homes along the coastal road. "Most of the time, I hear about properties before they come on the market. There are a lot of pocket listings—when an agent has an agreement with the seller but the property isn't listed—and there are also a number of investors who buy and hold. None of this is public, and those are usually the ones I want. But today, we're seeing a home that has been on the market for over a year and will happily sell below the asking price."

I pulled up at a graying Colonial that didn't look like it could limp through another winter. The location was magnificent; I could hear waves crashing against Swampscott's rocky shoreline from the driveway, and the Galloupes Point neighborhood was hot without falling prey to the trendy trap. If this home was waiting for a buyer after all this time, either the seller was inflexible or it was a sneeze away from falling off this cliff and into the ocean. Or both.

"Don't break anything," I said to Will as we approached the door. "No commando tactics, please."

"Your call," he murmured, his hands raised. "I was going to run some breaching drills, but hell, if you don't want me knocking down doors, I won't."

The agent spotted us and turned on his sales smile as he marched in our direction. "It would be best if you didn't," I whispered.

"Good morning," the agent called. "You're really in for a treat with this property. It was built in 1921, one of the first homes on the Point, all original floors and fixtures, and can you say ocean views? This neighborhood is always in demand, and it's wonderful for growing families, too." He smiled at us purposefully, and I reached into my tote for a business card. "What are we looking for today?"

He was wearing a shiny badge engraved with his name and agency, and I gave him a patient smile with my card. "My client here," I gestured to Will, "is looking for something to restore. He's a big fan of sustainable preservation, isn't that right?"

"Huge fan," he agreed. "The biggest fan."

"He's also looking for a place to wrestle whales and break rocks with his bare hands, so naturally," I said, gesturing to the beach, "this listing came to mind."

"Please, feel free to explore the home," the agent said, flustered. He handed Will a folder filled with glossy images of the home from all the right angles.

The first floor was as I expected: worn, dated, dark. As the agent promised, the views were incredible, and I found myself walking through the kitchen and onto the grassy patio that bordered the ocean. The home sat on a parcel of land that curved out into the sea like a hook, and it created a safe harbor from the choppy Atlantic.

"Those are killer waves," Will said from behind me. His chest was close enough to my back that I felt his presence, his warmth, but not his touch. "And I bet—" He pointed over my shoulder, to the craggy stone projecting into the sea, "—you'd find some shipwrecks out there."

If I leaned back, I'd be in his arms and...I couldn't decide whether I wanted that. "Why?"

"There's a sandbar out there." He gestured to the ocean, but I couldn't discern anything but waves. "It's probably only visible at the lowest tide. And that outcropping? The rocks? They extend about a quarter mile from the shore. No sailing vessels are getting into this cove in one piece."

"I'll be sure to add that to the marketing materials," I said. "I'm sure those are real selling points."

"This is not cheap," Will murmured, flipping through the folder. He pointed at the seven-figure listing price. "You can afford this?"

I spared the sheet a quick glance. "Me? Or the firm?"

"It's funny how you're recognizing a distinction now," he said. "I didn't realize one existed."

"Maybe you didn't look close enough." Turning back to the kitchen door, I said, "I wouldn't be here if I couldn't afford it. Me and the firm, but I'm thinking about this for my investment portfolio."

"That sounded really pretentious, peanut. Your *investment portfolio*," Will repeated. He watched while I opened the dining room's built-in cabinetry, and crouched down with me to study the underside of a shelf. "What are we looking for?"

"Original craftsman marks," I said. I found what I wanted, and stood, turning my attention to the window-panes. "It looks authentic, but I always check."

"Nothing here is straight," Will said, waving at the curved wall of windows. "That seems…different."

I ran my hand along the window sash, nodding. "Every room was designed to face the ocean. Typical in this area." I pointed to the staircase. "Come on. More to see."

Whenever I toured homes, I couldn't stop myself from thinking about the people who lived there. I wondered about their lives and their families, how they made it through good days and bad, whether they were content. I was always trying to nail down the *happy* home, the one that was well-loved rather than hard-worn, the one that breathed joy and comfort from the foundation up, the one that weath-ered storm and sunshine alike.

I couldn't rest my hands on a single reason to love this battered Colonial, but as I circled back through all four floors, I knew I did. This was one of those homes that spoke to me in little whispers, saying, "Show me some love and I'll sparkle for you." I elected to park myself in the butler's pantry and pull out my laptop to research the comparable sales.

"This is a decent place," Will said, opening the cabinets and looking inside. "Good tactical vantage point."

"What?" I murmured.

"Two hundred and seventy degrees of rocky oceanfront at the end of a cul-de-sac," he said. "Highly defensible, and the beach is prime."

"Well, when we're finished restoring it, I'll sell it to you," I said, scribbling some numbers in my notebook. "I'll even forfeit my commission."

"Ah, yes. There's that heart of gold I know and love," he said, moving onto another section of cabinets.

"Get out of there," I said, swatting his hands. "We've already determined they're legit. Your big paws are going to break something."

Will held up his hands. "My big paws are very nimble."

We walked out two hours later with the house under contract. I wasn't sure what I wanted to do with it yet, and gave myself the short trip back to the city to ponder. Will and I ate dinner while working through the rest of *Orange is the New Black*, and there was no debate about where he was sleeping.

He was a demanding pain in the ass, but he wasn't without his merits. He cooked breakfast after we jogged back from the gym every morning the following week, and there were days when I was almost too stubborn to eat anything. *Almost*.

Aside from him cleaning (and confusing the fuck out of my housekeeper by flashing her, paying her, and sending her home) and fixing things (and making comments about my useless brothers), we didn't talk about much more than my Netflix queue.

He started waiting outside my office in the evenings to walk me home. It was really fucking reckless, considering Lauren was a frequent visitor at Walsh Associates and she still didn't know he was in town, but I liked that he cared about me, even when I was shutting him out.

It reminded me of something I'd do.

Will: Do you like peas?

Will: I can't remember you ever eating peas

Shannon: Like, green peas?

Will: Is there another color?

Shannon: Would you like me to delegate that to my research assistant? It's not necessary for her to finish the property line analysis she's working on. I'm not waiting on that to file a conveyance or anything

Will: No. just tell me whether you like peas.

Shannon: I don't dislike them.

Will: You have a research assistant?

Shannon: Yes.

Will: That's new

Shannon: Yes. Many things have changed in the past 8 months.

Will: I'm making pasta with peas because you need more than cheese and nuts. I want to hear about these things over dinner tonight

Shannon: 1) Don't baby me. I don't need you to count my calories

Shannon: 2) I'm at a historic society convening until late. No dinner for me.

Will: Has anyone ever babied you?

Shannon: Maybe. I don't know.

Will: It wouldn't be the worst thing in the world to let me try.

Will: My quads are still feeling that spin class

Shannon: That's the idea.

Shannon: You should know…I go to barre on Wednesdays

Will: Ok I'm down

Shannon: You know barre is ballet stuff, right?

Will: You're not shaking me, peanut. I'll pick up some leggings this afternoon. Is a tutu mandatory?

Shannon: Yes. Pink.

Will: I fucking love pink.

Will: I especially like eating it

Shannon: Gross.

Will: I'm going to shred this ballet shit.

Shannon: Sigh

Will: Do your brothers do anything?

Shannon: Yes

Shannon: Many things, actually

Will: Fixing your bathroom sink isn't one of those things

Shannon: It's a little leak. I wouldn't bother any of them with that. They have far more important things to do.

Will: I'm sorry all I heard was you agreeing that your brothers are useless sacks of shit

Shannon: I'm worried about your powers of inference

Shannon: You didn't sleep well last night

Will: Did I bother you?

Shannon: No. but I remembered you getting up a couple of times

Shannon: Is everything ok? Did you have a nightmare?

Will: It's all good

Shannon: I don't believe you

Will: I'd be better if you were sleeping naked

Will: Not that I'd pass on sleeping with you under any circumstance, but…

Shannon: Don't go making it about the dick.

Will: I believe you brought the dick into the conversation, dear.

Shannon: The dick is part of every conversation

Will: True

Will: It's always popping up.

Shannon: Are you sure you're ok? You didn't have a good night.

Shannon: You sounded uncomfortable last night.

Will: Probably because you were rubbing your sweet little ass on the dick

Will: How about dropping the flannel PJs tonight?

Shannon: How about no

Will: I like that skirt you're wearing today

Shannon: Thank you

Will: I'd like to take it off you

Shannon: …don't go there.

Will: Sometimes I think about pulling the zipper down and watching it hit the ground, but then I think about ripping it off instead.

Will: Just ripping the whole fucking thing

Shannon: Your default setting is "brute"

Will: My setting can be whatever the fuck you want it

Shannon: How about off?

Will: You want me to get you off? get your ass on the bed and consider it done.

Shannon: I'm dealing with a probate issue today but thanks anyway

Will: No problem

Will: Kick the asses. Bust the balls.

Will: And when you're done, I'll rip the skirt off and get you out of your mind

THERE WERE ONLY a handful of people who knew I wasn't leading my platoon right now. It wasn't a secret but I wasn't publicizing it either.

Lieutenant General McGardil paid me a visit shortly after a pound of shrapnel was extracted from my arm, back, and shoulder. He notified me I'd received the Medal of Honor as well as the rank of Captain—neither of which felt deserved —and informed me I'd be taking command of a black ops team unofficially housed at a NATO base in Germany. The missions would be classified above top secret. The unit would be composed of the smartest, toughest motherfuckers in the teams. The tactical support would be unlimited but highly covert. The American government would not acknowledge our existence or rescue us if captured, so there was no room for error unless we liked the idea of a televised beheading or Third World labor camp.

But there was one condition: unit commanders had to be mission-ready, and my half-numb arm didn't qualify.

These opportunities didn't come around often. Considering the tragic end to my last mission, it was a shock to find this offer in my lap.

The only thing missing—aside from the fully functional arm—was the interest. I didn't want to load out for another mission. I didn't want to lose another buddy to an endless, bloodthirsty war. I wasn't interested in pounding my trident into another coffin or watching another family accept a crisply folded flag. I didn't want to spend another day staring down evil. I didn't want to live my life on one side of the globe while the woman I needed more than anything else was on the other.

Instead of me deciding where the road would end, the end found me.

I suggested as much to McGardil, and he made it clear he only wanted guys who jumped at the chance to sweat their sac off in his warzone. He sent me to the unit's shrink for a battery of tests. I knew none of this came from post-traumatic stress or survivor's guilt, and the shrink concurred, but McGardil wasn't interested in hearing 'no.'

The plan was simple: get home for some rest and relaxation, give my unreliable trigger finger some time to heal up, and put some hard thought into my future. In the meantime, the Lieutenant General was getting the team in place, and checking in on my ass almost daily.

Aside from McGardil, only Wes and Shannon knew I was hanging out in Boston.

I didn't have the words to explain to either of them why I was here. I only knew that I had to sort through all of this. Was I really walking away from nearly fifteen years of service? From commanding an ultra-classified strike force? What would I even do with myself if I left the military?

For the first time since who knew when —high school? childhood? infancy?—I didn't have a clear path ahead of me. Duty and service were sewn into my genes, and there was never a question about whether I'd enlist after college. I couldn't remember a time when I wasn't counting the minutes until I could be a frogman, and it was more than following my father's footsteps. It was a pure sense of responsibility.

My father—the man who donned the honorary title of commodore in retirement and didn't let a day go by without reading all the military community news and contributing his opinion on several special operations blogs—would find out about this soon enough. He always did. In most situations, he offered sharp insights and valuable perspectives, but I wasn't ready to talk it over with him. He believed in career military men, and while his satisfaction didn't drive my choices, I knew he wouldn't be an objective sounding board on this issue.

Wes was out of the question. Aside from the fact he was probably busy infiltrating the Kremlin, he would love a gig like the one I was being offered. He lived for that shit, and he'd insist I find a new shrink for a second opinion. He'd never let me hear the end of it if he learned I was spending my days washing Shannon's socks and vacuuming her apartment, and not back on base where I could get in the right head-space and train until I bled stars and stripes again. Regardless of how much spin class kicked my ass, it wasn't doing shit to fix my injury.

And Shannon…I suspected she'd spring into action if I told her about the nerve damage in my arm and the cross-roads in my career. She was a fixer. She was Harvey Keitel in *Pulp Fiction*. She'd go into her "I'm calm but this is a fucking crisis" mode, and it wouldn't take her more than a couple of calls to get me appointments with the best doctors in town. And it wouldn't end there. She'd designate herself my chief health advocate, and park herself by my side, taking verbatim notes and firing off questions. Then she'd thumb through her contact list and find someone who owed her a favor, and I'd have a job, or—heaven help me—she'd invent a job at Walsh Associates and put me on her payroll.

But I didn't want to get in line behind Shannon's brothers as one more person who required her to take care of him. I didn't want to rely on her to solve my problems, and not because I took issue with relying on a woman. The issue was with *this* woman. If anything, I wanted her relying on *me*. She already gave enough of herself to her family and their business, and I wasn't going to become one of the things she had to manage.

Someone had to make things easier on her, to lighten her load.

Not that she let that—or anything else—happen without a debate.

We were sleeping together (as in *sleeping*) but every night started with a negotiation of the demilitarized zone in the middle of the bed. I fought it hard at first, but quickly realized it was an unenforceable border. She wasn't accustomed to sleeping on one side of the bed, and always worked her way closer to the middle. I let her have her space, and more often than not woke up with her tucked right into my side.

I wasn't doing well with the post-deployment horny. Getting rid of the Douchelord and reclaiming my space in Shannon's bed were the first victories, but the game was essentially unchanged: she still needed to warm up to me, and she still deserved to be won.

It was good being close to her again. Even if it was jogging through the city or talking over dinner or arguing about a *Game of Thrones* episode, I liked the way she felt in my life.

Now I needed the rest of my world to fall in line with the one I was rebuilding with Shannon.

There was an email waiting in my inbox from Jordan Kaisall. From the subject heading, I knew he was looking for my opinion on hidden gem golf courses near Southern California. I'd take the ocean over greens any day, but he knew my parents were big fans of the game in their retirement.

Kaisall was good when it came to looking at issues from sides I'd never consider. I sent off a few courses to impress his prospective clients, and asked if he'd heard anything about the unit McGardil was assembling. I knew his response would come with another offer to run operation logistics for his private security team, Redtop, and though I wasn't convinced it interested me, I was curious about my options.

That's what I needed: *options*. Being thirty-six and not knowing what I was going to be when I grew up was fucking ridiculous.

Behind Kaisall's email was a message from Gustavo Granovsky. We'd started out in BUD/S together, and he quickly earned the distinction of funniest motherfucker to walk the earth. He found humor in everything, even the dive exercises where the instructors would swim up, put you in a strangle hold, and then tie knots in the oxygen tubing. It left you drowning while fighting off an attacker.

I'll never forget Gus crawling out of the pool wearing full gear, coughing and gagging on the hardtop, and then—with all the seriousness in the world—turning to the instructor and saying, "Sir, if you'd like to grab my dick again, please take me to dinner first. My mother didn't raise me to give it away."

We did two tours together before he was assigned to a different platoon. We never managed to be on the same continent at the same time anymore, but that didn't stop him from sending regular (hilarious) emails to our entire BUD/S class. He was big on staying in touch with people, and that was a quality worth having.

Gus was getting married later this month, finally making it legal with his long-time girlfriend, Aviva. They'd bought a ranch near Poway about seven or eight years ago, where they kept a couple of horses and dogs. A kid, too.

I didn't feel like typing any more emails with one hand, and scrolled through my contacts to find his number.

"How's it hangin', Captain?" Gus asked, his voice loud and tinged with laughter.

"Low and to the left," I said.

"As God intended," he said. "Where the hell are you? And when are you dragging your ass back to San Diego?"

I glanced around Shannon's dining room. It looked like the scene of a swanky dinner party. Light gray wallpaper with a raised velvet pattern covered the walls. There were heavy candelabras running down the middle of the table, and a glass bowl filled with cranberries and limes. *Fucking limes*. The table was long—easily fitting her entire family—and functioned nicely as a staging area for getting my life in line.

"Boston," I said, quickly continuing, "but I'm not advertising that. Just...dealing with some issues."

"Is that why you haven't responded to our goddamn wedding invitation yet? The nuptial event is only two weeks away and my bride is freaking the fuck out over these RSVPs, man."

"I'm monitoring a situation," I said. "I'll have to report back."

"Yeah, my bride's gonna love that," Gus said. "Do you have a timeframe for this situation report? Knowing that the long-term well-being of my testicles hangs in the balance? Literally *hanging*."

Flying to San Diego in two weeks meant leaving Shannon, and I didn't like that idea. "Not really."

Then it dawned on me: I wouldn't have to leave Shannon if she came to California with me. We could spend Thanksgiving together, just like we did last year. Maybe that was what we needed.

Gus sighed. "Do me a favor, man. Figure it out. I don't want to tell Viv that we can't give the caterer a final count yet. She'll make me sleep in the barn, and I won't get—"

"I'll be there," I said. "And I'm bringing someone."

Even if I have to kidnap her. Actually...that might make it more fun.

"Wes got his own invitation," Gus said. "That fucker hasn't responded either."

"Not Wes. A friend. A girlfriend," I said, and I hated the taste of that word immediately. She'd rip my spleen out of my belly button if she heard me stammer through that comment, but that was what I loved about her. She was completely unafraid of reaching into me, tearing out my bleeding organs, and making me look at them.

Women like Shannon weren't girlfriends. I didn't know what the right term was, but *girlfriend* did not fit the bill. She was too bold and sophisticated and independent to be anyone's girlfriend.

"Uh-huh," he murmured. "Should we celebrate you popping your cherry before hitting forty? And this lady isn't in Boston by chance, is she?"

"Yes, she is, but I'm not here because…okay, yeah I'm here for her," I said. "My last mission went to shit, my arm is fucked up, and I'm thinking hard about retirement. On top of that, I left things in shambles with my girlf—err, my Shannon, when I saw her before this deployment. Come back and she's dating a douchebag."

Gus was silent for a moment. "Is your arm okay?"

"Shrapnel. Nerve damage. Trigger finger."

"Shit," he murmured. "Didn't anyone tell you that you're supposed to be good to your lady before going down range?"

I yanked my baseball cap off my head and rubbed my palm against my forehead. "I didn't get that briefing, no," I said.

Another long pause filled only with the rustle of wind and trees on Gus's end. "You serious about retiring? What would you do?"

"Fuck if I know," I said. "On both counts."

"You could probably sell t-shirts at Quiksilver," he said.

"And those cute puka shell necklaces? You'd be good at that. You know, being a surfer boy yourself."

"Thanks for the advice, Gus," I muttered.

"Yeah, it's my calling. Career advice for ex-special ops. I'll give you this consultation on the house, but I'll charge a retainer going forward. Before you ask, no, I don't accept sexual favors." He chuckled to himself, and then continued, "The night before the wedding, a few of us are getting together at The Pub for drinks. Bring your Shannon."

I disconnected and stared at my hands. Aside from old scars and freckles, they looked like mirror images of each other but they couldn't have felt more dissimilar. I never thought numbness would hurt this much. It was like I slept in a strange position and my arm didn't wake up with the rest of me. I kept rubbing and stretching to shake off the prickly chill but it never stopped. There were moments when an avalanche of sensation hit me, and with it came dull throbbing or sharp, fiery pulses. It was awful, but I preferred it to the numbness.

I heard Shannon's key slide into the lock, and when she stepped into the apartment, she was a whirlwind. Spitting fire and five different kinds of furious. She was yelling at someone through her earpiece, and she looked like the most beautiful tactical commander I'd ever seen. Her eyes darted to me without reaction.

"Well I'm sorry, Patrick, but shit happens," she said. "Keep in mind that we're not talking about highly experienced or highly paid personnel. People with years of executive assistant experience do not want to work for a guy who goes through support staff on a seasonal basis."

She marched into the kitchen with her laptop tucked under her arm and started riffling through the refrigerator. It was full, a departure from her usual menu of yogurt and white wine. I took a strange amount of pleasure from engaging in domestic tasks like grocery shopping and fixing squeaky hinges. I even had dinner on the stove.

If all else failed, I was content being Shannon's personal chef and sex slave. That was a life well lived.

"I cannot oversee every single thing your admin does," she said, grabbing a bottle of Riesling. She held it against her body while she opened the laptop and started typing. "And as I've said before, if you can't find a way to communicate without screaming or glaring or otherwise implying she's dumber than stones, we're not going to stop this cycle."

God, I wanted to spend the weekend worshipping her. Tell her *everything*. Find my balls and act like a fucking man.

Instead, I snatched the bottle from her hand and crossed the kitchen to where she kept the corkscrew and glasses.

"I'll handle it. I'll handle it. No—" She dropped her head back and groaned. "*No*. No, Patrick. I'll deal with it, end of story. And if you don't mind, I'm going to hang up now. My patience for your absurd quantity of assistants is exhausting, and if I have to listen to you complain about Roberta for another minute, I'll find you and beat you with a brick." She stabbed her phone's screen repeatedly, and then tossed it to the countertop.

I set the glass beside her and grabbed the cheese tray from the bottom drawer of the refrigerator. There weren't that many markets in Chestnut Hill, and according to Internet commenters, only one with a highly rated cheese department.

"The minions aren't behaving?" I asked. I brought my hands to her shoulders, pressing my thumbs into the knotted muscles there. She leaned into my touch, sighing, and I dropped my lips to her neck. She released a slight purr, but before I could go any further, she shifted away.

"I have to go back to my office," she said, raking her fingers through her hair.

Hands braced on her hips, hair disheveled, and lips twisted in frustration while she tapped her foot on the hardwood, and I'd never been so turned on. I couldn't explain why I liked this girl fired up, but fuck, I did. I really did.

"And then I need to fire Patrick's assistant if I don't kill her first."

Covering the pans and turning off the heat, I said, "I'll come with you."

"Will," she sighed, swiping her hand across her forehead. "This isn't a field trip. Just let me deal with this drama alone."

"No," I said. I tucked her laptop into her bag and swung it over my good shoulder.

She wrapped her scarf around her neck and reached for her coat. "Simple as that? *No*?"

"Yeah," I said.

She wanted to argue with me, but crossed her arms over her chest, marched down the stairs to the curb, and walked toward the Derne Street office.

I followed her up and down several flights of stairs while she collected files, shuffled through a small desk outside a door emblazoned with Patrick's name, and finally settled in a wingback chair in her office while she made a couple of phone calls. This was her kingdom, and right now, she didn't look like a content queen.

She dropped her head to her hands after telling Roberta that she wouldn't be required at Walsh Associates any further. She blew out a heavy breath and turned to her computer. "I just need to reset the garage and door codes, and then shut down her email—"

"You don't have someone to do that for you? Where's Patrick?" He was the only one I liked. He rarely came up in her rants, and he wasn't sleeping with my sister. On that basis alone, he was tolerable. "Shouldn't he be doing this?"

"No," she said, her hands fisting on her desk. "At least, not right now. I handle this shit. That's what I do, Will, I handle all the shit because I'm good at it. Patrick is busy doing his job, and this just needs to get done. I'm not calling any of my team in to handle anything when I'm right here."

Shannon thought I wanted to change her, but that wasn't accurate. Saving the world was her gig, and I wasn't about to take that away from her. However, there was a difference between saving the world and cleaning out an assistant's desk on a Friday night.

I knew her family was everything to her, and I knew she was convinced that tending to their every need was her only purpose in life, and that was where I couldn't get on board.

While Shannon typed, I explored her office.

I was hungry for information about her, and since our conversations were only gradually moving out of superficial territory, I was forced to draw my intel from environment. I knew she had at least fifteen magazine subscriptions but didn't seem to read any. I'd first encountered her sin drawer last summer, but I dedicated an afternoon last week to categorizing the firepower and style of her sex toys. She had seven different types of salt in her kitchen—Hawaiian sea, smoked sea, flaky Maldon, fleur de sel, kala namak, black truffle, and kosher—but neither cinnamon nor sugar. She didn't like talking before dawn and changed out of her work clothes as soon as she got home. There were three different blow dryers and four different curling irons in her bathroom, and she kept a box of her mother's journals in her closet. I wouldn't have noticed the box if her pajamas weren't piled around it.

The office was equally intriguing. I glanced at the glass wall separating her office from the bullpen. From her desk, she could see Tom's alcove, the small room where her assorted assistants worked, Riley and Matt's offices, and the stairs. Of course she'd want to preside over it all.

There were photos from the Boston Marathon finish line going back six years, always with her four brothers and Shannon in the middle. Little geodes dotted her bookshelf. I spotted the framed magazine spread hanging near her windows and laughed out loud. It was classic Shannon—perfect red hair, perfect purple dress, perfect girl-boss pose, and the perfect headline. "'The Hand That Holds it Down', huh? Who holds you down?"

"That's pretty rapey, William. Thanks for that." She continued banging away at her keyboard.

"Not rapey," I said, frowning. Her body didn't lie in the night, not when she was unconsciously arching into me and wrapping herself around me. She was strung tight, aching for release, and I wanted her to let me take care of her. "Not even close. But tell me this: how hard would you come for me if I fucked you up against that glass wall? If you had to let go of everything and give it all to me?"

She was tapping her foot again, the heel clacking hard against the wood floor. I could almost see the disdain rolling off her in waves. "Like, how is that an acceptable comment?"

I rounded the desk and leaned in, bracing my hands on either side of her, my short beard scruff rasping against her ear. "When I can see how much you want it."

Her breath hitched and I knew—I fucking knew it—it was exactly what she needed.

"Finish what you're doing and then I'm taking you home." I didn't need to say another word. I didn't need to add that she'd be too busy surrendering to worry about anything else.

However, I couldn't think about that until we were home. It wasn't like I could stand beside her with my semi and expect anything more than an elbow to the nuts. She wasn't leaving until she was finished, and it was up to me to reconcile that reality.

I parked myself in a pale purple velvet chair and snatched one of the regional magazines piled on the small conference table. The cover boasted an exclusive peek at one of Sam's newest builds, and despite my biases about the man, I found it interesting.

"I need to leave a few things for Tom, and then we can go," Shannon said.

I followed her out, waiting while she marked files with sticky notes and arranged them on his desk. Pointing to a framed photograph, I asked, "Is that Tom?"

Shannon glanced over then went back to her notes. "Yeah, that's him at Machu Picchu. He likes going places to climb things."

"He's been with you a while, right?"

The air was crisp when we reached the ground floor, and wind whipped through the narrow street while Shannon set the alarm. "Six years," she said.

"You don't talk about him much." She yawned, pulled her coat tight to her chest, and leaned into me when I draped my arm over her shoulder. It was late and she was tired, but all I could think about was her skin against mine.

I'd settle for another celibate night if we could do it with fewer clothes.

That was a lie. There could be no celibacy with nakedness.

"It's not easy straddling the line between friend and boss," she said. "He's like family—of course he is, he lived with me—but he's also not, and that adds some layers. We had to suffer through some tense times before we found the right balance."

"He lived with you?"

"Mmm." She ducked deeper into her coat to avoid the wind. "His parents were terrible, hateful creatures. They sent him to all sorts of reeducation camps to pray the gay out of him. When that didn't work, they shipped him off to a boarding school that was basically hard labor and solitary confinement."

"That's awful," I said. It wasn't lost on me that this was the exact fear Wes lived with. There wasn't a labor camp in his future, but he was avoiding this reaction. And he wasn't a kid on his way to homophobic bible study; he was a thirty-four year old Navy SEAL.

"Completely. He tried to fake straight, but they were convinced he—and I quote—had the devil in him. They kicked him out and said he wasn't their son, and blah blah blah he lived with me for a bit."

"'Blah blah blah'?"

"I owed an assistant district attorney a favor, and one night she needed a public defender," she said. "He'd been arrested for trespassing. He'd been sleeping in a garage. I got the case thrown out and his record scrubbed, and I took him home with me."

In the elevator, I asked Shannon, "What else do you collect?"

"What do you mean?"

I shrugged. "You've got lost causes and dilapidated homes, broken souls, everything purple, and the geodes. And gourmet salt. Oh, and vibrators. And the bracelets! Those fucking annoying little bracelets."

She tossed her hair over her shoulder as she marched toward her apartment. "Don't be rude," she said. "You're one of my lost causes."

I leaned against the wall while she unlocked the door, watching the way her fingers moved over the knob. She glanced back at me when she stepped inside, and it was possible she was speaking but the only thing I could hear was my pulse hammering in my veins.

She hung her coat in the closet and kicked her shoes to the corner while I secured the locks. I noticed every one of the quick glimpses she shot in my direction, and I followed her into the bedroom.

She wanted this. She needed this. She needed *me*.

Reaching out, I caught her around the waist and dragged her against my chest. "You've been thinking about it, haven't you?" I asked. My fingers moved over her shoulder and down her chest, loosening her buttons until the shirt hung open. "About me taking you."

"Your ego continues to get in the way of rational thought, William."

She was working hard to keep her voice steady, but much like I could feel her body humming under my touch, she couldn't hide any of it from me. "Mmmm," I sighed, pressing my face into her hair and pulling in a deep breath as I shucked her shirt. "You don't need to worry about any more rational thoughts, peanut."

The skirt's zipper hissed as I drew it down, and when I released my hold on the fabric, Shannon was left in stockings and a bra. That bra was off and flying across the room before I formed a memory of the beige lace against her skin. My fingers dipped inside the stockings, pausing to press my fingertips into her hips for one sweet moment, and then I yanked them down to her ankles. "Kneel," I said.

"Your playbook is exceptionally limited," she said, crossing her arms under her breasts. "Kneeling or against the wall. It's really time to diversify."

My hands traveled up her torso, shifting her arms until she gripped either elbow behind her back. I cupped her breasts, groaning as my palms rubbed over her taut nipples. "You're adorable with your tough girl act," I said. My lips mapped her shoulders, neck, jaw, and it wasn't enough. I wanted to consume her, own her until I erased every minute of distance between us. Until she knew she possessed me in every way possible.

I walked Shannon toward the bed and pressed the small of her back until she was bent over, face down on the duvet. I wove the discarded stockings around her arms and shoulders, crossing them between her breasts, and tied them with a square knot. "All good?"

She murmured into the duvet, "This is new."

"You asked for diversification," I said. Two quick spanks landed low on her ass, and I panted as her skin bloomed with a bright flush. I wanted a million things right now—everything, all of it, anything to satiate the raw desire inside me—but what I wanted most was to feel her against my tongue again. "Remember that bed in Taos? When I tied your hands to the headboard with my belt?"

I dropped to my knees, and kissed from the backs of her knees to her ass, biting and licking and stamping every inch of this woman on my soul. She was moaning and wiggling, and issued orders to stop dicking around and lick her pussy already, but I made her wait. She was mad as hell and swearing into the blanket, and when my tongue circled her clit, I nearly came in my jeans.

Her legs were shaking within minutes, and when my fingers slipped inside, her words melted into a choked cry. I felt the pulse of her orgasm against my lips and the shock-waves on my fingers. She dug her shoulders into the bed as I licked her through the spasms, and she begged me to *stop*, to *keep going*, to give her *more* and *harder*, and *there* and *no, no, no more*.

"How was that?" I asked. I stroked her thighs while her breathing slowed, kissing my favorite freckle patches and dropping soft spanks on her ass.

Shannon's shoulders shook as she laughed. "Borderline hallucinogenic."

"Wait, was that a compliment?" I yanked my shirt over my head and kicked off my jeans, almost tripping myself in the frantic blur of arousal. I pressed myself against her, sighing as her skin triggered a burst of heat and affection into my blood. It was like the thrill of jumping out of an aircraft and tumbling through the sky, but better.

"Such a whore for praise," Shannon said. I spanked her backside a bit harder, and helped her shift to the center of the bed. Seeing her bound and kneeling...there weren't words to describe the jolting rush of adoration I felt for this woman.

"You know it," I said.

With Shannon's back and bound arms against my chest, I teased myself against her clit. Her hips rolled, quickly finding a rhythm, and I was sliding into her, a little farther with each pass. "Want you," she gasped.

"Me? Or somebody?" It wasn't the kind of question that belonged in the bedroom when light bondage and just the tip were involved, but it was the one I needed answered.

"What? You need me to unburden my heart before you'll fuck me?" she asked, angling her hips to take me deeper. "You want me to tell you how much I need you and crave you and can't survive without your gigantic cock?"

"I just want to know whether you want to escape it all with someone, or with me."

Shannon hummed as my cock slipped out and over her clit. She dropped her head against my shoulder as I positioned myself against her heat, and she whispered, "I've only *ever* escaped with you."

My brain wanted me to slam into her and fuck her until she couldn't walk right, but some other part reminded me to go slow, to enjoy this. She sank down, and we stayed there, kissing, muscles trembling, whispering about how good it felt until the urge to move was overwhelming.

We rocked together, *slow slow slow*, and my world was this bed, this woman.

"Will. More," Shannon groaned, clenching around me.

I found a faster rhythm, and brought one hand up to cup her breast and the other to her clit. The early convulsions of her orgasm were like a sexy, tingly embrace from an old friend, one that unwound the tension of space and time and brought it all back to the connection that was deeper than sex, deeper than desire. I felt it in my balls, and then that sensation spiraled up and down my spine, teetering on the edge of explosion. A hard thrust stole a groan from me, and I matched it with a quick slap to her clit.

"Come for me," I said against her ear. "Let go for me."

I slapped her again, and her sigh twisted into beautiful, breathy wail. The flood of heat and spasm triggered my orgasm, and I folded Shannon into my arms as I emptied myself into her. We fell to the bed, still panting and moaning, and not wanting to leave her constricted too long, I loosened the knot at her back. Lines and grooves marked her skin, and I dragged my lips over each one. Those kisses told her how much I missed her, how thinking of her got me through the worst of this deployment, and none of the issues in my life were greater than what I felt for her right now, even if my words didn't.

"Why do you do that?" she asked, her voice heavy with exhaustion as I kissed the indentation between her breasts. "Why do you like tying me up?"

I traced the crossed lines on her chest, and a touch of remorse gathered in my gut. I wanted to mark her in a primal, club-her-over-the-head way but I didn't want to hurt her. "Because it quiets you down," I said. "There's so much in your head, all that noise and stress. Forcing you to obey me turns it off, and I'm selfish. I want you all for myself."

"Damn," she murmured. "I was hoping for some story about discovering a rope fetish in your baby SEAL days. Or some *Top Gun* sexytimes with a hot instructor, and instead of fighter jets, it's knot tying?"

"Yeah, no hot instructors. No sexytimes," I said.

She dipped her chin down before speaking. "I'm selfish, too. For you." She hesitated and glanced away, her teeth pressed into her lower lip. "Before me...did you always?"

"No, Shannon," I said.

"No long, sordid history of breaking hearts and destroying tights?"

"None of that," I laughed. "You've broken hearts, though."

She shook her head, frowning. "The closest I've ever come to such a thing is blocking creepy boys on Internet dating sites." Her fingers brushed over my shoulder, and her eyes followed the jagged scars. "These are new."

Nodding, I rolled to my side and pulled Shannon to my chest. I'd ignored the pain in my arm while I was inside her, but now, without the pleasure of her body to drive it away, I was sore. "Not every mission goes to plan." She opened her mouth to say something but a low rumble from her belly beat her to it. "I made spaghetti."

"You are too freaking handy, commando," she said. "Fixing the bathroom sink. Cooking spaghetti. Bondage with tights. Destroying my vagina."

We ate in bed, sitting shoulder-to-shoulder, while watching the last half of the second season of *Game of Thrones*. Everything felt new, different, as if I'd only now—in *this* iteration of us—earned the right to steal tomatoey kisses or rest my hand on her inner thigh while debating plot points.

"We're going to San Diego," I said while the next episode launched, "in two weeks."

"Thanksgiving is in two weeks," she said. "I have commitments here."

"We're going to San Diego." I tilted her chin up and gazed into her eyes. "I recall you getting out of those commitments just fine last year."

"I'M GOING to murder your phone," I whispered into Shannon's hair. That buzzing was annoying enough to bruise my brain. "No more phones in the bedroom."

"Mmm, it's my alarm," she mumbled. She twisted away from me to reach for the side table. I caught her around the waist and hauled her back to my side once the noise ceased.

"Sleep, baby," I said. Her skin was warm beneath my lips, and I wanted to kiss every freckle on her back. "It's too early."

"There's a little something nudging my thigh," she said.

I shifted, fitting my cock to her backside. "Nothing little here." My hand slipped up her leg and settled between her hipbones, rocking her against me. "I'm keeping you in this bed all day."

Shannon reached over and patted my leg. "That's a really nice idea," she said.

Her hand ran down my leg, squeezing, and then her nails scratched back up. It was such a simple, unassuming gesture, and yet, it had my body fizzing with awareness. The battle for Shannon's affection was the hardest I'd ever fought, and it wasn't over, but it was turning the corner.

"But I have to meet your sister for lunch," she said with a sigh. "So, if you don't mind—" She wiggled against my cock, and laughed when I groaned into her back. "—I'll be going."

"I do mind," I said, sliding my hand between her legs. "I'll call Lo. Explain the circumstances. She'll understand."

"I'm in enough trouble with her over skipping lunches." Shannon arched into me, and fuck…she felt incredible. Hot and precious and mine. All mine. Always mine. "You really should tell her you're here," she said, her words breaking as I found the spot that made her mindless.

I leaned over to look at Shannon. Eyes closed, lips parted,

forehead wrinkled. Exactly as I wanted her. "You'd like me to stop? And call my sister? That's what you want right now, peanut?"

"If you don't fuck me right now, I'm going to beat you with a dildo," she said, her fists curling tight around the sheets. "You can call your sister later."

"Yes, ma'am," I said.

Twenty-Three

LAUREN and I started meeting for lunch on Saturday mornings more than two years ago. When we learned a local winemaker offered free samples at the farmers' market, we added that to the agenda. Basically, we were game for anything that involved weekend day drinking. Andy, on the other hand, was more interested in the fruits and vegetables and other farm goodies. Tiel didn't seem to appreciate the wine or the goodies.

Sometimes I passed on the market and met them for lunch. Other times, when I was open housing or pretending my best friend's brother wasn't quartered in my apartment and conquering my pussy, I skipped altogether. In my mind, my absences in recent months weren't noteworthy until Andy, Lauren, *and* Tiel all made it clear they wanted to see me today.

And I did miss spending time with them. I didn't understand how to make friends with adults until Lauren decided to teach me. Shy was the last thing anyone would call me, but after high school and college, it was really difficult to find friends. I wasn't especially good at it then, but without the structure of schooling to force people into social situations, I was stuck walking up to someone in the coffee shop and saying, "Hey, we ordered the same beverage. Shall we explore other commonalities?"

Growing up with brothers also meant I was less skilled in the area of female bonding, and working in a male-dominated field only compounded that situation. I didn't have much practice from childhood, either. Things were different when I was little, before my mother died, but there wasn't room in my life after.

But now I had these ladies, and they were expecting me for lunch. They didn't know that I had a demanding boy in my bed, and though I was occasionally desperate to unload this story on someone who could tell me what to do with all these wildly contradictory feelings, it was better leaving certain things unsaid.

I wasn't looking to keep secrets. Yeah, in the beginning, I didn't see any reason to bother Lauren with this, but that was when it was one night...and then things got messy and complicated, and it ended. And now—whatever this was, wherever we were in this loop of sex and insults and ocean-wide affection that I wasn't ready to address—I needed more time to make sense of these pieces. Even if I wanted to tell Lauren, why would I drag her into this chaos? There was no golden future for Will and me. This thing wasn't going to work out. Our lives were rooted on opposite coastlines. And I knew he'd leave again soon. My best guess, based on his complete lack of open communication, was that he'd be heading back to base after San Diego. I could cope with the continuous cycle of deployments and the heart-numbing fear they delivered, but that didn't change the fact that Will's life wasn't in Boston. That wasn't something I could ask of him, and leaving here wasn't something I could offer.

We had this morsel of now, and I didn't want to share it.

I was blow-drying my hair when Will edged into the bathroom. A towel was slung around his hips and beads of water sparkled on his chest, and there was nothing wrong with that picture. Nothing at all.

"There's someone here for you," he said.

My eyes traveled the hills and valleys of his abs, and I asked, "Should I interpret that to mean you opened the door like this?"

I gestured toward the towel. It was the biggest one in my linen closet, but it still didn't cover all that…girth. It peeked open mid-thigh and, if he moved the right way, showed off a bit more.

"It looks like you're having impure thoughts, peanut."

Very impure. "No, I'm just wondering why you're using a hand towel when there are plenty of bath sheets. Is this an illusion to make your dick look bigger? Oh, and don't talk to strangers when you're ninety percent nude. My neighbors already give me the side-eye, and now they're going to think I'm shooting porn in here or keeping a sex slave."

He rolled his eyes and hooked a thumb over his shoulder. "The door?"

I walked past him, patting his damp chest, and eyed the scars on his shoulder. They covered his back and arm, too. I noticed them last night, and they didn't look any less awful this morning. Long, jagged cuts traversed the rise of his collarbone and down his back, and there were dents and divots where smooth, strong skin once existed. It was worse than the flesh wound, much worse, and I wanted him to tell me what happened.

"We should get some vitamin E on that," I said, eyeing the raised, red lines that looked recently sutured. He grumbled something about real men not needing vitamin E.

"That's right," I said. "They just grab their nut sacks and will themselves back to health. Let me know how that turns out for you."

When I approached the entryway, I expected to find a delivery requiring my signature or a kid selling Girl Scout cookies. I didn't expect my future sister-in-law.

"Oh, hi," I said, shooting a fiery glance at Will. "How are you?"

Tiel looked between me and Will, a goofy grin on her face. "Didn't mean to interrupt anything…"

I pointed at Will. "You mean him? No. Ignore him. He's not actually here, and therefore you're not interrupting anything."

"Right, right," she said. We all stared at each other for a bizarre moment before Tiel held her hands out as if she finally remembered why she dropped by. "I drank the biggest cappuccino ever and now it's all in my bladder and since I was in this neighborhood I figured I'd stop in because Sam has me convinced that public restrooms are a breeding ground for all kinds of grossness and they probably are, but seriously, should I just not pee ever? No, that's ridiculous, so I stopped here. Can I use your bathroom?"

"Yeah, of course," I said. I gestured toward the hall, glaring at Will's glistening chest and the towel barely stretching across his thick thighs. His eyes followed Tiel as she darted into the bathroom, pinging back to me in question. "Sam's fiancée."

"Isn't Sam the preppy one?"

"Yes," I said. "And would it kill you to dry your chest?"

He ignored me. "And that's his fiancée?"

"Yes," I repeated, brushing the water away. It was also a fair excuse to fondle him.

"The same one? From last winter?"

"Yes," I said.

"So everything worked out after the near-death experience," he said. "He turned out okay, they got back together... the world didn't end?"

I ran my fingers over the beard that was coming in on his jaw. I couldn't stop touching him, as if I was starving for the feel of his skin under mine. "Yes, Will. Everyone lived happily ever after."

Tiel reappeared a minute later and paused in front of Will, who decided it was necessary to lean against the wall like he was shooting a goddamn cologne ad.

"Hi," he said. "Will."

"Tiel," she replied with a wide-eyed glance in my direction.

"Scheduled sex," I said, and her face morphed into a knowing—if not surprised—expression.

"That's why you've been skipping the farmers' market," she said. "You've got enough eggplant here."

"Aren't you a bundle of hilarious today? I'll meet you there," I said, my words giving her a firm shove out the door. She waved goodbye, and Will let out a low chuckle. "'Scheduled sex'?"

"Everyone gets a nickname around here," I said, heading to my room to finish getting ready.

"Whatever happened to Captain America?" he asked, following close behind.

"I don't think Captain America ever destroyed a pair of Wolford tights tying a girl up," I said from inside my closet.

He braced his hands over the door, and that position shifted his towel lower until the imagination wanted for little. "Nice guys can't enjoy some kink?"

I rummaged through a pile of jeans before I found the ones I wanted. "Are we talking about nice guys, or are talking about you?" I asked, snagging a pair of panties and a bra. "Because I recall you telling me that the last thing you were was nice."

Will moved away from the door and stepped inside the closet. He ran his knuckles down the lapel of my robe, stopping when he reached the knot at my waist. It loosened, and he trailed his fingers up my belly and between my breasts.

"You don't want nice," he said, his thumbs stroking my nipples. "You kick the shit out of nice. You fight dirty and you fuck dirty, and you only want someone who can operate at that level, too."

"And you're saying you're up for the challenge?"

"You still don't know the answer to that?" His hands shifted to my face and he kissed me, fast and hard. It felt like a punishment and tasted like a promise.

THERE WERE tiny bruises forming on my hips from Will's fingertips, my closet was a disaster, and I was very late for lunch, but the orgasm was worth it. Will smacked my ass and promised to fix the wreckage while I scrambled out the door. My phone was loaded with texts inquiring into my whereabouts and providing detailed directions to the group's table in the café, and it didn't stop chirping with alerts while I drove to the farmers' market.

I tugged my hair into a knot and hid the irritation on my

neck—a gift from Will's beard scruff—with scarf I found in the backseat, and hoped my appearance didn't scream "well-fucked."

The market was filled with slow-moving shoppers, and it drained every ounce of my remaining patience. When I found myself trapped behind a gaggle of hippie-stroller moms, I almost turned around and went home. If I wasn't completely certain Lauren would come looking for me, I would have been back in my car by now.

They eventually broke formation, and I made my way to the café. I slipped past the people waiting for tables, and spotted the group in the far corner. Andy noticed me first, and waved me over.

"I hate lube," Lauren said as I approached the table. "It's gross and I hate it."

"Hey, sorry I'm late," I said, settling beside Andy. I frowned in Lauren's direction. "And what the hell did you just say?"

"Why would anyone hate lube? It's glorious," Andy said. She handed me a mimosa. "We ordered for you."

"Yes, it's very useful, and I don't have a problem asking for a helping hand when I need it or when things are getting a *lot* of use, but..." Lauren held up her hands in frustration and wiggled in her seat. "Sometimes, it sticks around for too long. It feels slimy, like it needs to be power-washed off. Or worse, it dries everything out."

I watched while Tiel guzzled her drink, and I knew she was probably dying of Walsh information overload. She didn't realize that Lauren and Andy shared *everything* with each other, but that didn't make her subject to the same expectations. And it wasn't like this was easy for me, either. These conversations were only acceptable when I pretended these women weren't having sex with my brothers. In my mind, different celebrities or athletes happily warmed my friends' beds, and I didn't have to think about my brothers' penchants for growling or biting.

"Perhaps you're using too much," I said.

"Or the wrong kind," Andy said. "We only use coconut oil."

Tiel snort-laughed, then slapped a hand over her mouth. "Sorry, what the fuck did you just say?" she asked.

I watched while Andy turned a slow gaze in Tiel's direction. She was intimidating as hell, and there were still times when I found her chilly expressions and fierce cheekbones disarming.

"Coconut oil," Andy repeated. "It's completely organic and edible, and it's also antimicrobial and—"

"Okay, wait. You keep a jar of coconut oil in the bedroom?" Lauren asked. "You don't run into the kitchen every time, and oh God, tell me you have separate jars for sex and food."

Andy rubbed her temples and sighed. "Yes, we have a jar in the bedroom, and a completely separate jar in the kitchen. It never feels slimy and I'm told it tastes good, too."

Lauren sat back and tapped her fingers against her chin. "It doesn't make you feel dry or sticky afterward?" Andy shook her head. "Does it work for the backdoor, too? I need something that's good on both the backdoor and the downtown."

"All your neighborhoods and doors are covered," Andy said.

"I'm so confused right now," Tiel murmured.

"This isn't a vegan joke, right? If I go to your apartment

this afternoon, am I going to find a jar of sex-only coconut oil in your drawer?" Lauren asked Andy.

"No," she said, "you'll find it in Patrick's drawer. He's in charge of lube."

"Holy fuck," I murmured. I kept forcing that eye candy wide receiver from the New England Patriots into my mind but my brother, armed with a jar of all-natural lube, a wooden spoon, and a dumb grin, continued to reappear. "I might need to bleach my brain now."

Tiel caught my eye, and she sent me a sympathetic smile. "Do they know about Scheduled Sex?" she asked, gesturing to Lauren and Andy.

No no no no.

"Tiel, sweetie," I said. It was her way of changing the topic, and it was a kind gesture but it had my stomach audibly gurgling.

"No, you should tell them," she continued. "She has the hottest guy in her apartment right now. That man was delicious. Were those military tattoos? The anchor on his chest looked familiar, like a Navy tattoo, but the one on his arm, the frog skeleton—"

"Stop!" I sprung to my feet, my hands outstretched in Tiel's direction as I tried to catch the words tumbling out of her mouth and shove them back in. "Stop right there and don't ever say another word as long as you live."

The waiter chose that moment to arrive with our meals. He spent an entire lifetime setting the plates down, and then asked no fewer than six hundred questions before stepping away.

It took full minutes for my body to relax enough to return to my seat. Tiel was studying the tabletop as if her life depended on it, and Andy and Lauren wouldn't stop staring at me.

I picked all the avocado out of my salad and onto a saucer, then handed it to Andy before meeting their gazes. We were changing topics *now*.

"Why don't you tell us about the wedding plans, Tiel," I said.

Her head snapped up, her eyes wide. "Um," she started, "we're waiting until after we visit my parents in New Jersey to make any decisions because we don't know whether they're going to be happy and insist on a traditional Greek wedding or pretend I don't exist or some other, more ridiculous option. We're going there in a couple weeks, for Thanksgiving, or…the Greek version of Thanksgiving that my family does, which is pretty odd as far as Thanksgivings go and I'm worried that Sam won't eat the entire time we're there."

"Go to Juice Box in Southie and get some smoothies made up for the trip," I said.

Andy held up her hands for timeout. "Pause. Rewind. Who is this bare-chested, tatted man?" she asked. "Not Gerard, right?"

Tiel pressed her fingers to her lips as uncomfortable laughter bubbled up. These weren't the baby steps she preferred, not with the lube and the yelling. I was putting money down on her declining all future invitations.

"No," I said.

I made the mistake of looking at Lauren then, and her smile told me she was putting the pieces together. It was easy to underestimate her. She had the happy California girl thing going for her, and that came saddled with a sweetness that could rot teeth. But she was smart and perceptive, and pushed people exactly as much as they could handle.

She'd peppered a few off-handed comments about Will into conversations last summer, after Montauk, and then some more after the holidays in Mexico. It put me on guard at the time, but I'd convinced myself it was normal chatter and I was being hypersensitive.

"Right, okay. Since we're skipping *that* topic, let's go back to Greek Thanksgiving. That sounds a lot like Persian Christmas with my Jewish mother," Andy said, laughing. "And it's funny because Persians aren't usually hot on Christmas but I'm a mutt so it's all good. I'm a little obsessed with our secular version of Christmas, actually."

"Oh, okay," Tiel, said. "Maybe we can talk about our biracial holiday experiences some other time. I think I might have broken Shannon. Or, Lauren. Or both of them."

The way Lauren was staring at me now told me none of it was off-handed. "We're going to chat very soon," she said. "You and me, Miss Shannon. You and me."

———

"I HAVE A NEW STRATEGY," I said to Tom on Monday morning. "Patrick's getting two assistants. They can fight it out *Survivor* style." Tom rolled his eyes. "Here are their résumés—Dylan the Girl and Lissa Wynn—and I want you to block time on your calendar to train them."

"This will be amusing," he murmured. He was patronizing me in that *my boss is crazy and I go along with whatever she says* way, and it was a regular feature in our relationship. He passed me a stack of messages before I headed to the weekly status meeting.

I cursed every one of the steep stairs leading to the attic conference room. The stones were old and worn, some wobbled against the grout, and each one was a subtle suggestion for me to go home, crawl under the covers, and hide out with Will all day. After lunch at the farmers' market and an unusually radio-silent weekend, I had no idea what to expect from everyone this morning.

"I'm going to die on those stairs," I announced when I reached the conference room. Patrick, Sam, Matt, and Andy were already seated. "One of these days, I'm going to plummet to my death, just you wait."

"And good morning to you too, Shannon," Matt said.

"What exactly are you concerned about?" Patrick asked.

"Guys, I think some of these stones are loose," Riley shouted from the staircase. He bounded into the room and dusted off his knees before sitting down. "I slipped, and dropped my burrito." He held up a foil-wrapped cylinder. "It's a little smashed but I think it's still good."

I pointed to Riley. "That. That is my concern."

"Okay," Patrick said, typing a note into his spreadsheet. "No one die on the stairs today, please."

Patrick: isn't it a little early for you to be hitting the liquor?
Shannon: there are some legitimately loose stones. I'm not drunk.
Patrick: whatever…

The meeting churned along as they always did. Matt and Sam argued about structural issues. Patrick and Andy carried on an entirely silent conversation. Riley produced a bottle of hot sauce from his pocket and proceeded to demolish his breakfast burrito. He was set on bringing increasingly obnoxious snacks since the yogurt fiasco, but the rest of us were united in ignoring it.

Without fail, we turned the corner on the final twenty minutes of our time together, and business items were traded for family discussions.

"Tiel and I are heading to New Jersey next week," Sam said. He gestured to me, and I was suddenly curious what she mentioned about our time together this past weekend. She had plenty to work with, and those two lived under a ride-or-die honesty pact. "I know she told you on Saturday."

"Did she say anything else?" I asked.

Sam's forehead wrinkled and he shook his head. "No, I don't think so. She thought it was weird that you fed Andy your avocado, and then there was something about coconut oil...but that was it. Was there something else?"

"No, nothing at all," Andy said, and I appreciated the fuck out of her right now. "You know how I am about avocado. It's my favorite good fat, and you can blame me for the coconut oil, too."

"What did you do?" Patrick whispered to her. She patted his arm, smiling.

Shannon: I just want you to know, I survived the mother of all awkward conversations on Saturday and you probably owe me the biggest bottle of champagne or something sparkly because of it
Patrick: Yeah I'm beginning to understand that
Patrick: Sorry about that

"Are we doing Thanksgiving at your place?" Matt asked, pointing his coffee cup in my direction. "Is that still your show?"

Shannon: Don't kill me
Patrick: What now

"Actually," I started, "I won't be around."

Yelling was our native tongue, but when we tipped over from routinely unruly conversation into a verbal stampede, someone was always at the epicenter. There was nothing to do but ride it out. Words flew like grenades but the noise was such that the explosions often went unnoticed. It didn't happen often, but when it did, it was always preceded by a long pause, as if everyone was drawing a deep breath, squaring up, and gathering their fighting strength.

A quick assessment of the table told me that was exactly what was happening right now.

Tick, tick, boom.

Patrick: "What? Where are you going?"

Matt: "Why do you find it necessary to wait until the last fucking moment to tell us this, Shan?"

Sam: "Too many fucking secrets around here."

Riley: "What ever happened to our traditions? I demand turkey and pie and football and gluttony."

Andy: "Do you think you could give me your butternut squash pie recipe?"

Patrick: "Are we cancelling the pub crawl, too?"

Sam: "Since when did you become such a fan of traveling, Shannon?"

Riley: "We could go to Gigi's family's dinner. They have plenty of room and they aren't assholes who change plans at the last minute."

Andy: "I'll handle the pub crawl. It's not like Shannon's the only one who can pick out a couple bars."

Patrick: "Let's be reasonable: it's not like we were having

Thanksgiving at Shannon's place forever. We're not kids anymore. She's the only one who can manage a tradition."

Sam: "Wait. *Gigi*? As in Roof Garden Girl, Gigi? Magnolia, Gigi?"

Matt: "Shannon's blown us off two years in a row. We can't really call it a tradition anymore. More like abandonment."

Andy: "Everyone can come to us. We'll find the space."

Riley: "Yeah, Gigi's my bro. My homeboy."

Sam: "I'm suddenly thrilled to be spending the holiday in suburban New Jersey."

Matt: "Erin's in Iceland. Or Greenland. Wherever the volcanoes are, but it's relatively quick flight. I could probably convince her to fly in for the weekend."

Riley: "Nick will enjoy that."

Patrick: "Shannon has the best space for it, but it was fine at Matt's last year. Or the fire house."

Matt: "Why would *Nick* enjoy Erin flying in for the weekend?"

Sam: "That would not be my assessment of Gigi."

Riley: "Don't leave the good doctor unsupervised unless you have a shotgun handy."

Andy: "Tell me we are not still talking about Roof Garden Girl. I'm obligated to cut a bitch after what she did to Tiel."

Matt: "We'll do it. We have the space."

Riley: "Gigi is good people. Good people make mistakes. Let it go."

Patrick: "Motherfuck, how are we still talking about roof gardens?"

Riley: "Are we having Spanish food again? That feels like a real Throwback Thursday, and throwing all the way back to the Spanish monarchy. I like that shit."

Patrick: "We could get Korean barbeque. There's a little place that Andy and I love—"

Sam: "Stop it with the Korean barbeque. You're being ridiculous. Nobody eats kimchi on Thanksgiving."

Matt: "Someone tell me what we're doing so I can text my wife."

Patrick: "That seems like a generalization I'm not willing to make. Korean barbeque is better than turkey, hands down."

Riley: "I think I have a migraine now. A belly ache, too."

I set my coffee cup on the table and whistled for their attention. "All right. Listen. Patrick's ordering the meal. Matt and Lauren are hosting. Andy is handling the Black Friday pub crawl. Sam is going to stop being a mouthy bitch right now. Riley isn't dicking around with Roof Garden Girl because we *all* agreed to break up with her after she molested Sam. And I'm turning off my phone and going to California next Wednesday morning. Despite my travels, your delicate, tender lives will go on without incident, and you will realize that tradition has nothing to do with where your mashed potatoes are served. If anyone has any problems with any of that, I have a giant bag of old dicks rotting in my office, and you're welcome to juggle them until you get the fuck over it. Any questions?"

Matt raised his hand, and I definitely growled at him. "Can someone clarify why I should be watching Nick? And why I'd need a shotgun for that?"

I turned my gaze toward Riley. "Shut down the snarky comments." Folding my hands on the table, I looked to Matt. "You'd best be keeping your ear to the ground if Erin does make an appearance."

Shannon: My brothers just had a conniption about thanksgiving

Will: You can't tell me this shit and not expect me to hate them

Shannon: I want you to understand that I'm being pulled in different directions

Will: If there is anything I understand about you, it's that

Will: When you get home tonight, you're getting undressed, spreading your legs, and telling me all about your day while I lick your pussy

Will: No more worries about any of it, peanut.

Shannon: I've heard worse ideas.

Will: Question

Shannon: Yes, I am wearing panties.

Will: That wasn't the question but...I'll expect to have those panties in my hand when you're home

Will: Don't make me tell you twice

Shannon: Oh really?

Will: Are you looking to test me?

Shannon: Perhaps

Will: Do you have any flat shoes? Ones you'd wear to work?

Shannon: Yes but I really don't want you defiling my shoes

Will: Good. Just checking.

Shannon: Why?

Will: Because you're not going to be walking right when I'm done with you. Can't risk breaking an ankle in those heels

Shannon: Idle threats

Will: Hang on a minute. Let me add "buy rope and gag" to my list of things to do this afternoon

———

"HOW ARE Lissa Wynn and Dylan the Girl doing?"

Patrick turned a baleful frown in my direction, and I pressed my fist to my mouth to stifle a laugh. He was *hating* this. "They're my shadows, Shannon. They wait at the door when I use the bathroom. Seriously. They were standing there, with their little notebooks open, earlier this week, and I guess I should've been happy they stayed outside. What the fuck did you say to them?"

"They're attentive. Eager," I said. "That's good. Do you know which one is Lissa Wynn and which is Dylan the Girl?"

He squinted at the spreadsheet on his screen, and he murmured, "Not yet."

"Maybe you've needed two assistants all along," I said, pointing at him with my pen. "This could work out beautifully, and you can stop growling and kicking things. Just think of the money we'll save on new copiers."

"Yeah, we're finished discussing this," he said, rolling his eyes. "Have you talked to Sam much?"

"We checked in on the Turlan project last week," I said, yawning. Our regular budget meeting had been rescheduled three times this week, and now, late Friday evening, we were finally wrapping up cost structures for the Mount Vernon project. Matt was going hogwild with steel for the structural overhaul, and though we had the cash, it required a plan of financial attack.

"I meant life stuff," Patrick said, scratching his chin. "He seems good."

"As far as I can tell, yeah," I said.

He tilted his head to meet my eyes. "He's still not talking to you?"

I steepled my fingers under my chin, not wanting to revisit the cease-and-desist smackdown Sam leveled on me with respect to his wedding. "He's trying to establish some boundaries, and right now, that means he doesn't share much with me."

"That was diplomatic," Patrick said. "Are you doing all right?"

"It's hard," I confessed. "I'm happy for him—so happy—because he's found someone who loves him, and not only adores his quirks, but has her own to match. And I like Tiel, and I should have found a way to get to know her earlier."

"That wouldn't have helped," he laughed. "You can continue the self-flagellation, but the truth is, he needed to fall in order to find his way back up."

Snatching one of the anonymous geodes off the shelf beside my desk and rolling it between my palms, I glanced up at Patrick. "In a strange sense, it feels like I've lost a friend. Like, she's replaced me."

Patrick dropped back into the chair with a sigh. "She has," he said, "but it was time. He's not our problem child anymore."

"Well, we still have Riley," I said. "He's special."

"Oh, yeah," Patrick said. "I'm just happy Tiel likes him, and she doesn't mind him living at the firehouse with her and Sam. Let's keep our fingers crossed that things don't change after the vows because I do not want him sleeping on my couch."

"Does all this wedding talk give you any ideas?"

He glanced up from his screen, his brow furrowed. As expected, he was utterly confused. "I'm not sure I'd be much help."

"You are oblivious, Optimus. Oblivious." His scowl deepened. "What are you getting Andy for Christmas?"

He tapped a few keys and shut his laptop. "Haven't decided yet."

"What about a big, shiny diamond ring?"

Patrick held his computer to his chest while he considered this, his lips pursed, and then shook his head. He filed away his things, and slung the bag over his shoulder. "I'll take it under advisement," he said. "It's late, and I'm sure Andy's hungry, and this conversation is too complex for me. See you next week."

"You let me know when you're ready for a trip to Shreve, Crump and Low," I called as he left my office. "She's not a Van Cleef and Arpels girl. And for the love of God, no Tiffany." He raised his hand in acknowledgement, and kept walking.

I updated my cash flow spreadsheet and checked the corporate credit card balances to ensure we weren't up against our limits. We always managed to max out the cards on the days when we were taking clients to lunch, and that annoyed the shit out of me. It was Tom's responsibility to watch the charges, but I took a peek at least once a week to be safe.

"Closing time, peanut."

I shot back in my chair, yelping in surprise, and found Will leaning against my doorframe with his arms crossed over his chest. The pose did fascinating things for his biceps. And forearms. The whole thing was...fascinating.

"Patrick was here, like, two minutes ago," I said. My heart was skittering in my chest. "You're going to get caught if you keep stalking me like this."

He shrugged, and ran his thumb down the line of his jaw. His beard was getting thick again. "Maybe I want to get caught."

"Yeah, we'll deal with that issue in a minute," I said. "How did you get past the security system?"

Back before Angus died, there were a few incidents with him that necessitated a tighter approach to office safety. We'd selected a highly recommended—and very expensive—firm to outfit the building with limited access areas, cameras, and keypads at all the entry points.

Will pushed off from the door and sauntered to my desk. "Is that a serious question?"

"That's the best system on the market," I said as I gathered my things.

He helped me into my coat and held out his hand for my bag. He was insistent about things like that, and I usually hated all manner of chivalry but...it was growing on me. All of this was growing on me, and I didn't want to think about Will leaving for another deployment. That shadow was lurking around every corner, but I didn't want to look it in the eye just yet.

Not knowing when he'd leave made it easier. It wasn't until the clock was running that I had to reconcile my reality of small bites of time with Will.

"That system wouldn't stop someone who wanted to get in here," he said. He hitched my tote over his shoulder and took my hand. "You'd have the exact same level of security with a dead bolt."

"Lovely," I murmured. "Another unjustifiable expenditure. That's precisely what I need right now."

"What you need is a break," he said. "You're going to relax next week in San Diego. Hell, you might fall in love and decide to stay there."

At the top of Joy Street, I stopped to face Will. "Fall in love with San Diego? Or...something else?"

Will smiled and pulled me against his chest. "Let's find out."

Twenty-Four

SHANNON

"I'M ON TO YOU," Lauren said, leaning into my shoulder.

She showed up at my office late this afternoon wearing a bold, bright smile, slammed my laptop shut, and informed me we were going out. Apparently, barking orders ran in the family.

"What was that, Drunk Girl?" I asked.

The tavern down the street from the office was one of my favorites, and since I wasn't alone in loving The Red Hat, the place was packed. Matt tagged along, and was on the other side of the bar watching basketball.

"I said I'm on to you," she laughed. "I know what you're up to."

I'd been preparing for this. After everything that happened over lunch, it was obvious Lauren had a good idea—if not the full idea and most of the details—which bare-chested military man was in my apartment, and she was going to kill me with kindness until I confessed.

"Oh, so you're aware that I've been dropping engagement ring hints all over Patrick?"

Her eyes widened and she held up her finger. "We'll come back to that one in a second." She propped her hands on her hips and shot me a sharp look. "I hear you're leaving town tomorrow. What's the story, morning glory?"

This was the part I hated: keeping things from Lauren. She confided her secrets in me, and I dropped more than my share on her. She arranged my father's burial when I was too distraught. She changed my brother's life in too many ways to name. She brought Will into my life, and now...I wanted to tell her. This was like a jar filled with summer fireflies, buzzing and beating the glass to get out and live in a wide, open space, and my fingers were loosening the lid.

"There's not much of a story, Lo. Seriously, it's just—"

She waved her hands in front of my face and grabbed my shoulders. "Did you hear that?" she asked.

"What?" I couldn't hear anything over the dull roar of crowd noise and music.

She made an exaggeratedly impatient face and jostled my shoulders. "You just called me Lo."

Shit.

"You know who calls me Lo?" she asked.

I shrugged and studied my wine. White, chilled, average quality, not strong enough to get me through the beating she was going to issue any minute now.

"My brothers, most notably, my brother Will. My parents call me Lolo, and Wes, too. Everyone else calls me Lauren, or Miss Honey. Only Will—the one with the bone frog tattoo on his arm and the anchor on his chest—*consistently* calls me Lo."

"It's cute," I said, sliding my phone out of my suit coat and studying the newest emails waiting for me. "It fits you."

"It really doesn't, but let's deconstruct that one another

day." She squeezed my shoulders and hell, Drunk Lauren was strong. "Will is Scheduled Sex. You've been seeing him between deployments since…since when, Shan?"

There was an expression one of my torts professors liked to throw around—three people can keep a secret if two of them are dead—and I laughed out loud at the thought of it. This was *never* a secret. Riley, Erin, and Nick all knew the second night we were together. Everyone knew I was going somewhere and seeing someone. Tiel could draw his tattoos from memory.

There was no secret here, and there was some relief in that revelation. A shiver moved through my bones, and I didn't know whether I wanted to laugh or cry. "Will is Scheduled Sex," I confirmed. "And I've been seeing him since your wedding."

"You've been keeping this from me for more than a year and a half?" she cried. "Shit, I didn't think you'd admit it so quickly. Tell me *everything,* you dirty little slutbag."

A rush of emotion was rising up in my chest, as if giving voice to these realities made them more real and tangible. Will was mine and I was saying that out loud. "I didn't want to lie to you, but it just—"

"I know that I sound like I'm mad, and I'm not. I love you but I just feel the need to scream at you." Lauren's eyes narrowed. "Where is he right now?"

"My apartment," I said. I tangled my fingers around my long seed-pearl necklace. Every text from Will today was in reference to this necklace, and the thoroughly perverted things he wanted to do while I wore it.

"Mmhmm." She drained her drink and set it on the bar. "Mmhmm. Of course he is."

"It's not…" My voice trailed off, and I didn't know what I

was trying to deny. It wasn't more than scheduled sex? It wasn't going to happen again? It wasn't getting serious? None of that was true, and now that I'd drawn back the curtains on the history of Shannon and Will, I couldn't stomach another mistruth. I was going to stand there, twisting in my discomfort, and surrender to the reality that Will was mine.

Mine. Not for anyone else, not anymore, not ever again.

Lauren sighed, and I knew she wasn't mad. She was disappointed, and I was well-acquainted with that reaction. It was how I felt when Sam proposed to Tiel. I knew it made me an asshole for withholding some of my happiness for him because he didn't include me in his plans to get engaged, but we'd been through so much together. I was pissed that his life was changing in a way that excluded me, but I did the same thing to Lauren. I'd *earned* her disappointment.

"The first time it happened we decided you didn't need to know about it," I said, laughing. "The last thing you needed to hear on your wedding day was that your brother broke my vag...and the bed."

"You two must think I'm about as sharp as a spoon." My forehead wrinkled in confusion, and she continued, "He asked me a minimum of nine hundred questions about you while I was getting my hair done before the ceremony. And have you seen my photos? I had the photographer crop you two out of some of the images because it looked like you were molesting each other."

"Oh..."

"And let's not forget about that time when you two were at my house for dinner," she said, pointing her glass at me. "It was like a game of strip poker."

"He broke into my apartment that night," I said.

"Of course he did," she replied. "That's the kind of shit he does. He knows everything, he's bossy, and likes getting his way. I cannot imagine what the two of you see in each other." She ran her hand through her hair, sighing. "It's nice that he has some time off, even if he isn't sharing that news with anyone."

"I've been telling him to call you," I said, shaking my head. "We've been trying to sort some things out, and…he's a little stubborn."

"There's something to be said about pots and kettles, and birds of a feather, and taking one to know one," she murmured. "In other news: you two are going somewhere?"

I nodded. "One of his friends is getting married. In San Diego."

"Good," she said, and I looked up to find her smiling at me. "Good. I like this."

"That's great, but please don't announce it," I insisted.

"Shannon, this isn't my relationship to announce, and I'm a little insulted that you think I'd issue a press release or dump a long, babbling post on Facebook about my brother and my best friend. But please explain this to me: why is it a secret?"

I held out my hands to her, trying to conjure all the stress and drama of the past eighteen months into the space between my fingers. "We just wanted to disappear for a weekend, and then it turned into…I don't even know what it is."

"This is a ridiculous question but here goes: have you talked to him about this?"

"It sounds logical coming out of your mouth," I said, "but

in practice, it's rather to difficult to have those conversations."

"Don't I know it," she murmured. "Can I just say that I'm happy for you? I remember last November, when you came back from New Mexico. You saw him there, right?"

Nodding, I kept my eyes cast down, not wanting to see the joyful warmth in her expression. Any day now, he'd head out for another deployment. Things would return to the way they were before I knew what it was like to have him with me every day, every night. It wasn't something I was looking forward to.

"You were glowing when you came back, but then I didn't see that glow for a long time. Not until last weekend, when you came this close to slapping the shit out of Tiel."

"Please don't do this," I said. "Don't get invested."

"Did you know Andy almost bailed on my wedding?" Lauren asked, a petulant scowl on her lips.

"Wait—what are you talking about?"

"You remember. She and Patrick were going through their thing, and they were pretty much separated. So, of course, she thought I'd take Patrick's side because I was marrying his brother." She gestured toward me. "What I'm saying is: you'll always be my friend and my sister-in-law. I'm going to be happy for you and I'm going to get invested, but I can keep it to myself if that makes you feel better. I'll just be over here, quietly cheering for you."

Those words loosened the knot in my throat, and some stray tears spilled over. "You're a bitch for making me cry in a bar," I said.

"You're a bitch for keeping this from me for a year and a fucking half," she said, wrapping her arm around my shoulders.

"You're a bitch for figuring it out," I laugh-sniffled.

"You're a bitch for making me beat it out of you," she said.

Matt came up behind us and folded us into a hug. "Every time," he muttered. "Every time you two go out, you get sloppy drunk and run a bar tab the length of my arm."

"I totally thought you were going to say cock," Lauren giggled. "It's not your arm, but it's still pretty long."

"Your mouth, Mrs. Walsh," he whispered. "Still shocks me."

"You're a bitch for talking about my brother's junk all the time," I yelled.

"Says the girl with the broken vag," Lauren said, smirking at me. "See? You're already getting me back for it."

SAN DIEGO WAS Boston's opposite in every way. Where San Diego was sunny and bright, Boston in November was routinely gray. Everything here glistened and shined with newness, and my life back home was dedicated to preserving things that counted their age in centuries. The Pacific was a serene, sparkling sapphire when we touched down at the airport, nothing like the choppy, blue-green of the Atlantic. Despite the drought, bougainvillea vines edged the freeway, and there wasn't a barren tree in sight.

Just as Boston was all mine, San Diego was Will's, and I could have scooped a cupful of his happiness right off him the minute we stepped into the terminal. The entire cab ride from the airport was filled with half-complete stories about friends, beaches, high school, and SEAL training, each one piling on top of the other as he interrupted himself with a new memory.

"So you're serious about staying at your parents' house?" I said when we stopped in front of a classic bungalow in Coronado Village, complete with a white picket fence, Spanish tiles, and overflowing hibiscus bushes.

"They're on a freaking safari until the new year," he said, hauling our luggage to the curb. "If they weren't too busy petting giraffes for Judy's blog, they'd tell you that they want us to stay here."

"Yeah, and you technically live here," I added.

"I haven't been in one place for more than a few weeks since…since I was in college, Shannon. There's no reason for me to move out. I believe you'd classify that as unjustifiable expenditure."

"Yeah, but…" I gestured to the American flag waving in the light breeze. "It's your parents' house. We're in our mid-thirties. People in their mid-thirties don't shack up at their parents' houses."

"People in their mid-thirties don't wing limes at each other either," he muttered. He produced a set of keys from deep inside his backpack, and unlocked the front door.

I ducked under his arm and into the house. "Would you just let it go?"

The sun-washed walls were pale yellow with bright white moldings, and there was no missing the nautical theme. Seashells, sand dollars, starfish, anchors, ship's wheels…everywhere, but it was homey and wonderful and I loved it. An entire wall in the family room was arranged in a mosaic of photographs starting with Will, Wes, and Lauren as babies and fanning out to their college and military graduations. The white and navy kitchen opened up to a small patio overflowing with squat trees, vines and flowers, and a babbling terra cotta fountain.

I was staring at one of the trees when Will found me. "I don't get it," I said, pointing at the fruit.

He wrapped his arms around my waist and dropped his chin to my shoulder. "It's a fruit salad tree. Lemons, limes, and grapefruit, but don't get any ideas."

"That's amazing," I said.

Will's lips traveled up my neck and my eyes drifted shut as I melted into him. "Amazing would be getting you naked right now," he whispered, "and keeping you naked until it's dark, and then coming out here and fucking you under the stars."

"That might also be amazing," I said. "But I'm still taking a picture of that tree before I leave."

Will hauled me up, slapped my ass, and marched through the house. "Some people come to California and admire the beaches and ocean. My girl wants to photograph a fucking fruit tree."

He stopped inside a bedroom painted blue-gray, and sent me flying through the air. I shouldn't have been surprised that he threw me on the bed; picking me up and tossing me about was as routine to him as putting his jeans on one leg at a time.

"Such a meathead," I murmured.

Will laughed as he crawled up and tucked me into his side. With my head on his chest, I studied his room. It was simple and neat, and seemed to function more as a guest room than shrine to Will's formative years.

"I want to take you to the beach. I'll catch some waves and you'll decide you can't live without me and the Pacific Ocean," he said.

"It's a package deal? You and the ocean? I can't have one without the other?"

"You won't want to."

I pointed to the ceiling. "Riley would love all these exposed beams."

Will grabbed my hand and pressed it to his hardening cock. "Yeah, I've got an exposed beam for you right here."

I gave his shaft a squeeze and shifted to straddle his lean hips. "What's the agenda?"

"First, you're getting naked," he said. "Then you're putting your legs over my shoulders and insulting my moves while I fuck all that stress right out of you. After that? I'll show you around the island. Get something to eat. Do it all over again."

My hands traveled over his chest, mapping the hard lines beneath his t-shirt. "I'm not stressed."

Will shot a doubtful smile at me. "Says the girl who wants the agenda," he said.

"This is a first for me. Never been in a guy's childhood bedroom before." I nudged his ribs. "How many girls did you sneak in?"

"That would be zero," he said, planting a sweet kiss on my forehead. "My father would've had me doing fifty-meter dive drills until I passed out on the beach if he caught me with a girl up here, so..." He dragged his fingers down my belly and popped the buttons at my waist. "It's a first for me, too."

"If you didn't bring girls up here...there was a backseat. I'm guessing a truck." Will's hands slid up my thighs, squeezing as they moved higher.

"There was a backseat. In a truck." His hands traveled

down and then up, faster now. "And you? I'm thinking there was a lacrosse player. Maybe tennis."

I twisted away from him, immediately regretting this topic. "I don't want to talk about it," I said. It came out in an angry wail as I vaulted off the bed. "I don't want to talk about it."

Will watched me, his arm bent under his head. He nodded slowly, and though the twitch in his cheek told me he wanted more, his expression stayed calm and steady. "You don't have to be tough all the time."

"I'm not being tough," I said, dragging my fingers through my hair. I needed a shower. Something to wash off the grime of air travel. "I just don't want to talk about it. There are certain things I'd rather not discuss."

"You don't have to," Will shifted to sit on the edge of the bed, "but someday, you're going to tell me who hurt you."

Intent on stripping off my clothes, I turned my back to him while I stepped out of my jeans. "It's not like you can do anything about it," I said under my breath, and before I could yank my shirt over my head, Will's arms came around my waist.

"Because he's dead," he said. "I can't do anything about it because your father's dead. Right?"

It all came back to me like echoes bouncing off a cavernous space, and the memories—the worst ones, the ones I'd fought to forget—cackled through my mind, mocking, haunting. The disgusting sounds Angus would make as he invaded me. The names he called me. How he threatened to touch Erin whenever I'd resist. They rolled in like smoke, rising up around me until I was choking. My breath caught in my throat, and I was powerless to respond, tentatively bobbing my head instead.

Will's forehead dropped to my shoulder as he exhaled. "Every time you mention that bastard, I want to dig him up and kill him again. I hope he died peacefully because believe me when I say that's not the end he would've gotten from me."

I shivered, and he folded me into him until all I could feel was hard muscle and heat. In Will's arms, I was safe—I believed that above anything else—but a shimmer of doubt lingered along the edges. This wasn't information I disclosed freely. My brothers didn't know, and after all this time, there was no reason to tell them.

The one time I'd shared my history with a man I was dating, he buckled under the weight of it. He tried to look past it, but it was the only thing he could see, and he couldn't comprehend my desire for intimacy, especially the harder, rougher sort I favored. I was supposed to be damaged and I was supposed to find sex revolting, traumatic, and painful, and that was the only narrative he could abide. Everything else was evidence of my *issues*.

Will wasn't handing me the victim treatment, and I adored him even more for it. He held me, and not because I couldn't stand on my own, but because he wanted me to know that I didn't have to. He was mine to lean on, and right now, I knew that leaning didn't make me any less strong.

"Before he died," I started, "I told him that I forgave him. That he was a sick, sad man but he didn't take me down with him. He took a lot of things from me, but didn't break me."

"No, peanut, he didn't," Will said. "Not even close."

I'D FORGOTTEN the crisp pleasure of escaping with Will, and escaping to his town was even better than our previous destinations. Our nights were spent drinking and laughing in the backyard or tangled around each other in bed, and our days belonged to his favorite beaches, hiking trails, and taco shops.

We ventured to his preferred surfing spot—the southern end of Black's Beach—though he didn't mention anything about the breakneck cliff trail we had to descend to reach the shore until we were there. I didn't need new reasons to crave Will's body, but watching him emerge from the sea, surfboard tucked under his arm and water running through the deep cuts of his chest and abs, gave me a few more.

We argued about the existence of ghosts after he converted me to the splendor known as the Thanksgiving buffet at the Hotel Del Coronado. We joked about making this an annual trip, and each laugh we shared turned the words into small promises. Next year was starting to sound possible. Even likely.

An entire day drifted away while we wandered through the gardens at Balboa Park. It was sunny and balmy, and I was free to drag him into a shady grove and kiss him like I was a lust-hungry teenager.

"You can't wear that," he grumbled from the hallway while I straightened my hair in the bathroom. We were leaving soon to meet some of his friends at a bar near the base.

Gesturing to my skinny jeans and loose v-neck sweater, I said, "Be quiet. This is perfectly adorable."

"Yes, peanut, *you* are really fucking adorable." Will took the flat iron from my hand and set it aside, then slipped his hand down the front of the sweater. His thumb passed over my nipple, circling it until it peaked for him. "But if one of the guys gets an eyeful of tit, there will be a volume of bloodshed tonight."

"That's why you have balls. Just give them a twist whenever you think you're going to do anything homicidal," I said as I nudged him away.

"I'll remember that," he said. He dropped to the lip of the tub, his forearms braced on his thighs. I was a little obsessed with those forearms. Thighs, too. "Although, it is worth stating that I prefer when you give them a tug."

Will observed while I passed one section of hair after another through the straightener, and his gaze left my skin tingling. It was intimate, him watching me, almost overwhelmingly so. Less than an hour ago, I was flat against the shower tiles while he pounded into me. Now, I was fully dressed and making careful work of singeing my hair while our eyes met in the mirror, and I couldn't look away.

There was no urgent passion pumping between us, no timer ticking away the seconds until separation and distance robbed us of kisses, glances, skin-to-skin. This was different. It was everyday affection, and as it surrounded me, I knew it was sweeter and more satisfying than scheduled sex could ever be.

I wanted to tell him this, and show him that I was finished pushing him away, to explain that I was experiencing *other feelings*, but I wasn't the girl who lived for dramatic monologues or sentimental gestures. And there was no sense tweaking the rules of engagement, either. We shoveled a lot of shit at each other, and maybe it meant I was a new and improved brand of demented, I didn't want that to change.

"I like that shirt," I said, tilting my head toward Will. "I mean…I like it on *you*."

He looked down at the light blue Oxford, and smirked. "Was that your attempt at a compliment? That was rough."

"Yeah. I'm a lot like whiskey," I said. "Few can handle me, and even fewer can get it up afterward."

Will pushed off the tub and stood behind me, and I couldn't read his expression as his fingertips slipped through my hair. His hands tracked down my back to my waist, and when I expected him to lob an antagonistic barb in my direction, he dropped to his knees.

"You are the finest whiskey," he breathed. "Only the barrel proof."

My jeans and panties were skimming over my thighs before I could turn the straightener off, and Will's palm settled between my shoulder blades, bending me over the countertop. His lips mapped my backside, his short beard was hot, ticklish torture on my skin, and it only intensified when he widened my stance and ducked between my legs.

He traced my folds, licking just enough to leave me moaning and clawing for more. Rising up on my tiptoes, I arched back as his hand anchored me in place and his tongue speared inside me. His groan rumbled through me before I heard it, and that dark sound sent all the electricity in my body straight to my clit.

"Oh, fuck," he growled. He tugged me between his teeth, sucking and nipping, and I was rushing to the verge. Slack-jawed, cross-eyed, and teetering on shaking legs, that glowing ball of orgasm was throbbing low in my belly and ready to burst open. "Fuck, fuck, *fuck*. I can taste myself, inside you, and… I fucking love that."

Glancing down my torso, I could see Will's bent legs. His

impossibly thick erection was trapped against his thigh, under his clothes. "Take it out. Stroke yourself," I said, "but don't stop licking me."

"Like I could," he said.

His belt rattled as he whipped it open. He dragged his cock free, giving himself a slow caress down his length, twisting at the crown, and then jerking back to the base. With a strangled grunt that vibrated across every inch of my pussy, his hand flew back and forth over his cock in the purest definition of *beating off* I'd ever imagined.

Will's tongue matched that pace, and all of this—the naughty position, the filthy sounds, the hand holding me down, the lingering evidence of his last orgasm—had us careening toward the finish in minutes. My orgasm blasted through me, heating everything from my toes to my scalp, and leaving me breathless and quivering. He managed a few guttural noises that bore no resemblance to words before closing his teeth around my inner thigh and coming on the blue and white striped bath mat, and watching from my spread-legged vantage point was a new level of dirty.

"Shannon…" he sighed, his head resting on my thighs. "I want you. For a long time. A long fucking time. If you don't, I need you to lie to me, because there's a real possibility that I'll cry right now if you say no."

"Can we talk about this when your face isn't between my legs?" I raked my hands through his hair. "And since when is crying a commando tactic? I didn't think you even had tear ducts."

"We can grow them on demand, and I can't imagine a better way to have a conversation with you. You're amenable to most things when I'm licking your pussy."

"William," I said, my tone firm. "You're kneeling in a

puddle of jizz, and I'm pretty sure I have a perfect impression of your teeth an inch from my clit. I promise you we'll talk about all the things you said, but not now."

He sighed, and I was certain he was pouting. "I didn't mean to bite you that hard."

"It's okay," I said. "I kind of liked it."

"You're the toughest little peanut I've ever met. You're barely five feet tall, you weigh nothing, and you're small, but fuck, you are scrappy," he murmured as he pulled my clothes into place and carefully folded the bath mat. "I'm gonna wait for you outside. I might maul you if I stay in here much longer."

I required a few minutes to recover, and a few more to finish getting ready. By the time I met Will on the sidewalk, it was dark, and a heavy covering of marine layer was drifting in. It was a brief walk through Coronado Village to the tavern, and Will devoured the distance with rapid-fire stories about his teammates.

"Should I expect to see knife throwing, or kung fu and arm wrestling tonight?" I asked.

He paused at the tavern door. "Probably not," he said with some reluctance, "but it isn't impossible. There're always a lot of team guys here. Some I might let you meet."

"*Let me,*" I repeated. "It's funny because you think you're in charge here."

He squeezed my fingers as we approached a group clustered near the bar. "Oh, I like this," Will said, rubbing his hand over a man's head. "Keeping it high and tight for the big day?"

"Halsted," he roared, swallowing Will into a back-slapping bear hug. "Always good to see your ugly mug." A slow smile broke across his face when he spotted me behind Will.

When Will noticed, he stepped away and tucked his hand into my back pocket. "Gus Granovsky. The pleasure is all mine."

"Shannon Walsh," I said, meeting his outstretched palm.

Gus glanced to Will, his hand still clasping mine. "Are you blackmailing her? There's no reason why a nice lady like this would have any use for a frogman," he said. "What's he got on you, honey?"

"A little bit of everything," I said, laughing as Will placed his free hand on Gus's chest and pushed him away. "He's always catching me in weak moments."

At that, Will gazed down at me, smiling, and mouthed, "Showerhead."

"Don't go there," I laughed.

"Where's Viv?" Will asked. He craned his neck around, and it was then that I noticed the bar was packed with men just like him: big, chiseled, and with little more than posture and gaze, quietly broadcasting that they were the baddest of the badass motherfuckers.

"With her sister. You know, doing chick shit because you're not supposed to see the bride the night before the wedding," Gus said. He pointed at me. "Can I get you something to drink, Miss Walsh? Halsted has the manners of a dumb goat, and I hear he fucks like one, too, but *I* am a gentleman."

"Is that what your mother said about me?" Will asked. He brushed his hand down my back with an eye roll. "What'll it be, peanut?"

"I'll go," I said, nodding toward the bar. "You play with your friends."

The bar was a true SEAL haven. Black and white photos lined the walls, all featuring sailors engaged in beach drills or standing in formation, and there were cartoonish murals with frogs holding machine guns. A handful of men were gathered around a dartboard where they were talking an exceptional amount of trash, and the others were standing together, offering Will the same hearty greeting he received from Gus.

There were plenty of women, too. Some were in the wife or girlfriend category, and they were easily identifiable as they usually had one of those huge motherfuckers pawing at them. The rest were what Will liked to call tag chasers, and the decidedly predatory look in their eyes—plus their tiny scraps of clothing in spite of the damp chill rolling off the ocean tonight—made them equally easy to spot.

Also: three of them were leering at Will like they hadn't seen fresh meat in months.

"So you're Will's Shannon? I've heard a lot about you."

I turned, narrowing my eyes at the man seated two stools down. "Is that so?"

He wore a baseball cap pulled low and offered a lopsided smile. "Yes, ma'am. Lucas Quadros, but you can call me Quad."

I looked back at Will. He was deep in conversation with two men while his fan club engaged in all manner of hair twirling and come-hither glancing. He didn't seem to notice. "And what have you heard, Quad? Anything good?"

He nodded to the empty stool beside him, and I sat. "I heard about you for three days straight. If Halsted hadn't been talking my ear off, I probably wouldn't have made it out of that godforsaken desert."

My smile flattened. "I don't know that I follow you."

He pivoted, extending his leg out in front of him. A quick

yank pulled the leg of his jeans up, exposing a thin metal pole where a skin and bone should have been.

"Lost my leg in our last go-round. Helicopter went down."

I didn't know what to say, and what *could* I say?

"I'm sorry to hear that," I said, and it was possible that words had never been as inadequate as they were right now.

"We lost nine guys in that crash. Halsted got us out. The hostage and me. He ripped nine inches of shrapnel out of his shoulder with a pair of pliers, rubbed some dirt in the wound like a beast, and then dragged us through the desert for three days. Bitched and moaned about my lacking survival skills, and how he'd kick my ass out of the teams if I died." He laughed—that was some gallows humor right there—and I could only respond with a nod. "He was due home after that mission, and he made sure I knew it."

I leaned forward, my arms folded on the bar, and studied him. He was young, probably no older than Riley was, and blessed with a soft baby face. He saw it as a curse, I was sure, and was growing a thick, dark beard to prove that plenty of testosterone flowed through his veins.

"Why are you telling me this?" I asked. I didn't want to seem flippant or disinterested, but I didn't know how to handle this information.

"Halsted and I made a deal in that desert. I wasn't going to bleed out, and he was going to introduce me to the woman he wouldn't stop talking about."

I scanned the room for Will, and when I found him leaning against a booth, his eyes flickered to me, steady and unsmiling.

Why didn't you tell me?

"It was an ambitious mission by all standards," Quadros

continued, his fingertips running through his beard as he spoke. "He should have been commanding the op from base, but one of our guys rolled his ankle and Halsted refused to send in the rookie. The mission was high-value hostage recovery, and it had been scrubbed and rescheduled more times than I could track before the green light came in October. We had to act fast; all the intel pointed to the captors pulling the hostage's card any day."

He paused to sip his beer and I turned back to Will, my brows pinched in confusion.

Why didn't you tell me?

"It started with a long-range infil, which is a nice way of saying they dropped us on the far end of West Nowhere, and we had to get our asses to the east side without anyone noticing. We launched an attack on the hostage's location, got him out, and made it to the exfil site to meet the helicopter without as much as a sneeze. We weren't in the air more than a minute before the RPG blew us right out of the sky. Not my first helicopter crash, but..." He nodded toward the prosthesis. "But probably my last."

I glanced back at Will while this story unfolded, and we stared at each other across the room. Something passed between us...acceptance, forgiveness, understanding...something.

"He talked the whole fucking time. Said you're a damn smart lawyer and ass-kicking business lady. That you'd probably kick his ass for not getting home on time, and he'd probably like it, too. That me bleeding out in the middle of the desert would mean he was stuck carrying dead weight, and that would just take him longer so I wasn't allowed to die. Not on his watch."

You should have told me yourself.

"He should've left me there," Quadros continued. "He should've tied off my wound and gotten the hostage to safety, but he knew the insurgents would swarm the helicopter. He knew I'd be dead and he didn't give it a second thought when he tossed me on his back and got us the fuck outta there. It screwed up his shoulder and for that alone, he probably won't see combat again."

Those scars.

"I understand why he's retiring. I know it's not public knowledge yet, but…I've heard and I understand. This life… it takes a lot out of you. And he's given a lot. I don't know any more dedicated, hard-driving sailor than Halsted. He just gets shit done, time after time, and when it isn't getting done, he's there fixing it himself until it's right. "

For the second time in a matter of weeks, I wanted to hold him close, and then I wanted to slap the shit out of him.

"If you'll excuse me…"

Twenty-Five

WILL

SHANNON WALKED ACROSS THE ROOM, her eyes trained on mine, until she was right in front of me. She pressed a beer bottle into my hand and tilted her head, staring at my dick like it had insulted her country and faith.

"This thing you do," she said, gesturing to my crotch. "Where you tuck in a portion of your shirt right at the belt buckle? I know why you're doing it. You want everyone to notice your abs."

I glanced to Quad, and then back to Shannon. It was good to see him in town for Gus's wedding after everything he'd been through. All I'd lost was feeling in my fingers, and I couldn't make sense of life. This kid lost everything below the knee, and was already back to work. It was a desk job, but he was back at it.

"And here I thought they'd notice my cock," I said.

"That presumes there's something worth noticing," she said.

"That's not what you said last night," I said. "Or this

morning. Or a couple of hours ago, in the shower. Would you like me to continue?"

She plucked the beer from my hands and took a long sip. "Look, William. Your ego is very fragile. I can't go around crushing your self-esteem now, can I?"

"What did Quad say to you?" I asked.

"Why have you been parked in my apartment for the past month?"

"Because I wanted to see you for more than a weekend. I wanted to wake up in the same place for an entire month, and I wanted you there with me," I said, and that was the most honest approximation I could find. "And I have to figure out what I want to be when I grow up."

Her lips flattened as her eyes closed, her frustration with me as clear as day. "Why didn't *you* just tell me that?"

"I was going to." Shrugging, I snatched the bottle out of her hand. "Eventually. But, as you might recall, you weren't too interested in talking to me. You banished me to the guest room and threw fruit at me, and while you're at it, remind yourself there was a Douchelord in your apartment a few *weeks* ago. You're mine, and when I went to you, you were *with* that genital wart."

"We broke up," she said, her eyes flashing with anger.

"You're *mine*," I repeated. "Trust me; I was wise to your game. That little distraction to get you through? Did it help?"

Shaking her head, she stared at the ground. "No," she admitted. "Nothing helped, and when you didn't come back in September, that's when I knew it was really over."

Fuck. There was nothing I'd wanted more than to get a message to Shannon, to explain that I had to see the mission through, that I'd come for her when I was done. I could have called her when I was at the base hospital in Germany, but I was afraid she'd only take me back because I was injured, and I didn't want the pity-love she reserved for Sam.

"You know, Will," she started, her expression turning serious, "I let myself believe you were finished. That you realized I was too complicated and I'd pushed you too far, and you were done."

I held up a hand. "No, peanut, I—"

"I'm not finished," she interrupted. "You're mine, too. That never stopped. You're still mine, and I'm fucking furious that I had to hear about your injury—and everything else—from Private Ryan over there." Her eyes dropped to my shoulder, and her tongue swept over her top lip. "How is it? Are you all right?"

I shrugged, and right on cue, a bolt of pain zapped down to my fingers. "It's fine."

"It's nice how you're lying to me," she said. "Maybe you can tuck your balls back for a little while and stop being such a man."

I spread my arms wide, welcoming the onslaught. "Would it make you happy to hear that I can't feel these fingers—" I held up the last three "—and the nerve pain is an evil bitch?"

"Of course not," she cried, "but the talking goes both ways, Will. If you want everything from me, I want the same from you."

I reached for Shannon, but she slapped my hand away. She hit me with her most vicious scowl, but she couldn't hold it long. Her lips twitched, and she flew into my arms. "You have it," I whispered, holding her head to my chest. "You've always had it."

Shannon's hands fisted in my shirt, tugging me close. "What's next for you?" she asked.

I shook my head. This was one of my favorite locations on earth, and I was here with some of the best people I knew, but the only thing I wanted right now was her bare skin against mine. "I've been thinking about that, and I have some ideas, but...I don't have the answers yet."

"Then you should think about it in Boston," she said. "You should call Nick when we get home. He's a cradle-robbing asshole, but he's a really good doctor. He'll give you smart advice. And...you can always train the hedge fund wives or model for romance novel covers. There's no shame in either."

Surprised by the random compilation of ideas, I leaned back and studied her. "You're not going to jump in and micromanage?"

"No," she snapped. "You'll ask for my help if you need it, and you know I'll always give it to you."

My chest throbbed with the pressure of my affection for her and long unspoken words. "Shannon, I have to tell—"

"Not now," she interrupted, pressing her finger to my lips. "Not here."

She linked her hands behind my neck and pulled me down, touching her lips to mine, and when her tongue slipped into my mouth, it tasted like my eternity.

Twenty–Six

WE SPENT hours talking and drinking with his friends and teammates.

They were a big, rowdy crew, and they served each other a ton of shit at every turn, and I saw why this was home to Will. It was just like my big, rowdy crew.

They told stories about their training days, their deployments, and the never-ending series of pranks they pulled on each other. It was a facet of him I'd never seen before, and I adored it. His arm stayed draped over my chair, his fingers mapping the space between my shoulder and elbow, and for the first time, I couldn't grab hold of the darkness I felt when he was gone. As far as I reached, I couldn't dredge the anger and emptiness that simmered beneath the surface just weeks ago.

I didn't know whether that meant I'd let it go, or was allowing the steady pressure of his affection to slough it away for me. Or perhaps it was like he said while we watched the waves on the shore of La Jolla Cove this morn-

ing, "The best medicine is always salt water. It heals everything, every time."

I couldn't find any of it, so I stopped looking. I curled
into his easy touch, sighing in relief when his thigh edged
to mine and my body hummed with another point of
contact.

We were tipsy as we walked back to his parents' home,
and my mind was heavy with questions—was he really
leaving the military? After all this time? What was next?
What did it all mean for us? Was he in pain now? Was there
anything I could do? Would his shoulder ever improve?—
but the questions could wait.

Once inside the front door, his palms dropped to my
hips, squeezing, speaking the language that required no
words. I looked up at him in the darkness, smiling, and took
his hand. I led him through the house to the blue-gray room,
motioned for him to step out of his sneakers, and then
walked him backwards until his legs hit the bed. Wedged
between his knees, my fingers tangled in his hair while his
hands traveled over my back and thighs.

I threaded my fingers through his short beard, tugging
just enough to bring his eyes up to mine. "I have something
to say to you," I said. "And I expect you to listen."

"Yes, ma'am," he said, a smirk playing on his lips.

"I love you," I said. I could live for centuries, and I'd
never forget the way Will's eyes softened and glowed when I
said those words. "And you have to know I don't come to
that statement lightly, and—"

"Shut up," Will interrupted. His hands raced up my body
to cup my face. "I love you, too, and I'm not listening to any
opening remarks or qualifications on the matter. You are my
fire and ice, my calm and chaos, my *everything*, and I can't

remember life before loving you. Now shut up and strip, unless you want me ripping those clothes off."

He started unbuttoning his shirt, but I shook my head, wrapping my fingers around his wrist, and said, "Let me."

His gaze never left me as I peeled his clothes from him. With an arched brow, he watched while I undressed without ceremony and crawled into his lap.

My hand smoothed up his flank and over his chest, pausing at his scarred shoulder. "Let me," I whispered.

Will sucked in a breath as my lips feathered over his skin. I kissed every spot from his shoulder to his ear and back again, and I gobbled up each sigh and hum that slipped from his lips. Rising up on my knees, I pushed him back toward the pillows. He was quiet and obedient, and his eyes bathed me in the most glorious heat. I gathered him in my arms as best I could, my head on his chest and my hands flat on his back, and though his hips were bucking up in slow jabs and his cock was sliding against my center, hard and insistent, it was possible he required this moment exactly as much as I did. "Let me," I said. "Let me take care of you. Let me love you. Let me be yours."

"Shannon...you've always been mine."

"Are you sure I'm not too much for you?"

"How could you ever be too much for me when I can't get enough of you?" he said.

I reached between us, our foreheads bowed together to watch as he disappeared inside me. Our moans echoed around us when he was fully seated, and I held myself there, my eyes screwed shut and my hands on his neck with the beat of his pulse steady against my palms, his mouth a torment on my breasts and his beard tickling my belly, and my body moved of its own volition, knowing what we needed without conscious thought because we knew. We knew.

There was nowhere for these sensations to go but around and around, spinning and spreading out in waves that stole my words. The only sounds were of our shared murmurs and breaths, the creaking bed, the ocean.

He said my name in a long, content groan as he came, his mouth on my breast and those syllables marking me with a possession that felt boundless, eternal, permanent.

Our relationship was formed on the basis of really good sex, the types of which I hadn't known existed before this man. We knew hate sex, angry sex, quick and easy sex, dirty sex, lazy morning sex, slow sex, kinky sex, but none of that encompassed this night.

This wasn't sex.

This was love, and we both knew it.

Will: Thank you for breakfast

Shannon: Gross

Will: What?

Shannon: You can't call clit-licking your "breakfast"

Will: I can. I did.

Will: I'll do it again.

Shannon: Such a meathead.

Will: And remember which meathead left a handprint on your ass this morning

Shannon: Oh that? Barely noticed.

Will: Do not tempt me, little girl.

Shannon: Yep, blah blah blah you're going to spank me and tie me up. What else is new?

Will: You're real sassy until your wrists are tied behind your back and you have a cock in your mouth

Will: And let's put those vibrators to good use while you're at it.

"GIVE ME THAT," Tom said, coming up behind me. He tugged my outerwear off and tossed it to the chair beside my desk. "You've been standing there, muttering to yourself and texting for five minutes. Whoever you're talking to can wait but Patrick doesn't have that muscle, and you *are* going to be late. We don't need to start this week with an irritable Patrick."

Tom pushed a Starbucks cup into my hand, and pointed toward the attic conference room. A hearty discussion of last night's football game was underway when I arrived, and that distraction allowed my tardiness to go unnoticed.

Sam handed me a folder of documents I'd requested on one of his properties, and he pointed to my face. "Brought a little California sun home with you?"

A new swath of freckles covered my nose and cheeks, but thankfully, no sunburn. "Just a bit," I said. "How was New Jersey?"

Sam tugged at his collar and straightened his tie, grimacing before he spoke. "Not great. Tiel had warned me that it wouldn't be great, but…I figured I could handle a difficult family. Those people, though, they were *not* nice to her. I said something about it, and you'd think I was sticking up for Hitler and Mussolini." He blew out a breath and reached for his coffee. "We drove back Friday morning."

"I'm sorry," I said. "Is Tiel okay?"

Sam released a low, rumbling laugh and leaned forward. "Tiel's great, and it will be fine," he said with a nod. "It's unfortunate when you have a family but you can't go home because they're assholes. She has a real, living family—aunts and uncles, cousins, parents, grandparents—but they're complete shit. But we'll be fine without them."

He joined the unending football conversation, and I

opened my computer to a blessedly thin stack of unread emails. My calendar wasn't enjoying the same levity.

Shannon: Would it be possible to start this meeting?
Patrick: It must be really annoying when people have no regard for your schedule
Shannon: Yeah can we save the "Shannon's always late" comedy for another day?
Shannon: I'm prepping for the audit and closing on two investments today. You can speed this along, or I will.

"We should start with the beachfront," Patrick said, gesturing to me. "Swampscott. Riley and I walked through it last Wednesday to get a sense of the fundamentals. What's your angle on that?"

"It was a steal," I said. "I haven't thought through the restoration or marketing position yet, but they practically gave it away. And it tests new muscles for us. We'll run out of farmhouses and brownstones eventually."

"Probably not," Matt said. "Statistically speaking, we wouldn't. Not for hundreds of years."

"And there's your daily dose of *Matt Knows Math*," Riley said.

Patrick leveled an impatient glare in Riley's direction before turning back to me. "Get out there this week, or next, and decide which direction we're taking this." I made a note on my overstuffed calendar as Patrick shifted his attention. "Let's get into status reports," he said. "Matt, start us off."

While Matt detailed his plans for the Mount Vernon project and his excitement about us visiting the site on Friday, I pulled my laptop close and read everything I could find about shrapnel wounds and nerve damage. I had no

intention of project managing Will's injury—as if he'd let me
—but I wanted to get my facts straight.

The information was terrifying, and not because of what
happened to Will, but what *could* have happened. The
thought of him hurt, thousands of miles away, would always
be too difficult for me to swallow, and reading about devas-
tating injuries, lost limbs, widespread paralysis...it sucked
the air from the room and had a knot of tension high in my
throat.

I should have been engaged in the meeting, but pulled
out my phone and sent a text under the table instead.

Shannon: I love you.
Will: Because of the vibrator, right?
Will: I knew you'd like that.
Will: We should figure out how to use them more often if
that's how you're going to react.
Will: Let's get some other toys
Shannon: Shut up
Will: Ok, good talk. Love you too.

"Does that work for you, Shannon?"

My head jerked up, and I found Patrick, Andy, Sam,
Matt, and Riley staring at me.

"Um..." I glanced down at my screen, which was
currently displaying an article about nerve transfer surgery,
and noticed several messages from Patrick.

Patrick: You want to weigh in on this?
Patrick: I fucking hate the PR people attached to Turlan. It's
a decent property but I'm going to be thrilled when we don't
have to deal anymore

Patrick: Still with us?
Patrick: Did you catch that?

"The media showcase," Sam said. "For the Turlan project?"

I nodded, and motioned for him to keep talking. "Yeah, can you run that by me one more time?"

Patrick: Are you ok?
Patrick: You seem a little out of it
Shannon: Tired. Jet lag.
Patrick: How was California?
Shannon: Really, really good

Sam's lips twitched as he fought back a smirk. "The Turlans' publicist called me last week, and wanted to finalize details for the open house event they're doing in January. I'm just checking that you're still good with the date, and them handling all the arrangements."

"Yeah, there's no reason for us to take on any of that," I said. "We're down to the punch list on that property, right?"

"Yeah," Sam said slowly. "We were just talking about that. Riley went through all the remaining items."

Shannon: How was Korean bbq and pub crawling?
Patrick: What you're asking me is: How's Erin? Did Erin mention if she's ever coming home for more than a weekend? Did Erin discuss whether she's ready to end the war of silence?
Patrick: And the answer to all that is no because she didn't get here. There was a blizzard and her flight was cancelled.

"And I didn't pay attention the first time, so you're going to need to run it again," I said, pointing my pen at Riley.

He rolled his eyes. "Fine, but I need some sustenance," he said. He reached into his backpack, retrieving a spoon, a bag of hard-boiled eggs, and a jar of spicy pickle-and-onion relish.

"Riley," I said, my hand pressed to my neck. "Don't."

Then he unzipped the bag, and that thick, sulfuric scent swept across the table. The relish was next. "What?" he asked, his eyes glittering with the joy of behaving badly.

"*Riley*," I repeated.

"Dude," Matt groaned. "Don't be such a douche nozzle."

Riley selected an egg, scooped relish over it while smirking like the fucking sociopath he was, and popped the entire thing in his mouth. We sat there, staring, as he demolished six eggs and half the jar of relish.

"Motherfuck," Sam murmured. "Okay, Shan, I'm sending you the punch list report, and now we need to open some windows or maybe burn the building down."

"You win, RISD," I said, my hand pressed to my mouth. "You win. I'm never bringing yogurt up here again, and I don't think I'll be challenging you to a war of wills either. Now put this shit away, zip your goddamn pants, and get to work."

He pumped his fists in the air, a triumphant smile on his face. "It's because I'm the hero Gotham deserves."

Will: I had an idea
Shannon: First time for everything
Will: You're getting spanked tonight

Shannon: Was that your idea?

Will: No

Shannon: We're long past the stage where it's acceptable to be coy. Spit it out or shut up.

Will: You want to see a movie tonight? Maybe get dinner?

Shannon: Are you asking me on a date?

Will: Yeah, I think so

Shannon: Does that mean you're tired of Netflix and my sweatpants?

Will: No. I'm a big supporter of those things. I'd also like to take you out tonight.

Shannon: Ok. I'd like that too.

Shannon: How'd it go with Nick

Will: Meh.

Shannon: Words, please. No grunts.

Will: He slapped some electrodes on my arm and fired up the shock therapy.

Will: It was like SERE school.

Shannon: Lovely. Any outcome?

Will: He wants me to see someone else. I have another appointment tomorrow

Shannon: I'm fine with that. Nick treats children. You, commando, were probably born half-man.

Shannon: Have you apologized to Judy for that? It mustn't have been easy, birthing a dude.

Will: Are you amusing yourself right now?

Shannon: Actually, yes.

Shannon: Lauren just texted me about the holidays. She and Matt aren't going to Mexico?

Shannon: And – she says hi. She'd like you to call her.

Will: Judy and the Commodore are on safari. Kenya, Botswana, Rwanda, Zambia.

Shannon: Oh right.

Shannon: How's that going? Have you heard from them?

Will: They're loving the shit out of it.

Will: She made some suggestive Jane and Tarzan comments. I got the fuck out of that conversation real fast.

Shannon: So then…the holidays

Will: Yeah, you're stuck with me

Will: You have a list of your brothers' suit measurements. I found it when I was looking for paper clips in the kitchen

Shannon: Correct and paper clips are in the cabinet in the den

Will: Already found them but WHY do you have their suit measurements?

Shannon: It goes back to the great dispute over dry-cleaned trousers

Will: omfg. These guys

Will: There's even a note about which side they dress, for fuck's sake

Will: That's the line. Right there. That's the threshold between being involved and being fucking insane

Shannon: You might feel differently if I ordered you some suits.

Will: No

Shannon: Actually, I can call my gal at Neiman Marcus and have her pull some for you to try.

Will: No

Shannon: Why not? I like you all fancy pants. I love you all always but I'm very fond of you in a suit.

Shannon: You were hot as fuck at Gus and Aviva's wedding, and Lauren's too. You might recall getting laid after both of those suit-wearing events

Will: There are a lot of things I'll roll with. I'll let you pick which movie we're seeing. I'll make you come first. I'll let you leave the house in those Come Fuck Me heels and sexy skirts because I know everyone else can look but only I touch. I'll rub your belly when you have cramps.

Will: I'll be your protection detail when you go out drinking with the girls and get rowdy. I'll lick any part of you anytime you want. I'll keep my mouth shut when you work insane hours and come home half-asleep and growling. I'll let you dress me in a motherfucking tutu and take me to ballet class.

Will: But you know what I'm not doing?

Will: I'm not letting you give me the Black Widow treatment. You don't have to project manage me, peanut.

Shannon: What if I want to? Have you considered that?

Shannon: Taking care of people is how I show my love.

Will: I don't think you understand how much of that you do before you even start on the dry-cleaning.

Will: And I'm going to buy my own fucking pants because I'm the one who takes care of you

Will: And before you tell me you don't need anyone taking care of you – I love you. Deal with it.

Shannon: Shut up.

Shannon: I love you too.

Shannon: Can I come with you when you're buying your own fucking pants?

Will: Maybe

Shannon: I'd like to get you alone in a dressing room

Will: I'm listening.

Shannon: Something weird is going on

Will: Not your horoscope again

Shannon: Do not mock me.

Will: Not mocking. Just baffled that a woman with a law degree relies on mystical prophecies for daily guidance.

Will: What's the weirdness?

Shannon: I don't know exactly. There's something going on and I can't quite figure it out.

Shannon: Erin is flying in tomorrow.

Will: That's unusual?

Shannon: It's always last minute with her, too, like she's the queen of fucking England

Shannon: She hasn't spent Christmas with us since she was in high school. She was supposed to visit for Thanksgiving but something happened with her flight.

Will: Progress?

Will: Don't forget – even the Berlin Wall came down eventually

Shannon: You don't know my sister. She's stalwart

Will: Yeah. Wonder where she gets that.

Shannon: If you asked me to go to Mexico, I might say yes this time

Will: Too soon.

Shannon: …?

Will: It's too soon to joke about that.

Shannon: Ohhhh. Ok then.

Twenty-Eight

SOMETHING WAS unusual at the firehouse.

"Sam's wearing a tuxedo," I murmured. "A red tuxedo. Where did he get a red tuxedo?"

"Yeah, that's not making it easier for me to like that guy," Will said.

Miles of twinkling lights were strung across the old fire engine bay, a band was performing on a raised platform, and servers were circulating with champagne. It seemed over the top for our standard Christmas Eve gathering, and there were far more people than I expected.

Sam and Riley were huddled together on the landing between the first and second floors. Riley appeared to be adjusting Sam's bowtie, and repeatedly patting his lapels as if to reassure him. Perhaps more interestingly, Riley was wearing a kilt.

"Why is Riley wearing a *kilt*?" I murmured. "And that's… that's, what is her name?" I was staring hard at the petite woman with spiky dark hair. "She used to live with Tiel. Ally or Emma or something. She's supposed to be touring with her band. What's she doing here?"

I searched the space, not sure what I was hoping to find, and ended up watching Sam and Riley again. Riley's hand dipped into his jacket pocket, and he handed something to Sam, and then it clicked.

"He's wearing a red tux because he's getting married tonight."

Will glanced at me, frowning. "What about this scene says wedding to you? We've got a hipster band, there's a table of little cheeseburgers and corndogs over there, and red tuxedos and kilts. How is that—oh, no, I see it now."

"That little shit," I said, stabbing my sequined top with my finger. "I'm wearing white, and this is a wedding, and that fucker didn't even tell me. He planned an entire goddamn wedding and didn't tell me!"

With his hands on my shoulders, Will backed me into a hallway. "Sam planned a wedding," he repeated, "because you taught him well. He did this on his own because he learned how to grow the fuck up, and he did that because you showed him how. You know what? I'm gonna thank him for that, even if he is wearing a red tuxedo."

"He's still a little shit," I said, pouting. "We don't do secrets."

"Says the girl who had the secret lover," he said, pointing to himself, "for more than a year. They handled things maturely when you told them, didn't they?"

Mature wasn't the right term, but Will didn't need to hear the true events of my siblings' reaction to the secret lover story. It was only one step better than cancelling Thanksgiving.

"Shannon," Will said, his fingertip running over my

collarbone. "You are the sexiest woman alive, and I want you to enjoy this night. Do you want me to lick your pussy before we go back out there?"

I swatted him away. "Save it for later, commando."

"Yes, ma'am."

The music stopped, and we emerged from the hallway to find Sam on the platform with a microphone in hand. "They say you should marry your best friend," he said, "and that's what I intend to do tonight."

WITH DRINKS IN HAND, I made my way through the energetic crowd toward where Will stood with Patrick and Andy. He caught my eye, and held his arm out to me, an invitation to take my place by his side, to be his in front of these people, the stars, the sky, and the entire universe beyond this firehouse. It was an invitation I accepted without hesitation, and I did him one better by brushing my hand down his chest, stopping when my fingers met his belt.

"Did you know?" Patrick asked me. He eyed Will, still unsure of what to make of him.

"Not a clue," I admitted, shaking my head.

"That ceremony was…" Andy laughed. "That was unique. I've never seen anything like this."

I glanced up at Will, smiling. He kept his eyes on me while he tipped back his beer bottle, and I watched his throat bobbing as he swallowed. I knew how he tasted right there, and how he shivered when my nails scraped over his scalp, and how his breaths came in fast bursts against my neck when he was ready to explode inside me. And I knew he was all mine for right now.

"Oh God, he's going to talk again," Patrick murmured, gesturing to the stage. Sam was at the microphone, gin and tonic in hand, and Tiel on his arm.

I was still overwhelmed by the shock of this evening, but in a strange, wonderful way, it was perfect. This was Sam and Tiel, and I never would have been able to micromanage an event that came anywhere close to this level of quirky spectacular. And I was gradually realizing that I was okay with that.

"Tonight we celebrate my wife," Sam said, grinning down at her, "the most incredible woman in my world. Tiel, you are my sanctuary, my soul, my Sunshine." He pressed a kiss to her lips, and when he turned back to the audience, he was smiling brighter than I'd ever seen. "But I want to raise a glass to a few others who made this possible, who delivered me to this point, whether they know it or not. To the elder statesmen," he said, tipping his glass toward Matt and Patrick. "To the keepers of all the best secrets." He gestured to Riley. "And to the wanderers who know when to wander home, and…the cornerstones, the ones who hold us together. Without all of you," he said, sweeping his arm out, "I wouldn't be here. Cheers."

Looking up, my eyes landed on Erin, and I found her smiling at me. She glanced to Will, and then back to me with a quick nod. It was little more than eye contact, but it was the most we'd shared in years. She looked well, and my chest tightened with all the questions I ached to ask her. It still shocked me that she was a woman now, lovely and grown, and I wanted the best for her. I hoped she was happy and fulfilled, and that she was safe and loved.

"You should talk to her," Will said gently.

"Not tonight," I said with a sigh.

Nick appeared at her side, and she turned away from me. She tossed her hands up and bounced with the music, and our silent conversation was over.

"You were right. The rocks are from Erin," I said. "When my mother came here from Ireland, she had a little box of rocks. She always told us that they were like breadcrumbs, and they'd always help her find the path home when she was lost. I used to tell Erin that story every night before she went to sleep." I blinked away the tears that rushed to my eyes. "She's going to come home some day. The rocks are her way of leaving a path."

"Are you okay?" he asked, his lips brushing over my temple.

"Actually," I said, "I am. Let's pour some shots for the happy couple."

We stayed at the firehouse late into the night, drinking and dancing, laughing and celebrating, and there was no comparison to the sad, lonely Christmas Eve I spent at Sullivan's Tap last year.

We were all over each other on the cab ride home. Loose, giddy, flirty, desperate. The cabbie reprimanded us several times for getting too handsy.

And it felt good. Everything felt good and I never wanted it to stop.

I leaned against the door while Will dug through my purse for the keys. "Are you going to take me to bed?"

"If you're asking whether I plan to fuck you until the sun comes up," he said, "the answer is yes. Come here."

He motioned for me to wrap my arms around his neck, and then he lifted me, locking my legs on his waist. He dropped the keys and my purse to the floor once we were inside, and a trail of our clothes followed us into the bedroom.

"We go to a lot of weddings, don't we?" he asked. He tossed me to the bed and stepped out of his shoes and trousers. I pulled my shirt over my head and shrugged out of my bra.

"It seems that we do," I said, scooting under the blankets.

Will nestled beside me, his skin hot and his mouth urgent as he kissed my shoulder and neck. "When are we going to our own?"

His cock pressed against my thigh, eager for attention.

"Was that a proposal?" I asked.

Will laughed, and positioned himself between my legs. He wasted no time bringing his tongue to my clit and spearing two fingers inside me, and I arched back with a loud moan.

"Oh, fuck," I cried. "Fuck, fuck, yes, right there."

He popped up, his head on my belly. "See what I did there?" he asked, smirking. "You said yes."

Twenty-Nine

WILL

"CAPTAIN, I am looking at your discharge papers. Would you care to explain this shit to me?"

I knew this was going to happen eventually. Word was getting out, wheels were turning, and one irate Lieutenant General wanted my ass. There was no way for me to leave the teams quietly when my command of this new task force was a foregone conclusion in McGardil's eyes.

"The nerve damage isn't improving, sir, and I've decided it's time," I said. "I've fulfilled my service."

"Do I need to remind you that this country is at war?" he roared. "Men and women are losing their lives every *day*, sailor. I expect this shit from a bedwetting tadpole during Phase One of BUD/S, not a decorated officer when there's a team ready to load out."

I leaned against the refrigerator, softly knocking my head on the glass door while the Lieutenant General ranted about the need for battle-tested leaders, and expecting more from me, and the impact of my departure on critical missions. In the twenty minutes that he yelled and swore, he barely stopped for a breath. It was remarkable.

But it was hard to hear. Nothing he said was new—I'd been thinking the same things since this leave started last month—but the gravity of it was much greater coming from a man I respected as much as McGardil.

My decisions affected more than me, and this was the smack upside the head to remind me of that.

"You are a highly skilled operative," McGardil continued. "You are among the most lethal in the teams, and the United States has spent *millions* of dollars on your training. If you're not mission-ready, there are other critical roles to assume."

"I'm aware, sir," I said. "This wasn't a light decision."

"I should hope not, Captain," he said with a grunt. "Are you writing a book? A fucking screenplay?"

"No, sir. I'm…" I glanced around the kitchen, where I'd abandoned my lasagna preparations. I decided to keep those details to myself. Without a doubt, my newfound domesticity would land with a thud. "I'm exploring private security and defense contracting."

McGardil huffed out a breath. "Have you given any consideration to returning to Coronado as an instructor?"

And there it was: my least favorite option. I enjoyed working with SEALs who'd finished all their qualifying courses—the baby SEALs, as Shannon liked to call them—but the last thing I wanted to do was holler at a bunch of guys during midnight rock portage drills on San Clemente Island.

"Thank you, sir," I said, "though I'd rather not return to BUD/S. One visit was plenty."

"It's a loss," he said. "There aren't many men with your experience, even fewer with your cool head. This is a loss for the teams." I heard McGardil shuffling and tapping papers across the line. "Allow me to thank you for your service, sailor. It's been a pleasure, and I do hope you keep in touch."

The call ended and I was left banging my head against the refrigerator. Leaving the teams wasn't a simple decision. It was the only thing I knew how to do, the only thing I'd ever *wanted* to do, and it wasn't as though I could discard the responsibility like a pair of dirty socks. This duty pumped in my blood and gathered in my soul, and I would always live with the fire to push myself further than anyone thought possible.

When I'd banged myself right into a dull headache, I spied a new message waiting on my phone.

Shannon: I've been dealing with the most obstinate agent all morning. This guy is arguing every single point on this purchase and sale agreement. There's nothing special about the terms, either.
Shannon: This guy's just a dick
Will: When you get home, I'm taking your panties
Will: You're not getting them back until Monday
Will: Then I'm tying you to the bed
Will: Just keep that in mind as you're dealing with this fool
Shannon: Wow. That actually helped.
Will: Surprised?
Shannon: No…I don't know. Maybe.
Will: Also, I'm making lasagna.

Smiling, I swiped through my contacts until I found the one I needed. I'd been putting off this call—and a few others —for weeks, but I was ready. The pieces were coming together, and I knew what I wanted now.

"Halsted," Kaisall shouted when he answered. "If I didn't know better, I'd think you've been shopping my offer with the way you're dodging calls."

"But you know better," I chuckled.

Kaisall and I connected shortly before the visit to San Diego, and he shared plans to overhaul his firm, Redtop. He wanted to continue taking high-profile security details—gotta pay the bills—while branching out into kidnapping and smuggling cases, hostage negotiations, and the occasional clandestine task. In order to execute on this, he was reorganizing the company's structure.

"Are we getting into bed together?" he asked. Sounds of the airport accompanied his voice. Travel dominated his life, and it suited him. He liked the thrill of chasing down contacts and clients, and being in the know. "All toasty warm for me yet?"

He needed someone in the command center; someone who could watch all the pieces on the chessboard and make the right moves. The more I thought about it, the more I liked it. The work was still important, even when it included running background checks on an heiress's boyfriend of the month, and there was plenty of it.

"There's a strong possibility, yeah," I said.

"That's going to piss the special warfare command right off," he said. Flight announcements drowned him out, and he paused before continuing. "How long's it been for you? Two, three months now? You need to get back in the action. I bet you're playing *Call of Duty* at three in the morning and yelling 'hooyah' at the screen."

That was partially true. I missed the strategic nature of planning operations and working through variables, but I didn't miss a war with no end in sight, bullets flying at my head, meals in vacuum-sealed pouches, or the thousands of miles between me and the woman I loved.

"Let me sort through a few more issues this week," I said. "We'll go from there."

"You say that like you haven't already decided that we're going to be the best team in private defense contracting. This is the start of a long, profitable marriage," he said. Another flight announcement trilled through the line. "That's me. Talk soon, partner."

When we disconnected, I saw another message waiting. I wasn't ready to dump this information on Shannon yet. Given my contemplative mood, she'd launch right into problem solving mode, and I wasn't adding another issue on her plate. I'd think it all over this afternoon, and we'd take this to the next step.

Shannon: Does it make me old and boring because I want to stay in, eat lasagna and drink wine, and watch The Sopranos with you on a Friday night?

Will: No, but you forgot about being tied to the bed and fucked straight through to Saturday

Shannon: The whole package works for me

Will: Let's go to the beach tomorrow

Shannon: You're in New England now, commando. It's December.

Shannon: Beach season is over

Will: We can go for a walk

Will: I need some time near the ocean

Shannon: We jogged through the Waterfront this morning.

Will: That doesn't count. That's the bay. The harbor. I want a beach with dunes, sand, waves.

Will: Being in the city isn't even close to the same.

Shannon: Ok, ok, relax, we'll get you a beach
Shannon: Well…I was supposed to swing by that house I bought on the North Shore today, but since I'm dicking around with this asshole, I'm not going to make it up there. I've put it off a couple times now.
Will: The one where nothing was straight? With that rocky cove?
Shannon: Yep
Will: That's a great beach. We can do your stuff and then we can walk for a couple of miles and back
Shannon: Ok but seriously – I hate having wet socks. Being cold and wet makes me very unhappy.
Will: Good. I prefer you hot and wet.
Shannon: …
Will: I won't let you get cold and wet, peanut

WE WERE HEADED NORTH on Saturday morning, away from the city and all its congestion, and I was humming with anticipation. I loved being with Shannon; I could pack that parachute nineteen different ways and still come to the same conclusion, but I didn't love the city as much as she did.

There were the usual urban complaints: nonstop noise, pollution, close quarters, the *hurry up and go* mentality, but all of that was manageable. It didn't matter where I was, so long as Shannon was with me…and I got to hit the beach with some regularity.

"Talked to Kaisall yesterday," I said, turning off the highway and onto the coast road. "I'm going to give it a shot."

Shannon glanced up from the floor plans in her lap. "Okay," she said slowly. "So...that means you're moving to Washington, D.C.? Isn't that where Redtop is based?"

I drummed my fingers on the gearshift for a moment, searching the horizon for the right combination of words. We'd talked about me staying in Boston to sort out my life and deal with my shoulder, but we never discussed anything of permanence. Maybe that was embedded in each declaration of love that we shared, or the simple fact that we never discussed *not* living together, but this was where it stopped being temporary.

"No," I said. "I'm staying here."

She tucked her papers into a folder and filed it in her bag before responding. "How's that going to work?"

Veering into a residential area, I glanced at Shannon. Her arms were crossed, her fingers tapping her elbows, and she was staring out her window. "Logistics command isn't field work," I said. "It's about running comms, tracking intel, and monitoring operations from the eye in the sky." Reaching out, I caught her hand and laced my fingers with hers. "I can do that anywhere. We could share an office. Wouldn't you enjoy me, parked three feet away from you all day?"

"That's not a good idea. We can't be giving orders at the same time. We'd confuse the minions." She shook her head resolutely. "And this is what you want to do?"

Gray blueness shimmered in the distance, and despite the thick cloud cover, I breathed a sigh of relief. The sea did good things for my soul.

"I think so." It was the most sincere answer I had, and I accepted that I wouldn't know for sure until I waded into the work. "A couple years ago, Kaisall only did big game accounts—defamed CEOs with bounties on their heads, mid-scandal politicians, and the occasional foreign diplomat. Not my scene, but it worked for him. These days," I said, pulling into the stone driveway, "he's branching out. He's got some new contracts, and some of them are interesting projects. Human trafficking, small arms dealers, hostage recovery. I'd be into that."

Shannon's eyes cut to the side, studying me under her lashes, and she gnawed on her lower lip. "Are you sure about this, commando? You're not going to miss invading countries? Shooting the dictators? Blowing shit up?"

I brought her palm to my lips, leaving a quick kiss there. "I know what I want, Shannon."

She stared at me for a long beat, then blinked and nodded toward the house. "Let's walk first," she said. "I need to work off those pancakes before I deal with this place."

We hiked down to the shore, and followed the narrow strip of sandy beach. Shannon was quiet at first, and then started pointing out unique features of the beachfront homes. This area was growing on me. I never expected that I'd enjoy the cold, turbulent Atlantic, or its unforgiving coastline. Now, with Shannon and the sea on either sides of me, I couldn't imagine it any other way.

When we came to a sharp, rocky bend in the coastline where waves were beating against the shore, we turned around instead of trying to scale it. No wet socks today.

She stopped at the stone path leading back to the house, gazing at the structure.

We took the long way around, traversing the large lot and locating the property lines before arriving at the entry. "All right. Let's get inside."

I followed her, hanging back while she walked the first floor. She wandered through each room repeatedly, her fingers grazing the fixtures while her lips drew tight in concentration.

"What's our objective?" I asked eventually.

She settled on a window seat in the living room. "I don't know why I bought this house," she said, her words rushing out in a gasp. "The room dynamics are odd. The structure needs work. It's a nice piece of land and…it *feels* like a good place, but I can't remember what I wanted when I was negotiating this deal."

"Do you always know?" I asked.

"Yes," she cried. "The one thing I can do with any consistency is look at a property and know how to sell it, but…" She stood, shaking her head, and propped her hands on her hips. "The last time I was here, I loved this place. It seemed perfect for…I don't know. For something."

"Let's keep walking around," I said. "It'll come to you."

We climbed the stairs and walked through all seven bedrooms. She stayed quiet, occasionally making notes or running her palm down the walls.

"There's something about this place," she murmured from the center of a large bedroom that would surely bathe in the warmest morning sunlight. She held out her hands and turned in a slow circle, and it was right then, with her face tipped up and her green eyes wide, that I felt my forever winding around me. "I can't explain it, but it feels like people were happy here. It feels like a *home*. Is it just me? Do you get that vibe?"

"I think you're right," I said, and it wasn't without effort that I kept my voice steady. "It is a home."

But that sentiment owed nothing to the four walls and roof. This was about permanence. *Our* permanence and it was possible this was where it would start.

Our eyes met across the room, and Shannon sensed it too. She didn't know it yet, but she felt it.

"I know what to do, technically-speaking," she said. "Or, I know what the boys would do. Patrick would get rid of all the wallpaper, paint, carpeting. Anything that wasn't original. Matt would reinforce the foundation, pop out the dropped ceilings, and open up the layout. Sam would hit the sustainability features hard: rainwater catchment, solar, and tons of organic insulation products. Riley…" She looked around, her eyebrows pinching together as she thought. "He'd figure out how to replace the missing tiles in the entryway mosaic."

"And what would you do?" I asked.

"I don't know," she murmured. "I have no idea, and right now, I'm tempted to leave and not worry about this until spring." She leaned against the wall, her hands open and falling to her sides. "We have enough going on with the wrap up on Turlan, and starting Mount Vernon, and we still have the freaking Castavechias. And a dozen others on deck. My pet project doesn't need to consume everyone's time and energy right now. This can wait. I can wait."

Of course that was her reasoning.

She wandered out of the bedroom and toward the stairs leading to the third floor. Her fingers traced the intricate woodwork on the banister as she ascended. The rooms were narrower up here, but the views stretched off into the horizon for miles. There were small, rocky islands in the distance, and the faint outline of sailing vessels.

"It's a nice place," she said. "There's a lot of potential here. I just don't know what to do with it."

We'd share this home for the next seventy years. We'd

celebrate holidays and birthdays and everything in between here. We'd grow a family here. This was our escape.

I pointed out the window, drawing her attention to the grassy yard that rolled straight down to the beach. "Plenty of room for commando drills. Running, jumping, climbing. And those trees?" I gestured to the ancient oaks on the far edge of the lot. "They need tree houses, and a zip line. And down there? That old patio? We'll have barbeques and parties, and Lo will manage to pass out with a bottle of tequila every time."

It was bait, pure and simple, and I wanted her to take it.

Shannon's expression morphed from confused to curious to pained within seconds.

"You don't *want* to be here," she said. "You want to live in San Diego. You're going to get bored, and then you're going to resent me, and you're going to leave, and I probably won't survive it this time. So please, let me have right *now*. Don't give me a story about us, and zip lines, and barbeques. Don't play with me. Don't pretend."

Fuck. That. Noise.

"I'm not leaving," I said. "I'm not getting bored, and there's no way in hell I'd resent you."

Shannon pushed away from the windows and paced the length of the room. It was small, the ceilings vaulted, and it didn't give her much space to work out that nervous energy. "But you will!" she cried. "You're going to hate spending your days behind a computer screen when you're used to blowing shit up and being a badass."

"I knew I was ready about a year ago," I said, watching while she continued pacing. "I didn't acknowledge it, not really, but I knew I needed a change. I always thought I was career military, but I never saw a life beyond running special operations. That last tour was brutal, just fucking brutal. I'm ready, and even if all I do is cook you dinner, I'll be happy. I don't require much."

"Why didn't you tell me this?" she asked, stopping on the other side of the room.

"Because I needed to get it straight first. I needed a plan, and before you tell me that you would've helped, I know. I know you'll do fucking anything for your people, and sometimes it's crazy, but I love that about you—"

"You think you're one of my people?" Arms crossed over her chest, she marched up to me, her lips twisted in a smirk and eyebrow cocked.

"I'd like to be," I said. "You're one of mine."

"You might get bored," she countered.

I reached out, grabbing her ponytail and wrapping it around my palm. Tugging, I lifted her gaze to meet mine. "Shannon, I don't need much. Most of my possessions fit into a rucksack. If necessary, I can survive off the land for weeks. Maybe longer. All I really care about is being near the ocean and waking up beside you. I've had plenty of time to think this over, and I know there's nothing else."

She swallowed hard. "You're serious," she said, and it wasn't a question. "Serious about..." She waved toward the window, quietly gathering everything—the sea, the house, us—into the permanence we'd earned. "Why?"

My hands shifted to her waist, and I fit her against my chest. "I've spent too many months leaving you. I'm not doing that again."

"Are you sure about all this? I mean, we haven't—"

"Don't even start with that shit, peanut," I interrupted. "I am going to marry you so hard you won't remember your maiden name. I'm going to love you and protect you, and

I'm going to put up with your brothers and the violent citrus-throwing, too. You better get used to it because I'm here to stay."

At first, I thought I was she was crying when her shoulders started jostling. Then, I felt her laughter vibrating against my sternum. "Your proposals are about as good as my compliments."

Shaking my head, I pulled her closer. "It's not like you want roses and champagne, peanut," I said. "Was that a *yes*?"

"No," she said, looking up at me with her dark, dark green eyes. "It was a *fuck yes and let's christen our house now*."

epilogue
SHANNON

NINE MONTHS *later*

I WOKE UP ALONE.

I was exhausted, and needed a few more hours of sleep, but I hated lying there alone. And I had to pee. Again.

After heaving myself out of bed and hitting the bathroom, I changed into a sundress and headed down to the kitchen. Even though I had the air conditioner cranked as cool as it would go, this early autumn heat wave was hotter than Satan's balls.

"That better not be my wife on the back stairs. I've repeatedly told her that she's not allowed on those stairs alone, and if she's out of bed and on those stairs, she's not going to like the consequences."

I stopped and pressed a hand to my lower back. This baby was rearranging my bones and organs, and his father's voice only got him fired up.

We found out I was pregnant in March when I went to the doctor after a weeklong stomach virus wouldn't quit. As it turned out, the virus was a tiny human and Will's commando sperm was no match for my birth control pills. When the surprise of it all wore off, he was exceptionally pleased with himself and his apparent virility. The ultimate commando tactic.

I, on the other hand, freaked the fuck out. I didn't feel ready or qualified, and I didn't know how I'd manage something so delicate and important. The nausea and exhaustion of the first trimester hit me hard, but once I turned the corner into the second trimester, it was slightly more manageable. Slightly.

I stopped worrying about whether we were prepared, and surrendered to the fact that there wasn't one right time. My life wasn't composed of scripted moments. There were many things I could control—and I did—but everything else was out of my hands.

"What are you doing on the fucking stairs?" Will asked from the landing. I still hated seeing fresh surgical scars on his shoulder, those sharp red lines marring his golden skin, but it was the price for alleviating the pain and regaining some feeling in his fingers.

"Froggie is kicking the shit out of my bladder," I said. "Also, I'm starving."

Will jogged toward me, climbing two steps at a time, and put both hands on my belly when he reached me. "Froggie, we talked about this," he whispered. "You have to go easy on Mama." Another kick landed beneath his hand, and his eyes widened. "My girl's got some swimmer's legs."

"This is not a girl," I said, gesturing to the planet under

my dress. We decided to wait until Froggie made his or her arrival to discover the sex, although Will thought he saw a penis during the last sonogram. It was a leg. "This is an eight-year-old boy. I'm giving birth to a preteen."

He smiled up at me while massaging my bump. The shiny glint of his wedding band still caught me off guard, like a star I didn't expect to see in the sky. We took the ferry to Montauk in January, got married, and spent the weekend at Kaisall's house. We shared the news before returning to the city, and it set off a small firestorm of congratulations and some very loud grumbling from the family and friends who weren't invited. Which was all of them.

But a secret weekend was the only way for us.

"Let's get you fed. Then we'll talk about you hiking through a damn construction site while seven months pregnant."

He took my hand, and placed his other on the small of my back. Part of the Galloupes Point house that we called home was still under construction, but the master bedroom, kitchen, and the his-and-hers offices were finished. Froggie's room was next, although...I still didn't like the idea of him sleeping all the way down the hall. I wanted to reach over in the middle of the night and feel the rise and fall of his tiny— or not so tiny, such that I was enormous—chest.

"How's the water?" I asked, gazing at Will's bare back.

His hair was wet and he was wearing board shorts that hung from his narrow hips in a way that was nearly obscene. And I was good with obscene. Not long after we moved in, the ladies in our neighborhood discovered that Will hit the waves with the sunrise every morning. He accumulated a considerable audience, and they didn't even pretend they weren't lusting all over my husband.

They could look, but I was the only one to touch.

"Good temperature, easy surf. We'll get out there and go for a walk after you eat," he said. "Patrick called a little while ago. He wants to take a look at the progress in the dining room, and it's hot as hell in the city, so he and Andy are coming up for the day."

Somewhere between the college Bowl Championship Series and March Madness, Will and Patrick became best friends. They engaged in all manner of masculine activities together: surfing, sports viewing, distance running, ocean swimming, eating as if it was their last meal. They wouldn't let me hire a tradesman to restore the patio because they were hell-bent on doing it themselves. It was fair to say Will wasn't bored with his post-SEAL life.

I kind of loved the bromance between my two favorite guys.

It made it easier to scale back at the office, too. Pregnancy didn't agree with my seventy-hours-a-week schedule, and by July, I'd delegated more tasks than I thought possible. There were hiccups, and not everything ran smoothly, but Froggie didn't give me many options in the matter. I still handled all the buying and selling, all the finance and contracts, but I transferred much of the external affairs to Tom.

Will pulled a chair out from the table and held my elbow as I sat. Even though I had two more months to go, I couldn't see my feet and was known to knock things over with my belly. Everything about me was huge and uncomfortable, but I'd never been happier.

"What do you and Froggie want for breakfast?" He set a plate of pancakes in front of me and waited, knowing my meals included multiple courses.

"Scrambled eggs with spicy peppers. Bacon. Pineapple. And if there's any spinach dip left, I'd be excited about that, too."

"Yes, ma'am."

Much to my surprise, Will loved running command at Redtop. It was sexy as hell to watch him in his darkened office, studying the wall of computer screens, wearing his headset, and barking orders. His work was different now, and there were situations when he was locked in that office for several days at a time, but he adored it.

And I adored him.

I rubbed my belly again, reveling in the feel of Froggie's sharp kicks. There were nights when I sat in bed, my hands glued to my skin while Froggie rolled and hiccupped and fluttered, and I thought about my mother. I missed her terribly, and I would have given anything for her to sit by my side and smooth my hair, and tell me that I could do this. That loving and protecting my family came naturally to me, and this would be no different. That everything, everything, *everything* happened for a reason. That it would be scary but I was strong. That I'd know what to do when that baby was placed in my arms.

I hadn't seen any of this coming—the love of my life, the beachfront home far from my city, the baby growing inside me—and I wouldn't have wanted it any other way.

If you loved Shannon and Will, check out Jordan Kaisall's story, *Coastal Elite*.

JORDAN KAISALL HAS PROBLEMS.

Business problems, political problems, cheating ex-girl-friend problems. He knows that a week away from the Washington, D.C. Beltway won't do a damn bit of good for those problems, but his beach house in Montauk is exactly where he needs to be right now.

APRIL VEACH HAS PLANS.

Work plans, travel plans, try-everything-once plans. Montauk is keeping her plenty busy this summer between decorating wedding cakes and teaching yoga, and busy is good. But busy is also a lonely bed, and that wasn't part of her grand plan.

AFTER A WEEKEND TOGETHER, his problems and her plans take them in an unexpected direction.

COASTAL ELITE IS A STANDALONE NOVEL. Turn the page for an excerpt.

Join my newsletter for new release alerts, exclusive extended epilogues and bonus scenes, and more.

If newsletters aren't your thing, follow me on BookBub for preorder and new release alerts.

Visit my private reader group, Kate Canterbary's Tales, for

*exclusive giveaways, sneak previews of upcoming releases,
and book talk.*

also by kate canterbary

Vital Signs

Before Girl — Cal and Stella

The Worst Guy — Sebastian Stremmel and Sara Shapiro

The Walsh Series

Underneath It All – Matt and Lauren

The Space Between – Patrick and Andy

Necessary Restorations – Sam and Tiel

The Cornerstone – Shannon and Will

Restored — Sam and Tiel

The Spire — Erin and Nick

Preservation — Riley and Alexandra

Thresholds — The Walsh Family

Foundations — Matt and Lauren

The Santillian Triplets

The Magnolia Chronicles — Magnolia

Boss in the Bedsheets — Ash and Zelda

The Belle and the Beard — Linden and Jasper-Anne

Talbott's Cove

Fresh Catch — Owen and Cole

Hard Pressed — Jackson and Annette

Far Cry — Brooke and JJ

Rough Sketch — Gus and Neera

Benchmarks Series

Professional Development — Drew and Tara

Orientation — Jory and Max

Brothers In Arms

Missing In Action — Wes and Tom

Coastal Elite — Jordan and April

Get exclusive sneak previews of upcoming releases through Kate's newsletter and private reader group, The Canterbary Tales, on Facebook.

about Kate

USA Today Bestseller Kate Canterbary writes smart, steamy contemporary romances loaded with heat, heart, and happy ever afters. Kate lives on the New England coast with her husband and daughter.

You can find Kate at www.katecanterbary.com

facebook.com/kcanterbary
twitter.com/kcanterbary
instagram.com/katecanterbary
amazon.com/Kate-Canterbary
bookbub.com/authors/kate-canterbary
goodreads.com/Kate_Canterbary
pinterest.com/katecanterbary
tiktok.com/@katecanterbary